IZZ OF ZIA

THE FORBIDDEN ASCENT

THE WONDROUS ADVENTURE CONTINUES

WHERE FANTASY AND REALITY COLLIDE

TOM ICON

DARE TO ASCEND

Izz of Zia is an action packed fantasy adventure that embraces a deeper view of reality.

Tom Icon

Tom Icon

Published by TomArtCom 902 Delrey Drive, College Station, Texas 88745 USA
izzofzia.com

Book design copyright © 2017 by TomArtCom All rights reserved.
Front and back cover illustrated by Tom Icon.
Photographer Cory Dobson

Cover design by Tom Icon
Interior design by Tom Icon

Published in the United States of America
ISBN: 978-0-9987089-2-8

1. Fiction / Action & Adventure
2. Fiction / Romance / Fantasy

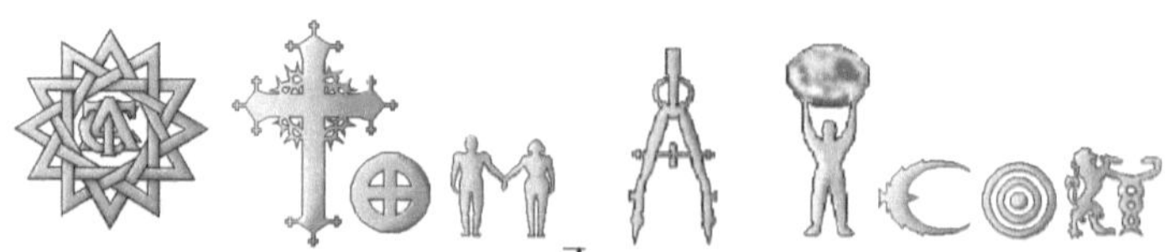

To my three sisters, Kathy, Julie and Kristina.

For further information, contact us at:

izzofzia@gmail.com

Or visit us at:

izzofzia.com

Tom Icon

Izz of Zia

CONTENT

INTRODUCTION

Once upon a time, long, long ago, there was a kingdom known as Edawn. It was a kingdom outside of time as we know it, in a parallel universe not of this world. It is the era of the Noble Kings, established in the First Age of the first millennia, in the year 111, in the days of Ozzdon Emperor of Xylenia, on the planet Zia.

It was written that in the age of the first Noble King, Mozar the Conqueror, there was an explosion of new knowledge among the children of the flesh. At the center of this expansion was a group of the most intellectual minds, who were known as the Enlightened Ones, led by the Grand Wizard Iwazz. Their cause was devoted to an unceasing endeavor to answer the perplexing questions that the universe entices every soul to ask. The greatest thinkers of their time began their quest for the meaning of life with noble intentions. But like most men who are wise in their own high regard, they slowly took a dark turn, making the wrong use of their perception and knowledge, drawing their own conclusions of reality. They intermingled half truths with evil thoughts for far too long, and somewhere along the way, they took the wrong turn and sank into a perpetual sinkhole. The workers of evil corrupted logic itself, so much so they made the truth seem like intellectual and ethical dim wittedness. Somewhere along their lost path, they concluded that the whole of creation—the sun, the moon, and the stars, the beauty of the seasons, the trees and their incredible variety of delicious fruits, with their flowers, the birds, the animal kingdoms—all happened by random chance. They reasoned among themselves that the whole of existence had come from nothingness, created by nothing, and thus they concluded that they had only themselves to answer to. Therefore, they rationalized that they were subject to no rules, no restraints, and no set of laws beyond doing whatever pleased them.

In their zest to discover the nothingness from whence they wanted to believe they came from, they probed behind the veil of the natural. Those that tourist they knew it all unwittingly unlocked the mysteries of ancient pathways between their world and a parallel supernatural underworld trespassing into the darkness to become part of that darkness. They splintered the existing order of reality along bizarre new patterns, bridging highways into ominous dark, chaotic dimensions. This corrupted power only served to embolden them to unleash the growing darkness within themselves, believing that they ruled over it. But in their drunkenness for power, it was the darkness that called the tune that the would be god puppets danced to. The minds of flesh were so wholly dominated by false beliefs that reason itself seemed like illogical foolishness and moral degradation. And quickly, the darkness bred within them and became a force beyond their control. From this new rule arose the Dark Priests, men enshrouded in darkness. Men who were given over entirely to the dark rituals dredged from the collective consciousness of pure evil. Before long, their demonic masters were demanding the sacrifice of their children's blood. And Soon they became drunk with the blood of the innocent. They corrupted anyone who ruled then brought them under their yoke, and a civilization of good moral standing was plunged into deepening darkness. They willed to make a paradise of Zia they christened the Order of the New Sunrise. But instead of the paradise, they promised the inhabitants of Zia; they only succeeded in making it a doorway into hell, devastating the fate of an entire people. And the masses of humanity only suffered poverty and enslavement.

The Dark Priests were responsible for offenses so disgusting that they became monsters too depraved to be tolerated. When opposition grew among those who refused to be enslaved by evil men; the secret brotherhood of Black Magicians, cleverly argued away or discredited anyone who threatened their beliefs.

Tom Icon

The minds of the Enlightened were so completely controlled by their delusion that their own lust for power enslaved them. They had everything—vast wealth, unrestricted rule, and ultimate power—yet they wanted more, much more. They wanted immortality. Soon they became even more treacherous, interested only in deposing those in honorable authority who openly opposed them for their cleverly spun lies. Their strength and riches grew as they attempted to become the sole masters of Zia. The oppressor's only law was that there was no law beyond following their selfish lust. Their twisted hope led them to surrender their souls to the dark side so that they, at any cost, might arise to tower over a new throne of universal empire in which they would appoint themselves gods.

The one book that brought forth good tiding and guidance for daily life from within its pages was the Great Book of Wisdom. Eventually, this divinely inspired book was collectively covered up and forbidden until only hushed whispers of its existence remained. They refuted the existence of a Divine Maker that they might convince the mind of flesh kind to turn away from their inward divinity and turn to the Enlightened for direction. In their arrogance, the so called Enlightened appointed themselves gods and exalted themselves above all other men. They created the secret ideals of their reality. They urged their spiritual leaders and their minions to conceal the obvious truth underneath the dredges of falsehood, blasphemy, and myth.

It was fortunate for the world of Zia that King Mozar had been born into the world at that place and time. Mozar, whose mind had not been rotted by the greatest lie ever told, sought truth and wisdom in solitary pilgrimage. Being a firm believer, he concluded that the Creator had not given him his senses, reason, and intelligence only to abandon their use to seducing spirits outside of sound logic. In his withdrawn isolation, through deep meditation and supplication, he sought knowledge from his Maker. It is written that Mozar humbled himself, and in his fervent quest within an explosion of light and power, he found his way to the fountain of truth. Whether in body or spirit, he knew not. Mozar embraced a reality beyond his mind; he made indirect contact with the Infinite Mind. Not much is known of the encounter, only that Mozar was given twelve crowns to conqueror and rule.

Led by Mozar, the Noble Kings went forth, in the name of the Twelve Crowns, slaying those who willed to rule through evil. There came a final battle between the conflicting powers. After a long and costly war, the heirs of the Creator crushed and disbanded the evil order, changing the course of history. For this Mozar earned a place in history forever, known to all proceeding generations as Mozar the Conqueror.

Most of the written records of the Dark Priest's blasphemous work and all their writings had been confiscated and destroyed when the evil realm fell. Any practice of this forbidden knowledge was outlawed and prohibited under penalty of death.

There were those of the secret cult, so thoroughly corrupted by the wickedness that they refused to turn away from the darkness. Sometimes one can be fooled into thinking that things that cannot be might be. Those who refused to renounce their wayward ways were driven into Noragore's deepest caverns where evil does not sleep; there they were entombed alive. It was said that their screams can still be heard echoing through the valleys in the dead of night.

It was written that there, their souls would remain lost throughout eternity. Selfish greed was their god, and it has become humankind's worst of diseases. For the afflicted, there would never be enough wealth, supremacy, or power to fill their empty hearts. In the end, their dreams will be unfulfilled, their names forgotten and no longer spoken, blotted out from the records of the book of life. They will eternally anguish because they did not set their desires on life's true riches: love, joy, and happiness. Their only reward will be to join the ranks of ruinous souls, neither living nor dead, eternally lost.

And thus began the Golden Dawning of the Noble Kings, and here is where our story continues.

ONE
DESECRATION

Hidden, completely, along the timberline at the edge of the woods among the brush, the master scout in command of King Ozzdon's volunteer reconnaissance party kept total vigilance as the sinister hordes retreated from Skymount. Through his spyglass, he could see the daunting advance guard riding ahead followed by the ground troops, the Zomborge handlers, and the slow moving catapult droves.

On the ground, maintaining strict silence, close to the advancing enemy was were the best scout spotters of the war games, scarcely visible except to the trained eye. Their mission was to gather information about anything said. It was a tedious, hazardous assignment; the greatest danger was that of being found out. These elite spies were exceptionally trained to be phantoms on the battlefield, spending hours in absolute motionlessness. However, if discovered, they were specially trained to be the most lethal phantoms on the planet.

As Baddlock and Dandork rode by, the closest spotter heard their ongoing conversation.

"Was it wise to be so brutal? Why risk pushing our hand too far?" Dandork asked, knowing that what had been done to the citizens of Skymount and its royals would result in global repercussions.

Izz of Zia

Baddlock, who was still ripping with shivering pleasure, held back his anger and hissed instead, "Do not be a dunce. This little skirmish was only amusement for our troops, for our ultimate battle is reserved for the conquest of Edawn and our esteemed King Ozzdon. You just keep thinking of the bright gold, and all those flawless, many faceted diamonds, plumped fat with carats."

The reminiscence of the slaughter was proving to be a difficult memory for Dandork to forget completely. Dandork then had a renewed thought of reward and booty. Subsequently, a vile, sappy grin came over his twisted face, and his evil demeanor changed infinitely for the worst.

Noting the change, Baddlock chuckled evilly and said, "The time for self congratulation lies ahead of us. There is much to be done, yet there is nothing like leaving a little tortured rotting flesh behind to make people think twice and let them know that those that oppose us will pay the ultimate price for their insolence."

Baddlock's next move was to strike at the very heart of the royal families of Edawn. Thus, a mad man's hate for everything good and the greed that not all the gold and gems in Zia would ever be enough to fill solidified their mutual fate more assuredly.

The master scout, well hidden in the tree line, turned his attention off in the distance to see the horrifying death shroud of black smoke ascending above the towers of Skymount. Once Baddlock's forces had moved away at a safe distance, the scouting party regrouped and, under cover of the backwoods, looped around the kingdom, driving on a carefully planned grid, checking for hidden enemy scout positions.

When they reached the battered rearmost gates of Skymount, they were all overwhelmed with a feeling that something utterly unpleasant awaited them within. The kingdom seemed abandoned; the scouts cautiously prowled through the kingdom's entrance, with their weapons drawn and their arrows nocked. Patches of thin black smoke rolled and obscured the scene like ink suffusing through water.

The instant they crossed the threshold of the rear gate, there were indications that atrocious things had taken place just beyond their sight. They all felt a wake of dread wash over them. Even the eerie silence seemed perverse. Their eyes were alert for any surprises, but no experienced misfortune could have prepared them for the unspeakable scene that was about to confront them.

There were signs of massive bloodshed, and the stench of death was everywhere, but where were the bodies? It was as if the ground had just opened up and swallowed every inhabitant. They held their breath and listened intently as if something extremely sinister was lying in wait for them. But the pounding of their hearts in their ears and the buzz of swarming flies as thick as fog were the only sounds they heard. The cracks between the cobblestones where they walked were filled with blood.

Without the hope of finding anyone alive, the master scout finally whispered, "They're all dead. There is no one left here."

Suddenly, at the turn of a lifeless tower that stretched skyward like a gruesome gravestone, they came upon a spectacle that made them stopped dead in their tracks. At first, it looked like a black fog as dark as pitch rolling back and forth, flopping against itself like a restless sea of inky slime. Then all at once, as if waking from a daze, it dawned on them all at the same time that they were thousands of vultures stirring like an ocean of black tar, jostling, pecking, and squawking over something as yet unseen. Suddenly startled by the unexpected approach of men, the mass of flurrying winged scavengers took flight in such numbers that the sky could not contain them, forcing thousands of vultures to flee on the ground.

"What in the world!" the head scout shouted over the roar of wind and wings.

The airborne birds of death created such a draft of dust and wind that it nearly knocked the scouting party's headgear off. As the air began to clear of dust and flapping wings, a veil was lifted to reveal a sight so unreal it exceeded anything any human being could expect to imagine, let alone believe. A putrid stench caught in their nostrils like a bad taste in their mouths that they could not spit out. They saw hundreds of mangled and mutilated bodies of men, women, and children hanging on a forest of wooden beams. The dirty birds had not been idle.

Transfixed, they all stood rooted to the spots in which they stood, eyes and mouths wide open. The only movement was in their horror filled eyes as they surveyed the gruesome carnage. They examined the scene, taking in the images that would be burned into their minds forever.

They looked upon the kind of things that caused hardened men to wake in the middle of the night, screaming at the top of their lungs. Bodiless human skins rippled on poles as if old tattered banners caught in the wind. Some bodies were nailed to the walls, disemboweled like rabbits, undoubtedly subjected to unimaginable pain. Others were impaled like chickens on a skewer. It did not take much imagination to realize from where the barbarian had inserted the beams. Hundreds of unarmed citizens were impaled, left pierced straight through and suspended in the air to die a slow, agonizing death. Their bloodcurdling screams of agony were still etched on their faces, and in their sightless eyes. Aqueous body fluids from half eaten blotting flesh dripped to mingle with their coagulated blood on the ground beneath them.

The senior scout opened his mouth as if about to say something but seemed suddenly at a loss for words. His face turned pale. Finally, he whispered, "The children..." With tear dimmed eyes, he stared at the twisted wails permanently frozen onto their innocent little faces. It was insanity. Like nothing, he had ever seen, not even in his goriest nightmares. He knew he would never be able to get out of his head what was now engraved into his soul, what he tried to say next deteriorated into unintelligible mumbling under his breath. Then his face lightened a paler shade of white. He became violently sick and had to turn away abruptly; he doubled over and spewed his guts out. The rest of the scouts followed suit.

Unexpectedly, one of the disemboweled men before them opened his eyes and choked painfully, almost drowning on the blood coming from his mouth. With trembling lips, soundlessly, he said, "Please...kill me!" His muffled whimpering and teary eyes begged release. Then they heard labored and pained strangulated breathing coming from several other men that had been impaled. The faces of the impaled were blue from near asphyxiation. Their mouths from where the beam exited bubbled with saliva mixed with blood. Drool sucked back as the victim took another agonizing breath of living death.

The stunned scouts stumbled back, tripping over each other. Appalled beyond belief, they quickly backed around the corner from which they came. They were ready to get the hell out of there when the master scout came to his senses. He held both arms out, halting the men about to flee and said, "Wait...someone has to go back and help those poor, unfortunate souls."

"Help them! Did you see them?" asked his senior scout. "They are impaled. They must be all torn up inside, and the other one has no entrails. There is not one thing on Zia we can do for them. The only unknown reason they have lived this long is that the nature of their mortal wounds have not allowed them to bleed out. And the one disemboweled is more dead than alive."

"There is one thing we can do for them," the master scout said grimly.

Everyone in the group knew what that meant.

Distracted by his own thoughts, Izz marveled at how the immediacy of death had helped him sort out his priorities in life. Here he was, risking life and limb for the love of his soul, and that was the single most important thing in his life. A cold gust of the high winds came from nowhere and blew refreshingly upon Izz. He felt a strange, powerful sensation that it was his destiny to be there, even with the possibility of dying, even that was somehow exciting. His mind shuffled through scenes marked with the memories of happier times as a child and Zuree, the crowning memory of his life, the one who was now making him tread where only crested eagles dared. In the face of death, he knew without a doubt that his love for Zuree was all that mattered. Izz could feel her soul pulling at his heartstrings.

He looked up the southern slop with determination; his mind was ready, clear, and open. Izz reached up across the face of stone for a handhold and continued to climb the towering barrier of time that loomed over him, once again willing to risk everything for love there could only one cure for. The tightness in his chest along with every joint that seemed to ache slowly loosened. With the presence of mind, Izz quickly scaled up the massive cliff face. Once Izz familiarized his fingers and acclimated his equilibrium, he settled into a rhythm as he slowly overcame the formidable opponent that rose in savage splendor. He scaled higher and higher, almost hastily, narrowly missing his foothold a few times in his impatience. Izz's one thought was to get to the top and climbed with a determination greater than any he had ever made in his life.

Despite the coolness, his face was awash in sweat. Suddenly the rock face seemed to become steeper, so much so that even the tufts of green moss and gray lichen had to struggle to secure a foothold on the crumbling wall.

One moment Izz was climbing a solid rock wall. The next moment, without warning, the whole mountain seemed to roll and jolt unexpectedly. He reached up for a rut and thought to use it to steady himself. He attempted to push himself off his stone footing with one great surge, but as he shoved off, he realized too late that the foothold had unexpectedly come loose. A troubled frown creased his sweating forehead as his probing foot encountered nothing but air.

As if things could not possibly have gotten any worst, the chunk of stone Izz gripped with his left hand suddenly snapped away from his fingers under his weight. The grip from his right hand came sliding down the long crack he had been holding on to as he hung on for dear life. Soon there after, the whole cliff wall began to shake violently. His other hand came scrapping across the uneven rock face, tearing his nails off the tips of his fingers, as he frantically searched to grasp on to anything—a crack, a slit, a chance—only to come away with a hand full of air and five bloodied fingers. His reflexes kicked in, and he balled his right hand, which continued to slide down the narrowing crevice. Luck was with Izz in that his balled hand suddenly wedged into the crack, riffing and closing around his fist like the jaws of death which in turn prevented Izz from slipping and falling to his end. As he swung out and slammed hard against the hard granite wall, he smashed his back with a cruel, noxious thud, leaving him hanging on for his life as the whole mountain face quaked.

Izz grunted with pain each time he was slammed against the cliff wall. He looked up to see dust plummeting down from every crevice. The intensity of the tremor continued to build. Stones fell from the walls, and then large slabs began to break and fall away. Below him, large stones toppled headlong zipping along the cliff. The falling rocks knocked against the cliff face as they plunged, bouncing off other rocks, and sending them tumbling too. The chain reaction caused a pile of stones to rip into a ground shaking avalanche. Then Izz heard the catastrophic crash of the rockfall as it echoed between the canyon walls below, reminding him which way was down.

Meanwhile, as Izz dangled in midair, he felt his fingers, arm, and shoulder strained to their limits. Terrible dislocating pain and pulsating spasms shot through his arm. As the deafening noise reverberated off the cliff walls and echoed across the desert floor, his remaining limbs tried in vain to latch on to anything. The mountain moaned in deep ground shifting tones and growled in piercing, deafening cracks as sand and pebbles rained down all around him, pelting his head and raining down across his face. As his fist began to ease, adrenaline roared through his veins, and he forced himself to keep his fist clenched despite the excruciating pain. Izz's heart was pounding in his chest, as terrifying visions of falling to his death flashed through his mind. Then unexpectedly, the earthshaking ended as suddenly as it began.

Izz dangled over the void like a twig twisting from a web in the wind. The muscles in his arm felt torn. He could feel a shocking, burning, wrenching pain in his arm as though it were yanked out at the socket. Eventually, Izz luckily managed to fit his boot into the break in the wall below him. He placed his other foot on top of it, to relieve some of the pressure from his wedged hand. But he was not well balanced and was reluctant, despite the pain, to release his fisted hand. Izz willfully calmed himself down.

Looking up, he saw that the crack in the rock in which his hand was lodged was his only option. Desperately, he struggled to reach his free hand up toward the crack, but his right arm did not want to work and would not do what he wanted it to. He felt as if his body had forsaken him. He gathered the last of his strength; slowly and painfully, his left hand went up as Izz felt pain sweep through his arm in shimmering waves. But it had to be done. It was now; if not now, not ever! His chest heaved with exertion; his arm burned with agony and sweat ran down his face in stream lets to burn in his eyes. With one brutally difficult surge, Izz forced all his concentration on his arm. Finally, ever so slowly, his hand inched up. There would be no relinquishing; it would take everything he had. But at long last, in spite of everything, he raised himself to clasp his left hand onto the crack. He jammed his toes farther into the cranny and made sure he had a secure grip before he shook his wedged hand to dislodge it. Finally, he was able to pry it out. He rubbed life back into it and then examined it. It was badly bruised and scraped, but nothing seemed broken. He placed his cold, battered hand against his pounding chest and thought of how that could have proven disastrous and how at these heights a fall would have inevitably crushed every bone in his body.

After Izz recuperated and the throbbing of his hand subsided to a tolerable level, he continued to climb but did not have the full use of his right hand. To make matters worse, the weather from the North began to deteriorate. Strong winds swept in from the East, bringing with them dense dark rain clouds along the mountainside. From the West came high altitude formations with narrow bands distorted by the winds, creating patches of fleecy long, turbulent clouds. From the North, an unusually fast moving cold front careened in with stiff biting winds that whipped down against the high mountain peaks and seemed to blow right through him. The three systems seemed to be on a direct collision course directly above him, and there was no doubt that it was going to rain; the air all around him reeked of it.

The skies above him began to cast configurations of menacing shadow patterns on the surface of the endless cliff face. A steady cold mist began to fall, bringing with it a harsh coldness. The chilly condensation filled sky pressed down on him like a roof. In a short time, the descending, engulfing mist turned to freezing drizzle and poured down on him, but that was not enough to deter Izz. Izz hastened his pace, but the faster he tried to climb, the more it seemed that he was going nowhere. He began to tire. He braced himself against the cliff wall and peered up through the deluge. The ceiling of thick clouds overhead obscured the summit of the mountain.

A cold gust surged through the black strands of his hair, giving Izz a new cause for concern. Icy showers pounded the cliff wall and pelted him unceasingly. Fortunately, the stone still held some of the warmth it had soaked in during the day. After a while,

Izz was finding it harder to catch his breath. He stopped and sucked at the air as he felt the intensifying ache of fatigue seeping into all his limbs. He held on tight against the rock wall as running water drenched him.

It did not seem to matter that his strenuous effort to climb was producing body heat; his body temperature continued to drop. The higher he climbed, the colder it got, and the harder it rained. The drizzle fell heavier and heavier until it was coming down in torrents. As his perilous climb weakened him, his love for Zuree strengthened him. Blasts of air currents periodically punctuated by whipping gusts of alternating wind directions sent rain careening from every angle.

In the howl of the wind, the recurring demons' voices in his head called his bluff. *Come hither, your fall will be greater.*

Rain soaked and weary, he worked through his fear and continued. Izz's mind forced him to painfully, bit by bit, move upward, letting the rainfall flow down over his back and down into the unending drop. It was dreary, and the pouring rain seemed to act as a wet blanket, sealing the chill right into Izz's weary bones. For a second, Izz worried about how the cold would affect his twisted hand, but the weather seemed to keep the swelling from spreading past a numbing sensation, which turned out to be a good thing since his hand had been in so much pain.

Ever increasing cold air began to creep earthward from above the mountaintops, braiding with the soggy air below, adding to his misery. The rain slowly became partially frozen droplets and then turned into intermittent flurries of snow and sleet. Strange enough, the snow fastened itself to the almost vertical face. His breaths frosted in the crisp air, and Izz began to shiver. Despite the pain in his frosty fingers, he probed the rock wall for his next handhold. The arduous climb kept Izz's fingers bloodied and his nails broken.

Many times, Izz had to pause a moment on the steep, rough tortuous route to clear the cracks by digging out the frozen snow, which made the handholds feel like razor sharp rocks against his freezing fingertips. Ice that clung to the wall broke away and fell in glittering shards. Izz knew the dire consequence if he did not keep moving, he would most certainly freeze to death. His back was to the wind as it howled over the mountain—cold, biting, and bitter. He braced himself against its onslaught as the wind continued to chill his body until Izz could not imagine being any colder.

Every so often, he shivered awkwardly, his teeth chattered uncontrollably, and his muscles twitched with the pain of pressing his hands and feet against the icy rock. He was in excruciating agony as bone chilling bitterness seeped in. Tough as nails, Izz pushed himself to the edge of human endurance. He could no longer feel his feet; they were so cold. They seemed like blocks of ice and felt like numb lumps of frozen flesh. His frosty fingers seemed chilled with a painful cold that seemed to run deeper than his bones. His sweat soaked clothes became sheathed in a layer of ice as rigid as a suit of armor, making his every move that much more treacherous.

Flecks of snow fell past him and disappeared into the endless drop. As he looked up searching out the summit, snowflakes lodged to his eyelashes and clung to every part of his face, cloaking his view. He could feel his cheeks cracking under the wind's freezing touch, taking his breath away, and siphoning off any body heat no sooner than it was generated. Eventually, his hands were encrusted with white snow, making him look as if he were wearing glistening gloves of ice. The cold air burned his lungs with every tortured breath, and then he puffed out mist in the frigid air. His body heat drifted away in faint, feathery trails in the sky below him as he moved up one more rung on the ladder to the heavens.

Every muscle in Izz's body was pleading for rest. His strength was failing him for pushing himself too far and too fast. He felt dazed. Fatigue swept through him in shivering waves more painful than the cold, but there was no way he could rest while clinging to the frozen wall.

The shorter path to the top had become harder than Izz anticipated, and he was more fatigued than he thought he would be. His mind and body ached for rest. His fingers and toes were numb after hours of repeated movements in the cold and miserable conditions. The climb and the elements had proven to be much more of a challenge than Izz had anticipated. Izz feared for his life for the first time, knowing that his life clung by a thread. The frigid atmosphere made his body shudder with cold. The wind that slapped his face was scornfully icy. Misty vapor crystallized on his hair and eyelashes. The wind had robbed all the warmth from his body. Izz began thinking that he would likely die of exposure, wondering whether it would be the cold or a fall that would finish him first. The unbearable, harsh cold and a sense of helplessness caused tears to flow, and as soon as they did, they froze and stuck to his face. When these thoughts of failure became too much, he choked them back and blinked away, sweat and tears from his face. Defeat was not an option; he had to keep going for her. *It does not matter how slow you go as long as you do not stop,* he tried to assure himself.

Izz of Zia

As blind luck or divine intervention would have it, up ahead just to the left, Izz spotted what looked like a small cave like opening—or was it just a shadow or was it just all in his head? He had to find out. It was his only chance. Izz was nearly frozen to death by then; his life clung to a wisp. In his urgency to reshuffle himself to the left, Izz reached with a trembling hand for the next crook, and his shaky footing slipped on some ice in the same instant. Only the fingertips of his left hand saved him from plummeting. The mountain had become an angry arbitrator set to punish his first careless mistake. Izz shrugged to steady himself, trying to shake some of the fatigue from his deadly tiredness.

The process of freezing to death was proving more terrible than death itself. If he could only make it to the opening, he would have a fighting chance. Finding the stamina from nowhere, he clawed himself upward. As he came close, he was almost delirious with gratitude as he realized that the small hollow was real. Izz pressed his palms against the rock's lip and slowly lifted himself over the edge out of the biting wind, out of the harsh howling and the patter of rain. He crawled up into the dry enclosure and crammed his legs in out of the freezing wind and wet snow. Light filtered through the opening, and the raw wail of the stiff wind suddenly screamed through the hollow, funneling with it its frosty breath.

The cramped, unappealing space was just big enough to be uncomfortable. The rock surface of the hollow was cold as a grave and offered insufficient shelter from the wind, but at least it was dry. After a moment of thanksgiving, Izz huddled up against himself; he pulled the flaps of his cloak tighter around him, grateful for the chance to rest.

Tom Icon

With the strength left in his arms, he dragged himself over to the very edge of the crevice and hung his head out over the abrupt plunge of the southern face. He peered down at the infinite vertical drop, staring blankly at the wet grayness. The height was dizzying, and it made him shudder. He had made it this far. Izz lean back as far from the opening as possible, up against the wall. He crawled into a fetal position to warm himself, but the cold of the hard stone floor beneath him and the stone wall against his back coiled around him like a freezing mantle. He could feel its frost level moving up and could not shake the chill that iced his bones and crept toward his heart.

Suddenly he felt desolate and unbelievably drained and utterly lost. Zuree was a painful ache in the core of his sorrowful soul. Outside, the roar of the wind seemed an even more ominous sound than when he was out in it as it moaned and whistled past the opening. Frost bound fog billowed through the hollow, bringing with it its bleak chill that filled the air with snow dust. It was thin, icy, and as it flowed into Izz's lungs, it set his teeth chattering. Sooner or later, this would all be over. Sooner or later, he would be before a warm fire again, safe and sound, and Zuree would be at his side. He knew that it was looking more and more as if it was going to be on the other side of this life.

He rubbed the palms of his frozen hands together and blew his breath on them. The contact was comforting, like the soothing breath of a warm fog. His fingertips were both covered with peeling blisters, and his right hand was severely scraped, bruised, and swollen, but thankfully, it was not broken. He flexed it out several times before him and balled it uptight. It hurt, and Izz winced in pain. It was severely battered, but at least he still had his use of it. He blew his warm breath on them again and then put one hand under each armpit. Finally, the brittle cold eased, and blood began to flow into his fingertips again. He thought of make a fire and curling up next to it, but all he just wanted to do is lie down and sleep. Only the wet and cold kept him awake.

His hands continued to warm up, and excruciating pain darted through him as he thawed out. His whole body throbbed from exhaustion as he cradled himself for warmth. He reached inside his shirt and held the stone; it was the only warm thing in his whole world. As he felt the stone, its touch seemed to bring healing. His heart responded to the stone's glow, jingling happily in his chest, warming his blood after almost being frozen.

He laid back and closed his eyes, listening to the droning of the wind outside. After a moment, Izz wiggled into a new position to gain a view of the outside world. It was still snowing heavily, and from what he could see of the sun, it was slowly inching its way ever closer toward the horizon. He did not have much time until it laid a foundation for its painted sunset. Once the sun fell, it would be brutally cold, unsurvivable on the wall, but Izz did not plan on stopping for long. He tried to stay awake, but his eyes kept drooping. His sluggish mind intermingled the dimming shadows of the presence with the sunshine of the past. He thought longingly about his warm bed, his soft pillow, and a hot, well prepared meal. He thought of Zuree. The possibility of failure entered his mind. It could be so easy just to fall asleep, succumb to hypothermia, entombed, never to wake up again. He closed his eyes and sighed deeply. He leaned his head back against his satchel and allowed himself a few moments of fragmented sleep, waking in a shiver repeatedly. He dared not fall into a deep sleep. He squeezed his tired, burning eyes shut, wanting nothing more than to roll into a ball for a few moments of oblivion. Yet he dared not. Time and again he shook himself awake, but weariness slowly took its toll. He willed himself to stay awake with all his willpower. However, his exhaustion quickly extinguished his resolve. He forgot for a moment how tired and cold he was. At length, he lost track of time and space and fell into an uneasy sleep. His frosted breath rattled in his chest like dead leaves rustling in the wind. His last thoughts were of Zuree; her spirit surged through him, kindling warmth in his bones, renouncing the cold.

Messengers had been bringing King Ozzdon regular reports of Baddlock's movement and atrocities. The world theater was set, the drama was written, the characters cast. War was the only path Baddlock had left King Ozzdon to tread. And so it would be. King Ozzdon had been collaborating with his council of elders and newly formed war council every waking moment. Preparing, at all cost, around the clock, the defense of his kingdom against the imminent attack. Every incoming runner was a bearer of bad news.

King Ozzdon had ordered barricades erected around the kingdom, hoping to prevent the invasion of Edawn. Elite teams were sent out to burn any bridges that lie en route, impeding Baddlock's encroaching advance in any way within their power. Messengers from within the empire came and went with in-depth accounts of how the final defense of the territory was progressing.

The northern tower watch reported, "An armed regiment approaches from the North bearing the eagle emblem of Skymount, flying the Ziaian golden eagle flag."

The main Skymount forces had arrived, escorting an exodus of fleeing villagers from the North, one step ahead of the utter brutality of Baddlock's killing machine, taking refuge within what they believed were the impenetrable, protective walls of the Kingdom of Edawn. Leading the Skymount forces was Arius, King Kozar's eldest son. Ozzdon and Arius had been friends since they were young boys. King Ozzdon greeted Arius with an embrace. "I am happy to see you, dear friend. It gladdens my heart that you have arrived safely."

Among the arrivals was Rayzar, a citizen of Skymount, Zandor's childhood friend, Zandor's second most favorite person in all of Zia. They both greeted each other like brothers with a hug. "Come," Zandor said. "Let us find something to eat. You must be starving." They were joined by Kondor who also greeted Rayzar warmly.

Inside the king's war room, Ozzdon and his war council updated the new arrivals on the present situation and their plan of defense. The Kingdom of Edawn had done everything they could have done to that point. They were prepared for war.

King Ozzdon sat at his throne, listening to his generals who offered their latest strategies for the defense of Edawn. He was surrounded by the most senior and influential members of his Inner Circle. His expression was grave as befitted the circumstance. He was tapping his fingers on the armrest, preoccupied with Zuree's well being, oblivious to the obscured truth of just how much danger the world of Zia was up against. Now and then, he made a short acknowledging sound as his advisers presented their proposals to enhance Edawn's defenses. However, it was Zuree's fate that dominated his thoughts. He knew one day, the treasonous ones responsible would regret their damnable decision. His only hope was that it would not be too late for his only child. He remembered Izz and thought of how he should have never allowed him to bear such a treacherous burden alone.

The king cast his eyes around the room, and wherever he looked, he encountered bleak faces that were trying hard to be optimistic. The entire court seemed to be struggling with the realities of a vicious and bloody war. The king sensed that his leadership now was critical. Ozzdon picked his thoughts back up. He forced himself to unclench his hands from his throne and rose slowly. In a measured, ominous tone of absolute authority, the king addressed the meeting by calling the governing body to order.

Everyone in the hall united their attention on their king out of respect. It was a respect that had been earned, not demanded, born of nobility, not manipulation.

King Ozzdon spoke with a loud voice, "As everyone knows by now, a vast inestimable army from the North has amassed and has mobilized itself. Even as I speak, this sizeable army is approaching from the North, out of the ancient fortress Kingdom of Phantomsdeep. I bear full responsibility for being taken unawares. I was apparently the last person in all of Edawn to know what was going on right under my very nose!" He paused long enough to let his admittance crystallize in everyone's mind, and then he continued painfully, "The empire's red alarms have been ignited to the ends of Zia, runners have been dispatched to alert our forces from the farthest corners of the empire, and scouts have been charged with observing the movements of this impending threat. If there is any good news, that is it. The bad news is that it will take days for our closest neighbors to reach us from the South and perhaps weeks before our outer troops can reach us from the East and west."

Izz of Zia

All eyes rested on King Ozzdon as he spread out a map of the region. Then he continued, "Here from the North through the Plains of Maggato and down the Wazoo Valley is where I expect Baddlock to advance." He looked down at the map for a moment as if he was studying a mathematical problem. "The tower guards have been placed on high alert, and this day, I have ordered the opening of the kingdom's reserve armories, and arms will be distributed to every able man in the kingdom."

A stir of hushed astonishment rippled through the overcrowded gathering.

"Mark my words. Because we are outmatched in numbers, I have concluded that circumstances call for a carefully planned defensive strategy rather than an all out confrontation or attack. Edawn is where we make our stand until reinforces arrive. If anyone has a better plan than mine or can offer any solution to the crisis that we face, you can join the war council in the great inner hall of the palace. We will defend at all cost everything our empire stands for and everything we believe in against this vile contingent that knows only evil. I do not know what tomorrow will bring. What I do know is that if Edawn falls, Zia will fall, and I am afraid of what would come after."

Izz suddenly stirred awake by the urgency of his heart rattling against his rib cage, warning him that time was of the essence. He hissed through his teeth. He had settled into a twisted; half turned aching position. He woke tired and queasy. The giant thumb of gravity held him firmly in place, and he did not want to wake, but he had to get going, and he knew it. Even though he was not fully rested, Izz dare not let himself get caught on the cliff face when the blindness of night fell around him. His arms and legs were stiff and ached when he moved them. His body hurt from rigidity, yet it was his concern for Zuree that gave him courage and strength to go on.

He had slept just enough to let the chill stiffen up his bones and muscles. He found himself still cold and weak, but a sense of urgency made him quicken. He had to move his stiffened body to circulate blood into his arms and legs. He suppressed a passing sick feeling and forced off the waves of pain and weariness. Even though he had not warmed up much, he had gotten some critical rest and had somewhat recharged his mind.

He peered out of his momentary shelter. The snow had stopped falling. It was late in the day, and the sun had reached the western horizon. The mountain canyons were already in deep shadow. The combined cloud systems had separated; one had lifted, and the other had dropped below him. The clouds below rode on shifting currents of misty white air, so pure, almost solid. It just about seemed to Izz as if he could have stepped out and walked right across it to the other mountain ridge. He turned his attention to the summit, the thinning clouds and the dimming sun revealed that the enormous silvery moon had already reached high into the icy blue roof of the world.

The summit was at hand. From where Izz stood, it looked like a fast vertical climb to the towering roof of Zia. For a brief period, Izz took the time to survey his plan of attack and observed several favorable irregular crack systems. Izz tossed his uncertainties aside, made his decision, and emerged from the cramped hole. With both feet on the edge of the hollow, he stood and quickly stretched enthusiastically. Once again, he was back out over the vast dizzying drop. On the sheer rock face, the clear, sharp, frosty air whistled past, buffing him against the stone wall, making him struggle. He felt his skin tighten from the dismal and bitter cold. It threatened to overwhelm his tenuous equilibrium, reminding him that one slip and his fight to win against his mountainous nemesis would be over. As he resumed his climb above the clouds, everything beneath him vanished from sight, concealed underneath a deep white sea of condensation. Izz felt the barren cold bleed into his body and allowed it to become a part of him. Looking up, he saw that the top was within his reach, and he felt a flickering surge of strength, resilience, and energy flow through him.

No sooner had he hastened his pace than he noticed that the grade had become even steeper. If it had been any more vertical, Izz was sure that it would have toppled over on him. The increasingly tricky climb quickly took its toll, and immediately exhaustion started to dig in, steadily nibbling away at his endurance. And soon, every muscle began to complain every time he forced them to move. The pain in his hands, behind his thighs and along his spine was so intense that he wondered how he could go on scaling such a treacherous incline. Between being overly cautious and pressing his luck, Izz continued his deadly trek. He ran his palm over the surface of the rock feeling for a groove. His fingers closed over nocks that almost did not exist. He inched along, looking desperately for anything he could grab onto.

The muscle soreness that had never left him almost all at once intensified. The already cold temperature plummeted in the promise of the setting sun. His breath chilled in the bitterly cold air, and even though it had stopped snowing, the icy wind still swept fierce and strong over the unbroken surface. Suddenly, a gust that could have blasted the armor off a rhinoceros almost slapped Izz off the rock face. He was left trembling with a horror that closed in on him, leaving him numbed with something more frightening than fear. His heart was pounding erratically; he could feel the throbbing pulse in his temple, and his vision blurred with every beat. His breaths were coming in gasps. The pain in the nerves and tendons of his fingers begged for release, and he was shaking so much that he could hardly hold his grip. But no matter what, some way beyond his understanding, he was able to hang on. The summit was within reach, yet it somehow eluded him.

He clung to the bone chilling surface of the rock with an ebbing panic that shook him to the core of his will to live. After a brief moment of rest, he managed to recover, enough to begin pulling himself up again. Relentlessly, he pulled and pushed one hand and foot over the other, squirming up the cliff that reached high above the clouds. Every step was an excruciating jolt of physical suffering to the muscles in his arms and legs. His joints felt red and raw, his bones burned, and his muscles twitched from exhaustion.

When he finally approached the very top, suddenly his legs and arms refused to move. A worried grimace creased his sweating forehead. Every muscle in his body trembled and quivered with paralyzing agony. Izz did not know if his heart could take any more strain; his brain had arrived at sensory overload. There came a threshold at which the body is consumed, and Izz had long since reached that juncture. The adverse conditions, fatigue, and stress had finally claimed their ultimate toll. He was losing his grip. He avoided looking down; the last thing he wanted at that point was to get dizzy. Instead, he looked up with a stiff neck; he could see that the summit was just beyond his reach now. But his muscles, ligaments, and marrow were emptied, having not anything else to contribute. He was at considerable risk. The only thing that was left in him was the love in his heart. Izz let out a bloodcurdling scream. Undulating echoes of his fury scaled up the face of the cliff to the crest above. He pounded his palms each in turn and kicked his feet against the rock wall until he beat the deadness from them. In his position, anything was better than numbness, even pain. Now it got nervy.

Ever so slowly, by some triumph of will, Izz reached up to climb again. By the time, he had reached the top; his icy hands were hardening to the frozen hell of the cliff wall. In a perpetual state of exhaustion, he urged himself to inch up with a tenacious sense of purpose. As he searched out the next handhold, he forced himself to relax, making sure he was choosing his anchors wisely. Never did Izz imagine that the human body could endure such affliction.

Two
Skullsdome

At long last, calling forth reserves of backbone he never knew he owned, Izz reached a jittery right hand up, gripped his tattered fingers along the top ledge, and pulled himself up with all his strength. In the end, the ultimate victory was finally within his grasp. Inch by inch, he continued to pull himself up; he struggled and finally wriggled over the edge like a crawling grub. As thin currents of air drifted below him, he clutched the stony summit, drawing himself over the jagged rocks along the ground with the hollow strength left in his arms. He could not have been more tired. He crawled to a safe distance from the drop and then slumped to the snowy surface, his lungs heaving and straining for the thin air that was almost nonexistent. His heart was screaming, echoing in Izz's chest like the final thumps of doom. Izz had finally conquered Skullsdoom, reaching the highest point on Zia in one piece, just as the sun kissed the southern horizon. Thus was the triumph of a mind made up.

"Thank you for allowing me to live through that," he whispered to whoever created this mighty mountain. Before him, a snowy slope immediately slid down into an airy fog. Patches of snow covered the top all around, gleaming in the low leveled light of sunset. Gusts of wind lashed at him from every direction. He fell to his knees and then slumped and collapsed face first. He rolled over once and crumbed on a finger's breadth blanket of snow. As he lay on the icy rock, his throbbing muscles unknotted themselves. He had undergone the ultimate test. He deserved the joy and exalting nobility he was feeling. Izz wallowed in a moment of celebration and bliss with a towering sense of satisfaction over his triumphant ascent—that is until he realized just how weak, miserable, and dead tired he was. He mopped his sweat drenched face with a swipe of his hand. He did not know that a body and soul could be so overburdened and not be dead. He just lay there, sprawled out in a heap, clinging to the stony spine of Zia like a tattered, worn out rag that had been wrung out one too many times. Izz was so depleted that he could not bear in mind what it was like not to be exhausted. He dimly stared into mid-space. His head emptied like a gourd that had been cored. A veil of darkness fell over his glazed eyes and everything in his mind when blank. In the snow and rocks, he swooned in a dead faint, panting as if sucking breaths through a thick, sweat soaked rag. Izz went limp, clutching Zuree's stone in his fist as the whole universe seemed to reel like a winebibber looking for a place to be ill.

In the great hall, King Ozzdon once more sat silently in the presence of the war council, but this time, it was not a game being played out. His expression was blank while so many thoughts raced through his head. Outbursts of recommendations erupted back and forth between the members of the war council as they fumbled through their maps and war manuals. King Ozzdon wondered to himself, "Just what are you after, Baddlock, you old buzzard?"

He thought of how Ammiz had objected to many of the proposals the Inner Circle had made regarding the appointment of exclusive authorities and liberties bestowed on Baddlock. He had been bothered all along that it was too much control given to one man without restriction or guardianship. But in the end, the truth was that the Wicked Warlock Wizard had made fools of them all. Through his carefully orchestrated lies and half truths, all but Ammiz who saw through Baddlock's trickery. Ammiz had been the only one to object to Baddlock's appointment as overseer of the Inner Circle. That had been the day Ammiz had fallen out of favor with the nobles.

King Ozzdon's thoughts were unexpectedly interrupted as a page approached. The messenger informed him that the northern tower watch had spotted a runner coming in from the northern frontier. Ozzdon rubbed his face and tried to regain his thoughts.

"Very well," he responded. "Escort him here as soon as he arrives."

The council murmured in worried whispers, and there was plenty to worry about. There had been nothing but bad news from the northern frontier, and no one expected anything to change.

King Ozzdon's forehead solemnly drew together, furrowing deep vertical lines between his eyebrows as he spoke, "My fellow guardians of Edawn, the chain of recent events do not make any sense, and I do not know what it all means. What I do know is that we must be fully prepared for the terrible aggression that seems to have been set in motion by madness. We must weigh our plan of action very carefully while we can. Our course of action will not only determine the fate of our people but that of our empire and the course of history itself. The defense of Edawn, above all other things, is therefore crucial. We must unite as never before and root ourselves to our commitment to preserving our celebration of freedom, justice, and truth."

The king was informed that the messenger had arrived. Ozzdon motioned the runner to approach. The messenger had to be carried in because he had run so far and so fast that he had collapsed before reaching the northern gate. The messenger could barely speak. "I bring word from the northern kingdom. Skymount has been sacked, my lord," he finally managed. Then his face drained of its color as he spoke of the inhuman atrocities that he witnessed and the enormous military force that was headed their way.

They all listened in stunned silence, their faces lengthening with every word as the messenger described the unimaginable destruction and most appalling carnage.

"One could not begin to imagine the slaughter—men, women, and children!" It was hard for him to recount the story.

The king looked around and saw that every unblinking eye in the room was fixed questioningly on him as if pleading him to gather them up and save them against a menace that seemed about to overwhelm them.

The messenger went on mumbling, his words running into one another, about weapons of catastrophic destruction and the demonic bloodbath that followed. The scout reached out and pulled the king in closer, almost frantic. "According to the deeper wheel prints and tracks, they are carrying much heavier catapults, equipment, and troops this way." The messenger concluded with an unexpected earful, "They're all dead. There is no one left alive. It is the end of the world up there!"

King Ozzdon squeezed his eyes closed, barely able to control a shudder as the deluge of horrible images cascaded through his mind as a result of the scout's ghastly account. His heart ached for his friend King Kozar, and he had to tear himself away to one side, not wanting to show any weakness, least of all not in front of his warriors. He struggled to retain his composure as fury welled up from within. When he gathered himself, he turned with his broad brow knotted and drew the great sword of Edawn, which hung from his silver belt at his side, and raised it high in the air. His complete being emanated the strength and authority of his eminence. In a loud commanding voice edged with frustration, he vowed, "In the name of all that is good, I for one pledge my life to defend, at any cost, the Edawnian kingdom, the Xylenian empire, and the Ziaian world against all aggressors." He spoke in a firm, disciplined voice, unmistakably in charge, as if suddenly tapping into a deep cistern of inner strength.

His generals rallied around him all of one mind, in one accord. The mettle of a true king fell upon the room; he was the rightful king, and every warrior knew that his word was law. The hall erupted into an unanimous roar of dedication and alliance. The sons of Edawn were ready and, if need be, were willing to spill their blood in defense of their world.

Izz came to with shivering convulsions as the penetrating frost woke him. The piercing cold had drawn vital warmth from him, making him even more miserable than ever. His eyes were frozen almost shut, and his lips had become a single twisted line. He could not move, could not see, and could not think. He had no way of knowing how long he had been adrift in the shadows of nod. He thought he had frozen solid but was finally able to pull his hand from the icy blanket of snow and felt its biting chill. He knew that it was much too cold to be lying there. His body was numb, his limbs felt half frozen, and he was sure his fingers and toes were frostbitten. Izz wanted to remove his boots and massage the chill from his feet, but he knew how ridiculous that would be.

Izz hobbled to his feet despite the agony he felt in his sore thighs. He tried taking a step, but his deadened legs refuse to bear his weight. He stomped his feet until feeling seeped back into them. With the first few slow steps Izz initially took, he wobbled like an infant learning how to walk. His muscles quivered as they unknotted themselves, gradually becoming able to move steadier and surer again. Izz thought about how he almost had not made it. And even though his strength was depleted, he somehow managed to stir up excitement just for being alive.

He suddenly realized his bladder was full. He walked to the edge of the cliff, stood atop the outermost jutting ledge, and peed a golden stream over the brink. He was standing at the rooftop of Zia, on the tallest mountain on Zia on which he yet prevailed! He had an unobstructed vista of the panorama that surrounded him as though he could see to eternity. The fantastic view transfixed him as he stood there surveying the world that stretched away to the South and fell away just beyond his feet. On either side, he could see with the help of the light of the setting sun that he was flanked by mountains saddled with sharp cliffs and dotted with wooded islands on all sides. He pulled out his long eye and cast his sight to Zia's farthest ends. He searched every direction and could not find one single mountain peak to rival his own.

To the West, below him, he saw a continuous chain of beautifully shaped triangular mountains with their rugged volcanic peaks reaching to the heavens. To the East, the Circle of Fire resumed with the likeness of a surreal scene resembling an echo of granite waves in the wake of the stormy high seas. Zia stretched out before him wider than the eye could take in, grander than anyone could ever imagine. It was too much to absorb all at once. Izz saw to the South the vast Wastelands of Woes was a wrinkled yellow blanket unfolding before him from wilderness to wilderness. The mighty Megacon River was a winding string of reflecting light. The Ring of Giants was mere twigs rising from a covering of green that was the Ebony Forest. Beneath patches of white clouds, as far as the eye could see, Izz could just barely make out Edawn, an angular speck against the backdrop of the Edawnian Sea. Farther out, Izz saw the perfectly circled edge of the southern world of Zia. He scanned the beautiful, silent world for the longest moment. He stared in awe and astonishment at the heart stopping view as the southern horizon unfolded before him like a magnificent blooming offering out over the sea and beyond the wind. Izz had risen above the clouds to look across the celestial body of Zia. He had seen a small proportion and perceived the overwhelming whole. It was as Ammiz had correctly affirmed, Zia had to be round. It was the mote of dust flowing throughout the length and breadth of the endless expanse he had seen in his dream.

Despite the fact he was still wincing, a sense of triumphant exaltation upstaged his pain. It had all been worth the journey to the top of the world, where he was suspended between the heavens and Zia. He was enjoying his king of the world footing, on the heights of this proud and beautiful mountain until he panned his eyepiece to the eastern horizon and noticed a movement. He focused his long eye for a closer look and saw the smoldering smoke towers of Skymount. The dismal sight of the once great kingdom and the dimming and the shrinking of the setting sun in the distance drew Izz back from his captivation. He backed away from the edge as the last pinpoint of the sun reflected its final signal of departure.

In the lingering twilight, Izz turned toward Skullsdoom. Natural beauty and cobbled together ugliness existed side by side.

What the fog had partially obscured now leaped out and stood threatening over him like something out of a bad dream. For the first time, his objective came into full view, the fabled lost Kingdom of the Noragore Rim.

"The forbidden realm," Izz whispered to himself.

It was Skullsdoom, the ancient ruins he had seen from the Ring of the Giants. The mountaintop abruptly unfolded before him into a disfigured inclining plain; the uneven footing was crusty and full of hairline fissures that hissed hot sulfurous gases all around him. The height that marked the remotest place on Zia was a mysterious and inactive inferno crater. The kingdom was built over a rift gouged into the mountainside. Perhaps where a devastating explosion of an ancient eruption had ripped the mountaintop in two.

Innumerous gas bubbles frozen in stone, cinder cones, and glassy volcanic rock fragments littered the landscape. Crackling, sizzling sounds hissed everywhere as geysers erupted boiling with steam. Bubbling black mineral waters and boiling mud pools sprouted rare and unusual thermal flora that displayed multicolored coppery browns, egg yoke yellows, and snowy white deposits. Rainwater that had seeped through the volcanic rock was forced back up to the surface in high billowing clouds of stream heated pressure, evidence of an everlasting fire below. A series of scorching hot springs along the ridge line spilled over, their water level dropping and rising again every time the geyser below the pool erupted. Newly forming silica terraces mingled with solidified lava and ash that cascaded over the sides of the mountain and kingdom frozen in time.

As the trail ascended toward the ruinous kingdom, the climb became steeper and harder. The sun was long gone, taking with it any warmth. The desolate, decaying kingdom seemed to loom over the jagged landscape like a long forgotten evil deity. Traditionally known as one of the oldest realms in Zia, the kingdom of death, as it became known, was, no doubt at least a thousand years old. Its walls erected during the renaissance of a dark period marked by radical dark changes, and wicked ideas. It was an era dominated by the self proclaimed Enlightened Ones—not an imaginary place after all—yet now it laid waste a dilapidated derelict lost in time.

The massive fortress of ruined roughhewn stone rose from the ashes of destruction. Like a monstrous anomaly stained on the side of the mountain marred, scraggy, and ageless as the weather beaten cliffs it clung upon. Towers and walls that rose ominously to formidable heights within a steep dormant domain were seized within its near vertical slopes of steaming cliffs.

With traces of twilight still glowing, the radiance of the moon, and the clearing mist, Izz could see the nearly extinct vent that supported Skullsdoom's badly deteriorating facades of masonry. Fractured, crumbling, and ascending to a final dome there the fabled kingdom of Skullsdoom stood frosty under the silvery moon. The dome, by nature or design, resembled a colossal skull topped with cratered eyes from which gases and steam eject into Zia's atmosphere. Izz stared at the massive fortress like kingdom of stone. It was monstrous, ancient, evil, reputed to prosper on human misery and sacrifice. At first, Izz moved slowly, yet maintained a steady pace. His weary legs forced him to stop every while until, in frustration, he commanded his legs, "Do not pester me anymore with your complaints." And finally, his brain grudgingly gave up on his bodily pains.

By the time full darkness had fallen, Izz had found that he could still see by the dim light of the moon that he was about halfway to the forbidden kingdom. Izz made his way forward as the moonshine interlaced itself with the evening haze and shrouded him like a cloak. Izz shifted his gaze up into the sky to see that the first pale stars had made their appearance. What astonished Izz was the constellation of shining stars that were strewn across the sky in a perfectly straight geometric line, something he had never seen before. Like harbingers, they dominated all the other stars to help the illuminating moon push back the enveloping cosmic dark. Izz's silent gaze fixed on the light display of the heavens and wondered if it could be the Great Conjunction Ammiz said would come. He questioned whether he would behold what the seer referred to as the glory of the Creator. He studied the starry display and sought to discern the mystery hidden in their brightness. He might just as well have willed the conjunction to spin back across the sky from where it came.

Izz knew he had only so much time to find Zuree. He pulled out Zuree's amulet and saw a faint pulsating glow, or was it just the reflection of the full moon? He returned the stone inside his garment and pressed it to his heart.

As far as Izz could see, he saw only shapeless mounds that were once walls and graceless heaps of gray blocks that had not withstood the sands of time. Izz forged ahead into a region blemished with fallen temples and monuments, crumbly and half buried, still marking where they once stood. Skullsdoom, named after the skull formation at its crest, was once the most powerful kingdom in Zia. It was interlinked to the lower world through a vast network of sky bridges and highways from the East. It was a kingdom built on top of the many ruins of earlier civilizations. Now it too was a decaying monarchy left behind by history in an obscure, forgotten corner of Zia.

Izz moved through the semidarkness as darkness continued to close in around him. The shadows thrown by the silvery full moon grew, and so too had Izz's uneasiness. As he neared the outer walls of the forbidden inner kingdom, Izz was half running even though he was short of breath from the lower oxygen levels. As Izz crossed the threshold of what remained of the outer walls, he noticed that most of the stones of its main gate had already tumbled down. As Izz made his way through, he was amazed at the size of the megalith blocks that remained standing.

The light of the full moon washed the summit with just enough light for Izz to trudge along until he reached the crest of a small rocky ridge. A sudden movement caused Izz's eyes to open wide with surprise as he reached for his dagger. A nocturnal marmot dashed for its den in the rocks and turned to peer out. From its entrance, it waited for the danger to pass so it could resume its nightly search for food where there was little food to be found.

Ahead was an ancient bridge that led to the ruins of the inner forbidden kingdom in the sky. The bridge seemed to be one colossal piece hewed out by the ancient rock cutters directly from the mountain's solid granite rock itself. The bridge spanned a deep fog enshrouded gorge. Izz studied the structure; it seemed as if it was on the verge of falling into the bottomless chasm at any time. Izz stepped onto the stone bridge, hoping that this was not the moment time chose to crumble the bridge into dust as it seemed it should have ages ago. As he walked out over the stone walkway, it cried out with abandonment and neglect. A sudden second tremor rattled the bridge, followed by massive jolts and thrusts. Although less intense than the first quake, it was an unnerving moment as dust and pebbles scattered and danced wildly on the churning bridge's walkway.

Pieces of bridge knocked loose by its weight plunged and bounced off the gorge walls as they cascaded down. Not daring to stop, Izz moved across the bridge, staying as close to the stone balustrades along the edge of the bridge where it seemed to be most stable. Izz peered over the side to see the steep walls of the gorge descend into the depths of obscurity. Gently undulating layers of mist rifting between the expanses of the two shelves made it seem as if the chasm dropped off the edge of the world. Izz moved quickly across the shuddering stone bridge, not willing to risk his life to the bridge one moment longer than he had to.

At the end of the bridge stood the inner wall's main gate that led into the inner world of Skullsdoom. The entrance was flanked on both sides by a gigantic limestone crumbling wall that stretched and surrounded the forbidden kingdom; it seemed to merge into the hard granite of the mountainside. It was a massive barrier built to protect a bygone domain. The fortified walls were battered with bad repairs in many places, ample evidence of a prolonged battle. The plaster covered walls were scarred by deep gouges and long claw marks, evidence of a sustained siege.

Tom Icon

As Izz approached the main gate, the shadows of the moonlit night deepened. The massive walls were covered with odd tangled brown and black ivy vines everywhere. There were darkened pockmarked blocks that had broken off and fallen into fragmented pieces. Jutting rusted iron pikes turned to the inside led Izz to wonder if this was a vault of confinement. The sky had too quickly turned from gray to purple to black. Izz searched out the strange string of stars and was amazed at how fast they had moved so far across the canopy of the heavens. What surprised him most is that they seemed to be shining more like miniature suns than stars and appeared to be coming closer together. As Izz rounded the wall, he felt his insides jump. The moon had suddenly cast its pale metallic glow over the rugged gate entrance. Set atop two crumbling black stone columns were identical pair of rough hewed carvings of gargoyles glaring down at him like evil demons from an ancient world. Their curved bodies, which almost seemed human, were covered with molded plates studded with iron spikes. Each wore a mysterious unearthly animal dragon face, and both bore a hideous grin from which protruded a grotesque snakelike tongue. The two sat on their perch overlooking the entrance; their menacing eyes bulged out at him in mock ferocity. Set around them were tall ornamented pillars and columns with deeply engraved lines, circles, triangles, and unholy symbols that seemed molded rather than carved on to their surface. Izz noticed warning signs etched into the wall, written in an old forgotten language. It was a riddle of obscurity and decay, leaving only an unreadable story. The wall reliefs seemed to indicate that the forbidden kingdom's kings had built their empire on foundations made to the overlords of the underworld. His courage was shaken. An overwhelming sensation of fear and darkness ran through him like a distant howl. Like an omen of forewarning, a foreboding feeling of something terrible about to befall him came over him. Suddenly overwhelmed with the strongest urge to run, Izz asked himself, *Should I be trespassing here? Should I even be here?*

Izz of Zia

As Izz passed, shifting moonbeams washed over the two gargoyles. The ominous light and shadows traversed over their sunken eyes, making them appear as if they were following him with their eyes. Their presence gave the impression that the two posted sentinels were daring Izz to enter the realm they guarded. As Izz forced himself through the gates, the menacing eyes of the terrifying gargoyles continued to follow him. The shattered remains of what was once an impenetrable oak gate now rotted away, only its massive hinges remained embedded into the stone gate frame. Long stained streaks of rust ran along the wall and through the barren ground below. Upon crossing, the threshold Izz felt the overpowering desolation that surrounded the entire kingdom.

As Izz passed through the crumbling gatehouse, he felt that he had traversed beyond some unseen fringe that descended him into the incomprehensible outer limits of another world. It was like entering into a domain that was tens of thousands of years old. Izz found that the outside was not half as cheerless as the inside. There was no sign of life, and no footprints marked the dust.

Whiffs cloaked with stagnant, hot, and humid air blew heavy across the frosty courtyard. Beneath its pungent odor lay a rich musky scent full of death and deep decay. In the atmosphere, Izz could sense a strange drone like the haunted sounds of evil, restless music that vibrated and lurked in the air.

Well inside the dilapidated remnants of a once great inner kingdom, Izz discerned there was something among the wall's buildings and rubble that spoke of a great breach and a dreadful battle. Tumbled down stones from the collapsed walls were scattered throughout the inside like an enormous gutted beast. There were scars of war everywhere. In many places, it seemed the mountain itself had heaved upward from its depths to reclaim its domain. Elongated limbs of vines twisted endlessly up the crumbling walls, interweaving wreaths of long unearthly tentacles.

Inside the inner court of the fallen kingdom, Izz moved along almost in a dreamlike state. He walked through the streets now empty and forgotten except for the spiders, centipedes, rats, and the unseen. So far, all he had seen were the shadowy outlines of collapsed ruins and empty dwellings. Shambling structures set amid a muddle of back alleys. It was as eerie and still as a graveyard, extinct without a soul, a place of the dead and decaying. Izz walked past a continuous progression of dark, empty, and dusty shells of buildings. He stood in awe at the enormity and complexity of the fortress kingdom.

Izz found himself at the center of a plaza where streets branched out in several directions. Some avenues seemed infinitely fractured and unstable, where the danger of collapse seemed to lurk at every turn. He stood at the center of the hub, wondering which way he should go. From the small clearing, he gazed up into the night sky and was awed that the unusual routed constellation was ablaze with a brightness that rivaled that of the full moon. The handful of white spheres was illuminated with a magnitude he had never witnessed before.

Izz felt the stone burn against his bosom when he faced what appeared to be a well worn boulevard that led straight up toward Skullsdoom's skulled summit. Izz drew the stone, and it rippled a bright blue light when he turned and started toward the main avenue. His footsteps quickened as he returned the stone and hurried up the dust laden path he hoped would lead him to Zuree. Izz moved along the fragmented cobblestone corridor through the darkened carcass of stone where flickering moonbeams threw tongues of dancing shadows high and low throughout the silent streets of a broken world. There was no sound except for the whistling moans of the wind's blowing pockets of wispy white haze that trailed through the weeping ruins. The streets were shadowy and barren, with internal decay strewn everywhere.

Coarse gravel ground underfoot as he peered into the maze of streets and alleyways, and somewhere, he thought he heard a sinister laugh, trailing off as the wind picked up. After a while, the street ended at a passageway that led up to a well worn stairway. Izz ascended the seemingly endless flight of steep stairs. Wide monolithic stone walls cut deep into rock ascended almost vertically and were badly damaged. Parts of the mountainside were strewn diagonally across sections of steps. Izz marveled at the workforce and the hundreds of years of toil it had to have taken to move those gigantic stone blocks and raise the colossal skull landmark. He could almost imagine the throngs of slave builders that had once pulsated through the forbidden kingdom's circulatory system, drawing and pushing the lifeblood throughout its streets. Izz's mind was boggled and could not imagine how a feat of this magnitude could have been executed. Skullsdoom's inhabitants had raised mighty temples and huge buildings where they gathered to worship the monstrosity of their skull god. And now the dilapidated monument was a forgotten work of man lost in the dark well of time, now only a burden on the ground it stood on.

At the top of the twisted stone steps, Izz saw that the path ended at the foot of the overawing skull topped mountain peak. Its ominous half buried skull seemed to be warring with the sky and losing as the mountain slowly reclaimed its stone.

Before the skull's dome stood a monumental archway, on either side atop two columns were two crouched stone gargoyles similar to the ones Izz had seen at the gate, but seemingly more hideous. They stood to watch like menacing sentinels before a vast dark edifice shrouded in the fog. Behind the imposing archway stood a gruesome altar like erection of cobbled up stone. Izz's anxiety grew as he approached. There was a different haunting, grieving sound in the air, an indefinable, strange noise barely discernible but constant, or did it only exist in his weary mind? Then he perceived a distinct feeling that he was being watched; by what or who, he did not know. All he knew was that there was something out there, waiting at the end of the stairway and it not of this world.

Preferring not to go this way, his hand went to Zuree's stone. He pulled it out and looked at it again. It gave a bright flash, and Izz knew he had no other choice. He came upon some sort of a monument encompassed by a cluster of lofty obelisks. The pillars were set in a five point star pattern that towered above the radius center of the weird edifice. As he neared the monolithic monument, its grandeur and massive form momentarily took his breath away. The construction of the decrepit giant was structurally sound but awkwardly asymmetrical, making the overall conception abnormal and unnatural. There was no way of knowing whether this was a result of destruction or some architecture's twisted idea of pleasing architecture. Long weeded vines choked the entire structure. If they should be removed, the whole architectural deformity, he was sure, would instantaneously come tumbling down into a dusty heap of ruin. The odd framework marked with weather stains and other signs of great age seemed to be of some significant ritual important in the era of the self proclaimed Enlightened Ones.

Deep, dark streaks showed on every side of the edifice, evidence to the concentrated power of incineration that had all but consumed it. At the altar's center was one solid black stone that rose from its flagstone base about half the height of a man and was roughly the length and width of a man. Along its sides were strange markings and pictorial symbols time had faded away, and only traces of its somber colors remained in the cracks. He seemed to sense something of its use, yet he did not know anything. The top surface of the platform was hollowed out into a shallow basin with two outlet groves cut at both sides of the bowl that were seemingly made to collect runoff. Izz moved in closer and looked inside one of the stone containers. He saw something caked and cracked the color of dried blood at the bottom of the large black stone urn.

He looked upon the raised images again and ran his fingers over its surface. Izz stepped back and carefully mulled over the strange thing. At first, it was difficult to understand what he was looking at, but gradually he discerned that it was a man being held down and his heart being cut from his chest. A priest stood over the victim holding the victim's heart to the sky while the victim looked on in horror. Izz felt the blood drain from his face, and his stomach turned; he realized it was a human sacrificial altar. Izz took several steps backward. The spell of intrigue he had fallen under was broken the realization that the corrupt hands of evil men had created the abomination that stood ominously before him. He was suddenly repulsed as if he felt icy fingers tighten around his throat as if it was his blood, the evil spirit yearned to fill its urns.

Izz stepped farther back, skirting the offering pedestal and quickly moved away from it, regretting having discovered its truth. Without taking his eyes off the altar, he quickened his steps away until he thought it was safe enough to turn and hurry away. He tried to wrench the evil from his mind as he distanced himself. His thoughts turned to Zuree, revolted by the idea that the person most loved by him in the world might die in such an ugly, grotesque way. He moved higher up the steps with an eerie feeling that he was being followed.

He hurried up the steep stone steps until he had arrived at the base of the grotesque skull monument. Stone was the medium of immortality, but the skull structure was earthquake battered with tumbled, fallen bluffs and overcast with cracks resembling lightning. Soot streaks, caused by a tremendous heat from an unknown source, had blackened the weather beaten surface of the skull like dome. Izz tread through fragmented rubble of shattered slabs and clumps of shapeless pillars that lay scattered about like the upturned rib bones of a giant monster. In many places, the ridge looked as if hell itself had heaved upward from its depths in its attempt to drag down the man made stone structures.

Against the mountain crest, was what was left of two chalky white grit covered battlement spires that had been destroyed by fire. Near dead vines climbed out of the poisoned ground to cling onto the crumbling structure. Hot steam plumes hissed from every rift into the thickened mist, sprinkling black liquid down from the dome of the skull formation. Stagnant water gathered here and there in tiny pools along the uneven surface. A whiff of ammonia wrinkled Izz's nose with its repulsion. *What is that revolting odor?* Izz asked himself. It was a rank and stale smell like that of some phosphorous bog.

As he came under the shadow of the unnatural skull like distortion on the mountain crest, the stench of charred, poison mixed with sulfur became more and more pronounced. As he came closer, the oppressive feeling of evil intensified in the air. Izz thought he heard a faint and prolonged echo of an echo that sounded like cries for help coming from the ruinous ingress before him. It was imperceptible at first, so much so that if Izz's senses had not been so keen, he might not have caught it.

In the background of the wailing sounds, there seemed to be an even fainter hissing sound: "Come, come, I have been waiting for you."

Izz tried desperately to convince himself that what he heard was not real, but the impression, however faint, continued to resound in his soul. Then a deafening quiet ensued. It was so utterly silent and deserted that Izz questioned whether he might not have mistaken what he thought he had heard.

At the base of the skull monument, Izz stood on the remains of what was once a doorway. He tore away at the dripping's foliage to reveal a thousand mysterious years hidden beneath and among the dust. Izz studied the graveyard of stone around him carefully and searched out any indication of an entrance that would lead him on his way to who knew what unthinkable doom awaited. What was left was the charred rubble remains of a keep or a stronghold where someone had mounted a last resistance. The entire side of the mountain was scorched, further evidence of some form of unearthly heat. The darkened glaze on its smooth ancient walls was now covered with moss, lichen, and creepers. Izz found rare traces of brimstone scattered everywhere. The steep and partially collapsed side of a huge crater remained as a testimony to an unimaginable cataclysm of utter destruction.

It was all guesswork; there was not one stone left on top of the other to indicate what had once stood there. What looked like a structure cut from rock, time, or war had caused it to collapse, though the head and the frame corners of an entrance still stood. Everything else had buckled into piles of rubble. What remained was just a flattened heap of fused ancient stone that lay in silent witness to the calamity that had destroyed it. Judging from the amount of ruin left, it had to have been a stronghold that now looked more like a huge ancient tombstone blasted out of time. Izz examined the surface of the rubble and could not fathom what tribulation could have heated granite to the point of melting. What was left of two columns of black stone, identical to the ones he had seen at the kingdom's gates and the sacrificial altar, flanked either side of the mountain. Whole sections of collapsed remains of an ancient entrance were now covered over with earth, rubble, and brimstone.

In the fading light, Izz saw perched at the top of each column two severely damaged stone gargoyles. The bestial guardians seemed to glare down at him. The same foreboding warning he had seen on the dead Warning Tree was written on the stone lintel over the top of what was left of the entrance.

DO NOT ENTER. THOSE WHO DARE NOT HEED THIS WARNING WILL MEET THEIR DOOM AND BE CURSED FOREVERMORE.

Despite the ominous warning, Izz wandered onward, in search of the entrance; that is when he realized that the persistent noises that sounded like moans were coming from beneath Zia.

Some ancient forbidden magic is kindled here. Izz realized that it was here that Abaddawn, the prince of the underworld, had first shown himself to man. And it was here where his most loyal worshipers had gathered to offer their souls to the darkness. He backed up, quickly stumbling over debris that was littered everywhere. *What happened here? Something horrid has taken place here!* Izz trembled and shivered as he frantically stepped away, almost losing his balance. *Something very, very bad, I can feel it in my bones.* He wanted to leave this place, but he dare not, without Zuree.

THREE
THE DESCENT

Izz pulled out Zuree's stone studied it, turning it this way and that under the full moon that stood straight overhead at its highest point. The stone's gleam reminded him of her eyes and the way they had gazed longingly at him. Again and again, came the unimaginable thoughts of the end Zuree might suffer at Baddlock's hands. The sheer thought of her demise left him stricken. The scene played over and over in his mind. And if he could not bear the mere thought of it, how could he go on living if it had become a reality? The ruins, the twisted altar, the destruction, and the skull added to his despair.

He replaced Zuree's stone and walked right up to the wall, but try as he may, he could not make out the entrance in the fragments that were left of it. If there was ever an opening, much of it was buried under finely ground black residue from the vaporized minerals that covered everything and gathered in small dust dunes scattered throughout. Izz dropped to his knees, and with his bare hands, he began to dig away at the finely pulverized pumice and piles of tumbled, broken stones.

After digging here and there, Izz finally uncovered the stone slab that had once sealed the entrance for untold centuries. The stone barrier was cracked down the center as if by some tremendous upheaval of nature. As Izz turned over the broken slab, a spine chilling sensation of evil seemed to leak out from the darkness inside. He was sure he was standing before the gates of hell. He wanted so much to leave this place, but fate had other plans. Izz pulled the neck chain from inside his tunic and held up the stone. Izz moaned mournfully when the gem gave mute evidence, brightening when he faced the hidden entrance and dimming when he turned away. This had to be the way to where ever Zuree was being held, unquestionably.

Izz stared at the dark and uninviting opening that seemed to be lying in wait for him like a set trap biding its time until he was well within its grasp. Izz's faith was for a lingering moment shaken; he looked apprehensively at the opening. Izz knew he had to go on. He could face anything, even his own death. But he could never face the haunting anguish of knowing that he did not do everything in his power to save the love of his life. Hopeful that the stone discerned more than he was capable of knowing, cautiously he poked his head inside, surveying the stability of the entrance. His gaze revealed the emptiness within. He warily wedged himself through the narrow opening. He felt as if he was crawling into his own tomb in search of faith. He was fully prepared to face the vilest horrors that could befall upon him. No one could accuse him of cowardice.

With propped up courage, intent on one purpose, Izz boldly clamored over the stony rubbish and squeezed between the cranny of the massive slap. Was the barrier meant to keep his intrusion out or prevent the escape of whatever was imprisoned inside? Midway through the slab, Izz remembered how much he disliked tight enclosures. He was not quite sure why, but he did with every fiber of his being. He had hardly completed that thought when his satchel got hung up on a jagged rock from above, and he could not advance. For a moment, he panicked, thinking he might be stuck there forever. He peered back into the moonlit world outside and was suddenly overwhelmed by the urge to turn around and go back. Izz lay there motionless between the thresholds of two worlds of light and dark. He was sure that it was a death trap, and he wanted nothing more than to leave this dreary place and go back to the world he knew. He hesitated and began talking to himself, "You know what I was just thinking? I was thinking that this was possibly the dumbest thing I have ever done. I was thinking I ought to get out of here and never look back." *Let them think I am a coward. Let anyone think anything they what.*

Frozen in place, he suddenly felt an equally overpowering feeling of self loathing for his miserable double mindedness. "No! No, I must find Zuree. I could never pardon myself if I ran off and left her to die alone. I am either going to find her or die trying."

There would be no peace for him if he did not do everything in his power to ever fulfill his reason for living. His mind finally adjusted to its befitting senses. With his blameworthiness somewhat purged, Izz relaxed, adjusted himself in the crack that held him, and wriggled his satchel free. Izz's longing gaze crawled along the tunnel ahead; then he took one last lingering look at the sky outside, his last look at the outside light. Taking in a deep breath, Izz quickened his spirit and spurred his courage on as he crawled forward. Still, he was perplexed by the nameless uneasiness that had swept over him. It had not been a mere sting of fear, but rather a bitter, nauseating apprehension that had wreathed and twisted about in his gut and choked off his breath. His only hope was that he did not run into any other tight squeezes. He hoped he could just slip in quickly and rescue Zuree while Baddlock was still occupied with sacking the northern frontier and celebrating his victory over Skymount.

He mechanically took the final plunge down, thrusting himself into the dimness of the gloomy underworld. He was about to find out what he was made of, for Izz did not know yet how scared he really should have been. The wind howled a bewailing lamentation outside as he slipped along the damp dirt into the darkness. Thick layers of undisturbed dust over a dark uneven rock floor—at least, he thought it was rock—showed no signs of intrusion. There were no signs that indicated that anyone had passed this way in eons. Everywhere he looked, he saw the ancient signs of a savage breach. There were traces of high resistance. Buried in dust were broken idols and the remains of the mangled resisters.

Izz of Zia

The instant Izz stepped through the threshold of Abaddawn's doorstep, the sadistic beast who ruled over the immense underworld empire of darkness was made aware. He sat upon a carved black throne made of a single slab of polished black stone. The enthronement was cut from a chunk of red streaked volcanic rock that looked as if it were made of shiny glass. At present Abaddawn could only fade in and out of the physical world. He allowed a slight mocking grin bare his fangs although his eyes kept their grimaced blaze. Abaddawn knew Izz carried the sacred dagger with him, and he knew that he was coming for the girl and nothing would dissuade him. Abaddawn had the princess, and very soon, he would have the very dagger he needed with which to sacrifice her. And now all the darkness had to do is wait for the exact moment when the long waited conjunction reached its zenith. How could it be more perfect? At once, Abaddawn began to indulge his most gruesome plans to lure Izz into the most elaborate death traps.

In that same moment, Izz heard within the depths of his mind a spiteful voice say, *You are going to be sorry in ways you could never have imagined.*

He had plunged his way into the underworld, or had the underworld plunged its way into him? Izz remembered what Ammiz had told him, "The lord of shadows is restricted, yet he remains powerful. Although he is constrained, he will attempt everything within his rule to destroy you." It was evident that the ground he set his feet upon itself seemed wicked. A rancid odor of evil that conjured up images of corruption and open graves seeped right into his pores. Izz stood where no human foot had marked its impression for perhaps millenniums. The depth of the uninterrupted dust indicated how long eternity was. Izz warned himself to be on guard. The first thing Izz hoped for was that nothing had taken notice of his entry.

Once standing inside, the first thing of significance Izz noticed was that the moonlight was not only coming in from the crack in the sealed entrance. There was moonlight also coming in from the many holes chiseled into the ceiling. Were they light portals, ventilation shafts, or both? Izz stared up through the perfectly hewn porthole in awe. He tried to envision a man wedged in the hole, methodically chipping away through solid stone, year after year after year, inching his way toward the surface. Rock bolts held the walls and ceiling in place, making the ancient man made tunnel look stable and fragile all at the same time. With apprehension, Izz peered past the ghastly gray stone that faded into the blackness and disappeared into the underworld. He looked directly into the darkness and beyond it, then quickly back as if sensing he had missed something. His eyes warily took in everything as the dampness and moldiness of the unknown pervaded everywhere and everything. Eerie vileness permeated through him as he cast his gaze all around, not knowing what it was or from where it came. Izz's skin tingled, and his hair all over his body stood on end. He almost immediately felt disoriented and misplaced, as if he had stepped out of a world of light and life and into a world of deep perplexity and dark secrets. From that moment, it seemed as if the man made passage did not want him to be there. The stuffy air seemed charged with hate and chaos, pain, and misery. His fierce sense of stabbing dread bore down on him early and never let up. Izz took a few hesitant steps along the flagstone path into the causeway and then stopped to allow his eyes to adjust to his darker surroundings.

Once across the main entryway, he saw before him a deep, symmetrical walkway cut through the solid granite of the mountain stretched out before him. Izz had no idea where he was headed. Inside, the rough hewed tunnel's air was warm, damp, and earthy. The only sound was that of water dripping. At first, he could not see three steps in any direction. Only slowly did his vision adjust to adapt to the dim moonlight cascading in from the many ceiling ports spaced throughout the ceiling. Each light port produced a small corresponding small circle of luminous glow on the eerie stone chamber floor. Nervously Izz took a few more steps forward and paused to look around again to let his gut sense feel things out. Izz reasoned that where he was had to be the place where legend had it that a whole civilization lived their lives out, never surfacing into the outside world. He could not rid himself of his building tension. Wincing, rigid, and uncomfortable, he stepped forward into the unknown, where Zuree was waiting for him somewhere in the darkness.

Izz followed the path into the underbelly of Skullsdoom in a spiral descent for a thousand paces or two into the underground empire. Along the way, moonlit beams continued to seep feebly into the inky darkness, just managing to pierce into the hidden chamber like the light of the moon viewed from the depths of a murky sea. Izz narrowed his eyes to a squint, trying to see through the dimness. Gradually his keen eyes fully dilated to get used to the dim moonlit corridor. It was not easy to see anything, but the pale light that lit the fusty, unoccupied tunnel was enough so that he could see in front of him and would not need to light his lantern yet.

It became evident that he was within an even older realm of a more ancient civilization entombed beneath the ruins of the forbidden kingdom overhead. The farther he walked downward, the farther it seemed he was walking back into time. The walls and ceiling were lined with rolls of arches that reinforced the chamber walls and resembled the inside ribcage of a giant serpent beast. The musky odor was as thick as a cloud. Beyond this point, he did not know what he would find; he set his jaw with determination, come what may and continued his journey into the unknown. He felt a shuddersome chill go down his spine, even though he saw nothing in the tunnel that posed an immediate threat. There was no rational reason for him to be afraid; he tried to convince himself. Yet there was that odd sense of danger and an overwhelming, foreboding feeling of intensifying wrongness that he could not deny. He knew that he did not have to see or touch anything to be aware that he was in the presence of a nightmare yet undiscovered. He sensed the steady glow of the stone against his heart. Izz felt excitement as he hoped with all his heart that Zuree might lay waiting in the next deep gulf of darkness. As he walked through the long tunnel that was all too swiftly retreating into the shadows, his hand inched close around the butt of his dagger.

Up ahead, Izz saw there was another stone door slab. A shadow revealed that a hole just big enough for a man to fit through had been chiseled into the stone barrier. The seal had been broken. Just then, Izz remembered how an older sailor on one of his many sea voyages had spoken of ancient tombs and tomb robbers. They spoke of those who were masters at setting hidden traps that guarded against those who might raid their tombs and sacred places. They told stories of booby trapped entrances with arrow propelling devices. They gave accounts of deep pits covered with straw and filled with needle pointed stakes sometimes poisoned meant skewer any person who fell in them. They talked of dangerous, deadly snares with hair trigger mechanisms that made every path a potential avenue of death.

Perhaps it had been tomb robbers seeking the fabled lost treasure of Skullsdoom that had gone before him. No sooner had Izz crawled through the opening than he felt something inconceivably ominous, seemingly stirred up by his presence, suddenly jump out to envelop him.

Along the darkened passage, he came upon yet another doorway. This one was open and welcoming, and Izz just knew it was trouble as soon as he laid eyes on it. The closer Izz got, the more he feared something awful was going to happen. Something about the way the odd looking threshold was quarried into the made him uneasy. He warily stepped into the unusually wide and strangely cut doorway. As he entered, he wondered if such booby traps existed, and if they did, what were the odds that any such ancient device would still work after thousands of years? For no apparent reason, midway through the threshold, Izz suddenly hesitated, unable to dismiss the dread he felt. He cocked his head, trying to sense what was amiss. But by now, he was so well acquainted with fear that he ignored his misgiving as just another misconstrued feeling. He cast a final glance forward and from side to side and then continued cautiously.

Izz of Zia

When he stepped into the next corridor, he thought he had felt the stone flooring beneath his foot give slightly. While he was trying to decide whether what he felt underfoot was real, he heard the clang of metal on metal. He froze when he heard a grinding sound behind him. Instead of jumping back, Izz jumped forward to get out of the way as a massive rolling stone rolled, intent on squashing the intruder. As the stone settled into place, an opposing wedged stone slid down behind it to lock in place. Izz stared in shock as the stone doorway rumbled and shook as dust cascaded from everywhere, and the room seemed to inflate and then deflate with a shudder. With all his weight and strength, Izz pulled and pushed at the unyielding stone. He was unprepared neither for the helplessness he felt now nor for the terror that engulfed him.

He turned to consider his options, his fear evident on his face as he looked about apprehensively. The thin air in the corridor eddied with narrow shifting layers of swarming dust. An aura of malice, a change in the very atmosphere, weighted down on Izz's spirit and touched chills along his spine. Izz could not quite put his finger on it, but there, just up ahead, he could sense something ominously wrong.

Izz's anxiety mounted as he moved away from the blocked passage. He could see little from his vantage point, despite the dim moonlight bathing the chamber from the portals above. Izz could feel fear rising in his belly. Drifting motes of fine particles danced against ghastly moonlight like realigning constellations in the nearly stagnant air that surrounded him. Izz pushed his way through the cobwebs that infested the passage. His sense of foreboding forcefully intensified, causing the hair at the back of his neck to rise higher and higher on their ends with every step. He brushed away another layer of cobwebs that entangled him like strands of torn tentacles.

What he saw next before him seared a jolt of both shocked and terror within him. As the moment of totality grew, his eyes locked in disbelief on the gruesome scene before him. His mouth was moving, but his words were stuck. Before him were hundreds of long, razor sharp, two edged blades descending from holes in the ceiling. Skewed in the blades outlined in dust were six men's skeletal remains. Izz gasped with infinite terror as he felt their ghosts leap out toward him, warning him to go back. All the while, he was thoughtlessly backing up until he found himself leaning up against the rolling stone slab with both hands spread, pressed flat against its rock surface. In all likelihood, they had been the ancient grave robbers that had breached the second sealed door. Perhaps they were explorers in search of relic treasure, the vast fabled treasure that had vanished at the fall of Skullsdoom. They had somehow managed to avoid the first trap. Unfortunately for them, they must have unknowingly tripped the triggered mechanism that set in motion the fatal contraption. The death suddenly closed upon them like a monster's teeth to end their lives. What kind of inherently heinous mind could have come up with such a gruesome implement of death? A depraved mind of evil, no doubt!

Izz's mind methodically analyzed the situation, racing over and separating into parts the possibilities and consequences. He then studied the interrelations of both and concluded that it was impossible to go on. Furthermore, his analytical mind pointed out to him that that could have very well been him, pierced through like a skewered chicken. Izz suddenly found himself wishing that he was anywhere else in the universe than at that particular corner of the world at that specific time. A horrible, overwhelming clash of willful resolve pushed its way to the forefront of his mind. Overpowering fear rooted in doubt and indecision. "What am I doing here?" he asked himself, trying to justify why he was there and not at home. "I am just one man. What can I possibly do? This quest is indeed a fool's mission. It was a fool hearted attempt at heroics like the one that got these men killed. I have to get out of here!" Full blown panic rushed over him. His spine turned to jelly.

Izz turned back to the enormous rolling stone that had cut off his only escape back to the outside world. Closing his eyes to concentrate, he tried to get some kind of grip on the stone; his brute effort to move it was just as unavailing. Izz let out a roar of fury as he tried with all his might to budge the rolling stone. Izz grunted and groaned, pulled and pushed at the rock in vain. The massive stone would not even dislodge a fraction of an inch from its inert position. He struggled to keep panic from engulfing him as he realized that he was cut off.

The first thing he came to terms with was that he had no other option than to go forward, deeper into the abyss. That was his only chance in the world, and he might as well face it. He cautiously made his way toward the maze of blades. He stood before the murderous implement, staring at its victims for the longest while. The flat edged shafts were made of an alloy Izz did not recognize. He ran his fingertips along the edge of a polished shank, and to his amazement, it had remained surprisingly razor sharp. He had to traverse this deadly quandary of blades somehow.

Izz removed his backpack, held it at his side, and entered the labyrinth of lethal steel. Ghastly moonbeams from the outside world spilled down from their portals to mingle with tiny illuminated dust particles like snowy white powder seemly suspended in the nearly stagnant air. The limited light was inadequate at best, yet the moon streaks, which leaped and danced off the reflecting blades shimmered like a thousand tiny refractions. The flickering back and forth off a thousand tiny mirrors, offered just enough light to allow Izz to navigate the problematic gauntlet.

As Izz gingerly twisted and squirmed forward from one ingress to the next, his concentration was centered at its cutting edge. His senses were as keen as the razor sharp blades that surrounded him on every side. His lips were pulled in tight against his teeth, his stomach drawn, his shoulders set. Izz had to meticulously analyze his every move with precise accuracy, for he perfectly realized that he had taken his life into his own hands and risked being shred into pieces if he made the slightest mistake. Small beads of sweat formed on his forehead and ran down into his eyes, causing him to squint hard against the salty perspiration burning in his eyes. He desperately tried to wipe the stinging sweat from his teary eyes. He raised his shaky free hand, knowing that his life hinged on the balance of his optical and nimble exactness.

Tom Icon

One by one, with his heart pounding in his throat and his insides cringing, Izz bypassed the skeletons of men who had died so violently. Tattered and disintegrating pieces of clothing in various stages of decay still hung from their dried out bones. Their possessions remained untouched. The skeletal remains of the first man were festooned with cobwebs and covered inch deep with the dust of the ages. He was crouched down to the lowest possible position on the stone floor, where he was pierced through the chest, thigh, and left hand, like a rabbit on a rack. His jaw was gaping in an eternal scream. Suddenly, something uncanny and snakelike crawled out of one of its eye sockets. It was an unusually long flesh eating centipede that slithered across and disappeared into the shadow of the other socket. The next skeleton was frozen in a kneeling position with the blade driven through its right hand held up in a protective posture. The futile attempt did not stop the blade from stabbing the victim through the torso. Fragments of dried, decayed flesh and hair still clung to bleached out bones that dimly reflected in the eerie moonlight. The same agonizing scream was petrified on his skull. The others were all equally twisted in a last ditch effort to save themselves. One had the bones of its arms tangled on the blade, indicating that the sufferer had died a slow, excruciating death. Izz wondered how long the looters had been there, years, decades, or centuries. Their once bright fleece clothing, now disintegrated and faded by time, gave no other indication other than it had been a very long time.

At long last, Izz made it to the other side. His clothes were sliced in several places, and he had sustained several razor cuts on his shoulders and arms, but nothing too serious. Just outside of the perilous deathtrap, Izz fell to his knees. He had no realization until then how mind numbing it had been to maintain such an intense degree of concentration for so long. Izz pushed himself up against the wall, hugging his backpack to his chest as he listened to the blood pounding in his ear. At that moment, he wanted nothing more than to slide down to the dusty corridor floor and to rest, perchance to sleep, but he knew that was not an option that he could afford. A growing knot of urgent despair tangled deep within him, leaving his nerves raw and exposed. Izz glanced wearily around the vaguely illuminated chamber. The light shafts offered just enough lighting to see down the long tunnel. There was not much to see in the thick dust laden air, only that the passage dropped at a steeper grade now toward Zia's bowles

In the deepest underbelly of the netherworld, Zuree had been in the pitch blackness; ever since the metal door had been sealed shut. Within this insidious darkness, she had no clue of the passage of time. All she was aware of for sure was the thundering of her pulse in her wrist encased by the manacles that shackled her to the darkness. Her body ached from the positions she had been forced to assume to relieve the excruciating pain in her wrists. She was surprised that she had been left alone for so long. Her mind had become a jumbled mess. Zuree was very scared to be down there alone. She was sweaty, weary, and in throbbing pain, but most of all, in throbbing pain. She feared she would go mad or that she would be down there until death came to take her.

In the darkness, Zuree heard weird things—a ruffling in the air, the grating of stone, and the odd sound of footsteps. In the blackness, she began to see transparent, apparitions made of smoke or some strange liquid like substance. There were other bizarre phantoms in addition to the peculiar black figures.

Just then, she felt the familiar pull of her amethyst stone from afar, and for a fleeting moment, she thought she could feel Izz's presence. But she could not reach out to him or hold him. In anguish, she cried out, "Izz...Izz, I am here! I am here." Just the thought of him a far way off brought bitter lamentation to her heart.

As Izz stared down the sinister dust colored corridor, he studied the walls, roof, and floor; his mind became distracted. He reached back to his first memories as a child. His recollection was like a bothersome dream, dredging up hidden perceptions that he was all

alone. The feeling of being unprotected came crashing down on him. Suddenly he thought he heard in the silence a dim and faint resonating echo of Zuree's voice calling out to him now. All at once, the memory of Zuree's eyes took his thoughts away from the fixed condemnation of his circumstances. He felt a slightly cool draft on his face coming from the opening just beyond the darkness that caused a sliver of hope to ripple over him. If there was anything worth winning, it was her that would make him strive to tread through the pathless unknown. His inborn dream of a future with Zuree resurrected and became more real than ever, never to be destroyed, never to die, and never to be doubted again. He had to keep his strength up. As he ate what was breakfast, lunch, and dinner, he wondered to himself, *How can I ever hope to find Zuree in this tangled quandary?*

The point of no return had been indelibly cast. Baddlock relentlessly drove his Norticlan armies to the South, day and night. His monsters war machine quickened its march trampling over the face of Zia as Baddlock intensified his quest to bring Zia to its knees. The Wicked Warlock Wizard's surprise attacks were serving all of his evil objectives. Baddlock quickly boarded his expansion, dominating a long section of the northern roadways essential to their advance. He simultaneously cut off Edawn's northern supply routes.

Along his path of annihilation, the Wicked Warlock Wizard destroyed not only man and beast but also the land itself. Without stopping to rest or sleep, his narcotic driven army burned and pillaged everything in its wake. His wake created a surreal world founded on fear, bathed in blood, and tainted by atrocities and destruction. He cared nothing about life or those who possessed it. He brutally exterminated thousands, indifferent to their human condition as if they were something pitifully insignificant. He valued only those things that were offensive to the living and hated everything the human heart cherished. With every conquest, his wish to reign grew infinitely more devious, consuming him with the selfish desire to be worshiped as his dark underworld god promised.

To rule the world of Zia was Baddlock's most enticing obsession. His insatiable ambition drove him beyond greed, covetousness, and madness. The dark fires of his mind awoke to seducing beliefs of his own godhood, allowing demonic powers to unleash the vilest bidding of its beguiling master. As it has been said, if one tells a lie that is bold enough and repeated long enough, there will be those who will eventually come to accept and believe it. Such was the alluring effects that poured through the mind of a willing participant, one based on the hatred of humanity and self loathing. The only thing that seemed to survive Baddlock's intellectual decay was his cold, brilliant, military objective to rule in the four corners of Zia.

Those who fell victim to Baddlock's murderous onslaught, those who were without head wounds and those who were not too damage would be added to the ever growing legions of Zomborges. All the while, the most powerful demons, including the prince of darkness himself, impatiently awaited their appointed hour. At the Great Conjunction that their dark energy might be set free to rule over the heavens. At the exact moment the blood of the princess was poured out upon their dark altar demonic portals throughout the universe would open.

The dead bodies were gathered and stacked like firewood onto wagons. Arms and legs bobbled grotesquely over the side as they were moved along the uneven northern road on their way to their next camp when darkness covered Zia.

The few young males who had been spared were drugged and turned into the living dead, eager to do whatsoever they were told. The old, the young, and the women were disemboweled, disfigured, dismembered, or impaled along the roadway. Many were left along the roads squirming in agony as a symbol of Baddlock's reign of terror. It was sure to send shocking horror up the spines of any who happened upon the gruesome sight and would, in turn, send fear coursing throughout the land.

From time to time, a pawn was allowed to escape, ensuring that detailed news of their new master's awesome supremacy was spread. The fear of an unimaginably cruel and heartless death was the Wicked Warlock Wizard's grand design and most powerful weapon. Its effect laid siege to the imagination that expanded wide and far like a contagious disease before the wake of a world, which was rapidly becoming Baddlock's empire.

By the time Izz finished the last of his meager meal, he had finally concluded to himself. "I have no other alternative but to go onward; there is no other choice." As he sat there, his eyes searched the darkness before him, which seemed just to dangle there suspended in time and space. Izz could sense that unearthly things were waiting for him there. Izz knew that he should get going.

Nevertheless, he remained, lingering another brief moment, very much like a moment of reverence. Then he found himself whispering a prayer from which he somehow drew strength and courage. He bolstered his legs, got back to his feet, and strapped his satchel to his back. With a tether tied to his heart, Izz approached the foul darkness, prepared to fulfill what was his unwavering fate. Izz could see that up ahead the passage was dimly lit with a dark grayish glow that seemed to darken at his approach. He shivered as much with hope as he did with fear of the unknown that waited for him. The path quickly turned into obscure uneven rock. Izz drew the gem, it flickered mysteriously with eerie green blue clarity. It brightened as he faced the unknown passage ahead and dimmed when he turned any other way. So be it. The stone made his faith endure, giving him the courage to keep going.

As Izz descended along the ever declining path of Zia's undersurface, he shifted his gaze constantly, alert for any unexpected motion. There was just enough moonlight penetrating from above for Izz to make his way. There was no rational reason to indicate that anything tangible lay in wait behind every shadow.

And yet he felt threatened by a sense of constant peril as if evil was riding upon his shoulders.

Izz walked along cautiously, his eyes glancing in all directions. His fingers fumbled on the hilt of his dagger. He looked to the rock ceiling to see that even at this depth, portholes were somehow bored into the solid granite from above to let in shafts of moonlight that filtered in from the Ziaian surface

FOUR
THE GAUNTLET

e came to a bend in the passageway; all appeared quiet and lifeless. Yet Izz could feel wickedness waiting in every dark corner, watching him through eyeless sight. An oddly warm breeze blew sultry cloaks of air through the passage. He could not see very far, but because he was running low on lamp oil, he thought it best to conserve his lamp oil while he could. As Izz moved along the path, he could smell the stench of decay.

Just ahead, there was another arched doorway cut into the rock where the unknown waited for him. The source from above gave him just enough light to see that beyond the doorway, there lay a human built shaft that led through a carved archway and farther into another passage. As he walked toward the arched entry, an uneasy feeling tore at his belly from all sides. He reached the first eerie threshold of the two. Each one fixed with its own death trap, no doubt.

Izz peered in to see that just beyond the entrance, a long corridor stretched out before him. Cobwebs clung from above, waving in the currents of air. The walls displayed the precision work of man. Something about the hand of man upon the stone made him uneasy. Then suddenly, he just knew—something was amiss, he could feel its wrongness trilling in the air in front of him. Izz's keen eyes noticed some unusual rows of walnut sized holes bored into the wall in patterns of threes. The holes were aligned from about eye, chest, and thigh level, sequenced from one end of the passage to the other. That could mean something or nothing at all. On the opposite wall, there was the exact perforation pattern, slightly offset from the other.

A sense of trepidation seized Izz as if a pair of eyes had suddenly focused on him. His confidence was shaken; his suspicion, exposed. He knew that this had to be a trap like the ones canceled at every other corner ahead of him. Izz had to go forward. There was no turning back even if he wanted to. After all, he had been through; he was prepared for whatever lay ahead, ready to do or die. "Besides, what were the chances that any of these rusty mechanisms still worked after all these eons," he whispered to himself. Then he thought, *Where have I heard that before?*

Despite his better judgment, Izz moved on. Of course, he suspected there was danger there. Of this, he was certain. What Izz did not know was that each hole was fixed with a powerful magnet. If the magnetic field were interrupted, a magnetic lever would trigger three metal crossbows exactly where the field was broken. Izz wiped away the strands of sticky cobwebs. Stiff necked and rigid with apprehension, Izz stepped forward.

Izz crossed the first set of holes. There was a sound, a click; the sound was very real, not just the figment of his imagination. Then there was a simultaneous screech of rusted iron and a sharp clank of metal on metal. The golden hair trigger mechanisms were tarnished and covered with just enough dust to delay an explosion of arrows a fraction of a second. Izz gasped a breath as his heart evoked a pounding warning. In a purely reflexive move, Izz took a step back with blinding speed. He caught himself from stumbling as the six arrows zinged passed him crisscrossing like dueling swords, trailed by six jets of dust. The arrows came at him faster than Izz could have believed possible. The barrage of shafts stuck hard against either side of the corridor, sending stone shards and wood splinters in all directions. Each arrow narrowly missed him by a breath, except the one bolt that ripped his heavy wool cloak across the upper part of his body, leaving a razor cut from one end of his chest to the other. Izz felt a trickle of blood spill from his wound, but in his terror and shock, he felt no pain. Without thinking, Izz reached for his chest and wiped across the rip on his cloak and shirt. He looked down as he ran his thumb from finger to finger to see and feel the blood between them.

While he was recapturing his breath, whatever was left of it, he felt dust floating down from above. For the first time, Izz noticed the same three hole pattern on the ceiling. He looked down to see the remains of three more arrows shattered on the dust covered floor. *That was close, too close,* he thought as he allowed himself to breathe again. Yet not close enough to turn him from his mission. Just then, a crazy idea entered his mind. Noting the triggers were just slightly delayed he might be able to sprint across the corridor fast enough to avoid being pierced through. After all, he was the fastest man in Zia.

Izz focused all his attention ahead. One false step and all would be lost. He dug the tip of his boot in between two base stones and concentrated on the other end of the passage across the death zone. There was no room for error. Izz cleared his mind and allowed his body to take over, relying totally on his muscle memory. With one explosive jump of preloaded elastic energy, he launched himself forward like a bolt of lightning. Hope and fear ran alongside, hand in hand, as Izz's boots lifted little swirls of dust into the air, kicked into life animated clusters of dust motes sent meandering through the shafts of light behind him like galaxies drifting away through the cosmos. He quickly got into an accelerated rhythm and almost at once reached his maximum running speed. Arrows systematically fired in sequence, each just barely missing him by fractions of a breath. Izz could sense the projectiles as vibrations of displaced air swished past him. He heard the bolt's high pitched whooshing sound as they crossed and smashed themselves on opposite walls, splintering into thousands of fragments as he sped through the threshold of sudden death.

When he had crossed the last magnetic sensing set of eyelets, he felt a trickle of falling dust brush against his face and felt the whole tunnel tremble. There was a horrible rumbling of granite scraping against granite as two huge rounding stones began to roll into place, covering the entrance and exit on either side of the passageway. There was no way Izz was going to be able to stop his full tilt run; thus like threading a needle, he dove for the lower corner of the rolling stone and squeezed through the viselike closing by the skin of his teeth.

Izz landed shoulder first on the solid rock floor. After a half bounce and a full roll, he was sprawled face down in a twisted position on an unforgiving floor covered with centuries of accumulated dust. He lay there catching his breath, creating horizontal plumes of dust with his nostrils, and then Izz rolled over laughing outright, thrilled at his narrow escape. "You missed!" he roared. "You missed me!" His voice echoed defiantly throughout the chamber. Only an eerie silence answered him.

Izz dusted himself off as he stood. He squinted into the ever darkening moonlit passage that disappeared around a bend in the rock wall. Bursting with adrenalin, he wasted no time in moving on. His boots left behind a set of footprints in the thick dusty floor as he headed straight down toward a place that would have best been sidestepped, but there was no way to avoid it. He continued across the rough, dusty stone floor into the next corridor and almost immediately began a steeper descend. As Izz continued down the shaft expecting the unexpected, he became aware that the air started to change. There was a strong gassy odor of a flammable mixture and sulfur. The passageway's grade steepened sharply yet into an even steeper descent as it curved on a corkscrew path into a seemingly bottomless narrower passage cut into the bedrock. Deeper and deeper into a dark world beneath Izz went down. The farther he descended, the darker and warmer it grew. Izz wiped the sweat from his forehead. He had no idea how deep into the hidden bowels of Skullsdoom he had gone.

The lack of moonlight filtering in forced Izz to consider digging his lantern out, but then he noticed that the far end of the passage below was lit. He walked toward the light, tracing its illumination forward like a lifeline through the haze. Izz drew Zuree's stone, and as far as he could tell, he was on the right track as its glow pointed his way toward the light at the end of the tunnel. The only sounds he heard along the way were the occasional muted echoes of soggy water dripping slowly from the ceiling and the crunchy sound of gravel under his boots. Izz reached the light source and walked into the middle of a circular space with a light vent cut into its ceiling.

Izz moved on until he had come to a junction with three tunnels leading in three different directions, one branching off to the right, another to the left, and between the two was a spiral stairwell that led down deeper still, into the recesses of Skullsdoom's underbelly. Again Izz drew Zuree's stone. It was the only thing that he could trust, the single link to Zuree in this dark and mysterious journey toward the center of Zia. The stone indicated that the stairwell was the way he should take. The dim moonlight from the space above faded as he walked down level after level of ancient foot stones carved into the rock solid granite of the mountain. The passage seemed to twist down into total darkness. The stone again led him down into the mysterious depths underneath, doubtlessly full of secrets and untold dangers.

Izz was beginning to wonder how far into the shadows he had gone when up ahead, he made out another island of faint light. The portholes of light had led him deeper and deeper into the bowels of the deep. He picked up his pace until he came to a huge circular subterranean chasm filled with thick, warm, stale air. He moved along the wall to the edge of the tunnel and discovered that the passage led into another underground cavity.

In contrast to the darkness he had emerged from, the moonlit hole in the center of the chasm seemed bright. Izz walked to an overhanging edge to stare deeper into the strange opening. What he saw astounded him. From top to bottom, it looked like a giant wormhole that burrowed straight down into infinity. Clinging against the wall, Izz peered into the void's great depths and saw a sheer drop that seemed like a sort of window that reached toward the centermost parts of Zia. What he was looking into was the seemingly bottomless black hole of an ancient volcanic opening of some sort.

Izz of Zia

Izz then leaned out as far as he dared, craned his neck, and looked up to see the source of light that marked the vent's rimmed opening. The circle of moonlight reached down as far as it could and was lost in the blackness below.

His eyes penetrated through the obscurity to see toward the bottom. There close to the farthest reaches of infinity was a reddish glow that indicated volcanic activity of some kind. Inside, along the wall, he saw what seemed to be the start of a spiral staircase. As his eyes became accustomed to the changing light, a set of immense stone steps of a stairwell was revealed descending, almost vertically, along a stone clad wall that coiled down into the brink. Izz stood indecisively at the top of the stairwell, keeping his eyes trained on the steps below him. The brightness of the volcano opening was not exactly what he needed, but it was the best he could get. The light showed a dark, empty pit below him. Izz nervously drew Zuree's stone and held it out toward the stairwell. His guts jigged a dance under his ribs when the stone burned brightly. He was not at all sure that was what he had wanted, but he considered trusting the stone his sworn duty. He had sworn a vow, and nothing this side of heaven was going to keep him from keeping it.

The stairs were lichen scarred and severely damaged. Izz set his best foot forward and stomped on the first worn step to test it. It felt sound, not too crumbly under his boot. And thus he continued his descent. Surefooted Izz descended the twisting steps that clung to the internal surface of the vent wall. Every inch of rocky surface was crusted over with eerily brilliant colored minerals of different chemical combinations. He ran his fingertips along the sheer rock faces of the vent. It had the feel of marble with streaked layers of black ash and bleached patches of white. The stone stairwell appeared to be ebbing down into the darkest heart of the mountain. Moving quickly, Izz tried not to stay too long on the same stepping stone. He descended deeper, not having the slightest idea where he was headed or what he would find there. His anxiety mounted with each step as he navigated the circular stairway as if somehow he knew something terrible was about to happen.

Small holes and fissures along the wall released chlorine and fluorine gases. Other vents let off steady plumes of scalding steam. Now and then, dense clouds of sulfur dioxide gas roared upward from the lower vent, enveloping Izz in acidic fumes that swirled so thick that Izz's vision was obscured. Each time the heaviness of the gasses passed, Izz refocused his watery eyes on the receding steps below him. He leaned into the wall and felt along the face of the increasingly hot stonewall as he tried to make out the lay of the steps below. Off balance at times, he guided himself downward, moving as quickly as he could.

The air grew thicker and heavier with every descending step down. Izz's heart thumped with anticipation as the stairs seemed to moan and groan under his weight. As the stone stairwell took a sharper descent, he heard a dim and faint voice. "Your next steps will be your last. You have sealed your doom."

Izz's pace wavered in purpose, and he staggered to a stop, flung back against the vent wall by what he heard. He stood there frozen. He lifted his foot but discovered he could not maneuver himself downward. He listened intensely, but only a deep, deafening silence ensued. He finally exhaled a long breath. The only sound that came after was his pounding heart beating in his ear. Izz questioned whether he might have merely imagined the reminiscences of a forgotten fear. The dim glow from the single source of light from above bounced off uneven walls casting grotesque shadows that seemed to leap out at him with every step as he forced himself to continue.

Halfway down, he felt a pang of apprehension and paused, feeling that all was not quite right. From the step below his foot, he felt the slightest vibration through his boots and up his legs; then it intensified, feeling the shock through his whole body. "What now!" Izz groaned.

In the next pulse of time, Izz felt a remote fluctuation in the weight of Zia. There was an almost noiseless sound of stone grinding on stone coming from below, followed by what Izz could barely distinguish as a whooshing sound. The wall seemed to be vibrating as if a swarm of giant bees was swarming, their tension building, just on the other side. Strong, hot winds belched from beneath, and Izz felt pressure in his ears. The whole vent shuddered. He heard milling and snapping of the stone around him. The stairwell was making a long rolling sound, rumbling loudly, grumbling and threatening to come apart altogether. The walls of the vent began to clatter; the steps shook forcefully jiggling him from the inside out. It seemed that the whole world of Zia was shaking. Suddenly being inside the vent was now like being on the inside of a dragon's mouth. Izz was whispering a solemn prayer just under his breath, hoping that the dragon did not decide to roar!

Then in a heartbeat, a wall of thick gas blew up from the pit, and everything around him turned into a world of grayish red. Izz was forced to shut his eyes and drew his scarf around his head to protect his eyes and lungs. An instant or two later, a noise from deep beneath the bowels of Zia, a rumble, filled the vent; and in the next terrifying moment, the stairwell groaned and shifted beneath his feet. When Izz stepped on the next footfall, his heightened senses detected instantly that the step under his foot would give way under his weight. Without stopping to think, he jumped to the next set of steps. Then Izz heard a crashing sound from overhead. Instinctively, he sidestepped and pivoted so forcefully that he slammed and collapsed himself flat against the wall just in the nick of time to dodge a huge stair section falling from the dimness above. Several massive blocks came smashing down on the very spot where he had been standing. He pressed up against the wall and braced himself as he saw another stone block pulverize the section of stairwell below him just inches from where he was standing.

Izz stared in terror as the stone section disappeared underneath him into the enveloping darkness. As the stone block continued endlessly into an unimaginable depth, Izz heard its echoing rumble as it bounced from one wall to the other, creating such an ominous sound, as if all of Zia was crumbling all around him. The vent was in convolution, and Izz had to hold on to the wall to keep himself from falling. He leaned back and looked up along the length of the shaft as far up as he could see. From above, Izz watched in panic as he saw yet other sections of the stairwell appear. Suddenly at that same moment, the steps under his feet cracked in several places. The vent rattled and heaved up with a terrifying motion. For a startling instant, a dizzying image of his death flashed through his mind.

Most of the steps above him were gone. A crippling fear came over him so intense that his heart almost failed him. Izz desperately struggled to assess the instantaneously shifting situation mounting all around him, but there was no time to think. In the next click of time, he surrendered totally to his gut instinct and made the instantaneous decision, then and there, to move down and fast, or die. At breakneck pace, he ran down the steps to the next level. Izz heard more stones falling and was forced to move even faster with superhuman stealth and care to avoid being smashed like a cave cricket. At that instant, Izz heard the first stone section when it finally reached the bottom with a shattering crash that shook what was left of the stairwell below him. The air trembled violently as enormous projectiles of fire spatters and bursts of fireballs glistened through the shadowed air. As Izz raced down on the only path that was open to him to where he did not know, another stone section hit just in front of him, forcing him to leap to the next lower segment of the stairwell. Stones continued to rain down. It was like an aerial beast closing in on top of him. Death was nipping at his heels. Each impact sent shards of fragmented stone in every direction and ejected clouds of choking smoke and fire. To merely survive seemed almost impossible, but to walk away unscathed from this would be even more so.

Izz was moving at breakneck speed, faster than he believed was humanly possible—with the agility of a hunted cat, his wits increasing tenfold as he shuffled down, balancing on the knife's edge, taking stone steps two and three steps at a time, trying to stay one step ahead of certain death. The entire vertical shaft was buckling and shaking madly as if the whole underworld all around him was going to come completely apart altogether suddenly. Waves of pressurized air fluttered as choking clouds of smoke rose past him. It was at once an unearthly scene as reality seemed to lapse into an altered space and time that unwound in slow motion as the foundations of the mountain itself seemed to be moving out of their place. The fact that he had half expected to face this exact prospect did absolutely nothing to ease his mind. Izz's heart slammed against his chest, and his body quaked with the hot buzz of adrenalin as he clamored down several collapsing stair sections. He breathed in fear and regret as he somehow continued to race down the steep grade. Izz moved down to the next flight of steps sidestepping a hail of falling stones and bolting over crumbling gaps in the stairwell below him. He found himself frantically trying to look in two directions at once. He looked up at the falling blocks above and then down at the crumbling steps beneath.

Suddenly a convulsing tremor came from somewhere far, far below, followed by a massive haze of sparks billowing up from the boundless depths. A thundering crash sounded from far below. The endless rumble reverberated all around him. The disorienting noise was becoming unbearable, grating, and malicious. It was followed by battering heated air from below that had been whipped into a wild frenzy. The stairwell he stood on suddenly splintered and fell away in every direction almost instantaneously. The upheaval felt like a great wave of terror, drawing him under as gravity seem to pull him under and sweep him away. The vertical vent gave way. Izz shuddered to think where he might land. Terrorized out of his mind, he yelled words he thought he never even knew as he fell. If he went down with the stone slab, his remains would never be found, if there was anything left to be found.

As he dropped with the section of stone, he caught sight of a platform still attached to the wall. His last and only chance was for him to jump to it at precisely the right time. Izz knew he had only a timeless twinkling to make a decision. The slightest miscalculation would cost him his life; he had to jump without hesitation at the precise time or plunge into the abyss. In a wholly reflexive move, Izz executed an almost perfect headlong lunge and managed to hurl himself toward the platform below. Izz fell head over heels. He screamed and cursed as he completed a full flip; he would surely break his back or neck. Soot that had remained undisturbed for countless sun cycles suddenly gushed up like jetting black geysers from everywhere as most of the human fixed stones of the giant hollow cylinder fell away into the enormous pool of magma. Izz saw the world of Zia swell, fracture, and come apart beneath him to crash with an impact that thundered, echoing up through the caverns, in a blazing burst of flames that seemed to shake the entire planet of Zia.

In the same instant, Izz's momentum sent him hurling through midair, overpowered by feelings of the gut panic of certain doom as he fell. Izz closed his eyes tight and held his breath against his impending crash. Izz covered his head with his hands to keep from splattering his brains on the rocks below. It would be his body that would be broken, if anything, probably every bone. Yet somehow he managed to maneuver his center of gravity, allowing him to make the first contact on his feet. As he was forcefully sent somersaulting forward, Izz tried to break his fall with a shoulder roll. He landed with a terrible, deadening thud. His breath was knocked out, and his vision exploded with starbursts from the numbing impact. Izz tried to tumble with the acceleration of his fall to soften the sudden collision but was unable to do anything more than bracing himself for the blow. Finally, he slammed on the balls of his heels, and the flat of his back, stumbling for a foothold. His momentum sent him flipping, scraping the skin off his hands, knees, and elbows across the rough, hard stone. Finally, Izz came to a rolling stop as if broken to pieces. The collapse sent showers of dirt and rock and shattered fragments falling from the cave ceiling as dust pounced out of every connecting shaft.

A heavy curtain of surreal silence in the dust choked air followed the sound of fragmented stone cascading down the vent's vast depths. Shaken and without breath, Izz slumped down with his face to the floor, half covered with dust and stony rubble. Several rocks had dug deeply into his body where he had skid over them, and blood trickled from his mouth and nose, but at the time, that was the least of his worries.

Izz listened to his grating respiration as the dust marred air became harder to take in. He realized that the ground was still shaking. He exhaled with a whistle as he let out a cautious, muffed cheer and wondered how he could still be alive. Izz just laid there for a while as an aftershock sent a hail of coarse stone fragments pattering down on him. Izz wondered how he had done what he just did. Then for one edgy instant, he found himself laughing with a crazed sense of excitation for having survived against the all odds.

When the stone floor had stabilized, when his unsettled stomach had steadied, and the ringing in his ears had subsided to a steady buzz, he raised himself to his hands and knees. Nothing seemed broken, but he was badly battered and bruised. Izz rose to his feet, and again the world of Zia began to spin and roll beneath the stone blocks of the floor, yet it was only in his head.

Izz unknotted his scarf from around his face and pulled it down around the lower part of his neck. He tried to move, wincing and gritting his teeth with pain as he did so. He had had more than enough of this gloomy subterranean world. Izz sighed. He lay there for a moment, trying to gather his strength, trying to recover from the injuries he had sustained in the fall. Things looked bad and would most likely get worse before they got better. However, it was not over yet. It would never be over as long as he drew breath. As long as his heart had a beat, he could hope that his dream of finding Zuree would come true.

Izz slowly regained his strength and began to rise from the rocky rubble; exhausted and exhilarated at the same time, he pushed up on all fours, dangled his head as his long hair fell forward in thick strands. He shook his head to clear it, but to no avail. He quickly realized that he had not gathered all his wits. Izz took stock of himself, making sure he did not have any broken bones. Izz slowly stood upright on wobbly legs, ignoring the aching numbness of his back. One narrow escape after another left him physically and emotionally spent.

His back was disjointed; his elbows and knees were a mass of scrapes and bruises. There was blood and dust encrusted along the side of his grazed face. Izz braced his hands against the nearest wall as he considered how to proceed. There was nothing before him but shadows, and there was no way he could go back the way he had come. It took everything he was, but after a moment, Izz straightened up and shook the dust and despair off. His unconquerable human spirit refused to give in. He took long, deep breaths of comparatively less tainted air. He did not have time to feel sorry for himself; he told himself firmly. He had to find Zuree.

As he continued, like a malignant thing before him, Izz could feel foulness in the depth of his bones as if demonic legions were waiting to pour upon him like a raging sea. It was frightening, but he could not resist fate's beckoned call, daring him to come forth. He felt his feet carry him forward almost against his will as if they had minds of their own. Something called to him from beyond like an evil spirit luring him to his death. He was pulled along as if by a thread tied to a ring in his nose.

FIVE

BESIEGED

Up ahead, Izz was met by yet another ominous arched opening that led to yet another chamber. From every dark shadow, it seemed that something was watching him. He stepped through the archway's threshold and entered a hall from which several corridors twisted and forked into a network of human built shafts that splintered into what must have been many secret passageways. Izz felt awestruck by the stark scene before him.

Just beyond the entry was a marble platform interlocked to a steep flight of steps made of countless polished stones. The platform was dimly lit by the pale moon's light that seeped through the portholes on the ceiling. Izz was more than confounded that they could reach this depth. He refocused his attention on the gloomy subterranean world surrounding him. There, there seemed to be an enormous congregation of evil gathered in this place. Cut into the solid rock ceiling was what looked like an interlocking backbone with ribbed brace supports that arched across the upper limits like a web that extended down along the walls to the marble floor. He observed that the chamber circled beneath a vast geodesic dome was hundreds of hand spans high and thousands of hand spans in diameter. It was a cavity that looked remarkably like the inside of a whale's circular rib cage, perhaps more like that of a monstrous dragon.

All along the ceiling, there were strange, intricate shadow patterns that Izz could not quite make out. As his eyes raked the circular length of the upper span, he saw dark connecting passageways leading away in every direction. Below him, the dim lights from the portholes caught something at the bottom of the steps. Izz focused on what he recognized to be another sacrificial altar.

As he began to descend, Izz stepped onto a stone; and when he put his full weight on it, it slowly grounded down a few inches and then stopped abruptly. Izz somehow knew that this could not be a good thing. The trap that had been set was sprung Izz groaned. Why did he keep making the same mistake over and over again? Once again, Izz felt his stomach muscles tighten; his skin began to tingle unpleasantly as warning bells rung out in his mind. He tottered down a few more steps. At first, nothing happened; then there was a hesitant metallic clank. Izz did not like the sound of that at all. Almost instantly, he felt an awkward tremor building in the stone underneath his feet, which spread all around him and through him. Dust and tiny pebbles started to dance on the platform surface as the ground under his feet began to shake.

In that same instant, he heard a weighty, dull rumbling sound, like convulsions from every side of the chamber. From beneath, a series of dust plumes came rushing up. Izz glanced hastily over his shoulder and saw a stone slab descending over the arched doorway from which he entered. His gaze flicked to see the rest of the stone slabs were simultaneously rumbling down to seal every exit. Izz turned to escape, but when he reached the marble archway, it was too late. The stone slab grated down over the entrance before him like jaws snapping shut with a disconcerting thud of eternal finality. He was sealed in, vaulted down. Then to make everything worse, as if the situation had not been bad enough already, he caught a glimpse of each light port each, in turn, sealing shut. Then lightlessness descended like a cloak of total blindness, spreading like a stain until every vestige of natural light had disappeared from what appeared to be quickly becoming his tomb. Like a succession of falling dominos, his opportunities for blundering into one trap after another seemed limitless.

Whether designed by the trappers of men or from overbearing weight held up for far too long. Suddenly, ominous crackling reverberation began to build from deep within the depths of Zia, proving that things could never get so bad that they could not get worse. And when the rumbling reached a crescendo, the marble platform began to crack open from one end to the other, with long fractures, like lightning strikes from an angry sky. With a sudden shock of discovery, Izz realized that the whole platform he was standing on was going to collapse. The platform began to come apart beneath his feet and fall away in chunks as the entire underworld seemed to be coming apart all around him. Silently he cursed his dreadful luck. His face filled with uncertainty as his heart dropped directly into the pit of his stomach. No longer able to see anything, without stopping to think, Izz dropped to his hands and knees as the marble slab all at once shifted at a fortfive degree angle. Suddenly, the foyer behind him burst with an undulating, convulsive tremor that showered Izz with its crumbling debris. He heard a loud whooshing sound and then he was plunged downward as the crest of a platform section tilted and tittered; he wildly shifted his weight to keep from rolling off the center. A thick carpet of dust heaved up and was stirred into life. As collapsing stone careened into a weird, underground world of sudden dangers, the scream of stone sliding on stone filled the void. Large blocks began to fall, closing in fast from different parts of the chamber. As Izz rode the avalanching tons of milling stones, he could hear large segments of wreckage grinding so close that he could feel their crushing force pulverizing everything all around him.

Izz was riding the raging marble slab when it unexpectedly came to an abrupt stop, and in a flash, he was hurled forward onto his feet. He suddenly found himself racing, at break neck speed, straight down an avalanche of bone grinding stone blocks. It was like trying to outrun a monstrous cyclone intent on swallowing him up. He did not so much as pause to think how he would stop himself when he reached the bottom. For a sickening endless moment, horror stabbed at his heart as Izz struggled to retain his up and down equilibrium. Izz was so disoriented that almost immediately he lost all sense of whether he was right side up or upside down. He whispered a prayer as he was hopelessly swept along the great lash of rippling wreckage. While Izz tried to zigzag down the sudden rush of falling mass, there was no time for thought, no time to focus on what to do next, suddenly gravity made the decisions for him. As blocks of stones grate in unison all around him, in a fit of concentration, Izz tried to pinpoint in an attempt to dodge each loud crunch of grinding gravel that surrounded him. He awkwardly maneuvered himself around the enveloping rubble. Frantically trying to avoid the heaviest stones rolling end over end, high and low, and all around him. He was careening through the air so fast he had no time to stop to think things out. All his instincts were screaming as tons of crushing stones careened on every side. He tried to fight the building acceleration, but its grasp quickly overcame his best efforts. Helpless to halt what was unfolding, he realized that his hopes could suddenly be shattered at any moment; he braced himself for the worst.

I am not going to make it! He no sooner completed that thought than he felt his feet leave the ground and were thrown up and tossed forward as his body twisted in the air. In the same blink of an eye, plumes of fine powdery dust rose and became tumbling walls of suffocating dust that engulfed him. His desperate shouts were swallowed in the rumbling storm of dust and stone. It felt as if the whole world was oscillating violently from pole to pole while it's groans vibrated through the air. Izz took several deep gagging breaths, then clamped his teeth shut tight and tried to hold his breath. Instinctively, Izz knew that he could quickly suffocate if he inhaled too much fine dust into his lungs, so he tried desperately to breathe through his nose when he had to.

Izz sensed that he was almost at the bottom, and all he could do is curl up and shield his face. A glint of dauntless hope sparked. Maybe he could make it. He might very well break a leg, fracture an arm, split his skull wide open, or even perhaps break every bone in his body, but anything would be better than being buried alive. Then in an instant, Izz found himself crawling on all fours as fast as his feet and hands could carry him. There was a trembling of loose ground roaring down on him, frightfully building until the noise was deafening. Suddenly he was flung headfirst into the swell of churning debris. He flew across space, tumbling head over heels over and over, overwhelmed and frightened by the realization that he might die. A million thoughts careened through his mind. *If I roll when I hit...if I use my feet if I land flat, will it soften the impact?*

At long last, in the slew of ever thickening darkness, in a tangle of thrashing legs and arms, he felt his forward motion begin to slow down. All the while waves of fist sized stones pummeled him with unyielding cruelty. Suddenly, Izz landed stiff legged, bounced once, then twice. A second later, he smashed into the ground with an abrupt and bone rattling bump too soon to have prepared for it. Izz unwaveringly held on to consciousness. He slammed onto his knees, bounced over on his back, and jackknifed off the stone floor in a forward direction. He balled up onto himself like a falling spider, feeling for the existence of the rock solid ground somewhere far beneath him. A trailing tidal wave of dust and stone came crashing overhead. From out of the dust and rock debris, Izz's grunts of pain and yaps of fright came to a sudden stop. The air from his lungs was knocked out of his chest. A black cloud ballooned inside his head, blotting everything out. For the longest moment, everything went blank.

A blistering pain burning inside Izz's chest quickened him suddenly; he found he had a mouth full of bloody dirt and realized that he had drawn in a lung full of dust. He repeatedly retched until the entire load of smothering dirt, rock, and the dust finally came to rest. It was all over almost before Izz realized anything had happened. After a final settling movement, all was still, and everything went suddenly deathly quiet. Izz was buried under what seemed like a ton of hard and unyielding rock and dust. The only sound was the thundering of Izz's heart. It's pounding somewhat reassured him. The vacuum of silence compounded by the abrupt uncanny calm was now somehow even scarier than the roaring motion of the cave in even at its height. Still shuddering with the aftershock of the sudden impact, Izz continued to cough violently, unable to catch his breath.

Tom Icon

Izz's eyes snapped open to the dominion of the perpetual darkness as he quickly assessed his situation. He was alive, and once again, miraculously it seemed that he had not sustained any significant injuries, at least nothing seemed broken. As the settling debris weighted down around him, Izz found that he could not move his legs, and the lower part of his body was bound tight. Izz was sure he had cracked at least a coupled of ribs. He could hardly breathe under the weight that held him fast, but as far as he could tell, even though he was completely buried, there was some breathable air. Luckily, he had cradled his head with his right arm, creating an air pocket, which allowed him to take in oxygen. Izz could taste the dry dust smothering his tongue, irritating his throat and nose, and he could feel stone fragments scraping against his teeth. He was buried alive!

Disaster had befallen him; distress took hold of him and held him in its death grip. Izz was encased in rock, trapped, and left to go crazy. In his desperation, he tried madly to claw himself out from under the heavy refuse that held him. His heart began to race again as he frantically tried to set himself free. But his struggle to free himself was doing him no good. His lungs were on fire with oxygen depletion, and soon he realized that struggling would only deplete the little air available. Izz forced himself to calm down. Izz head began to clear, and his breathing slowed.

After a moment, he compelled himself to relax and to think things out. He began to use his right hand to dig out more elbow room around his face. Izz bent up from the waist and rocked back and forth, using his body as a lever to push himself up to give himself a little more clearance. The best thing was not to panic; he kept reminding himself. Izz fanned his elbow up and down, like a wing, and moved his shoulder back and forth. He painstakingly squirmed one part of his body at a time, which allowed him to work his arms loose and was able to slip out of his satchel. Izz wiggled and dug with his hands until he could reach it upward. He doubled up his right hand, made a fist, and pushed his twisted right hand up, punching it through to the surface. Only through an extreme force of will did Izz manage to lean back and loosen himself. It took the greatest effort, but he was able to stretch out his legs to push himself up. Retching, gagging, and groaning, Izz summoned all his might and forced his body up through the strangling heap of dust, blocks, and rock. Grimacing with effort, desperate for breath, Izz forced his soot covered head toward the surface, as if from a grave, and emerged into a darker world.

Still encased up to his neck in rocks and pebbles, Izz shook his battered head to remove dust and debris cluttered around his face. Izz took a choking gulp of dry dust laden air. He could not have lasted very much longer in the oxygen poor confinement that imprisoned him. He shoved several heavy stones off himself and was barely able to squeeze his foot out from under a massive boulder that narrowly missed squashing him to death. Almost in tears from exhaustion and anger, Izz squirmed out of the trap that held him. Furred with dust, Izz shook his head to clear it, and he rolled away from his own would be grave.

Crawling free, he turned on his back, exhausted and covered in grit, and took in a few shallow breaths. The air smelled foul and was thick with clouds of dust that hung in the air; he used his shirt as best he could to filter the air he could not help gulping in. Dry and gritty eyed, Izz coughed with an agonizingly racking that seemed as if it would never stop. He rubbed the dirt out of his eyes. In the enveloping darkness, Izz cautiously felt for blood. Everything, it seemed, was still in one piece.

It had been yet another narrow escape. Izz had managed to survive only by the skin of his teeth. He suddenly felt bitter. Death seemed to be stalking him at every turn like an overpowering shadow that seemed to be relentlessly pursuing him. Izz just lay there, stunned, feeling practically broken in half and wondering what else could be waiting for him beyond the next unforeseen bend. His mind began to batter him hard with unanswerable questions.

The dark voices in his mind echoed back, *This is a foolish, vain, stubborn, impossible attempt at the unattainable. Your fate is sealed! You are doomed, to be sure this time.* Wicked laughter sounded in the background.

The images and the possibilities of never returning to the outside world alive swooped down on him like a hawk taking its prey. Silence closed in again, more oppressive than ever, and shook him to the depths of his soul. The sensation of darkness descended upon him.

Izz had emerged from darkness into deeper darkness still. The bad dream was finally over, but it was just the beginning of an encroaching nightmare. There were no portholes that remained open. The world of sight had been swept away beyond his grasp, and it seemed there was no escape. The chamber felt closed and oppressive. Izz stared wide eyed, unsettled into the lightlessness, and pondered why something as contrary as darkness was ever compelled to be. He was utterly cut off under tons of dust and rubble from the rest of the world, interred in a labyrinth of an inky blackout. The booby trap or the cave in, or both, had sealed all the entrances and all the exits, entombing Izz completely in the subterranean pitfall condemning him to an inevitable slow death.

There was a slight aftershock that caused several large loose stones to fall from the ceiling. Then there was silence once more, deep and suffocating silence. Like a death shroud tossed over a dead man, the darkness seemed to close in all around Izz. A stale smell circulated like a cloud of smoke through the dense, dusty air. He strained his eyes to see, but the darkness only deepened; everything was as black as a bat's wing.

Darkening thoughts flooded his mind, and Izz began to wonder if he would ever see Zuree again. His guts felt as if they had dropped right out of his belly. He was failing miserably at his hopeless struggle to maintain his faith in the face of disaster. Izz cringed at the thought of his faithless weakness. No! His heart screamed at the disloyal reasoning being screwed into his head. The first self and second self warred, two natures trying their best to convince the other of what was real and what was sheer lunacy. With every bit of strength he possessed, he drove away and held at bay the thoughts that threatened to consume him with despair. A change came over him too deep to put into words. By some workable understanding that was not his own, Izz realized at that very moment that there might be something worse than death. "Zuree, I will not...I cannot...live without you!" He stood to his feet to make sure he was still in one piece, that no major bones were broken. Finding he was not severely hurt, he screamed into the darkness. "Kill me if you can!" Izz mocked in bleak defiance. The presence of something evil lurking in the air was his only reply.

Izz blinked his eyes over and over again, trying hopelessly to focus on something, anything, as he grumbled and complained about the string of disastrous events that had befallen him. But he was reminded that things could not be so bad that they could not get worst. Izz's eyes showed him nothing but spots and whirls as he aimlessly groped in the darkness, hoping to find he knew not what. Finally, in the contrast of the heavy jet black veil that folded over him and smothered over everything, Izz's eyes slowly started to adjust. He noticed purplish shadows cast by only the dimmest hush of light coming from somewhere up above. Without forethought, he slowly stumbled forward partly dazed, groping his way through the blackness toward the suggestion of light, knowing nothing of the mystery that surrounded him on every side. As Izz stepped forward, to his horror, his left foot found no resting place. Losing his balance, he fell forward. He instinctively arched his head and spine backward as he pivoted on his right foot at the same time. He rotated his body and swinging his arms around as he shifted his weight away from his fall. He stretched out both arms in the opposite direction of whatever it was that was about to swallow him up. Izz's elbows smashed hard against solid rock, and he dug his fingers in even harder, resulting in two busted elbows and ten bloodied fingers. His left hand found a dangerously unstable grip, and his right hand slipped away. Izz raked his fingernails hard against the rough stone surface to no avail. He clung to the rim of the jutting stone. Izz's legs dangled over the edge below him, which was cloaked in the black mist of dead space, unable to make contact. The fear of falling into the empty air underneath him made his one handed grip tightened instinctively.

Izz hung precariously suspended in emptiness, scared gutless that at any moment, he would plunge into the black void. He did not bother to look down into the lightless emptiness. Instead, he scrambled to find a foothold but found none. Acute primordial fear seethed forth from the core of his soul as familiar sensations of foreboding doom spawned within. Izz fought off his panic and inched up. Somehow he was able to anchor his chin over the edge of the drop. Then by hook or crook, with a death defying explosion of effort that could only come from a combination of shock and terror, Izz pulled himself up with Herculean strength. He threw his right leg over the rim, pulled himself over its edge, and rolled away from the drop off. He pressed and molded himself against the solid face of the rock floor as he slightly raised his head, desperately trying to drag air past his heart lodged throat. Izz gulped life in as he unconsciously dug his fingers into the dust and debris littered the floor as if at any time he was about to be sucked back into the opening. Izz rolled over on his back away from the drop. After a brief time, he finally convinced himself that he was safe for the moment. Izz gathered himself together and edged his way back to the brink of the hidden drop. He felt the heat rising from an unknown source. Izz peered farther over the side and saw nothing except what appeared to be a bottomless pit of deeper darkness with no top or bottom.

After a long time of staring down into perpetual darkness as far as his eyes could see, he caught a faint suggestion of something down there. It was a glimmer of reddish flux. Izz suddenly realized that he was staring down the throat of another ancient volcano vent. The dim glow was molten magma flickering and fluctuating in the deepest entrails of Zia. He felt a large rock at his side; he took it in his hand and cast it down into the pit. It fell with no evidence of ever reaching the bottom. The only indication of its depth was a far off wall to wall bouncing rumble. At the thought of nearly falling down a bottomless abyss, Izz felt his stomach tie into knots. He rolled over on his back once again and glared into space where light refused to cast its power. Izz sensed an overwhelming feeling that he was in the wrong place at the wrong time. A thousand thoughts tumbled inside his head.

You must go back. No one will be the wiser. You have made a disastrous mistake. No one will ever know if you turn and run away.

The thoughts kept repeating in his mind. Among the rushing feelings of confusion, one thought came and drove every other thought from his mind. *You shall find her. You have only to look with your whole heart for it to be so.*

What Ammiz had spoken stirred hope within him. Izz remembered Zuree. The mere recollection of her smile sent a raging tidal wave of courage racing back through his veins. He thought *Darkness is darkness alone, nothing more, nothing less.*

His mindfulness of Zuree became his light in the darkness. Izz recovered himself. Cautiously, he crept away from the deep crypt on all fours for the most part. When he did stand up, he trod very carefully, testing his footing before resting his entire weight down. Guided by the shadows, he returned to the place where he had been buried alive, and with his bare hands, he dug up his satchel. Izz stumbled around in the dark until he reached what seemed like an outer barrier. Izz pushed himself up against the wall, clutching his backpack and huddling up against himself. There was only so much a man could take. With his head in his hands, for the longest time, Izz lost himself in his mind.

Eventually, Izz was able to regain his composure. He opened his satchel and fumbled around for his lamp. After he found it, he pulled his flints from his pocket and struck an igniting spark from them. After several attempts, a hot spark kindled the wick, and suddenly the dim flickering lamp fractured the intense darkness. The light radiating from his animal fat lamp was not at all what he wanted, but it was the best illumination he could get from the small lamp. Izz held his lantern as far out as he could reach, but the dust had not completely settled. He was only illuminating the dusty haze from within like a glowing reflection in a thick fog, which only added to the surreal atmosphere. For a moment, he was unable to see anything.

Then out of nowhere, Izz felt this uncanny feeling that he was no longer alone. There was something there as he stared into the dimness beyond. Izz's eyes adapted themselves to the obscurity of the creeping dust laden darkness as much as his dim lantern would allow. The air felt heavy in there all of a sudden as if just ahead, death lay in wait for him. Slowly, he began to make out the shapes at the edge of his lantern's light as his eyes adjusted to the mix of light reflecting out of the gloom.

The vision before him knocked Izz back into a state of absolute shock that grew with each hammering heartbeat. The blood drained from his face. Nothing could have prepared Izz for what his questioning eyes refused to believe, for what he saw was beyond anyone's darkest imagination.

Before him was a spacious expanse with a lofty height. The first thing he was able to distinguish was that thousands upon thousands upon thousands of eyeless skulls were staring back at him. From the base of the floor to the crest of the ceiling, the walls were covered with the bones of thousands of skeletons. Pile upon pile of meticulously arranged skulls, femurs, ribs, tibias, and spines. Most were assembled in a multifaceted wicker design, not unlike prehistoric ornamentation. Countless bones of men, women, and children were stacked one upon the other. Izz could not tell how deep the bones were stacked, but he did know there were incalculable skeletons all arranged in orderly patterns. Transfixed where he stood, Izz panned his lantern to the right to see throughout gruesome arrays of every bone of the human body fashioned into the most macabre arrangements.

From the part of the ceiling that had not collapsed hung, what looked like a grisly giant bone candelabrum. The branching skeletal fixture hung from the center of the room by a huge iron fettered chain and dominated the chamber. The chandelier structure was sculpted with a bewildering array of skulls, pelvises, tibiae, femurs, and other skeletal parts morbidly designed and fastened in monstrous patterns.

From the ghastly ceiling fixture strung out to every corner of the almost cylinder chamber were suspended strands of backbone sections, skulls, and rib bones looped like chains of celebratory ribbons. Most were sorted in an intricate woven pattern resembling that of a long brooch. It covered the ceiling everywhere, all arranged to someone's notion of uniformity. Everywhere Izz turned, he saw towering stacks of human skulls heaped in pyramids that rose to the heights of the roof. Such vast numbers of dead, every fleshless skull represented a person who had once lived. Why were they here, and who was responsible for their death?

All at once, every pair of eyeless sockets, with its toothy grin, seemingly turned and focused on Izz. Out of nowhere, a sense of death seemed to rush in on him with its tormenting shadowy whispers of ancient agony. Suddenly he felt as if he heard from deep within the cavernous tomb thousands of voices screaming all at once, echoing the same warning, *"Run! Run! Run!"*

Mounting alarm quickly grew into a staggering panic; Izz stumbled backward, tripping over the waste strewn floor. His boots raised little puffs of animated dust as he staggered over the uneven surface with bone fragments crunching underfoot. Izz left heel suddenly got caught between two stones, and he went crashing down to the dust and stone marred ground. The force of his fall caused him to lose his flickering lamp, extinguishing its light, and plunging the chamber of death into darkness again. Scrambling on his hands and knees, Izz crawled around the mountain of rubble that had spilled down into the hall from the upper level. Izz frantically groped about like a blind fool, probing with his hands the wreckage in search of his lantern, his only link to sanity. He felt his lamp from behind a fallen block. Izz nervously drew his flint stones. His hands were trembling hysterically, and his heart was pounding when he struck a feeble spark. There was a noticeable flash of light in the oppressive well of total darkness, bringing forth faint hints of row upon row of staring gibbous skulls, then there was complete darkness again. Izz took a deep breath to steady his hands, repositioned his brass lantern, and struck his stones again. This time, the lamp's wick lit and struggled against the darkness, sputtering as it sucked up fuel. Izz nurtured the flame until its fire flared to life, stabbing its piercing beams into the lightless gloom as if it were pushing away pure evil itself. Izz trimmed the wick of his lamp, and once again, the geometric patterns of human bones encompassed him.

Izz stood his ground, trembling and shivering. Time seemed to stand still in dust laden limbo while he struggled to regain control of his nerves after being shaken by what he had discovered and thought he heard. The warning he heard had sounded unmistakable, but he reasoned, *The assault could have just been inside my head, where those kinds of weird images and sounds often originate. Or at worst, only echoes from the entombed past kept alive by the walls of this forsaken place. Echoes cannot hurt me, nor can the dead.* Izz tried to assure himself, yet he kept his lantern focused there, where fleshless heads covered the walls and vacant ghostly eyes stared relentlessly into nothingness.

At that instant, Izz remembered how Ammiz, the Seer, had recounted stories of vast armies who went forth to capture suitable human sacrifices to satisfy their greedy thirst for blood. Victims were amassed for ritual slaughter. Warriors captured young, innocent victims or gathered as tributes from vassal kingdoms who offered up their sons and daughters for sacrifice to appease their demonic masters. Ammiz had spoken of the demons of the underworld and their insatiable appetite for death, misery, and blood. He had spoken of how the cruel rite of a primitive religion promised unlimited earthly riches and boundless supernatural powers. The most terrible and frightful thing was that this eerie account had been real and was carried out on a vast scale of thousands upon thousands. Could everything the old man spoke of be right? And what about the things he had spoken of Zuree? Before him was the ghastly evidence eternally resting in mysterious patterns in this grisly bone mausoleum? He had to find her, and soon!

Izz's skin was crawling all over him as he back up slowly, wishing he had never had to come there. There were ghosts there, where time stood still. The spirits of the ill fated patrolled the dead kingdom in the heart of the darkest nights. A great heaviness settled in Izz, giving him a sense that death was a terrible thing and that it desired to whisk him away before his time. For one thing, Izz was not ready to go, not now, not here. He panned his lantern over his head as he turned deliberately searching the upper level for a way out. His fragmented light revealed that every visible exit had been sealed tight.

He had unwittingly crashed down by chance into the burial place of Iwazz, the last king of Skullsdoom. A burial chamber that seemed untouched by time was meant to be permanently locked away in the past where untold millions had been ghastly sacrificed at the king's death. It was an enigmatic zone of profound mysteries, possessing the indefinable dimension of unfathomable evil powers. Izz tried to think about what to do next. He had survived the wolf attack, the Wastelands of Woe, an insurmountable ascent, the arrow booby trap, the sword gauntlet, the collapse of the stairwell, and the wreckage of tons of stone that had not killed him. Only to be trapped in such an impasse in time and space, a yawning chasm swallowed up entirely in darkness and death with no way out, or so it seemed.

Izz shone his lamp along the margins of the subterranean vault, its glow sliced darkness, splashing great pool of shadows along the outer limits of the tomb walls. As he walked, Izz directed his light into the dark space beyond where the walls receded past the limits of his small lamp. Izz's light suddenly reached a section of the tomb where overlapping stone tablets along the wall loomed up toward the roof. Izz walked over to the nearest wall moving closer to examine the protrusions of polished slaps. Its surface was covered with a confusion of carved symbols and objects commemorating the reign of their tyrannical rulers and their unrelenting taskmasters. His eyes fell on something complicated and boldly depicted on the walls. Izz could make out mystifying hieroglyphics covered with dust and cobwebs encrusted with mineral stains and a glaze of streaked residues. The carved stone sheets still had the clarity to astound, as imagery of the wicked king's many atrocities came to light. Moving closer, Izz used his lantern to trace their outlines. His face was so close to the panel that his nose was nearly touching the raised images. He ran his hand over the tablets shrouded in spider web, sweeping layers of dust away, searching out their meaning. The stone had the slickness of metal. Pieces of stone crumbled away and fell to the ground where other scattered chards and chips lay. A grievous sensation lightly touched the outer edge of Izz's consciousness. He pulled his hand back quickly as if he had suddenly been burned.

Izz stepped back to examine the intricacy of the carved figures and forms thoughtfully. It was difficult at first to make out the scenes that were represented, but little by little, a clearer picture began to emerge. He saw half silhouetted human figures twisted in frozen postures of agony. What Izz discovered troubled his mind. He had never expected such a truly gruesome and heinous display of bloodletting, debauchery, perversion, and depravity. Izz's eyes bounced from one image to the other. Throughout were carvings that told of unspeakable horrors and hideous tortures. Izz recognized the portrayal of ritualistic murder, showing the shackled broken bodies of thousands of overburdened slaves no longer able to work, dragged away, decapitated, and dismembered. After centuries of silence, the illustrated story unfolded with ample evidence of a ruthless cult who thrived on human sacrifice. Carnage was the central theme in Skullsdoom's ritual and worship in which blood was the factor that bound their world together. Their victim's souls ultimately offered up by unhallowed grand sorcerers in honor and tribute to their gruesome demonic masters. Sickened, Izz turned away, forcing his growing nausea back down.

He went on groping his way around the tomb, searching out an escape. Zuree was the heart of his intent, the price of his dream, and nothing else mattered. Izz pulled out her stone necklace. It was unresponsive, and his heart sank. Vigilantly he moved along the rough bare stonewall, feeling it out in search of an opening. He knocked on the wall and listened for the hollow sounds of any kind that indicated an exit. He found nothing. All the while, the inky blackness threatened to overpower his lantern's ebbing flame as its glow disappeared past its limits along with the browns and yellows of rock strata.

Izz seemed to be carried along with a circular waft that extended all around him. Mold spores and dust motes meandered in and out of his lamp's light as he stumbled against the walls of what was looking more and more like his tomb. With escalating desperation, Izz's eyes and fingers searched out holes, cracks, nooks, and crannies for a hidden escape. Moments that passed seemed like hours of bitter vexation. There was no secret passage, no hidden trapdoor. His fruitless search for something, anything, that might offer him some chance of escape left him at his wit's end. He swept his lantern across the chamber in frustration. In the murkiness, his eyes caught a glimpse of a flashing reflection. Thinking he had imagined it, he panned back quickly. Again, there toward the hidden center behind a shroud of vexing darkness, his lamp once again glinted off something smooth and reflective. Izz warily made his way toward it.

Six

The Tomb

here, facing to the North, a rectangular monument rested at the top of a black granite pedestal. The faint spectral light emanating from his lamp caused the huge box to glow suddenly bright as if daring his approach.

The probing light revealed the lower end of a curved black stone stairway that led to the base upon which a coffer laid glimmering down on him. The faint odor of death still lingered around the tomb of stone. At the footing of the stepped platform, Izz's lantern flickered and wavered behind its glass chimney as its yellowish gleam spread itself over the sight before him. He saw a self contained world of earthly goods as he stepped over a jumble of artifacts. Izz treaded gingerly upon the lower steps in front of him, hoping not to trigger another booby trap. At the top, he found a massive vessel of solid gold. Izz's face filled with astonishment. Moving closer, he used his lantern to discover that the receptacle had no seams, which meant it had been cast all in one piece. That kind of technical knowledge was unheard of as far as he knew.

Everywhere, the metal walls bore the skull crest of the dark lord that was entombed within. He was once reputed to be an immortal, but ultimately, time had exposed his deceitful claim to godhood. Around the golden sarcophagus, there were copper tablets with the same writings, and there were idols with evil looking faces, seemingly standing guard at every corner. One figure was missing its head; another was missing an arm.

Izz of Zia

Izz noted the crafted design of intricate cryptic patterns of inscribed symbols etched symmetrically around the upper part of the box's edge that coiled toward the middle. Every golden side of the coffer was covered with mysterious inscriptions, strange markings written in the most mystical characters. Most of the letters looked like random squiggles; others were like crossed sticks—all symbolizing an evil influence, no doubt. Izz could only speculate upon their many symbolic meanings. It was an extraordinary thing with illusory, bizarre makings that paralleled the other diabolical designs throughout this infernal region. As Izz moved his lantern along the writings, the light of his lamp revealed a diagram he had seen before. It was a design so complicated that it dizzied Izz to look upon it. It was a replica of the planetary system Izz had seen hanging on Ammiz's wall. It showed the lining and the ancient astronomical movements of the planets. It was like a great universal clock of time pointing to the hour when the fullness of the conjunction would come.

Around the planetary image were strange, indecipherable markings, calligraphy like patterns, and delicate lines of a complex lettering system. It was a pictogram, an extinct order of words that bore witness to the first written language. He remembered Ammiz referring to it as the oldest written tongue known to man, writing that had not been used for more than six thousand cycles of the sun. Izz tried to get his head around the whole bizarre message, but the enigmatic markings might as well have been chicken tracks. He attempted to figure out what the inscriptions meant, by what Ammiz and his old schoolmaster had taught him. It was from an era of savage, barbaric kings that reigned in absolute power and terror over an oppressed people. Izz recognized some of the markings from Ammiz's books. He had learned just enough of the ancient tongue to acknowledge a few syllables. "Concurrent creation and destruction, universal portals, altar markers, dark strongholds, matter and energy, secrets brought to fruition; chains are broken, precious, pure, royal blood, innocence's taken."

Other than that, the message was incomprehensible to him. The strange writing raised more questions than it answered.

Suddenly, Izz's unsettling feeling grew stronger. "Pure, royal blood, innocence's taken," he whispered.

Izz's lantern cast its faint glow over the engraving as Izz studied the illustrations. He walked along the images as he carefully swept his fingertips across the solid golden surface as if it would somehow help him unlock its secrets. In someway, he touched upon the bereaved world of the dead emotionally, mentally, and spiritually, and his skin crawled to touch upon its past. All at once, a weird sensation came over him like that of being in someone else's dreams. A force rumbled through him by way of his mind; its undertow carried him away across bygone eons to a lost time and space, to a world of long forgotten atrocities. Somewhere in his head, he heard, like a whisper ringing in his ears, "At the exact moment of the conjunction, the pure blood of the royal virgin must be spilled upon the black altar. At long last, the heavy chains of heavens will be broken and cast aside. Thereupon lightlessness will come together to rule the universal womb and give birth to utter darkness."

Instantly, Izz was aware of an unsettling feeling, like a warning of a heavy evil curse. And he could not imagine why, nor could he say what. But neither could he deny the foreboding premonition of secrets snatched from the other side of infinity. Turning the corner, he withdrew his hand as the wall that served as the backdrop of the golden box unexpectedly leaped into view. His eyes fell on something intricate and boldly decorated. It was a wall upon which image words were written in blood, and once again, what he did not want to know shouted out at him. The entire breadth of the plastered walls around the burial box was covered with mottled and discolored images that faded with the age of time. The more Izz saw, the more extremely brutal, unbelievably grotesque, revolting, and savage the ritual painted scenes became. Bizarre representations detailed fierce masters of war brutally skinning, boiling, roasting, blinding, strangling, decapitating, nailing, disemboweling, burning people and hacking off their organs and limbs. The unfolding story exposing the truth was too much, too hard to comprehend the extent or rationale of it all. Its meaning became blurred and tangled and was lost in Izz's mind. The stone reliefs, murals, and writings clearly showed the practices of unspeakable torture, unimaginable mutilation, and sacrilegious sacrifices beyond comprehension, all in the name of their false gods. How could the human conscious plummet to such bestial decay? Could the truth possibly be real?

What caught Izz's eyes next struck him like a bludgeoning blow. As Izz swung his lantern upward and downward, the wall seemed to step toward him. Everything around him faded as all his senses suddenly concentrated on the image before him. At the centermost part of the mural, carefully depicted in a series of illustrated images, a fair young maiden was spread upon a flat round stone ritual table with her back arched over an altar similar to the one Izz had seen at the entrance. Each limb of the victim being offered was held down while a priest wearing a hideous death mask with strange symbols cut into his face and body used a razor sharp two edged blade to cut open her diaphragm. With steel tipped fingers, the slayer then ripped out the victim's palpitating heart while the young maiden looked on in horror, still alive and her upraised heart still beating. Arcs of blood fountained everywhere as the yet throbbing heart was placed on a dish of smoldering coals and offered up to what appeared like the Great Conjunction of the seven sister planets. The victim's blood was collected and drunk by the priests. The victim was then decapitated, and the body was taken to the meat pots to be eaten by the bloodthirsty royals and lords of the underworld. Izz wanted to be sick.

As Izz withdrew his lantern, it became painfully evident that Zuree was the intended sacrificial victim. Sharp pangs of disgust slew his heart and a deep riff of repugnance splayed open in his mind. Surrealistically, the thought of Zuree being in the hands of like-minded beasts forced him to let out a loud excruciating moan. The idea walloped him like a sharp blow to the temple. If he could not force this thought from his mind's eye now, what would become of him if he could not stop it from happening?

"No!" Izz screamed as if a stake had suddenly been repeatedly driven into his heart, piercing it through and through. The unraveling horror turned to disgust, twisting Izz's stomach with absolute indignation. Izz staggered away and leaned against the tomb, sickened. Izz doubled over, his hand clutching his stomach, as he heaved dryly, but his empty stomach offered nothing. It was too much for Izz to bear. It was like having spikes driven into his eyes. He did not want to spend one more moment in the same room with the remains of someone so diabolically dominated by evil and hate. Someone who slaughtered tens of thousands shedding their innocent blood to deities, which did not exist. He rushed down two steps at a time from the burial box, wishing nothing more than to put as much distance between him and the images of bloodlust and death.

Izz made his way to the farthest corner of his prison, a few hundred paces away from the crypt. He stopped when he reached the dead end at the edge of the cavern. His eyes had seen too much. Izz extinguished his lamp, and instantly everything thickened into the darkest well of jet black until its pitch seeped into his soul. He felt his way to the ground and flopped up against the jagged rock wall. Izz sat with his knees drawn up and his head between them. A vast heaviness settled in on him as he felt all optimism wither and die. For the longest time, he was thinking in the silence as if waiting for something unthinkable to happen. His mind struggled for a way out, but he saw plainly that he was trapped. Moments that passed seemed like hours. Things looked grim. It was all so hopeless.

With his head in his hands, Izz was feeling cursed, ruined, doomed, forsaken. He was huddled up against the wall. His dark eyes were heavily circled, his face was lined with grief, and his thoughts were left disconnected.

It was no good pretending that there was a way out. When he realized this, he eased himself into abandonment. Izz reached down and clutched two handfuls of dust, squeezed it in his fists, and then let it sift slowly through his fingers. His expectations of ever finding Zuree were translucent, formless shadows. His dreams were the granules of dust slipping through his fingers. He was locked in a prison of failure and self pity, banished from the face of Zia. He would never see the natural light of day again, but most grievous of all, his greatest loss would be never to see the one he needed more than his next breath. There was no worst loss than that of his hope.

Izz laid his head back against the rock, enveloped in the blackest depression he had ever known as if his very soul had stepped inside of a deathly nightmare. Helplessness and hopelessness swept over him. Izz was beaten physically, mentally, and spiritually. What did living mean anymore? What did anything mean anymore? What did anything matter now?

This is as good a place to die as any, Izz thought as his heart and mind broke. Tears welled behind his eyes, and he wanted to weep like a baby, but he could not. That would not be manly. But then, he did not feel like much of a man anymore. He felt hope wither and die. His mind was battered, his spirit crush and his heart hacked to pieces. The notion of going crazy in utter lightlessness eclipsed his soul. Darkness had him, and his only escape was to admit that there was no escape.

<hr>

At about the midnight hour, Baddlock had reached the southern borders of the Ebony Forest where he rejoined his main forces. His track to Edawn was well marked in a trail of blood, carnage, and desolation. Everywhere he lay foot; the woodlands were reduced to blackened stumps. Every water well had been poisoned. Everything that could burn was set ablaze. He destroyed all, scourging the land without a second thought. The Wicked Warlock Wizard's reign of terror advanced rapidly across the land with frightful acts of destruction.

There had been pockets of resistance, but they were no match for the brutal Norticlan savages whose wills and hearts were hardened in the ruthlessness and cruelty of revenge. Those who had not reached the protection of Edawn continued to fall victim to the lawlessness spreading across the land. The onslaught went on mercilessly, day and night without ceasing, visiting destruction and mayhem upon every hamlet and farm in Baddlock's wake.

The advancing armies did not stop to rest; instead, they spent the night pillaging and burning every vestige of civilization in their path. Work crews worked around the clock widening a beaten path through the tangled landscape for their oversized catapults. The tallest, straightest, strongest trees were collected along the way for the throwing arms of the bull catapults.

Baddlock's wicked priests, the mind molders, made sure that every man had plenty of the Wicked Warlock Wizard's concoction. The effects of this vile narcotic were similar to that of the adrenaline produced by the body. It triggered an elevated state of alertness while at the same time reducing the subjection to pain, hunger, and thirst. But most of all, it reduced their need for sleep. Man and beast were pushed to the brink. By near dawn, the hordes had reached the southernmost borders of the Ebony Forest. All were breathing heavily, all but the Zomborges.

Under cover of darkness, Baddlock's most ruthless Norticlan assassins had eliminated the outermost lookouts, Edawn's first alert towers. Concealed along the forest's edge, with just enough light from the full moon, yakoxen pulled forth the overburdening catapult wagons. They struggled to follow the arduous trail up the base of the steep foothills before Edawn. Every tree was cut down. Enormous spaces were cleared. Hour after hour, the equipment essential for the monstrous invasion was amassed on the dark side of the northern ridge of the foothills encircling the Edawnian Kingdom. Baddlock immediately seized control of all of Edawn's main roads, bridges, and trade routes coming in and out, isolating the kingdom from the rest of the world. Baddlock's underwater divers, in unison, covertly boarded the warships that were docked in port, seizing the Bay of Tranquility, blockading the kingdom from the sea, cutting off all supplies. Baddlock now ruled the southern coast, hoping to cripple the kingdom, expecting an early victory.

Izz of Zia

In the still of the night, under the full moon, for some time for no apparent reason, the royal dogs had been howling and baying. Their fur was bristling as they faced toward the North. Then the same dogs bred for hunting down full grown grizzly bears began to eerily wail and whine almost hysterically. It was as if at the moment, a giant monster had cast its terrifying shadow across the kingdom. After that, almost back to back, scouts from the northern innermost posts began to pour in with the same report, "The enemy is upon us!"

The Wicked Warlock Wizard's lone figure sat atop his pitch black warhorse, Midnight, like an overgrown vulture waiting for something to die. With barely a movement, his inherently evil stare fixed on the kingdom of Edawn. Baddlock knew full well that he needed Edawn as a foothold for his massive invasion of Zia. His objective was to conquer the strategic territory and port to establish an anchor from which he would become the master of the world of Zia. Therefore, victory at Edawn was essential, and he was prepared to commit everything at his command to destroying this stronghold. The acquisition of Edawn would eliminate the empire's most potent strategic defense. More importantly, the victory would shorten the war, dashing Xylenia's hopes of victory and weakening her resolve.

Dandork approached and joined Baddlock at the top of the shadowy hill. "All our equipment and weapons are at the crest of the hills. What is your command?"

With a preoccupied expression seared on his face, Baddlock continued to stare at Edawn as if Dandork was not even there. Several rigid moments slipped by; finally, Baddlock spoke, "Assemble the long range catapults, all of them."
The low loaded wagons, on which the bases of the huge dismantled catapults were carried, together with the towering timbers hewed along the way, were moved to the front lines.

Tower guards caught sight of torches being lit along the rim of the hilltops. In the northern towers, watchmen stared in alarm as suddenly one by one bonfire appeared all along the entire length of the highlands of the North.

At once, the watchman on the tower cried out, "Edawnian brothers, the enemy is upon us!" The outcry was urgently bellowed. Alarm bells at once sounded in the watchtowers across the whole Kingdom, shattering the stillness that had fallen over the anxious realm.

Ammiz raised his head from his desk where he had fallen asleep over his books. He looked over his shoulder and whispered, "The dark hour has come upon us." Then he turned and thought of Izz and wondered about his whereabouts as one would for his own son. Ammiz shuddered at the image in his mind and whispered, "Rise and be who you are."

Inside the walls of Edawn, an erupting quagmire of activity was spreading.

The watchman on the tower reported, "If I could count them, their numbers would be more than the sands of the sea."

Troops on guard along the high walls of Edawn converged on the northern battlement. Soon the swarms of combatants on standby joined them. Having heard the warning bells, Baddlock broke into a mocking and hideous grin. "You are too late! I wield power now to trample you into dust!" His eyes danced with delight. "By the next setting sun, not one stone shall be left standing up on the other in Edawn."

As trees were cut down by the hundreds for the assembling of the catapults, several surrounding camps were being built. Chains of continuous embankments, trenches, and barbed throne barriers were added to fortified each joining a camp. Even though Baddlock's forces far outnumbered that of Edawn's and his weapons were vastly more superior, Baddlock left nothing to chance.

The king soon joined his warriors on the parapet overlooking the heavily occupied northern heights. He wore his tightly woven metal mesh, his braced leather armor. His golden crown seemed to droned on his head foreboding what was about to befall them. Through his long eye, Ozzdon could see the many figures running around the northern hillside like roaches against the dancing, crackling flames of their campfires. He was able to identify the Norticlan armies by the horned helmets they wore. King Ozzdon looked on in perplexity at the massive monstrosity assembling itself over the hills that flanked the East and northern walls of Edawn. A force that no one in the kingdom could have ever possibly foretold was fanning out around the horizon and positioning itself to descend upon them.

As Ozzdon looked over the menacing threat, attempting to tally the situation. Zandor and Kondor appeared, their bulky muscles fully encased in armor, both with their long dark hair tied back in a warrior's braided tail. The pair stood together by their king like two towering pillars staring out on the plains, defiantly waiting to meet the battle.

King Ozzdon's eyes raked the horizon from side to side, searching through his long eye as his dark eyebrows wrinkled with concern. In the receding twilight, King Ozzdon spotted Baddlock on the hilltop like a scab on an ulcerous sore, moving to the front of his troops to contemplate how and when he would unleash his stormy beasts of war. "There he is, that maggot filled sack of puss," Ozzdon said with a biting tone. "And there at his side is the boil on a pig's rump, Dandork." The king grimaced in disgust.

Zandor was the first to speak in the silence that ensued, his hand resting on the hilt of his sword. "We are all ready to fight to the last drop of blood."

Every warrior responded with an overwhelming sense of unity and patriotism, vowing their lives and their allegiance. The king fought to hide his anxiety as he addressed his nervous knot of generals. "I do not know what this day will bring. What I do know is that it will be a day to remember. It will not only determine the fate of our kingdom but that of our empire and the course of history." Worriment stole unintentionally into his tone.

The king held his warriors in the highest respect, and his warriors were loyal to him, and he knew that they were prepared to fight to the death as he was prepared to die by their side. He was also well aware that their fearlessness was the sublime courage of those who had never been at war, thinking they were prepared to engage in battle and face down death.

The king looked about them and saw many champions, the bloodline of brave men who had competed in the tournaments and won many courageous victories and countless flags of valor. But this was not a game. Their lack of experience was the rule rather than the exception. Equipment was another problem. Essential weaponry was either in short supply, outdated or lacking entirely.

Having scraped together everything, almost every man carried a sword forged for ancient wars beyond their memory, long since forgotten in the pages of time. King Ozzdon took his crown from his head, handed it to his page and called for his polished gold plated armor designed for ceremony now meant to protect his chest, back, arms, and legs. He donned his golden war helmet adorned with the eagle crest of his noble forefathers.

He turned to his troops. "I say we wait for them to come to us. Prepare for battle and remember that the future of Edawn, of Xylenia, of Zia itself, depended on the outcome of this great battle."

As the sun rose slowly, lighting up the sky, its dim glow revealed the ghostly silhouette of the amassed force arriving on the horizon with dust and thunder. Zandor interlocked and flexed his fingers and cracked his knuckles. He would defend the walls to the right and Kondor to the left.

In the belly of Zia, in complete darkness, there echoed a chipping sound at fixed intervals. In the upper level of the tomb, a small fire flickered and cast weird shadows against the featureless, barren wall. Izz had collected some wooden artifacts and a few metal implements and was chipping and whittling away at the stone slap that had blocked the passage from which he had entered. The obscured light from the small fire allowed Izz to see that he was getting nowhere. Bathed in sweat, weary with exhaustion, and drawing long, heavy breaths, he examined the hard granite stone. After working on the stone slab for hours, he saw that he had barely managed to scratch its surface with the blunt tools he had used for a chisel and mallet. He shook his head and sank back down into the corner. He mopped the sweat from his face with the back of his hand and disillusioned he threw his tools on the dusty ground. Izz looked at his hands and saw that he had only managed to gain a few more blisters on his already blistered hands. He took in a long jagged breath and asked himself, "What is the point? What am I doing here? At least I should have the good sense to admit. For all I know, Zuree is already..." Izz's whisper died on his lips. Izz wanted to believe, but the seed of doubt had sent out its root to strangle his last shred of hope.

Izz moved into a sitting position. He leaned back against the stone slab to conserve his energy. Izz sat for a long time, pondering his options. He had already walked the perimeter of his entombment searching for a hidden passage, doorway, or stairwell, only to find no way out.

As the unattended fire died down, the walls around him became lost in shadow. Then the fire went out completely, and again deep, dreary, and oppressive blackness pressed in on him on every side. Once more, he shivered with the horror and fear of a trapped man. He stared for hours, it seemed into the eternal darkness, reflecting on how hopeless his circumstances had become as he lost all sense of time. He rested his head on his folded arms on his knees. Izz sat in the dark without bothering to relight his fire. His quest was over. He did not know if it was day or night, nor did he care. Izz was tired, hungry, and frustrated, feeling bitter and alone in the underground empire of the dead.

Without having slept, hallucinations slowly began to creep in through the edges of his mind, causing fleeting thoughts to manifest themselves as reality suddenly. He could see faces of the entombed as if they were with him in the darkness. His mind began to torture him with Zuree's pleading whispers. Izz opened his eyes wide, and he stared into the darkness as fleeting visions of Zuree being set down on the sacrificial altar trembled through his mind.

Izz backed into the wall and used his shoulders to crawl himself up. Suddenly overwhelmed with shock, he screamed, "Please noooo!" to the highest heaven as the anguish of his vision slashed through the innermost depths of his heart. Zuree had become a reason for living, needful for breathing.

Shaken, Izz stood there, staring into the middle space of nothingness. After countless moments of silence, once more, the evil voice in his head came crawling up to torment him. *You will soon be dead, and Zuree will be forever mine.*

Izz tried to clear the haze out of his mind as he straightened his backbone and weakly retaliated, "No...no!" The words passed his lips a bit more resounding and full mouthed. "It is only darkness, nothing more. It is nothing to fear." Over and over again, he muttered those words into the void. He had come so far, endured so much; he was not going to surrender to hopelessness now. "Come and get me if you want me!" he screamed into the darkness in defiance and then slumped back down again.

Like a whisper of Ammiz's voice inside his mind, he heard the question, "Have you truly sought her with all of your heart?"

"I shall find her. I have only to look for her with my whole heart for it to be so," Izz weakly vocalized the words that seemed to fortify him. So far, it had all been true—every word Ammiz had spoken. He had to find Zuree! And soon!

Izz pulled himself back from the brink and stared the darkness down. Somewhere in his heart, he found hope. "Darkness is nothing more than a place without light," he whispered to himself. "And fear...is only a notion, just an impulse, simply a concept, a state of mind. In truth, the only thing to fear is fear itself. I will leave no stone unturned!" he vowed.

Then in the next moment, a fantastic thing happened. Izz's eyes began to dilate, adjusting against a low level light that seemed to be slowly seeping into the sealed vault from somewhere in the ceiling. The mausoleum was lighting up by an unknown source that sent strange shadows dancing all around him. A drawn out cracking sound came to his ears like the sound of fingernails on a rigid surface. *Another hallucination playing tricks with my mind,* Izz thought.

Nonetheless, through the haze, his eyes followed the glow of light to its brightest point. Carefully he climbed down the landslide that had almost entombed him alive. Up ahead, the overhanging roof was glowing with an increasingly bright ring of light. He walked up to where he had first unexpectedly discovered the rim of the gapping pit and looked up into the waning glow of light from the volcano's open crater above. *It must be the next morning, Izz reasoned to himself.*

In the shadows of the volcano throat, he could see several vent openings lining the walls. The central vent opening, was just a tiny dot of light above him. Blissful brightness, the beam of the sun, even what meager amount of it, found its way into this gloomy vault! It had to be close to noon. Izz had lost track of time; he had to make a decision despite his serious misgivings. The vent could be his only way out; there was no way up unless he suddenly sprouted wings. He had one of two choices. Climbing down the pit was going to be risky, but his only other option was to relinquish and die. He had, it seemed, eliminated all the possibilities—except one. It would appear that he was facing one last option, and that option looked dishearteningly bleak, to say the least, but what other alternative did he have? Izz tried to reason it through. It is too dangerous, of course, but the choice was clear. He would rather give up his body, his blood, and his life than to never see Zuree again.

Izz turned his attention to the bottomless pit. He dropped to his knees, kicked his feet back, inclined his weight toward his toes, and leaned as far forward as he safely could. It was like looking into the inner depths of hell itself. Izz suddenly felt weak; he sat up and scrambled from the edge of the drop. Izz's stomach turned at the mere thought of going down there. Izz suddenly felt frail and had to brace himself to keep from toppling over. The thought of Zuree in the hands of those filthy beasts made Izz set his jaw. Izz pushed himself away from the wall and reeled back to the edge of the abyss for another look. Blinking and squinting, he peered into the vast well of mysteries. Izz strained with his inadequate sight, trying to penetrate the blackness. Searching with his insight, he felt a sudden strange assurance that there was a horizontal vent hole just beyond his view. He inched out a little farther, and when he did, Zuree's necklace slipped from under his shirt and dangled from his neck. From the lower corners of his eyes, Izz saw that the tiny facets at the center of the stone were radiating, pulsating brighter than ever before. At the same moment, he perceived an uncanny, unexpected prickling sensation that caused him to shake involuntarily, followed by a spasmodic vibration in his heart. Izz glanced down at the gem and knew it had detected Zuree's presence as the Seer had promised it would. Izz rolled to the side on his back. Zuree was down there somewhere, and he had to get to her somehow.

Izz repositioned him and studied the depth of the pit again. Izz tried to measure the distance and direction of what seemed to be the only way out of this guaranteed death trap. He could feel the heat rising against his face and smell the faint odor of sulfur from the lowest point of the pit. He did not have the slightest idea of how hot it was down there or if there was any air to breathe. He reached down and explored the possibilities of a handhold. The surface was once molten but cooled and solid now. There were no reliable indications of handgrips. At best there were a few lava overlays, and most had been worn down into smooth rounded groves by untold eons of rainfall from above. Izz was not prepared to stake his life on these edgeless contours. A frown waxed on his face as he turned back and sat up. The wall was vertical, with slick sides and only a few strewn out handholds at best. How could he scale that? Once again, his confidence shook as shadows of regret crept through his mind. A sense of inevitable doom from within and the whisper of a faceless fear coiled itself around his soul and began to crush any hopes of escape mercilessly. His shoulders slumped in defeat. Izz desperately searched his mind for another option and found none. The pit was the last resort, and that did not exactly offer him much of even a glimmer of hope. Izz did not like that, but he did not see any way around it.

Even as all those thoughts, doubts, and feelings of doom poured through his mind, he refused to relinquish all hope. There was a great question to be answered here. What were his priorities? The only answer—much worse than death—would be dying knowing that he had not done everything in his power to rescue the only one he had ever truly loved. Izz knew even if he ever got out alive that he would never love again, not the way he loved Zuree. As that thought firmed up in his mind, it led to another. What else in life could be more important? He would rather die with honor than live with dishonor if he had a chance to live at all. *I would gladly give my life,* Izz thought as the last of his fears fell away from him. "I swear I will not leave a single stone unturned." He had sworn his oath, and one way or another, nothing was going to stop him from keeping it.

Izz turned his attention back to the black circle of the pit. As he stared intensely at the bottomlessness, studying it for a possible way down, a tiny light suddenly winked red in its depths. Even if there were a way down, how could he possibly see his way? Then he remembered the strange headlamp Ammiz had given him. Izz scrounged through his backpack, and there, at the bottom, he felt the odd gadget and brought it out into the ever brightening light from above. He carefully studied it as he tried to figure out how to light it. Straps were attached to an oil filled ceramic bulb. A cork covered its opening at its top, and a square cork block at its back would keep it from burning a hole in his head. In front of the block of cork a concaved, polished silver reflector and a cupped glass bowl, which fit around an adjustable wick at the top of the ceramic oil bulb, were attached. Izz searched his pockets for his flint. After finally finding his flints, by some wonder he still carried, he lit the unusual headlamp, and the lantern's wick ignited up, and as the flames flared, it began to glow brightly. The round flame emitted a strange acidulous odor, making Izz wrinkle his nose. He quickly adjusted the wick, closed its vented glass cap, and strapped it to his forehead. He turned one way and then the other and was amazed at how mirrored surface behind it doubled its brilliant beam.

Izz directed the beam downward and observed the flickering shadows cast by a reflective lamp before the pitch black yawning utterly swallowed the light. He concentrated the beam on the smooth walls as far as his bright light could reach. The light beam flattened itself against the pit's wall surface as Izz scanned it, searching for anything he could scale down. He stared into the middle distance beyond the reach of his shaft of light. On and on ever deeper, without end, the pit was swallowed by the darkness like a shroud cast to conceal the very edge of time itself. Encroaching darkness engulfed his heart as he stared down into the vast depth below him that reached downward where a tiny pinpoint glow marked infinity. The deeper Izz stared, the deeper the darkness filled him. "It is only darkness, nothing more than darkness," he whispered.

Perspiration broke out over his entire body. Exposing himself to such a precarious situation is not what he wanted, but circumstances left him no other choice. Suddenly there on the other descending side, he thought he saw a crack. He could not see where it ended. There was no right choice here, but he had to take a chance, he had to have faith. He was too desperate, too firmly fixed, to not to. Izz took a few short drinks from his skin of water and ate a hurried fistful of what was breakfast, lunch, and dinner, all in one gulp.

Izz strapped his backpack on and stared into the bottomless drop as he carefully weighed the risk he was about to face against his love for Zuree. He drew extended breaths down into his lungs. He knew climbing down would be easier but more treacherous than climbing up. Izz licked his dry lips, knowing that he was about to begin a delicate dance with gravity and death. It was a chance he was willing to take. For the last time, he plotted his descent and tried to think everything through before he lowered himself into this underground brink of the unknown. He had put the final decision off as long as he could, yet the conclusion was simple yet frightening but the obvious choice.

"I made a solemn promise, a promise bound in love and honor. Even if I die in this noble attempt, the attempt will be worthwhile," he reaffirmed as if he wished his last words had remained unspoken. *One mistake, one slip, one faulted step, and you are a dead man,* he thought to himself.

Izz cautiously positioned himself at the brink of oblivion. He knew full well he could not afford to be careless, acutely aware that his life was on the line. His senses said no, but his will said yes. This climb would be the most dangerous thing Izz had ever attempted, but even though Izz felt the ominous warning, he showed no indication of relenting. After a moment of hesitation, he hung one leg over the ridge and then the other, and then he slid backward, tipped himself over the rim, and eased over the edge. As he swung himself over the threshold, he heard some stones fall and skip down the infinite void beneath him. His legs dangled, and his feet probed instinctively for a foot hole in the obscured gloom as he began his descent. Slowly he lowered himself into a world of sudden danger.

Izz took in a deep breath and then another. He had run out of time to consider further. It would require all the courage Izz could summon to ease himself down and away from the ledge completely. Once his hands left the rim of the pit, he whispered to himself, "I hope I do not live to regret this." *That may have been a poor choice of words.*

He clutched at the smooth rock, selecting each handhold with exact precision and as Izz pushed his luck to the limit, the danger of falling mounted. Every downward move he made, he knew could be his last. Death was the last thing he wanted to think about at the moment, but only a fool climbs with no thought for the unthinkable. The one thing he was sure of was that there would be no gain in doubting himself now. He climbed down lower and lower, gripping anxiously onto the lava rock, descending into the near darkness; the only exception was the steady beam of his small headlamp and the tiniest red glowing speck of light at the very bottom of the abyss.

For better or for worse, he had decided to go after Zuree; the hunger to see her again would not be denied, even if he had to go to the ends of Zia, even if it cost him everything. Even if he fell to his death in his pursuit, at least he would die trying; it would be worth it. *If I have to risk everything in the hope of gaining everything, so be it.*

Izz of Zia

Izz set his jaw and gathered his courage with absolute conviction, trusting his already overextended luck rather than his common sense. He moved very cautiously; he examined each handhold, clamped his fingers firmly on it, and tested every foothold before putting his full weight on it. Izz found that the texture that covered over the smooth fused wall was like a carpet of solidified moss, which made his hand and footholds more secure. All the same, caution was the key. Steadily he descended, continually looking over the side to map his way down. By now, he was gaining some confidence. Concentrating the full capacity of his mind and skills, he pressed on.

Izz reached the crack he plotted out from above and used it to hem himself into the rock. The seam continued steadily downward, not changing in direction, with only the slightest indication that it was narrowing. The deeper he descended, the smaller he became until the blackening shadows slowly swallowed him up. He lowered himself down into a level where faint wisps of smoke hunted the upward waft, where an acidy edge tainted the air he breathed. The first thing that struck him was that the atmosphere's temperature was getting oppressively heavy with heat, and the last thing Izz needed was for his fingers to start sweating. The next thing that struck him was that the crack was definitely narrowing, and the pit's surface was quickly proving to be the most dangerous face he had ever scaled; but at that point, his purpose was more important to him than his life.

He found he had reached a point where he could no longer insert his fingers into the crack. All at once, it became apparent that if he lowered himself to the next level, it would be virtually impossible for him to climb back out—something he had not given any thought to at all, until then. However, for Izz, the time for turning back had long since ceased to be an option. *If I make a mistake, the consequences will be instantaneously deadly and in all probability extremely painful.*

It was getting hotter in the pit, and he was starting to get tired. He dug his fingers hard into the almost ridge-less rock wall, crystallized by molten magma. Already he was beginning to regret his decision, but it was too late to wish he had taken more time to consider the consequences. It took fierce concentration to maintain his balance. Izz knew he dared not falter. He craned his neck to look back up across the abyss to the upper end of the vent. He could barely make out the eclipsed pinpoint of light far overhead. As he lowered himself farther into the encroaching blackness, the surface of the wall was becoming increasingly difficult to scale. The unsteady grip under his sweaty fingers felt like burned molasses covered with slick black stone soot that Izz had to wipe from his hands continually. Izz probed the stone's external surface frantically for the slightest crack, reef, or jut, anything he could get a hold on. His hand and footholds were reduced to nothing more than bumps on the pit's wall. Izz paused a moment to recapture his breath, collect his strength, and gather his thoughts.

Izz looked up above him. The vestige of natural light coming from the crater's opening receded as though a cloud had swept across the sun, making the pit seem all the more unfathomable and making his descent slower and much more dangerous. When Izz took the next hold on the rock before him, he felt something skeletal and spiny crawling in his grasp. He pulled back his hand to find a huge flesh eating centipede clinging and injecting its venomous poison into his right hand. Izz nearly let go in a moment of panic as he shook the nasty creature off. Then his worst fears were realized. His feet began to slip dangerously from under him. He quickly stabbed at the slippery, glassy ceramic wall with his fingers. Hand grasp after hand grasp slipped away. Izz frantically began to claw at the cliff wall; he arched his back to pin himself toward the pit's face, attempting to defy the laws of gravity. His eyes widened with alarm as he desperately tried to cling to the rock face.

Finally, Izz's searching right hand found the smallest folds of rock as his feet lost their footing on a crumbling edge of the drop. The muscles in his right shoulder and arm, bruised and torn from his first near fall, stretched to the breaking point. His joints and ligaments snapped and crackled in protest as they were strained to their limits. Izz felt something in his arm rip inside of him. He moaned in agony and stark fear as his tendons tore. Izz let out a low pitched shriek as he reached up with his other hand only to grasp at nothing; he was jerked back down by the irresistible pull of gravity. The snapping sound was displaced by an appalling grind of breaking cartilage all over the right side of his chest and shoulder. The pain in his shoulder and arm reached and surpassed the utter agony of his previous near fall, shooting fire throughout his entire right side. Izz dug his fingers into the fold harder as he struggled to keep panic from engulfing him. His feet thrashed about searching out a foothold. He tried to place a trembling foot on a jut that he expected to be secure, but when he shifted his body weight onto it, his foot slipped away. For an eternal moment, he perilously dangled from the pit's wall. Just then, out of nowhere, Izz heard someone, or something, whisper his name. "Izz...Izz, we have been ever so patiently waiting for you."

At that precise moment, the entire world of Zia seemed to tremble. Then the unthinkable happened: his bitterest horror was realized. One by one, his sweaty fingers began to lose their grip. Izz bit back the curse on his lips as he wavered, teetering on the edge of oblivion. Repeatedly he tried to brace his feet up against the volcanic rock wall, but instead, they danced in empty air. He was swinging in emptiness, hanging from the ends of fingertips that were turning numb. Just then, Izz heard a gentle voice from within say, "Do not be afraid to let go."

His precarious position hit him all at once, causing a moment of pure panic. *No! No! Help me! Help me!* Izz cried out over and over to no one there until his heart seemed to fly into his throat. There was absolute agony in his frantic movements as he slowly slipped closer and closer toward the unavoidable certainty of death, and there was nothing more he could grasp for and nothing left to resist with any longer, from within or without.

Izz had assured himself time and again that he had come too far, given up too much, to fail, that he would see Zuree again, that he would hear her voice once more, and that he would hold her in his arms at long last. Izz had believed it with all his heart. But now, he realized, that the certainty that had been with him as he had lowered himself into the pit, had misled him. It was too late for a remedial comeback; the inevitable irreversible was upon him. *I will die knowing that my best efforts were in vain,* Izz thought. Izz did not have time to consider another thought. In one heart stopping instant, there was a question-less resignation.

All at once, Izz drew in a sharp breath as the dismal fragment of slag his life clung to suddenly gave way. His wide eyes fixed on the darkness below. As though suspended in midair, Izz tensed for a fraction of a heartbeat, then plunged headlong toward the center of Zia. Izz found himself grasping a hand full of air as gravity betrayed him. He reached out madly with both hands to save himself, only to drop like a stone into the vertical emptiness. The terrible moment of falling had happened so quickly, but it seemed like it had happened so slowly. A belching scream escaped Izz's mouth as he plummeted. Izz at once went into a panicked tailspin as he was thrust through weightless space. As Izz's plunging body picked up speed, his mind whirled out of control. White hot dread flamed through him with an all consuming intensity. There was no feeling on Zia quite like knowing there was nothing he could do to alter what was about to happen.

Izz's first reaction was to resist the unyielding law of gravity that had shackled him in its downward grasp. His face froze into a grim expression of terror. In his opposition, his heart rate dramatically increased, and his stomach muscles tightened. Izz windmilled his arms and scissored his legs as he tumbled head over heels as if that would somehow slow him down. Fighting and kicking against the fall, thoughts flashed through his mind. In his hysteria, Izz had the state of mind to pull out of his plummeting tumble. He forced his limbs in opposite directions, spreading himself out flat and wide against the buffeting wind, attempting to find with every fiber in his body the resistance that was not there. "What good does this do?" he asked himself. Izz was plunging in free fall hundreds of feet a second on the way down into the waiting arms of death. His last shred of hope for living fell away and receded before him into the dark cavity of the immeasurable drop. Izz was falling so fast everything around him was a blur as the dead air rushed around his hair and clothes like an angry storm screaming in his ears. His cheeks were pressed up again, his cheekbones, and his lips were gaping as they flapped against his teeth.

The fall was so vast, so deep and unending that Izz seemed to have been suspended in free fall forever. He fell faster and faster through the atmosphere that seemed to be growing thicker and hotter layer by layer. By now, Izz was falling so fast he thought that at any time he would burst into flames. Suddenly his body seemed incredibly heavy as the forces of gravity pulled on him. The resistance of the air causes the blood in his body to be pushed back in the direction he was falling. His heart had to work harder and harder to get the oxygen to every part of his body, especially his brain. Disoriented by weightlessness, Izz felt faint as a result of this temporary imbalance. His free fall velocity had reached its peak, stealing his breath away and causing him to lose consciousness.

Moments later, Izz's body somehow adapted and reawakened. He instinctively jerked himself out of his unconscious tumble and swung himself upright, gradually bringing his mind and eyes back into focus as his body seemingly hovered endlessly, motionlessly, in the void. All he could see was the sweeping walls of the huge chasm as he shot past them. Miraculously, the wick of his headlamp had somehow managed to stay lit behind its shielded crystal. Izz looked around in the ominous darkness that absorbed him and saw its blurred light cast on shades and patches of grays, blacks, browns, and yellows. As he spun on the resistance of the buffeting gale against his body, he realized that even though he was falling fast, it seemed to be happening in a prolonged dream like state. Izz hoped against hope that it was all somehow just a bad dream.

The sides flashed on by as the jagged rock face swept upward on either side. The only sound was the whooshing of his body dropping through the air into a vortex of darkness down, down into the infinite drop. In a blind panic, Izz became temporarily confounded by the afterimages racing past his groping fingers, and he reached out to touch the rock face. The contact shattered his fingernails off his fingers. It was not a dream! The next few immeasurable units of time were sheer delirium. He was engulfed in mind twisting shock. Something in his mind broke, and his thoughts bled utter terror as he inhaled and exhaled death. As a consequence, the only power left to him was to wait for the sudden deathblow.

Izz's eyes glazed, blinding him to the present. Neuroelectric chemical compounds all at once flooded his brain, exploding into thousands of inward and outward trajectories. Suddenly he found himself drowning in a staggering sea of mental images. His mind flashed fleeting mirrored memories across the multifaceted tapestry of his mind. As if for the last time, some kind of primordial recall system surged through his mind. Flashbacks raced across his recollection from his first processed thoughts in his mother's womb to the now and then.

As if in a time lapse, infancy weaved into childhood, then flickered into youth, to the present. Spontaneous multilayered flashbacks of his lifetime shimmered through Izz's mind. Hodgepodge imaginations of faces baring every expression and gesture he had ever observed of everyone he had ever met—from laughing to weeping, from happy to angry—flashed through his mind. Every feeling he ever felt, every idea he ever conceived, every scheme he ever hatched, every good deed, every wrong mistake—all hurled through the universe in his head in every minute detail.

Izz's whole life up to that point in time flickered through his mind, lapsing behind him, receding further and further into his past with each fleeting instant that rushed by. Events great and small came swarming upon him like bubbles in an over boiling cauldron until his mind had no more room for another thought; then his intermingling thoughts rewound and replayed, again and again, front to back and then back to front, without the sense of the passing of time.

The one memory that stood out and surged through him like a deluging storm over a thirsty field was the reflections of Zuree, memories of the special moments spent with her. It had been the best and most beautiful thing that had ever happened to him. Every thought of her and every way she had come to mean everything to him played out so vividly and repeated without beginning or end.

Then it was over as suddenly as it started. All that was left now was the inevitable pulverizing impact with the unknown below. Pure guesswork told Izz he only had a few moments before he hit bottom. He hated pain a lot more when he knew it was imminent. He had enough of his wits left to wonder if he could aim to land feet first. Perhaps his crumpling feet, legs, and pelvis might provide some protection to his major internal organs. No sooner did this fleeting thought complete than he realized how hopeless that would be. At this frightening velocity, he was sure to hit with such force that all that could be left of him would be a gruesome stain of splashed blood, splintered bones, splattered guts, and plastered flesh no matter how he landed.

It began to seem as if he was destined to fall for the rest of endless time until he thought he saw something coming up fast out of the smoke and darkness. Black and crimson shadows flickered on smooth curved stone walls, and then suddenly, flames began to shoot up, skyrocketing from the yawning fissures below. Izz thought he was staring directly into the lowest point of hell itself.

His final thoughts were that of a jar of clay shattering into a thousand chards, his heap of mangled flesh and bone pressed to the solid rock, his insides torn, and his heart collapsed, twitching and jerking as his lifeblood pumped out in fountains of squirting jets to mingle with the dust and darkness.

In anticipation of what was inevitably going to be one horrific impact, and unable to stare death in the face at the last moment, Izz managed to flip himself around and arched his back up as if he could somehow run away from his unfortunate end. His voice strained against a scream as he tried to decide if the end was only a few feet away or several hundred. Izz clamped his lips and braced his face, and his stomach muscles tightened with resistance in an involuntary reflex. Instinctively, every nerve constricted, like coiled springs, wound up too tight. A long agonizing moment passed. Izz closed his eyes in anticipation of the final, fatal impact. There was an instant of heightened hysteria as he locked his jaw against a last cry of distress and terror, and then Izz landed with a sickening, bone jarring, tooth rattling jolt that violently shuddered his entire body and stunned his mind. It felt as if a crazed mule had kicked him in the back as hard as it could and smashed the air out of him. At that moment of collision, he lay there waiting to die as his eyeballs whirled around like two peas spinning in a hollow gourd. Emptiness surged all around his mind. Izz fought off unconsciousness barely long enough to realize it was the end.

Just before his mind went completely black, he was almost inconceivably aware that he was still careening downward. Somehow, he kept going beyond the impact point in slow motion until his acceleration stopped for the briefest moment. Then within the next fraction of time and space, Izz felt a most unearthly sensation, as if he was being slung back up, back toward the heavens. Once again, he sensed he was slowing and then once more suspended. Then back down, he went falling again. This repeated falling and rising continued in diminishing intervals. *Perhaps Ammiz's Creator cannot determine whether I am yet dead or not,* Izz tried to rationalize.

Then he seemed to come to a vibrating stop with a single, final pull. The sensation lasted only another moment. But at that moment, it appeared that he had died a hundred times. Izz felt suspended and weightless. *Is this what it feels like to be dead?* He wondered to himself. Dizziness turned into a whirlpool of what first seemed like little colored dots becoming white then black. As his body rang with the prickling of a billion tiny needles, Izz's mind and consciousness took their departure. A loud ringing roared in his ears, and then almost as though he was not even there, as if he were in the final throes of dying, everything went blank.

For the longest time between wakefulness and oblivion, Izz could not tell if he was dead or alive. Izz did not know how long he had not known of himself. He had no way of knowing how much time had passed from then to his next semiconscious thought. Minutes or hours may have passed away without his recollection. In his mind, he came awake kicking and screaming, but in reality, he lay motionless. Deadly quiet surrounded Izz. He did not move. His legs, arms, back, and neck hurt terribly, but he could feel, breathe, and move his fingers. Nothing seemed broken. He just lay there, tuned into the pulsating of his own heart still pounding in his throat, urging him to wake.

Izz's eyes finally, cautiously opened just a slit; his first overwhelming impression was that of bright patches of whiteness. His mind and body were wholly stunned numb. Dazed, Izz could not tell if he had died in midair from heart failure or had been smashed like a worm against some mantle. He did not move or breathe. Was he even still alive? Izz believed he had to be dead, but incredibly, he was alive. He was too battered, too shocked to feel any pain. He was aware of the whizzing of air in and out of his lungs. If this was not death, how could he have possibly survived the incredible fall?

Izz's mind was still somersaulting as feeling returned to his body. He felt a tingling rigidity in his muscles, and suddenly his head was throbbing, and his whole body felt like one big welt. The ache was intense. If he was in truth dead, how could he be in so much pain? For a moment, he regarded his implausible survival in a state of skepticism. If he was alive, how could that be humanly possible? Izz opened his eyes wider, unable to focus. "I am...alive! But how?"

All in all, the falling sensation might have lasted less than a few heartbeats. It had only felt like a dream locked in endless time. Izz found himself wishing that he was waking from what had all been only a terrible dream. But like scraps of illusion, his remembrance told him he had not been dreaming. In a painful collage of images, he recalled in every detail what he had just gone through; the nightmare of the fall had been a reality.

As his vision slowly cleared, everything seemed so unbelievable. In the process of his wonderment, he saw something he had never expected. There was a piercing white blazing thing shining down on him from far, far above. Miraculously his headlamp was still burning. Izz realized that he was suspended on something like a huge cobweb like festoon that covered the entire circular depth of the vent from wall to wall and disappeared into a cavernous opening to his right where any vestige of his light beam receded into nonexistence. What seemed like a giant crisscrossing web that supported him and had broken his fall was thicker than a ship's mooring lines.

Somehow, Izz had managed to land on an intersecting section on his back in a tangle of arms and legs. The rush of deceleration had strained all his muscles to their limit. With a groan, he struggled to lift his head, and he tried to move, but Izz found that he was held fast against some substance that clung to him like an iron fist. His effort to move left him feeling as if every one of his joints had been jarred out of its place. Every bone in his body felt rubbery as if they had been shattered into a million fragments. His brain felt as if it had been scrambled like an egg inside his head.

He lay stunned, drenched in viscous sweat and gasping for breath. Feeling queasy, he waited for his heart to calm down and for the stark reverberating bewilderment to leave him. He closed his eyes a moment as he drew breath deep down into his lungs, attempting to regain some self possession. The initial shock subsided, and the full realization that he had somehow survived, against all the odds, settled in. A weak smile played over Izz's lips, and he found that even that hurt. What he really wanted to do is to break out into hysterical laughter, to roar, but that would have been too painful.

Far overhead, the patch of brightness still blazed, leaking down onto him through the great distance of the ancient vent opening. Izz blinked as he stared up and realized that it had to be the high noon sun shining straight down on him like a watchful eye. The vent along the walls to the left just within the bounds of his peripheral sight from below was aglow; it turned pale orange with the light that seemed to be coming from a burning whirlpool beneath him. There were colors of lead, zinc, copper, silver, and gold created in the furnaces of volcanic activity. Beneath him, there was a faraway roaring, a roiling undercurrent of violence that sent mysterious sparks of lights drifting and dancing up from the depths.

Izz could not quite put his finger on what so suddenly turned amiss. He blew at the loose locks about his face. He felt around himself to discover that he was caught in something sticky that had immobilized him. He dug his fingers through the goop and felt something like thick silken fibers twisted together to form a rope like strand. The fibers were soft, almost delicate, but he could not break them. Izz lifted his head as far as he could to see that the strands were wound in a spiral orb around an intersecting V-shaped netting set on a horizontal plane.

Now that he was fully awake, Izz rationalized for a moment as he rubbed the gluey substance between his fingers. *Sticky... web...predator*! He was afraid even to think of that possibility. Izz felt his throat tighten as a heaviness grew in his chest. He felt a few moments of panic. The thought gave him an unsettling feeling, like hundreds of crawly feet running up and down his spine. The hair on his head was entangled, but he could still raise his head to take another look around. Above him, on the wall, he saw strange orange glowing shadows everywhere. Izz could see fumaroles smoking and hissing, and steam swirls coming from all around him. From below, he could smell an unpleasant scorched odor and see a smoke cloud with a hazy red radiance rising. From beneath the ancient underworld, heat beat against his back in pulsing waves. Izz craned his neck as far as it would go as his eyes darted around, and from the edges of his vision, he could see underneath him, in the distance, dazzling red and orange molten fire blazing with incredible power. Magma splashing back and forth with vigorous undercurrents bubbled and sloshed like thick, chunky gravy. From his viewpoint, he could barely see anything, and he had not heard any sounds apart from the ones he was making himself.

Suddenly there was a noise! Izz shivered. It was like that of teeth clacking and clicking together, which made Izz's empty stomach churn. He looked up sharply with a shuddering jerk, trying to stretch his neck around to see what was lurking in the darkness to his right. "Who is there?" Izz asked, unable to twist around to see beyond his headlamp's light. He thought he had felt a slight vibration on the sticky radial of the web like spiral. Then he felt a sharp jolt. "Wh...what was that?"

Izz held a jagged breath as he felt his insides tightening, aware of the warning of danger. His stomach flipped upside down. Izz struggled to free his tangled arms from their tacky grip. Something was out there probably watching him at that very moment. Fear uncoiled itself through his veins as if suddenly every horror that had ever haunted his darkest nightmares had all at once found him out. His jaw muscles were clenching and unclenching with anticipation as he desperately reached for his dagger at his side. The web's glue like substance was remarkably strong, but Izz could feel it weakening as he continued to stretch it. He could feel the hilt of his dagger at his fingertips. Slowly, he slipped the razor sharp blade out of its sheath.

Izz finally was able to shine his headlamp toward the farthest corner of the web. The beam from the headlamp managed to catch the flecked reflections of eight eye like spheres glinting in the darkness. Izz narrowed his eyes to a squint to see through the black obscurity. There hiding at the edge of the web with one foot on a single line of the web network was the outline of the biggest spider Izz had ever seen in his life. It was a completely unknown species, nothing like anything he had ever heard of in the wildest sailor tales. As far as he knew, they were not even supposed to exist. A sudden fear more lethal than death ruptured through Izz.

Izz of Zia

The crusty, gory, multi eyed monster oozed poisonous slime from its fangs. It had not moved an inch, and then it suddenly stepped out into the light like the embodiment of some nightmarish prehistoric creature. It had a huge hairy head with eight eyes, enormous fangs, and eight long, furry legs with claws on each end. It just sat there watching and lying in wait as if assuring itself that its prey was helplessly trapped before moving in to snag its meal.

Ignoring the pain that racked his body, Izz wildly scrambled to get a firm grip on his weapon. At long last, he had the hilt of his dagger at his fingertips and in his hand. Once he had the blade secured, Izz let his arm snap back against the stickiness that held him, causing the strand to jiggle.

The spider had sensed the jolt and now the struggle of its prey. Izz held the dagger firmly in his right hand; bending his wrist toward himself, he deliriously battled to free his clothes from the gluey strands of the web that held his right arm down. The giant malformation came at him with a vicious string of mock attacks and sidestepped to get at Izz from his most venerable angle.

Undaunted by the mutation's ferociousness, Izz continued to cut away at the sticky strands, contorting his wrist and elbow until he had freed his arm to his shoulder.

The oversized spider prepared to inject its venom into Izz. It would either paralyze him or kill him; either way, the venom would slowly turn his insides into jelly. She would then consume him later at her leisure when Izz was fully digested. The spider stomped toward Izz, its fangs repeatedly scrapping together, dripping milky white venom as if in great expectation of gorging itself on a tasty feast. The thing came closer, paused, oscillating its front pair of legs at him as if testing its prey's defenses. Izz was trapped in a tangled mass; he could not even move enough to kick at the beast. The eight legged monstrosity positioned itself over Izz, towering over him like a giant, and prepared to dip down to bite and inject him with its paralyzing poison. As Izz struggled, the tendrils that held him captive were beginning to relinquish their strength and rip as Izz sawed the sticky web away. The monster's powerful legs grabbed and pulled Izz toward the dangerous fangs in its mouth. Izz swallowed in horror and felt sick to his stomach as his mind fought to cope with the impending danger. The spider thrust its head forward, targeting Izz's chest, and as it bore its fangs to deliver its lethal injection, his headlamp made it possible to see the creature's ghastly mouth flanked by its two dagger like hollowed fangs, oozing with venom meant for him.

Temporarily blinded by the flash of light, the beast hesitated. At that moment, with the superhuman strength of desperation, Izz pulled himself up on one elbow and struck at one of the arachnid's eyes with his dagger. The razor sharp blade perforated the multifaceted eye up to its golden handle. Enraged, the creature reared its head back, its remaining eyes bulging with shock. Its injured eyeball dripped with yellow gunk and squirted out spider blood. The wounded giant stomped its front legs in rage, raised its head to the ceiling, and unleashed a vile howl in agonizing pain. Suddenly, the deadly predator sprang toward Izz and returned with jabs from its four front hooked feet.

The outraged spider positioned itself over Izz, covering him with strands of sticky strands from its abdomen. There was no time to think, no room for mistakes. In that instant, Izz had become both predator and prey in the chain of survival where there was only life or death for one or the other. Izz plunged his dagger up into the soft underbelly of the spider and ripped with a downward thrust. Izz withdrew his blade and did not miss his opportunity to slash at the underbelly again and again. The spider's reflexes caused it to somersault backward in midair, inducing it to implode into a giant spindling mass of spider legs. The wounded beast lumbered slowly away, dragging its entrails along as it staggered away, leaving a slimy snaillike track behind it. It struggled for stability as it continued to slither away on its hemorrhaging gore into the shadows, into whatever darkened hole it crawled out of, as carnage oozed out, forming huge droplets on the cavern floor.

Midway across the expansive web, the abnormality collapsed, pulled its legs in under itself like a pile of sticks, and turned into a quivering mass clinging to the web with its last vestige of life, spewing streams of inner goop from its furry body that spilled onto the cave floor below. As the hideous creature lay dying, it seemed to be tapping out some sort of alarm with its two front legs onto the web strand that was connected to a large sack like nest woven from fine white silky cobwebs. Off to his right, spiderlings came pouring out of the funnel of a translucent cocoon by the hundreds. The encroaching spiderlings moved around their web quickly and with relative ease.

Upon seeing this, Izz began to slice and chop frantically at the gluey web that held him in its death grip. Spiderlings, each with its own set of poisonous fangs, came at Izz from every direction as Izz tore at the web around his torso and then his legs. Being careful not to entangle himself again, he rolled over and dropped himself to the underside of the web, but he found himself still within reach of the aggressive spiderlings. Izz pulled in a deep breath. This was going to be a serious test of his obedience to his faith. If he ever had to believe in miracles, this was the time. He fortified his heart against his doubts. In a desperate final attempt to survive, Izz hastily proceeded to saw away at the main web strand above him. It was the only way he could stay alive one more moment. When he had nearly cut through to the other side of the strand, it detached itself from the central web, sending Izz, barely in the nick of time, just out of reach of the spiderlings. In frustration, they reached and clawed at Izz as they stared menacingly with their glistening eight, catlike eyes at him.

As Izz felt a sudden sag in the web strand, he quickly placed his dagger between his teeth. Looking up, he saw that the fibers where his lifeline was jointed began to stretch under his weight, pulled tautly, and tore away, setting off a circular chain reaction of detaching links. Suddenly Izz found himself slinging around and dropping in a counterclockwise rotation, bringing him closer to the glowing lake of fire below. The links continued to break, and Izz could feel the incredible heat bearing up over him as clouds of sulfur dioxide, chlorine, and fluorine rose all around him. Izz prayed that the stretching web strand would not break while he was over the blazing abyss. The web strand continued to detach in a wide circular downward jerking motion, and Izz was sent soaring around toward the dark side of the opening on his way to an uncertain end. The integrity of the web had been severely compromised, sending many of the spiderlings toppling. All the while, the mother spider continued to cling desperately to the web with its final once of strength. It was as if it knew what waited below on the cave floor. Some spiderlings fell away into the churning waves of fire, and they burst into ghostly red puffs of smoke, their screams sucked away from them as the bubbling lava swallowed them. The web stretched from one side of the vent to the other as it continued to unravel. The centrifugal force would soon cause Izz to lose his grip and slide down or fall altogether.

In a life or death instant, Izz thought of jumping as he reached the dark side of his descent, but there was no way of telling what lay at the bottom end of the inky darkness or how far down the cave floor was. Come what may, anything was better than a fiery end. Izz took a desperate gasp of air, braced himself for the worst, and released his grip as the line continued on its rounded return toward the blazing abyss. Bubbles of molten rock ascended out of the scorching depths and erupted at the surface with a splashing display of fire hotter than popping grease.

When Izz reached the cave bottom, his feet hit first, sending him tumbling head over heels onto the cave floor. He had plummeted through the darkness, landing with a crashing topple, with enough bone shattering force to render anybody a crippled, collection of brokenness, but Izz's fall had somehow been cushioned by what seemed like large, long sticky bundles of cotton. His headlamp's flame went out as he came to a jumbled stop. Izz immediately checked for broken bones, and incredibly, other than a few rivulets of blood running down his chin, a few additional bruises, multiple scraps, a sprained ankle, and three dislocated ribs, everything seemed to be all in one piece and working order. As he tried to get up, he felt a sharp pain in his right shoulder and arm. He rubbed his shoulder gingerly; it was probably dislocated, but at least it was unbroken. The impact of surviving the fall, the vent, the spider attack, and now this, it suddenly hit him—what were the odds! Once again, he had cheated the grim reaper, against all odds. As Izz stared up into space, he wondered if Ammiz's Creator conceivably watching over him, what were the odds?

TEN
THE HORDE

The underground vault suddenly dimmed as Zia turned on its axis, and the sun traversed the sky. As Izz slowly sat up, the first thing he noticed was that the air around him was foul and disgusting, like the smell of rat urine, causing him to gag. Izz tried to feel his surroundings out only to find more sticky cotton like bales. Something wickedly furry brushed against his leg, and he jumped in alarm. With one hand, his fingers tightened on his dagger; with the other, he reached up for his headlamp only to discover that it had been crushed in the fall. Even though he could still see, from the glow of the fire pit where he was, the darkness all around him was absolute! Its completeness pushed up against his eyeballs, burrowing its way into his mind, and eating away at his courage. The silence broken only by the sound of an isolated drip was complete.

In almost total darkness, he removed his backpack and searched for his broken lamp with shaky hands. Izz placed the lamp in front of him and lit it with his flints. He adjusted the wick and held the light up high. He heard and felt nothing as he stood and waited for his eyes to adjust to the light of his lantern. To his surprise, he saw that the bundles were bound in webbing, wrapped around the boney empty shells of men like a ceremonial dress of a spider's web. An unspeakable vision of human sacrifice shot through his mind and seized his heart like a strangling fist. Izz quickly backed up on all fours, only to discover to his mounting horror that the web caskets were everywhere around him, and each one held a skeleton clothed in garment fragments. Izz noticed that every skeleton had its hands bound with leather straps behind their backs. This could only mean one thing: these men were bound and fed to the monstrous oddities on the web above him. Izz reasoned, *If these men were brought here, then there has to be a passageway out of here.*

Izz held his lantern up high again and scanned every foot of the sub-terrestrial den. His lamp cast such a dismal light that he could not be sure of anything except that everything on the cave floor was covered in cobwebs.

As Izz picked at the strands of web dangling from his hair and clothes, all he could think of was how close he had come to ending up as a dissolved, rotting, hollowed out corpse. He could have ended up wrapped up in web fibers left in the vastness of nothingness, in the middle of nowhere, never to be heard of again. He could not seem to get that thought out of his head.

Izz was only beginning to clam his traumatized nerves over the close call he had had moments before. And just when he was starting to think that things could not possibly get any worst, Izz's skin began to tingle unpleasantly. The overpowering feeling broke his train of thought that he was not alone. He was being watched. The powerful sense was an impression he could not dismiss.

Then Izz thought he heard something—a faint noise. He stopped to listen. Soft chronic scratching sounds off to his left rearward toward the far end of the cavern. Yes, he was positive that he heard something—a clicking, grinding sound of teeth meshing. Farther to the right came more scraping sounds. He noticed that the noise was growing louder as if magnified by the in existence of light. Izz's skin began to tingle dreadfully.

All at once, his senses called out with alarming warnings. The uneasy feeling of foreboding grew stronger with every heartbeat. There was a strong, distasteful odor of rodent urine and defecation drifting in the warm air. His stomach seemed to churn. Izz held up his lamp out before him and started in the direction of the noises. Desperately he tried to see something, anything, but the light was not shining far enough to do him any good. He saw nothing moving where Izz thought he heard the noise. The sound grew as he listened, and he wondered what other hideous creature or creatures could inhabit this warm, moist, and lightless area of the underworld. Izz's eyes strained against the blackness of the cavity. He heard a muffled pattering somewhere. Something was moving toward him.

Izz held his breath and listened intently. The minutest sound of tiny footsteps was amplified in the hollow space and coming closer. Izz stood trembling. With every moment, he became more aware of the relentless sound slithering all around him, just beyond his limited field of vision. He supposed that the lamplight was all that kept whatever it was at bay. Izz began to back away from the noise; the sounds grew louder, closer. His pulse began to race as the raking sound filled the cavern.

A shadow on the floor suddenly moved against the darkness. Izz panned his lamp, and in the same instant, the phantom skittered away to escape discovery. From the sound, he suspected it had to be some kind of a rodent. Whatever it was, it was too big to be an average rat, too small to be a spider, like those he had just escaped. Something stirred in the darkness nearby. Izz scanned the floor with his lantern, and his eye caught movement on the floor at his feet. Out of one of the cocooned cadavers, Izz saw the head of one of the biggest rats he had ever seen, with a matted black snout and tattered black ears. It had chewed into the body cavity. The rat, the size of a small dog, crawled out of the carcass's chest and wiped its snout with its grisly paws. It snapped and crooked its head in Izz's direction and bore its teeth at him. The half starved rat was missing one eye and seemed to be covered with hundreds of tiny teeth marked scars. The emaciated rat sat back on its hind legs with no signs of fear. It sniffed the murky air, oscillating its whiskers, twitching its nose and grinding its large glistening incisors on its oddly humanlike face. Izz could feel the thin and wasted black rat's hungry eyes upon him, gloomily waiting with expectation for any opportunity to stuff its face. But little did Izz know that in the deeper darkness, the whole smelly rat colony stared from the shadows. They were gathering to the hunt, drawn out of their hiding places, attracted to the anticipated feeding frenzy.

The lone rat suddenly let out an eerie squeaking alert to the rest of the colony, as if urging them to join in the impending attack. Izz shuddered in response. A wave of shrill squeaks suddenly pierced the darkness. He swept his lantern glancing around, trying to look in every direction at once. Then out of the darkness, Izz saw the frontal attack of the rats, a few at first, then more and more. "Rats!" Izz choked. Suddenly, in great numbers, ravenous rats poured out from seemingly everywhere—hundreds of huge rats, perhaps thousands, squirming and pushing, shoving and jostling one another. A tidal wave of fury, rats, rushed at Izz, each one aroused, expectant, and on edge.

On the cave wall to the far right along the ledge, a procession of hungry rats ready to bear down on him crawled over the twilight edge, scampering upon the overhead ledges on their little gray hands and feet. They stared down at Izz with their unblinking eyes glistening wetly, all the while salivating crazily as an easy meal for the taking was before them. Other rats came out of the surrounding corpses. Izz did not know how many rats there were; he only knew that he had to get away from there and fast. Izz drew his dagger and backed up slowly, not wishing to trigger an all out attack. It was doubtful any weapon could save him were they to attack suddenly all at once.

Izz continuously peered behind him, looking for an imagined ambush. The rising and falling layers of rats on the ground and walls made his skin crawl. As Izz tramped over the sponginess underfoot, he unexpectedly sensed something scurrying at his feet and stood still. Izz swept his lamp along the floor. He noticed movement near his feet and all around the fringe of the cave floor. At first, the rats on the floor scurried out of his way but showed no real fear of him. Suddenly, at the base of his steps, he caught sight of several giant rats sniffing around, bobbing their heads up and down. One grabbed at his pant legs, waiting for the others to arrive. Izz slashed out with his dagger and kicked viciously back at them, trying to throw off their pursuit. Every muscle in his body tensed as he retreated from the threat. There were more, and thousands of them, crammed more and more tightly until the visible cave floor appeared to be enveloped with drab, disheveled fur that writhed and undulated. Incalculable beady black eyes stared hungrily out at Izz. Soon, clusters of rats would be all over him, attacking him, eating him alive! Izz readied himself to take flight at the first sign of attack.

Unexpectedly, all movement ceased. Everything went instantly still, as deathly quiet ebbed across the cavern. Then the lead rat reared up high on its hind legs and froze, its whiskers bustled and shuddered as it stiffly sniffed the air, then scampered off into the shadows. Izz swiveled the lantern around but could not see a single rat. Then suddenly out of nowhere, there came a new more massive moving sound in the dark. Jostling sounds, sickening, dragging sounds that repeated and rapidly grew louder and louder. Nothing sane or of this world could exist in any other place but this utter darkness. Izz's pulse quickened from fast to racing, and his mouth dried so that his tongue stuck to its roof.

Suddenly there were fulsome scratching sounds by the thousands coming closer and heavier from every direction at ground level. All at once, out of the darkness, there was a loud squeal from the recesses of the shadowy backdrop. A prolonged shrieking filled the cavern and resounded from end to end. Startled out of his wits, Izz jumped and trained his trembling light in the direction of the bloodcurdling shrill. With his teeth set on edge, he concentrated on the growing sound that was headed his way. At that point, there was a multitude of life-ending squeals; then all hell seemed to break loose as rats bolted in every direction. The stampeding sound of rats running for their lives was drowned out by an eerie deepening advance of thousands of tiny scraping feet. For a moment, Izz stood paralyzed, vainly trying to calm himself. He could feel something coming, drifting in the warm air. It's sound seemed to keep getting closer and louder. There was some entity closing in on him from every side with predatory swiftness. But he did not know which way to run.

The light from his lantern soaked into the darkness and was blotted out just short from where the sound was advancing. Izz strained his eyes against the blackness of the cave. And in his mind, he saw death coming at him from every direction. Out of the impenetrable gloom and doom that his eyes could not pierce, something scary beyond imagination was hunting him. Something was watching him, targeting him, something hungry and unnatural. The increasing clicking noise of feet and fangs filled his heart with overpowering fear. The sound of movement intensified as Izz tried to determine from which direction the main attack was coming from, and which direction to run. The sound rose up to the roof of the cavern, echoing and roaring until the walls themselves seemed to tremor. Izz could see individual shadow shapes that formed one encompassing wave of churning agitation. It seemed that the whole cave floor was alive with commotion.

Finally, whatever was stalking him crossed the twilight threshold of his lantern and came into view. What Izz saw was one approaching movement, a form that was closing in fast, very fast, and immediately, he noticed a strange brownish red like blob. The mass was made up of armies upon armies of glossy little mechanical creatures completely swallowed up under the sheer crush of endless numbers. Millions of them poured out of every shadowed hole in the cavern. They were too big to be worms, too small to snakes. They were hordes of predatory flesh eating centipedes! The carrion beasts were coming at him like a tumbling flood of wild wolf packs, thousands of thousands of them! The noise the mass made as it moved was that of a frenzied attack as each centipede scrambled to be the first to descend on its prey swiftly.

A sudden and uncanny wave of fright rushed over Izz. He wanted to run rather than wait around to discover what a countless number of small predators could do to him. A voice in his head screamed, Run, run now! But Izz was frozen where he stood and could not move a muscle. He was caught in the iron fist of overwhelming terror and confusion. Izz watched in horror as a rat fell from the upper ledge and disappeared in a swarming whirlwind of gruesome killers. Izz's heart leaped to his throat, strangling an impulsive scream.

Izz reached his lamp over his head and looked up for a place to climb before it was too late. He swiveled his lantern over every nook and cranny, searching out any possibility of escape. He saw on a ledge overhead an enormous, well fed rat, scrunch down on its hunches encircled by its wiggly tail. It glared at Izz as it ran its sticky tongue over its clawed clutches; its saliva dripped from its sharp pointy teeth. It sat there on its rump as if savoring some slaughter to come.

Other rats gathered, sniffing the air from the banks above. Meanwhile, the twisting mass of elongated forms continued to press in toward him with the rhythm of crackling kernels of corn. There was no place to run, no place to hide. Izz began to back up slowly, trying to formulate some kind of strategy. With every step he took backward into the darkness, he became aware of the crunch of pulpy skeletal organisms underfoot. The smashed nocturnal creatures secreted a strong, unpleasant odor from their glands, and their death permeated the air. Izz glanced around in the half light and kicked away at aggressive scavengers that crawled up and clung to his pant legs. It became increasingly evident that he get away as soon as possible, if not sooner.

The moving heaps of centipedes continued rising from the cavern floor and shadowy corners, swelling in numbers as they closed in, drawn to the kill. The clustered frontal horde was almost upon him, so close that he could see the millions of eyes focused on him. Soon, he would be overrun with ravenous predators, and Izz wondered if he had not been better off back up above with the spiders. All at once, there were shuffling noises everywhere near him with the rage of an oncoming storm. Above, on either side of the bluffs, more rats were gathering. Like spectators, they rose up around the rim of the cavern, in mounting rows higher and higher until they faded into the blurred darkness of the distant ceiling. By now, they were vibrating with excitement and impatience, sniffing the air for blood, hoping to be spared a scrape of flesh or a taste of gore.

Izz tripped, and as he fell back onto the darkness of the cave floor, his hands instinctively tightened on the hilt of his dagger and the handle of his lamp. On the cave floor, he saw hundreds of bones picked clean—rats bones and bat bones that had fallen victim in times past.

Pumped up with adrenalin and driven by fear and his instinct to survive, Izz quickly got back to his feet, fighting to keep his balance. He fell again. He got up and bolted for open ground without thought and stumbled on the uneven cave floor. Everywhere he looked, the voracious meat eaters were attacking. Their millions of legs moved forward like the rippling, onrushing waves on a restless sea. The gigantic swarm suddenly overwhelmed him by their sheer numbers of hundreds of thousands. They climbed all over his body, trying to find a way inside his thick cloths to get to his flesh. Soon he was entirely overshadowed by centipedes. It was terrifying! Izz's mind was racing fast, concentrating all his efforts on protecting himself. He covered his face in his hands to prevent stings. Izz swiftly donned his hood, pulled his scarf from his neck, and wound it tightly around his face and head. Izz eyes were wide ovals of terror. He could see in his lantern's dull glow the individual centipedes as they rushed to engulf his face, eyes, nose, temples, and mouth.

Out of the corner of his eye, Izz saw up close a fishtailing head, a mouth, antennas, and a pair of pincer like jaws searching out their mark. Izz swept the hideous creature away with his bloodied hand. With the flat edge of his blade, he scraped and slashed off centipedes by the hundreds. Millions of tiny skulls, mostly all teeth, sharp and bloodstained, swarmed over him. Izz panicked and tried to tear the creatures away. With his extinguished lantern, he tried to pound at the assailants on his back. Quickly, the onslaught of individual marauders became a smothering blanket of little clinging feet, twisting bodies, and stinging fangs. It was a living nightmare. Izz flailed his arms, swatting at and trying to knock as many of them off him as possible. Smashed centipedes fell to the ground to be eaten by other centipedes. Overanxious rats reaching too far over the edge found themselves dropping and quickly being covered in centipedes.

Suddenly, as if all at once, Izz started receiving hundreds of aggressive centipede bites, extremely painful, similar to that of a bumblebee sting. Thousands of powerful, sharp fangs delivered their poison from venous glands. Izz screamed in pain and fright, "I have to get out of here!" as he felt engulfed in a furnace of angry stinging fire. He fell and rolled over, smashing hundreds of exoskeletal bodies at a time. But the sheer numbers were overwhelming as crushed centipedes were instantly replaced by the waiting hordes that immediately resumed the attack. Izz's fingers were slippery with blood as he plunked away at the hundreds of yellow legged, scarlet horrors. Somehow many had managed to cut through his thick clothing and had begun relentlessly to chew away at his flesh. Everywhere Izz was bitten, a stream of blood ran freely. The flesh eating assailants trembled with pleasure as they drank their fill and fell away only to be replaced. Izz's tattered clothes were drenched in blood, which ran down his leggings and onto the dusty cave floor. Centipedes were all over him, all over everywhere, as Izz was slowly being drained to death from hundreds of tiny razor bites. With his bloodstained hands, he did his best to protect his face and eyes. In raising hysteria, Izz flailed and swatted his arms the more, felling centipedes by the hundreds with the repeated sweeps of his dagger and heavy swats of his lantern. Having tasted blood, the flesh eating mass's attack intensified; they readily inflected their venomous bites and moved very quickly to replace the fallen continuously. They were not about to relent.

Every moment that passed substantially lowered Izz's chance of escape. It seemed the more he tried to ward off the multi legged monsters, the more it felt their savage attack intensified, seemingly gathering in greater and greater numbers. Izz suddenly calculated his chances of staying alive and came away short. Out of desperation, Izz executed a final surge to get to his feet.

The vicious meat eaters finally penetrated Izz's headgear and were stinging and biting his face and neck repeatedly. He pulled the vicious creature off, and a trace of his skin tore away with it. Then Izz's feet slipped out from under him, and he went down hard. He managed to get to his hands and knees momentarily but soon fell back to the cave floor where he was finally overcome. Izz looked like a cave beetle groping around the cave floor, breaking its back to live, but losing the fight. No matter what, he refused to let go of his lantern even though it had gone out. Izz's weapon hung from his hand as if it was too heavy for him to lift. His strength was fading. With chilling effectiveness, the throng continued swarming over their victim. The beast kept forcing Izz back down to the ground by the weight of their sheer numbers. Its sound was like that of millions of pelting raindrops in the middle of a raging thunderstorm as millions of small feet danced to the rhythm of death.

As the frenzy increasing, Izz's chances of survival decreased dramatically. Soon he would be centipede fodder, and they would be able to feast to the full at their leisure and liberty. As the venom built up in his system, Izz thought, *Why fight? Life is a struggle that everyone eventually loses. What is the use? Death comes to us all. Why bother?* Izz let loose of his lantern and stopped rolling and swatting at the centipedes. The flesh eaters covered him like a death shroud, like a swarm of flies over a corpse.

As the toxins began to shut down Izz's system, his life clung by a thread suspended in limbo between life and death. Just when Izz thought this was the end, the giant spider clinging to its web lost its fight to live and fell to the cavern floor with a great splat. On impact, its insides spilled out of its belly wound onto the cave floor. The bloody smell was overwhelming. Suddenly Izz sensed a shift in the momentum of the attack as thousands of hunters turned their attention to the disemboweled spider. The smelly gore had been too much for them to resist. As centipedes peeled off Izz layer by layer, he instantly felt the weight of thousands of predators lifted. He sensed a window of opportunity, his last fighting chance to live. Izz found his lantern and held it to his chest, then instinctively spun as hundreds of smashed centipedes fell away. Without a second thought, he got to his feet reaching for a place to run, as if trying to escape a fire, and made a dashing bolt for open space.

He blindly ran until he collapsed, sobbing, choking for life, safe for the moment. Numbed by the toxins that were taking their lethal effect, Izz tore the remaining centipedes from his flesh and crushed them between his thumb and the rock floor. From beneath the web, there came a slopping sound, followed by a low hissing then a high pitched squeal as the giant spider's body jerked and twitched a dance of death. Finally, there was a prolonged squall and then nothing

Izz's escape was short lived as the overflow of centipedes returned to overtake him before he had expected. He clenched his teeth, and with a final convulsive heave, Izz turned and scrambled to his feet, fighting to keep his balance, and started running. He fell again. Izz took a deep breath, trying to bring his reserve up one last time. He stumbled away, squeezing out whatever was left of his survival instinct; he tried to breathe between his screaming wails of pain. Izz could feel streams of blood running down on every side as he used the wall for support. He pushed himself off and made it to another wall. Izz pushed off again, all the while hoping to avoid the misstep that would send him to the cave floor and his death.

Izz's whole body and head were once again covered in centipedes. He brushed as many centipedes off his face as he could while they pick up where they had left off, biting and stinging him all over. With a savage vengeance, Izz launched a formidable assault of swatting and flailing arms. Centipedes clung to his legs and climbed onto him as he tried to kick them away. He was yelling and screaming, attempting to get the remaining centipedes off him. Izz was just barely getting the advantage over the remaining attackers when the rats saw their opportune moment to reap their good fortune. Crazed by the smell of blood and gore, the rats went into a frenzy. As if on cue, the entire rat colony surged downward like a raging flood over a broken dike. For a mind numbing moment, sheer panic anchored him where he stood.

Knocked from his traumatized inertia, he groped wildly with fear rearing up in him, pushing him to flee. He turned to run at full tilt. He had no idea where to run. His feet pounded the uneven cave floor as he wondered if there was even any point in running. The starving rat pack was instantly on him. Then as he took the next step, the cave floor beneath him unexpectedly gave way and collapsed under his feet. And once again, he found himself falling. It took the life out of him. "Oh, no! Please! Not again!"

For a long moment, time stood still as Izz flung his arms helplessly and thoughts of plunging to his death glutted his mind. But before he could get another thought out, he suddenly hit the skin of a surface that splashed away from beneath him. One moment, Izz was falling, and the next he was submerged in icy coldness. He had broken through a thin layer of cave ice, a smooth, deceptively thin crust barely concealing what mostly resulted in certain death. It was an underground water basin, landing with a large and loud jarring plunge. Those centipedes that still clung to him fell away. Since they depended on their external environment for body heat, the cooler temperature quickly immobilized them. The few that managed to make it to the surface swam out stunned by the cold water.

At first, Izz found it hard to determine which way was up or down. He finally gained his bearings, and slowly he seemed to float to the surface from the depth of the lake like a lifeless fish might rise from the floor of a stagnant lagoon. Izz could barely stand the pain. His face contorted into a grimace of physical suffering. He was greatly relieved to find that the chill of the water was soothing the burning pain of the thousands of bites and tears he had suffered. In the coal black space, Izz resheathed his dagger and swam toward the water's end. The stone of duller black marking the shore was barely visible against the water's gleaming dark surface. He swam in the blackness in a straight line with the ring of his lantern between his teeth. When he reached the shore, dripping and shivering, his relief was intensified. Izz tossed his lantern forward and peeled off his satchel, which had helped to protect his back.

Izz's teeth were chattering; his two hands felt spongy and swollen as he swiped them across his face. His face was numb. His arms and legs were aching and deadened with stings, bites, and the cold of the water. Every inch of exposed surface along the length of his body was covered with the raised bumps. Thousands of little blotches and bites marked his flesh from head to toe. His clothes were tattered and stained with blood. He laid there in the cold water as bluish welts began to swell, followed by intense itching all over as if he had been dragged over a field of stinging nettle.

Then a heightened tormenting pain set in as the venom began to break down the cell walls of his flesh around every stinging bite. Jolts of agony shot through Izz's tortured body. The venom seeped and circulated into his bloodstream, and even though he was cold, his body shook as he started sweating from every pour in his body. Izz went into a convulsion of dry heaves over and over again. With his body still half in the water, his head drooped, his eyes fluttered as he succumbed to the pain, exhaustion, and the poison. Izz screamed out as he clenched his fists, and his eyes glazed over with fever. Eventually, he closed his eyes, and feebleness swallowed him up as he groaned and squirmed. Izz's last thought before unconsciousness overtook him was that he would rest for just a few moments and regain his strength. And then he would again get up, and there would be no height in the world above or depth in the world below that would keep him from his quest to find his beloved.

Before long, the battering ram and catapults were assembled and leveled along the hillside facing the northern walls of Edawn. The drums of war sounded out their ominous omen. Hundreds of death skull banners filled the skyline. A dense timberline of spears spread across the landscape, and a wall of innumerable helmets and shields filled the horizon. The enemy had circled the land with evil. The hillsides were a solid mass of activity, heaving and rippling with so many moving men and animals, with so many implements of war and supplies as far as the eye could see.

Mounted at the Wicked Warlock Wizard's side on the field of battle were Dandork and Darkon. Behind them, amassed along the horizon, was his myriad of Norticlan warriors, weather beaten, vicious looking vagabonds whose compassion for any other human beings was impossible. Behind them were the hordes of Zomborges looking like mysterious monsters, incapable of mercy, mindlessly transfixed, and seemingly thirsty for blood.

On Edawn's northern battlement, ready to answer the threat of aggression, the kingdom's troops watched as it all unfolded. The invading army was like a darkening shadow seeping through the rising sunshine, emerging into an ominous and frightful presence. All were on edge, struggling to calculate the full extent of the wrath that was about to descend upon them. The worst moment was waiting for the sting and clash of the great assault. They could hear the unnerving commotion of their enemy's drums from afar as the moment for the unknown grew near, but it was just the calm before the storm.

Baddlock stared over the jewel of Edawn with covetous eyes and was suddenly overwhelmed with gluttony for it all. He turned to Dandork whose greed knew no restraint. "Bring up the bull catapults. We will now lay waste to the remembrance of Edawn and their so called King Ozzdon. Every written record, every commemoration, every monument will be wiped out. Every teacher, scholar, artist, seer, and scribe will be blinded, and their tongue ripped from their roots. From this day forth, anyone who ever even whispers the word Edawn or Ozzdon will be immediately executed along with every member of their family. When the sun sets this day, history will never even know Edawn ever existed."

"Excellent, Lord Baddlock," was all Dandork could manage, remembering for a fleeting instant the friends he once knew in Edawn. That fleeting thought had flown by him with as little enduring effect as the passing of the wind. The fact that Edawn was holding a vast deposit of valuable treasure was the one thing he could not ignore. His mouth twitched at the corner as his face brightened with greed.

Darkon impatiently sat upon his mount as if he was more than ready to kill. His thick and hairy black brows were furrowed with hate. His square jawed face was twisted into a vicious, animalistic look. His long black hair flowed from under a horned helm. His shoulders were shielded by something that looked like human skulls that shrouded his rippling, furry shoulders.

On the horizon, the enemies' encampment was alive with motion, boiling like an anthill. At first, the maneuver looked disorganized as everyone seemed to be rushing frenziedly around. But soon after, the confusion gave way to an orderly scurry of activities as Baddlock's generals synchronized to their assigned tasks. They orchestrated the movements of their catapult handlers with the smooth precision of a finely tuned killing machine.

Thousands of Zomborges pulled the massive catapults along their treks into their killing positions where they caught the rays of the rising sun. Hour after hour, the equipment necessary for the massive assault was slowly amassed and lined out. A forest of monster framed structures built with rough hewed timbers weighing ten tons each arrived and were positioned along the highest ridges of the hillside. The maniacal offensive was about to begin. The huge timbers groaned as they were bowed out of shape in opposition by geared winches designed by Ammiz the Seer, and was stolen from his secret libraries. The specially geared winches allowed a team of catapult handlers to concentrate a greater load of energy on the throwing beam. The click-clacking winch gears pulled back against springs made of tightly wrapped bundles of sinews and ropes. Every fiber creaking out under the stress as the release mechanisms were latched into place. Teams of Zomborges then centered enormous stones that weighed almost a ton onto the wooden throwing beams of the catapults. One by one, the massive machines were systematically armed with their monolithic test loads.

The kingdom had been waiting in vain for the main reinforcement forces to arrive, but none came. That is when the weighty realization dawned on King Ozzdon, he had waited too late against Ammiz's demands to light, the red alarm towers. Now they were all alone and cut off from the rest of the world. King Ozzdon ordered Zandor and Kondor to reinforce the defensive line on the northern wall. They added extra parapets to the northern wall and began to fortify the fortress bastions. Ozzdon concentrated on formulating the best ways to use their limited supply of weapons and manpower to defend the most threatened front of the kingdom. Watchmen remained posted along with every high tower; their eyes were ever watchful for the first signs of engagement.

The king watched from the battlement. His defensive strategy and tactics were all based on the books of the great ancient wars. He drew on the knowledge he had gained from the war games and hoped that that would be enough to defend against the onslaught that was guaranteed to come. Everyone within the kingdom watched and waited for something to happen. But what that was, they could have never imagined. The moments felt like hours, and King Ozzdon could barely stand the tension, much less the suspense. His hopes diminished considerably while he anticipated the arrival of reinforcements and sufficient weaponry.

As ever, the scribes, guardians of the official history of Edawn, witnesses to the fateful truth, positioned themselves in parts of the upper keeps facing the attacking forces and began to gather their papers together. Equipped to the teeth with their quills, inkhorns, and scrolls spread out before them, they readied themselves to record with unwavering testimony the epic battle to come. They scribbled notes on the pages of their parchments, writing everything as it unfolded, recording every milestone as they were captured in their thoughts. Quills raced over their parchments in loops, squiggles, notched lines, and crisscrosses. To anyone else, this method of rapid handwriting would have looked like nonsense. But these marks on paper would be committed to ledgers, then eventually to the official annals of war. Ultimately, these historic moments, if Edawn survived, would be preserved in stone for all future generations as a warning down through the ages yet unborn.

Nine

FIRST SALVO

Despite the delay; everything was finally ready as Baddlock surveyed the situation in the rising tension. He had every intention of becoming the new master of Zia, and nothing was going to stand in his way. The Wicked Warlock Wizard reviewed the details he had premeditated for years to bring the kingdom to its knees. Hundreds of times, he had studied the landscape tactically, running over in his mind the finishing touches on his plan of attack. What army could stand against him? Finally, Baddlock signaled for the opening volley meant to gauge the range and set the sights for the coming deadly volleys. At long last, a metallic click rang out, and the armed catapult released its heavy payload. The colossal stone arched high and fast across the envelope of the sky, creating a whooshing sound as it bristled through the air.

There was a crackling noise in the upper atmosphere as the heavy target stone was sent buzzing through the air like a giant mad hornet. The large stone struck the ground just short of the northern gate with a terrible, shuddering impact. The ground quivered noticeably as a large crater erupted, peppering the surrounding earth with dirt and stone shards. Baddlock's surveyors quickly adjusted their trajectory. Kuvazo, the senior catapult overlord, gave Baddlock a reassuring nod. An evil incarnate smile flashed across Baddlock's withered face. "Grind them down into dust. Pulverize them until they cease to exist."

All of a sudden, a myriads of mechanical clangs tumbled, and a multitude of metallic rings rang out like a forest of machines let loose a terrible accelerated cataclysm of unimagined violence. A deep, eerie tremor vibrated through the air as hundreds of catapults had instantaneously discharged their first cyclonic onslaught. Soon thereafter the first incoming shot crushed with a pounding impact as it landed with a pulverizing crash. The stone then ricocheted off the turret wall and tumbled to the wall walk beneath, crushing several bowmen posted at the North wing. Soon huge stones began to rain down all over the kingdom with a devastating impact. One of the first incoming stones struck the upper turret wall with a pulverizing crash, then ricocheted and tumbled down to the lower floor below, crushing several bowmen posted on the North parapet walk.

Several other men were squished like worms against the inner wall where the massive stone finally came to rest. Edawn's fortified outer wall shuddered but stayed intact. Nerves stood on edge as eyes darted every which way, and in the next instant, more huge stones were falling from the sky everywhere. Immediately after each launch, the rattle of *click-clack-clickety-clacks* grew into a fierce repeated churning rhythm as the thick grove of catapults were quickly reloaded and readied for another major strike.

The sound of the incoming stones sent a wave of terror throughout the kingdom. The mysterious, indefinable sound gradually intensified in volume and pitch as the tumbling stones approached from the northern compass. The sounds of the enormous projectiles that tore into the blue sky at first sounded like the rush of a faraway whirlwind, then; it grew into a roaring surge like mind numbing wails of impending destruction.

Wham! Another stone struck, and then all at once, chaos broke loose as stone after stone rocked the kingdom, causing catastrophic destruction and confession. Those unfortunate enough to be caught beneath the crushing weight or careening path of a plummeting stone were smashed beyond help.

As the continuous bombardment of deadly strikes found their mark, the surface of Zia shook, and the screaming of incoming projectiles tangled with the screams of men. It did not take long for everyone on the wall to realize that they were not only outnumbered; they were also out weaponed. Zia's crust and the hearts of men trembled with an unbelievable intensity never imagined possible. Relentlessly, the hammering wave after wave of devastation rained from the sky. The remorseless and unforgiving annihilation repeatedly descended with catastrophic wreckage and carnage. Most warriors quickly learned to determine the murderous trajectory of the falling stones from the noise that they made as they crisscrossed the sky. Some were able to duck for cover just in the nick of time to avoid the ferocity of the storm that came upon them. Others ran around in circles, unnerved, waiting for instructions, praying for deliverance. But no such salvation came as heavy catapults fired, at will, over and over again.

One megalithic stone struck the base of one of the North side towers, causing it and everyone in it to come crashing down. Rock hewed blocks and chipped stone came crumbling earthward wreaking havoc on those below. When the dust finally cleared, survivors gasped in gut wrenching horror as they saw their countrymen crushed by the stone's terrible destruction. Blood oozed out from under rock piles, and men were crushed like bugs underfoot, smashing the life out of them, yet still barely alive, begging for relief.

The bombardment was seemingly stepped up; destroying numerous targets throughout the city and battered the kingdom. The catapult stones bore into the thick Edawnian guardian walls, and the screams from the wounded men mounted. King Ozzdon looked intensely over the mounting cataclysm from atop the battlement of the main keep. He saw the broken bodies of hundreds of men. He saw how their crushed bodies flopped and jerked as the life drained out of them. His eyes tightly closed so that he could see nothing more. Generals knotted around him, wanting to hear their next orders. At long last, the king called out one command, "Sons of Edawn, stand your ground! Stand your ground for the love of your children and the love of your wives." For the love of their families, they would fight for them, tooth and nail, to the last if they had to.

The king cautiously made his way to the outer wall and stared out at the continuing storm, watching the wretchedness and destructiveness of the attack slowly but surely desolating his beloved kingdom. Shards of stonewall scudded past as catapulted projectiles crashed all around him. Fragments of a near misses ricocheted off the wall beside him, pelting him with debris that sliced a cut across his cheekbone. King Ozzdon desperately, tried to organize the defense of his kingdom against the obliteration that was about to overwhelm them. He shouted encouragements to his dazed troops, "Sons of Edawn, stand and hold your ground! If you fail, all will come to darkness."

Frantic men momentarily froze where they stood and looked to their king.

"Have any walls been breached?" The king drew a deep breath. "And if so, where and how badly?"

"The northern wall has sustained excessive damage, my lord," came a hectic response from the northeastern watchtower.

"Fortify it with anything and everything you can get your hands on," the king responded resoundingly.

A wave of men carrying anything that was not nailed down rushed to fill the gaping holes ripped through the infrastructure by the slaughterous catapults. They were able to repair the preliminary damage, but the foundational damage would take time. Moments seemed like eternities as the barrage of massive stones furiously continued pelting the kingdom's walls like a hailstorm trilling in from the North. The doom they faced was proving to be the greatest disaster on record, and it was nowhere near its end. Catapult warriors determined to defend their king and kingdom fired a sporadic barrage of stones that hurled with terrible force against their enemy. But too soon they discovered to their disheartenment that the dreaded foe was out of their catapult's range. The beginning of the end of Edawn had come.

Izz lay face down on the wet cave floor. His body was still sprawled out in the frigid water, which probably saved his life by slowing down and drawing out most of the large proportion of centipede poison. Fortunately, the good news was that the pain had been the worst of it. The cold water had also helped immensely to reduce the swelling and had slowed the damage of the venom. Thanks to the chilling water, the centipede bites had not been toxic enough to be deadly. Somehow, the cold water, or the minerals in it, had also prevented the paralyzing bites from becoming painful open sores. Izz's chest rose and fell with a faint breath.

His first awareness was that of trying to open his crusted eyes. The second was feeling the impression of every sharp rock he had been lying on for who knew how long. Instantly he was wide awake with a startled gasp. Piercing tentacles of pain shot through both sides of his head, splitting his brain straight down the middle. The pain pierced down through the center of his backbone to the tips of his toes. He felt as if he was having a nightmare.

Izz's inebriated brain resurfaced from a none too sound but badly needed rest, forlorn and forsaken, in a cold, darkened world. He was shivering and vomiting on the hard cave floor. He flopped over on his back, feeling like a drowned rat. No position he twisted into relieved his pain. So far he could breathe—at least something was still responding. Izz just laid there on his back, his eyes open and staring vacantly into the darkness. He longed for nothing more than to lie there and go back to sleep.

At first, all he could manage was to lay there staring into middle space, listening to the echoing sound of the steady drip of water. *Drip, drip, drip,* he focused on one dribble for a drawn out moment as it marked the passage of each brief moment like a precision timepiece.

He had no way of knowing how long he had been out; all Izz knew for sure was that he was losing precious time. His chest felt tight, his eyelids were swollen, and he was having difficulty breathing. But by some wonder, thankfully, despite it all, he was still alive. He pulled his sore and swollen self farther out of the water, all the while vomiting poisonous stringy green slime. Izz touched his swollen hands. They felt like two inflated pufferfish. Izz probed gingerly with one finger around the lacerations on his face, thankful that the bleeding had stopped. Izz ran his hands over the painful bites and stings. Some felt raw. *I am sure there must be at least one fraction of me that I have not managed to injure,* he thought to himself. It was just a hundred other blemishes to add to his already mounting inventory of injuries.

Izz's hair was caked with mud. His skin was full of lumps that looked like giant goosebumps. The centipede attack had been extremely severe, and Izz had received thousands of poisonous injections. Izz buried his head in his hands and waiting for the agonizing throb to end. But it seemed that it would never stop. He suffered from chills, fever, nausea, and a splitting headache that felt as if someone was pounding on his head with a sledgehammer. Izz had many welts and bloodied cuts on his face, but they were not disfiguring. His body was stiff, but as he began to limber up, he began to warm up his joints.

Up to that point, Izz had never realized the human body could endure such affliction. The attack was still fresh in his mind, and he shivered at the recollection. Unable to walk, he slid on his belly. Eventually, he rose to crawl on all fours to the water's edge where he hesitated. In complete darkness, Izz gathered his belongings, his backpack, and his lantern. He searched his breast pocket and found his flint still dry in its waterproof, oil treated leather bag. He wiped the excess water from his lantern. Luckily the oil had repelled the water from soaking the wick. After many failed attempts, a bright spark jumped from his flint, and a small flame timidly danced like a lone star in a vast lightless universe. Its faint illumination was nearly swallowed up by the encroaching darkness. As the flame dried and heated the chimney of the lamp, it gained strength and pushed the darkness back.

Izz splashed cold water on his face and rose ponderously, dripping and shivering all over. He just stood there in his lantern's ring of light as he steadied his equilibrium. His body was rigid and sore; his muscles painfully ached and radiated different kinds of misery from every part of his body.

Izz felt as if a sloth of mountain bears had mauled him, but at least he was still alive and able. With that realization, he experienced an utter feeling of gratitude. Izz pulled out Zuree's stone, which indicated that the long corridor to the left was the way to go. At that fleeting instant, he latched on to the love that had burned within him ever since the first time he laid eyes on Zuree. The beautiful dream fastened and locked in his spirit, and his heart would never let it die. Despite his many serious injuries, Izz continued his trek. He felt squeamish. His head, back, hips, knees, ankles, and feet hurt, but as he walked, his blood got going, and he felt somewhat better. Reenergized by passion, driven by love, Izz reset his iron will on the grueling journey ahead. He aligned himself with the most potent power in the universe—the power of love, and nothing else mattered. After a short while, most of his strength had returned to his marrow. Every trace of pain that had burned in his bones seemed to have faded away. Even the intense hunger pangs that had consumed him from the pit of his stomach were somehow nourished.

Izz stamped his foot against the cave floor now and then along the treacherous narrow path that lay before him, making sure it would hold his weight. There was no reason to mark his path at every turn and corner to indicate which way he had taken, because Izz did not have a clue where on Zia he was nor where he was going. He only knew that he was somewhere beneath Skullsdoom, under tons of granite in the evil forbidden heart of the Noragore Rim. Every twist and turn vanished from Izz's memory as soon as they fell behind him. But there was one thing Izz knew for sure: he did not have to worry about getting lost. No one on Zia knew where he was, except maybe Ammiz. No one would ever come searching for him. The best he could do for himself is to stay calm and keep moving.

With lantern before him, Izz followed the contour of the underground lake. Despite his fears, he followed the mysterious insight of his instinct. As he walked through the deep cavern, Izz thought he heard a rushing sound, like wind maybe. Izz cocked his ear to one side. He held out his hand before him and felt not a breath. What he had heard was a faint, distant cascading sound. As Izz ventured farther, the rushing sound got louder until he was sure it sounded like the rushing of water barreling swiftly over its rocky banks. Izz realized that the water in the reservoir was flowing and that if he followed the current, he would more than likely find his way out. But that would take him, as far as the East was from the West, away from his mission.

Izz raised his lantern to the cavern's roof. Its uneven surface had the look of something like living rock. He instantly sensed something out of the ordinary about it, but it was an alluring oddity. Water was leaking through the cave ceiling everywhere. As he moved along, Izz watched as big droplets built on the tips of huge hanging cave formations. Each droplet pulled long with weight, broke free, and splashed its perfect liquid crown to deposit its limestone sediment on the growing formation from the cave floor up. Izz swept his lantern into the interior of the cavern and allowed his eyes to adjust to the dimness. What he saw was a magnificent crystallized limestone cavern all about him. It was like coming into an enchanted world of strange colored crystal like creations. An alien world of vivid brilliance immediately transfixed Izz. In every direction, he beheld a vast configuration of natural limestone structures spearing down from the vaulted ceiling as their counterparts reached up from the cave floor. Some formations of stone came together to form milky white, almost translucent columns that stood like cave guardians frozen in time. Izz drifted slowly through the deepest recesses of the impressive landscape, lost in the indescribability of the cavernous wonder.

Izz turned his attention to the far corner in the direction of the rumbling water. The cave seemed to brighten up in the reflecting light of his lantern. Izz could see the chamber come alive with the diversity of colors, shapes, and forms. The sound of dripping water was all around him, creating a rhythmic sound clear and soft. Absolutely nothing on Zia could have ever prepared him for the jeweled crown of glass like structures that covered the inside dome of the cavern everywhere. To the left and right, the walls were covered with huge natural crystals and translucent beams of gypsum as long as the tallest obelisks he had ever seen. Izz was standing in an undiscovered world, one of nature's phenomena that had taken eons to create where no other man ever stood.

Delicate beauties dotted the surrounding walls of this deep cave system. Every corner of the whole chamber was filled with big crystalline formations, and imposing pillars framed the largest and most beautiful mind boggling grottoes. The most astonishing crystals flickered and glistened off the cave roof, walls, and floor as it reflected the light from his lantern. Everywhere Izz looked was alive with reflective light. The walls had been transformed into gemmed rifts in two parallel corridors that covered the length of the room. Dramatic, luminous views of traversing pools and ponds along the cave wall receded into obscurity. Their surfaces were transparent as glass, so clear Izz could see the bottom. From certain angles, their smooth face glittering in the light, reflecting the dazzling jeweled ceiling like a flawless mirror.

Izz paused for a moment to examine one particularly complexes crystallization, a most exquisite and unique geometric configuration. "It is beautiful! If only Zuree were here to see this," he thought out loud. "Zuree!" he whispered as he reached out, but upon touching it, the hallucinogenic beauty turned into fine crystal dust particles. Something that had probably endured since before the dawn of civilization simply disintegrated before his eyes. The excitement suddenly faded out of Izz's eyes. He gazed somberly about him. Izz hastened his step quickly, made his way past the formations, and headed toward the direction of the sound of rumpling waters. The rest of the underground chambers would have to remain a mystery forever.

As he hurriedly continued, the flow of water disappeared around the bend where the walls of the spacious chamber were lost beyond the limits of his small lamp's penetration. Izz could hear the echoing of running water gurgling in the distance darkness that had no discernible end.

Izz quickly meandered his way alone the ledge through the maze toward what he thought was the sound of the cascading waters. After his last fall through the cave ice, he stepped gingerly as if he was walking on eggshells over thin ice. Up ahead, around the bend where the rushing sound of falling water came from, his attention was drawn to where he thought he saw a faint glimmer of light in the dark chasm. He lowered his lamp and in the half light, could see more clearly the unnatural glow in the distance shimmering as if it were coming from an underground moon. Izz's flustered mind teemed with questions for which he had no explanation. Izz could not imagine how, at these depths, there could be a speck of light, where sunrise had never shined. Yet the next chamber was lit up and growing in intensity as he neared it. Izz followed the bluish light through the haze like a moth caught under the control of a mesmerizing flame. At first, Izz thought he was walking toward another vent. Or that he had reached a tunnel that somehow led to the outside world. As he rounded the bend, the unnatural light poured in on him through the thin atmosphere, bathing him in a glow that felt sacred in its halo. Izz gazed out across the curved canopy of a vast cavern that seemed to be brightly kindled with thousands of tiny dangling candlelit crystal chandeliers.

Dotted across the cave ceilings like a star spangled night were silk threads that hung down vertically emitting a blue-green light brilliant enough to light up the whole chamber. As Izz entered this extraordinary vault, he examined the source of light up close and observed small droplets of very sticky mucus over a silk thread line. Beautiful star studded globes burned bright with a beautiful natural light that danced around the room. What he was looking at was cave glowworms, colonies in masses that made cave ceiling's their home in the blackest, deepest places of Zia. Creatures in impressive numbers, naturally capable of discharging spellbinding light in a lightless environment, birthed into life right before his astonished eyes. The light was the result of an incomprehensible chemical reaction produced by these light emitting organisms in varying intensities. Izz had heard about them from old retired gold miners, but he always thought they were fables from old men that had way too much time on their hands. They were beautiful.

Izz of Zia

He noticed that the silken treads were coming from the mouths of the glowworms like strings of white glowing sticky pearls. Each worm produced hundreds of strings suspended from the ceiling alongside thousands upon thousands of others. Once the lines were set, the worm waited patiently with its bluish light glowing from its tail. Izz watched as an unsuspecting cave moth lured by the irresistible light became instantly entangled by the sticky silk strands. Once caught, there was no escape. Izz watched as the worm slowly sucked the line back into its mouth, reeling in the catch and eating its prey alive. Izz at once felt ill at ease, reminded of the spiders and centipedes. His skin crawled, and his bites and stings ached numbly. This underground labyrinth had given birth to some of the most bizarre living things he had ever seen on Zia. These were weird creatures that had never see the light of day or would ever set foot in the outside world.

So utterly out of this world was the magical glowworm spectacle, that Izz had not noticed the illuminating reflections the curve of the cavernous hold had hidden from his sight. To his right, a glint caught Izz's eyes. He flashed his lamp about, as he looked around. The light diffused all through the chamber, reflecting off something shimmering off the floor and walls. Little by little, like the bloom of a glittering jeweled flower, an inconceivable sight came into focus. There, something dazzling, metallic, and heavy laden within, Izz gasped and caught his breath. He could not have possibly been more utterly stunned by the vision that embraced him. The guttering light from the glowworms shone on and reflected the room's content over and over again. He held the lamp toward it, his eyes wide and disbelieving. How could he possibly believe his eyes?

Izz stood before a vast treasure hidden in the deep caves, heaped up piles of treasure stacked to the ceiling. Incalculable wealth yet undiscovered that had allured treasure seekers throughout the centuries. It all had to be an illusion, a trick of the light. The cave floor was dimly lit, but his eyes adjusted to see what the darkness was hiding. Izz saw mound upon mound of gleaming gems, jewel coffers, and trunks, ingots of solid gold, porcelain, temple carvings, and silver objects everywhere. The inconceivable treasure reflected streamers of light casting a dull glimmering deluge of brilliant. The fabled riches of the ancient wars of sat there flashing golden and silvery colors over the trove hidden in the depths of the Zia throughout the ages.

As Izz moved in closer to take a better look, he flicked his lantern wildly from one thing to another over the tantalizing sight. The room's content sent prisms of refracted luster shimmering and dancing over everything with the brightness of starlight. Then his dazzled eyes suddenly made sense of what they were looking upon. "The lost ancient treasure of the Forbidden City," Izz whispered to himself. It was not just a fable after all.

Suddenly Izz was made keenly aware of every wondrous thing that surrounded him—heaps of rare giant flashing diamonds, emeralds, sapphires, rubies, opals, garnets, topazes, and many other rare gemstones. The immense horde glowed like the color of a moonlit rainbow such as Izz had never laid eyes on before. There were gold, silver, and copper coins and vessels, relics, and artifacts of every size, shape, and form everywhere. Crowns of conquered kings, vases, bracelets, rings, pendants, clasps, adornments, locks, jewelry, masks, swords, spears, earrings, and even shields all decorated with precious multicolored gemstones. It took his breath away, a thing of fantasy, the crazed dream of an opium eater. Forgetting all else, Izz became overwhelmed with excitement. His eyes lit up as bright as the treasure trove that reflected in them. He picked up a diamond that was as big as his fist that shone like a miniature sun, almost too bright to look upon. In his other hand, he held up in his closed fist a handful of golden coins. There was no way of knowing how vast the span of time since the splendorous fortune had remained untouched by human hands. The secret of its whereabouts taken to the evil king's grave and buried along with him.

For one staggering moment, Izz's eyes bulged wildly, bloated with awe tempting lust. The allure was irresistible. He trembled with excitement, "I am wealthy!" Izz screamed and then abruptly fell silent as if someone might somehow overhear him and attract unwanted attention. He abruptly peeled his satchel off his back, emptied its content on the cave floor, and greedily scooped up gems and gold coins by the armful. *I am rich, I am rich, I am rich beyond my wildest dreams,* Izz thought as he loaded up and looked around suspiciously as if his precious discovery might unexpectedly be found out. He dug his hands into the gold coins, seizing them as if they were of the highest importance.

Then out of nowhere, Izz felt an intense stab of pain that slash like a razor sharp blade through the center of his soul. He suddenly came to himself and was horrified by his own selfish, desires. His lust for riches shamed him. "What is such treasure to me? Gold and jewels it is merely cold metal and lifeless stone. My only treasure is Zuree. She is the only treasure more precious than gold or gems that could ever enrich me beyond my most beautiful of beautiful dreams."

Izz dumped his satchel at his feet and dropped to his knees. He gathered his meager supplies. He was amazed at how the allure of material riches had almost turned him into a fool. He hesitated for a moment. "With this boundless wealth, I could ease the suffering of the poor, build orphanages and schools in a hundred forsaken corners of Zia." Conquered by his higher calling, he slowly turned and trudged away without another word, abandoning his whimsical covetousness. Without Zuree, the treasure was worthless and could remain hidden forever for all he cared at the moment.

Ten

Entombment

Without looking back, Izz continued through the breadth of the cavern along the amazing wonder world. He passed a maze of formations that led toward the sound of sloshing water. He made his way through chasms and inlets that angled away in different directions. There was a mysterious dampness in the air, and the thundering sound of a waterfall was growing louder as he advanced. Izz heard the roaring deluge and knew he was so close he could taste the water in the air. The bodies of pools narrowed and turned into a rush of running water with an ever increasing current of a stronger stream. Izz approached a cool, dimly lit cavern filled with the sound and scent of rushing water. The tears of a cascading waterfall suddenly rippled and speckled him with its outthrust fingers of wetness reaching to spatter against him. In the shroud of gray, the smell of moisture was heavy in his nostrils, and the sound of running water roared in his ears, with its powerful flow it bellowed.

Around the ridge of the cavern, to Izz's amazement, he saw the high waterfalls in full view for the first time. It poured itself over a table of solid rock, in long ripping veils of silvery curtains. The falling water thundered into a large pool where it sloshed against the rocks below and ran into its connecting pools. As Izz approached, the amplifying sound of rumbling echoed in his hearing. He raised his lantern and scanned the falls that looked like a roll of shimmering silk cascading down from the top of the bluff, glistening and reflecting the light from his lantern. Effervescing bubbles rose up, clumping together on the surface, sending rippling circles out against the stone shoulders of the pool. Izz reached the pool's edge and splashed a few cupped handfuls of refreshing water from the underground pool onto his face. He stooped to fill his water skin with pure life giving liquid and saw in its crystal clear depths a fish that had neither eyes nor color. He drank gratefully and swallowing noisily as the cool, wet mist in the air bathed his face like millions of liquid butterflies. His supply of food was gone, but he had plenty of water. He had enough lantern oil, and the welts that covered his body had shrunken considerably.

He looked up and down the bluff wall. His keen eyes picked out a zigzagging path that seemed to have the hand of man in it. The obscure path led to just beneath the mouth of the fountains of life and disappeared. In the opposite direction, the trail ran along the upper wall away from the falls and vanished into the darkness. It only seemed logical that he had to go up, and the only way up meant that Izz would have to, once again, climb. He set his mind on the climb ahead, to ascend forever if he had to. With his lantern hooked on his thumb on the one hand and his life hooked on the other, he scaled the bluff with his belly pressed to the wall. The footing was slippery, but once he overtook the lower wall, it was not too difficult to climb. When Izz reached the timeworn passage, he made his way over the narrow ledge to where the waterfall plunged from atop the bluff before him. He did not intend to backtrack, so he did not bother to look back at or mark the trail from which he came.

Above Izz could see the fountainhead of the spring bubbling up crystal clear from its icy depths. Before him, the waterfall cascaded into the sink below. When Izz reached the spring head, he thought the passage had abruptly come to a dead end. But when he peered behind the waterfall, he found a hidden tunnel with just enough room to walk under the onrushing water. The shaft was manmade, cut into the solid granite. With his lantern, Izz took in its depth. Water dripped from its ceiling all along its length. At the other end, Izz found a concealed exit built into the outside wall in a way that was not meant to be found. As Izz emerged, a mysterious fog surrounded him that seemed to be reflecting a blurred light from beyond. Izz wondered if he had reached an opening from the outside world. He quickened his pace, maneuvering around the cloaking bluffs, snaking his way around the jagged rocks that concealed the opening to the waterfalls.

Izz's jaw dropped in awe as he emerged into a mammoth span of space yawning with an airy height from floor to roof before him. The realization that there was such a vast cavern at such an immeasurable distance underground was such a surprise for Izz that it took his breath away. He found himself in the most spacious underground world he could have ever imagined; its sheer physical scale overwhelmed him.

From the ceiling above, the strange illumination filtered in a light that cast faint shadows like those seen in a dense fog. The glowing source was coming from the ancient volcano's throat. As Izz made his way under the opening overhead, Izz could see sinkholes and hidden openings everywhere threatening to swallow him up. He looked down the vent and below he could make out the web and the molten glow just within the bounds of sight. He realized it was the same pit from which he had fallen. Izz looked up the giant vent as he drew his compass. Izz saw that the darkest shadow along the vent was on the West side, which told him that the sun had dipped way past its midway point, which meant that the time to find his beloved Zuree had shortened against him.

His heart quickened as he wondered which way to go. Izz reached for Zuree's amulet. He held the gem out at arm's length and slowly rotated around the humongous subterranean space. The stone noticeably burned a little brighter when he pointed it toward one of the many limestone cavities on the northern wall. As Izz trekked his way across the mammoth cave, his thoughts turned to visions of falling through to his death. He assured himself that each step was intact before he entrusted his weight to it. He dare not rule out the possibility of stepping onto a pocket of cave ice again. Next time he might not be so lucky. Izz safely reached the northern wall riddled with mysterious openings. As he approached, he was greeted by a particular shadowy opening that was lined with rows of jagged rocks that jutted up and down like monstrous teeth. The entrance resembled a predator that was anticipating his arrival so that it could suddenly gobble up and swallow him down into the bottomless depths of its belly.

Knowing full well that time was slipping away from him like a fist full of sand, Izz pulled out the stone once more, for he could ill afford to wander off on a wild goose chase in the wrong direction. The amulet once more pulsated when pointed toward the peculiar opening and then glowed steadily. As Izz entered the spooky hole, Izz might have guessed—it led downward along a declining path. The ceiling was unfortified, and the bare earthen floor was uncertain. The ground thankfully felt hard and unyielding under his boot. Izz managed to set his doubts aside.

Almost immediately, the last of the natural light disappeared behind him, and he was surrounded by uncertainty. It was stuffy in the passage due to the lack of circulating air. He extended the wick in his lantern and trimmed it for maximum illumination. Izz's eyes adjusted fully to the dimness as he and his lantern's light were assimilated into the encroaching pitch blackness. He did not have a clue where he was going; Izz only knew that he just had to keep moving and trust that the stone was pointing him in the right direction.

The only thing Izz worried about was getting disoriented and wandering through the cave network of passageways in intertwining circles. Getting lost at this depth was a very hazardous reality that would surpass any nightmare that had already befallen him. The deeper he went, the more complex the tunnels, corridors, and passageways wound and forked into a chaotic puzzle of interlocking bewilderment. Finding his way was unquestionably a needle in a haystack situation. One single mistake, if he lost his lantern, he was dead; if Izz went the wrong way, he was dead; if he got lost, he was dead. As if there was any way he could get any more lost. Izz's only hope was Zuree's amulet. Izz held his lantern up high, but its light was impoverished in the subterranean labyrinth of extraordinary complexity. The tunnels were so dim and dusky that his eyes could not penetrate its interior more than a stride or two ahead of him.

As he probed deeper and deeper, the light given off by his lamp seemed to be getting fainter and fainter. With every step as if an extra proportion of darkness had been poured out into the air. Each shadow seemed vaster, murkier than before, and more sinister in some unfamiliar way. The air continued to feel heavy and laden with ominous foreboding. Izz felt strange and not at all comfortable like a mouse on a wild goose chase, trying to find order in disorder. He was hopelessly lost in a black maze of dead ends, complex paths, and matrix systems that emerged and then disappeared into daunting innumerable interconnecting tunnels. Izz traversed through tunnels, buried cavities, vaults, galleries, and corridors as if cutting random paths through the universe. After a while, he came to a narrow opening.

Izz was about to get caught in a labyrinth as twisting, and hidden tunnels unexpectedly confronted him. Corridors emerged, crisscrossed, and led off in all directions then disappeared. Fear that he would fail in the end began to seep in. Izz clutched Zuree's stone that he now wore in the outside of his badly battered shirt, its perpetual signal urging to go on and on. Acutely aware of his race against time, Izz cast caution to the wind, moving at a breathless pace, bestowing his full trust in the power within the stone. He pressed on through the interior of the mountain along the winding tangle, of narrow entranceways that were quickly becoming a very perplexing riddle, a complexity of complexities. The narrowing passage the stone marked led into a honeycombed muddle of further confusion. Izz navigated by instinct in the limbo of interweaving darkness, but his life he entrusted to the stone that glowed brighter and brighter as Izz continued his descent.

It seemed to Izz that the passage he followed was becoming narrower, with irregular walls of rock and stone flooring, closing in on him as it were with every step. From time to time, he had to crawl forward on his hands and knees around craggy rocks as he endured. The tunnel was proving to be increasingly challenging to negotiate. He bent to peer into a dark crevice between two huge boulders before him. Izz stared down the empty tunnel as if the answer lay there just beyond his reach. He had to stoop to get inside the tunnel, so he did not bump his head against the roof. Izz squeezed through into the next passage that appeared even narrower. He hesitated at the next tunnel's entrance; the ceiling was uncertain at best. The probability of disaster tightened around Izz's chest. He kneeled at the opening and peered into the narrow passage. The top of the tunnel was also getting lower. Closing his eyes, he leaned against the rock wall; he hated tight enclosures more than anything.

For a moment, he was undecided what to do; he felt like a mouse about to enter the cat's mouth. Izz looked into the unsure space a second or two, deliberating, incapable of calculating any of the consequences that might lurk around every dark turn. He looked as if he were going to be sick. The thought of getting wedged coursed through Izz's mind like a death sentence. He was a mess of apprehension, anxious that precious time was being wasted. He held his lantern out as he fingered the stone with his other hand. The decision Izz made he hoped never to regret. Izz just shook his head and continued as if he were being quickened along by some unearthly power.

Before long, Izz had to stoop over lower as he squished through a tight spot, scraping off his skin as he slipped through. The dark stone walls were closing in all around him. By and by, he found the enclosure was so low; he ended up reluctantly bending down on his hand and knees, cramped into a crawl space and starting to feel claustrophobic. Izz scrabbled forward on his knees and one hand as he tried to keep his lantern in front of him. His hands and knees became nicked and gouged by the many razor sharp shards along the uneven floor. Izz looked down on his bloodied, scarred hand, rough and ingrained with tiny red stained shards of rock. He winced against a dull ache in the joints of his throbbing knees as he was desperately trying to remain positive. The tunnel continued to close around him so tight that his backpack was repeatedly snagging along the ceiling. Izz unstrapped, his backpack, drew his water skin and took a long pull. He emptied everything he had in his pockets and placed anything that he could in the satchel, including his dagger. Izz took off his belt and tied the satchel to his right ankle so that he could drag it behind him as he went. Then he turned with his lantern held before him and continued crawling forward for what seemed like hours. If only the universe were not such a faithful timekeeper of time, he could stop to rest. But he had no time to lose, and the great rotating clock of Zia would not miss a beat for him.

He trimmed his lantern's wick to conserve his lamp oil and then crawled forward until he reached a skirted cranny. Izz could tell that from that point things were about to get very cramped. He thought about turning back, but he had no intentions of quitting. Destiny bound his bones, and the stone and his love for Zuree gave him the courage he needed to forge onward. Izz slid his lamp through the confined opening up as far as he could reach, then jammed his shoulders against the rock wall and then wriggled and twisted his upper body through to resume his trek. The stone, like a glowing coal, continued to shine brighter and brighter, and Izz crawled in deeper and deeper into the substratum bedrock of Zia. He would never stop, could never, ever stop.

From time to time, he paused and thought of the tons of rock that separated him from the surface, and his chest constricted. All around him was gloomy and quiet; moist from seepage dampened the dirt floor. The heavy stale air had a strong smell of mildew. Up ahead, the ingress was tightening around him, and Izz did not know if he was going to be able to make it through or not. He only knew that it was going to be oppressively close. Izz pushed forward into the bowels of Zia like a human shrew clawing into the darkness inch by inch. The squeeze squished the breath out of him as he used his lead arm to pull and his trailing arm to push forward; rotating his hips into a suitable slant, he worked past the squeeze. Once inside the next crawlway, he could move around more freely, but in every direction that he turned, he could see that he only had a few inches all around him.

Izz of Zia

The passage he continued through was becoming even narrower and tighter. Izz clasped Zuree's stone with his shaking hand and wiped his thumb across its face as if that would help him read it more clearly. The stone continued to radiate brighter than ever.

Izz reached a point where he had to make a critical choice, knowing that if he kept going, he would not be able to turn around. With the little light he had, he could see that the passage continued to narrow. If he went forward, he could get stuck or run up against a dead end. On the other hand, if he turned around while he still could, perhaps he could find another way. Izz pulled out his compass and held it in his hand up to his face. The tiny needle bounced back and forth much in the same manner as the pivotal decision he was about to make. The compass's needle came to rest, marking his direction as due east northeastern, deeper into the mountain range's core. He wondered how knowing what direction he was on was going to do him any good. Izz took another longing look at the stone. He rotated it in his fist. There was an odd tingling feeling at the touch of the blue amulet; every cut seemed to be reflecting its internal light. The thing began to throb faintly in his hand. Excited that Zuree could be very close, Izz tightened his grip on the stone and held it close to his lips. The stone's magical glow filled the air around him; its light made it easier to see. Instinctively Izz knew he had to go forward. He secured the stone and continued until he found himself crawling forward on his belly, dragging against stones, like a human mole through a dark rock rift.

The entire time Izz was thinking about how he was going to backtrack if he had to if he ran into a dead end. Izz reached the point where his back was scraping on the top of the tunnel. He was having a terrible time trying to keep his chest from painfully grating on the rocky flood as he belly crawled forward. If he turned back now, he could still worm his way back inch by inch, if not, soon it would be too late, and there would be no second chance. He took one last long look at the situation before him and knew that no one but a crazy man would dare persist. But Izz was a willing victim of love and was determined to move heaven and Zia to find the source of a passion he had never felt before.

Izz decided that it would be less torturous if he turned onto his back. He wiggled, squirmed, arched his body as much as he could and finally was able to turn himself onto his back. He breathed heavily from the effort it took him to turn. Several minutes passed before Izz recover enough to press on. After moving several more foot spans, he realized that the four walls around him were slowly hemming him in, like the jaws of death clamping shut. Yet Zuree's stone glowed brighter and brighter, and it gave him the courage to take a leap of logic just to push through. On his back with the encroaching stone ceiling a breath from his face, Izz pushed himself forward with the heels and toes of his feet, painfully over the jagged points of irregular rock. The passage was so terribly reduced that he would no longer be able to change his position. With one arm forward and the other one back, Izz threaded himself through worming and wiggling forward inch by inch through the twists and turns. His left arm now became worst than useless. He used his shoulders, toes, and the fingertips of his right hand to writhe himself forward, every inch along the way scratching and scraping his shoulders, arms, and face. He had yet to crop into a bigger space, and he did not have a good feeling about it. However, he knew that even if it meant his death, there would be no stopping and no turning back, if he could have turned back.

There was no other way out now but forward. Izz sweated and strained, punishing his body with every painstaking finger's breadth of the squeeze as powerful jolts of pain reminded him of his encounter with the centipedes. He could feel his chest pressing hard against the top of the squeeze every time he inhaled. Izz felt sharp edged gravel rolling under his back as he slithered along. Every inch seemed to take forever. The music of trepidation began to swell in his head. There was very little room to move around, and he would have to stay in the same position whatever lay ahead. He struggled along, disparate with the idea of emerging somewhere, anywhere, and soon. Izz's hair was damp, and he had sweated through his shirt and pants that now clung to his skin. In the narrowing crevasse, Izz was in a near panic stricken frame of mind, and as a result, he was banging up his head and peeling off the outer layer off his arms and legs. His back was nearly numb with the pain of all the abrasive grinding, and his arms and hands were bleeding from dragging and pulling himself through the jagged tunnel. Yet he pressed onward as if in a dream, obsessed with getting through.

Izz reached a juncture where he could feel the walls shutting in too close all around him. But still, he went on squeezing into the crawlway, knowing that frequently the wildest, crazed, unthinkable inklings are the best decisions. And if he had to risk it all in the hope of gaining everything or die in the attempt, that was a consequence he was willing to face.

Suddenly out of nowhere, Izz felt the rock bed beneath him begin to tremble unexpectedly, barely discernible at first; then a lurch and an eerie granite groan rumbled throughout the underworld. The underbelly of Zia shifted with a terrible shock that ran through the tunnel and produced a vibration that rattled his teeth. In an instant of insanity, Izz felt the floor heaving and knew that the ceiling could come down at any time. He was scared to death, crucified with a fear that almost stopped his heart. Then after eternity past, it was all over as suddenly as it had started.

He was still alive, still in one piece. Izz forced himself to calm down, and when he was finally able, he crept forward, dragging his decimated courage alone. He could feel with his head that the passage was becoming dangerously crowded. With one arm cramped in front and the other pinned beside him, Izz found he had reached an impassable point where it was a hair too small to pass his body through. He could feel the one thing he feared most of all staking upon him—the fear of getting stuck! But not even that was going to stop him. Rocks and dust fell on to his face and into his eyes. Izz paused for a moment, trying to blink the dust out. He was unmistakably wedging himself in tighter and tighter. He got his lead arm through the opening with minor effort, next came his head. By keeping it turned sideways, he was able to get through until he reached his shoulders. He tried to think about what to do next. Izz pressed himself forth. The jagged stone wall dug painfully against his left shoulder as he streaked bleakly beyond the full capacity of the gap. He tried to push forward, scraping every inch of his shoulders and back against the unyielding rock until he felt utterly wedged in! Izz could no longer move forward, much less backward. Desperately, again and again, he tried to move. "No! I must get through," he mumbled woefully. But the cranny was too narrow for him to force his body through.

He craned his head back as far as he could manage and then swiveled his head to the right as far as he could. Rotating his eyeballs on the upper rim of his eye sockets, Izz could see in his lantern's light that he had crawled himself into a dead end. What he had dreaded most had come upon him. This was not going to end well. He shivered as fear rippled through his body with the realization that his most terrifying fear was confirmed. He was hopelessly trapped, draped like a cocoon encased in stone, unable to escape! Izz felt as if a huge stone was crushing him as if its weight was compressing down on him from all sides. Convinced that he was going to die, after all, he could contain himself no longer. All the aggravation, dread, and pain of this day exploded from the top of his lungs. He screamed to the silence around him, *"Noooo!"* Izz's mind had reached a point somewhere between terror and hysteria. He was done for!

His lead hand released the lantern in front of him and clawed feverishly at the rock. Hopelessly he tried to widen the gap until his fingertips were a bloody mess, to no avail. With his right arm stretched out over his head and his left arm pinned at his side, his heart began to thunder in his chest. Izz panicked as he suddenly felt the boundless weight of the whole granite mountain of Skullsdoom crushing down on him. It was as if all of Noragore was bearing its load on him. He felt strangled from all sides as if the enclosure was smothering the life out of him. Izz started to pound his fist into the wall above him. He turned his head to look further ahead but could not see past the twisting and curving walls of solid stone. No longer finding any need to light his way, he extinguished his lamp.

Darkness struck its blow seeming to echo with the silence that was somehow more terrible than that of his heart slamming against the solid rock over him. The sense of it all took his breath away, and Izz limply fell back as the silence, the stone, and the darkness crowded in on him. His most distressing nightmare was unfolding, turning out worse than he could have ever imagined. As Izz reached the limits of his endurance, his spirit darkened as if the shadow of death had come to claim it. He laid there, heart and soul, entombed in rock, hopelessly locked forever within, forced flat to the underbelly of Zia. Izz was all alone, nothing more than a small dot under the Noragore Rim, trapped under tons of rock. Of course, no one would ever find his body. He would just be missing forever, just another lost soul. And Zuree, what of Zuree? At the very thought of her, a desperate wave overcame him. Izz struggled over and over to free himself. As time wore on, the shadow of failure enveloped him. Bereavement was the final challenge he faced. That is how things are: if you want something too much, then it cannot be. It was not right. It was not fair. With this, as it were, Izz's world had come to an end.

As fatigue set into Izz's tightening muscles, their dull ache intensified all over. With hardly a breath of wind to breathe, his mouth went dry. His distress caused his temperature to rise, and clammy sweat broke out profusely all over his entire body. His lightheaded mind began unraveling, paralyzing him with fear until he did not even know his name. Izz could stand it no more! The torment was completed. Driven mad by his inability to move and the darkness, at that point, death would be a relief. If at that moment he had not mercifully passed out, his heart would have exploded, or he would have virtually gone irreversibly insane. Izz's eyes closed, succumbed to the numbness of failure. Izz's perception went into a spin that hurled him beyond the deepest recesses of his primordial cognizance. Izz puzzled doubtingly.

Tom Icon

The last thing he heard before the darkest haze crushed in to shroud over him was Zuree's voice echoing his name from a distant world somewhere.

"Izz, I am here. Please come to me."

ELEVEN

THE DARKEST HOUR

It did not take a fortune teller to know what was waiting out there. Ammiz the Seer had set up a medical station to assist the wounded in the innermost palace room where the great hall was bright with daylight, and from where the wounded could quickly be moved, if need be, into the inner keep. Every available healer laid out their instruments. Tables were stacked with piles of clean woolen cloths and herbal medicines, and treatments were placed onto nearby trays. It was going to be nothing short of a true nightmare. Then too soon, the wounded started pouring in by the hundreds. Those that could still walk dragged themselves along as they helped others with broken legs or grievous wounds. Women and men too old to bear arms carried litters that bore those so smashed that they were unable to walk.

Ammiz directed those that were most gravely wounded onto tables where an overwhelmed staff of healers stood ready to attend to the injured. Nurses and midwives, in turn, stood by, prepared to assist the healers. A large basin was placed on the floor next to each table, to collect blood, amputated limbs, and other mutilated flesh that had to be cut away. Sheets and blankets were spread out on the floor to soak up the blood that fountained and seeped out of gaping wounds. Around the tables, fire cauldrons were lit to sear wounds that could not be sewn up. The queen and her handmaidens, including Atta, joined Ammiz to help in any way they could.

Ammiz, with tears welling in his eyes, attended to the worst off among the victims. Some had to be forcefully held down by three or more strongmen, with little or no anesthesia, so that crushed limbs beyond repair could be removed and cauterized before they bled to death. Men screamed and cried, wailed, whimpered, and sobbed, while their bodies convulsed and contorted in pangs of yawning woe. Pain pulsated from the holes that riddled their bodies while blood squirted everywhere. Arms and legs too maimed to save were severed with razors at the elbow and knee joints. Limbs smashed at mid bone were removed with saw and cleaver—a slow, grisly, agonizing process. Hastily twisted tourniquets were fixed on amputated limbs that were then seared. Broken bones were reset, foreign objects were dug out, and bleeding wounds cauterized, by the healers. A veteran warrior was brought in with a fractured leg beyond repair. When told that nothing could be done to save it, the old hand grabbed the healer by the collar and said, "Just sever it. I would prefer to live without it than die whole. Better to be disfigured for life than be departed."

A round wooden rod was placed in his mouth, a tourniquet was applied, and he was held down. He was given a strong narcotic, but because of the profuse, full flow bleeding coming from multiple severed veins, the procedure began immediately. The surgeon skillfully used a sharp knife to slice through the skin and muscle. He removed all the damaged tissue and sawed off the crushed bone, leaving as much healthy tissue as possible. As he quickly worked, he attempted to shape muscles so that the stump could later be fitted with a peg. Blood vessels and nerves were then seared off. The surgeon closed the wound by sewing the skin flaps. All the while, the strong warrior fought back—slashing, swinging, screaming, and cursing. Finally, the anesthetizing numbness of the powerful tonic spread mercifully through him. His arms dangled off the table, and his eyes fixed on the dull light washing in from the ceiling above.

Those whose lives were smashed out of them were immediately taken out to be cremated according to the ancient wartime rules of war, lest the sight of the mangled cause panic among the living. Blood and pieces of flesh filled buckets. Ammiz called out for any and every clean cloth that could be used as bandages in an attempt to maintain a sterile environment.

Healers stained with blood were ill prepared for the hundreds that cried for their help. Ammiz was elbow deep in blood as he tried desperately to knit a young warrior back together. His chest had been crushed, and his broken ribs had punctured his lungs and damaged his major blood vessels. Every vibrating wave of anguish beat against Ammiz's senses as he shook his head like a healer about to tell a patient's family that their only boy was not going to be coming home. A compassionate faint finally blacked the boy out. Just as heart wrenching yet were the cries of those waiting between life and death, smashed, crushed like bugs underfoot, barely hanging on in unbearable torment before wretchedly dying. While Ammiz feverishly worked on the young warrior, who was little more than a boy, the barrage outside continued with a series of earthshaking tremors, reproducing themselves in successive repetition. He was wiping blood and sweat from his forehead when suddenly, the catapult onslaught came to an abrupt halt, ceasing as suddenly as it had begun. And then an eerie sense of suspense fell over the room. However, very soon, that would all change.

<hr>

Baddlock's eyes blazed with impatience; the desired effect had not been attained. His soul burned with the willful desires to crush all life in Edawn. He gazed into the sky above him and spotted the ever present flock of buzzards circling overhead. Dandork was deep in thought, thinking about all his old friends who would have never turned on their king. The Wicked Warlock Wizard's fixed stare slowly shifted to Dandork, catching the treasonous general's attention. "What is the matter with you? You look as if you are about to wet yourself. Pull yourself together." His remark drew no reaction from Dandork.

Baddlock looked at Dandork only briefly before he turned away, cocking his head skyward. "A favorable omen continues to foreshadow us everywhere we go. Edawn will fall to its knees before us this day, and then the whole world of Zia will be ours." Baddlock's fearsome black mount, Nightmare, sifted its weight from one pair of legs to the other. Its ears perked forward, and its square nose quivered as it sniffed in the odor of blood in the air and snorted. No longer aware that Tigbone was still crouched at his mount's feet, Baddlock cruelly spurred his warhorse's flanks, violently reining it around.

Tigbone's globular figure scrambled for dear life. The stallion bewailed a grieving sound that resembled more the screech of an eagle than the cry of a horse as Baddlock reeled his mount Nightmare to face the Catapult Warlords. Suddenly greedy for it all, Baddlock commanded, "Prepare to launch the incendiary cisterns," as his face broke into a fiendish grin, and his eyes glazed over with lust for death. All at once realizing that he had almost trampled Tigbone, he turned Nightmare towards Tigbone who was now crouched to one side into the smallest heap he could make of himself. With a sardonic twist to his lips, Baddlock rolled his eyes, as if unable to believe Tigbone's lack of common sense. Heaving a deep, half mocking sigh, Baddlock said, "You do these things just to irritate me."

Tigbone let out a deep, unmanly sniff, relieved his master seemed more disappointed than angry.

The command to bring forth the incendiary pots was relayed back through the ranks. A chasm was opened in the midriff of the military masses as numerous wagons that had seen ages of hard use were sluggishly rolled toward the front lines. Each wagon was loaded to the hilt with ceramic pods. Each large ceramic cistern was packed with a mixture of pitch, oil, and rosin. Sulfur was added to create noxious, toxic fumes. The catapults were readied, the large pods were loaded, and the range calibrations were adjusted to accommodate the lighter weights of the volatile weapon.

The first volley had been by far the single most destructive attack ever, but despite the thrashing trial by stone, by some miracle, the kingdom's walls and gates, even though severely damaged, had somehow withstood the first attack, in defiance of the unbelievable assault the kingdom defenses held. Clouds of dust still eddied and wafted, high and low, throughout the battered kingdom. And in the momentary calm before the storm, there was a prolonged unsettling, ghostly stillness that caused fear to seep into King Ozzdon that penetrated deep beyond the bone. Even the screams of the wounded seemed to echo from a distant reality. Lurking fear began to overtake him, and the king realized that he had to get a hold of himself. Amid the silence, the king shouted at last, "We must, by no means, be caught off guard. Reinforce the damaged walls and make preparations to secure the kingdom by any means we have left to us."

The Catapult Master quickly adjusted new distance coordinates. A mock shot was fired off to measure their accuracy, puffing into orange smoke at the apex of its flight. The blazing ball of fire, correctly ranged, smashed into the targeted Northern Wall. Flames leaped up from the pod's white center upon impact and splashed out like a starburst of consuming light. The bright sputtering smoke instantly ignited into a raging blaze that burned in the swell of the billowing smoke. As the loud cracking inferno threw sparks high into the air, its flames devoured everything and anything that would burn.

Once again, the Catapult Lord gave his vile master the *All is ready* nod as the fiery pots were ignited simultaneously. The Wicked Warlock Wizard twisted his hands together in anticipation, then slashed a hand through the air as a crazed amusement played over his weather beaten face. He shouted, "Let them taste the whirlwind of fire, like chaff before the tempest. Let them perish in flames." He cupped his right hand so that only his bony index finger pointed toward Edawn. "Overburden them with your torment and strike fear into their hearts with your deluge of fire." Then he commanded, "Consume them, belly and bowel, heart and soul."

From the kingdom, everyone on the wall had seen pods being lit all along the ridge line. The tension suddenly shred into fragments as hundreds of burning cisterns lurched and filled the sky like an inferno singeing the heavens. Each pot tumbled end over end in midair as it arced its way at an alarming speed toward the kingdom. Streaks of fire, with their trailing tails of boiling smoke, marked each frightful trajectory.

With watery eyes, King Ozzdon watched the fearsome attack with mounting hopelessness as the nightmarish holocaust converged on them. It seemed the air itself would fracture and rift apart under the swelling stress as the fierceness of the onslaught whistled toward them. Suddenly, fire rained down from the sky with apocalyptic voracity as the reign of terror continued. The sound of descending pods shook the air just before the plummeting incinerators struck at the heart where the gem of the empire crowned Zia.

With thunderous impact after impact, the clay crucibles smashed into the kingdom, repeated at fixed intervals, stabbing with great flames, shaking with exploding fires, their brazing contents splashing in every direction with surging waves of devouring destruction. Flames shot up everywhere, joining and spreading until there were huge plumes of smoke, billowing into monstrous black clouds of fumes that rose to blot out the light of the sun. Engulfing fires fanned into raging flames that swept across the kingdom like rushing winds upon the inhabitants of Edawn. Firefighting brigades were organized, but water only made the flame spread wider. The only way to smother the flare at their source was to throw earth on them. Scalding smoke and blistering flames singed the hair, scorched eyebrows, and burned the throats, airways, and the lungs of those that tried to extinguish their fury. Men engulfed in flames danced a grotesque jig, running around in circles, flailing their arms and stomping their feet, which all ended with a whistling cry of pain. Others bolted as if trying to outrun their all consuming flames, ultimately falling and rolling around until they lost their battle for life. Each man that shrilled out in pain was another weight on the heart of the king.

The hellish inferno spread across the kingdom with alarming speed until almost the whole kingdom was on fire, smoke was everywhere, and the air was scorching hot. As flames soared high into the sky, heavy black clouds continued to roll across the furnace like atmosphere that lit the kingdom into a flickering nightmare. The once mighty northern gate, splintered and cracked from the first brazen onslaught, had reached its flash point and was now ablaze. Frantic firefighters worked feverishly to extinguish the gate's blaze. But the madness had yet to abate.

Baddlock's Catapult Masters continued to press their savage attack with blinding efficiency, making every moment seem like hours; and the hours seemed to last a lifetime. Edawn quivered, and the black smoke boiled, while the Wicked Warlock Wizard shook with crazed laughter. From his vantage point, he heard the roar of war and could even see the leaping flames belching and dancing along the rooftops. The fire leaped up all around the kingdom, its flames spreading quickly in every direction. Buildings went up like tinderboxes, and the smoke of their fire stretched to all the ends of Zia. In a surge of excitement, Baddlock dismounted and danced with glee in spinning circles. "Bring the calamity. Soon all of Zia will be mine. All mine, all mine, all mine," he sang with demonic insanity.

Meanwhile in the bowels of the deep, beneath the depths of Skullsdoom, Izz was still wedged within the impassable tunnel the seemed to be squeezing the life out of him with each passing moment. He found himself caught in a strange state of stupor, drifting halfway between consciousness and unconsciousness. His heart was beating erratically, and he felt short of breath. His third eye peered internally and externally and saw naught. With nowhere to go, time passed with agonizing slowness, and the silence went on as each excruciating juncture of time crawled by. Suddenly, out of nowhere, he thought he felt he was in the grasp of someone holding him from behind.

He smiled to himself when he thought he could see the thought of Zuree embracing him flashing in and out of his mind. But then he became deeply distressed. When he tried to turn and face her, he was held fast by her encircling arms, which seemed to have turned into a desperate clasp that screamed out for help. He tried to jerk himself free after hesitating for fear of what he would see. Izz finally opened his eyes and stared blindly into the stores of darkness. There was no radiance, not even a suggestion of illumination, only the deep shadows of death.

For a moment, he was disorientated as he came awake trembling and sweating at the same time. And he wondered in his delusional, altered state of consciousness where he was. The next conscious recollection of wakefulness brought him back with a terrible, awful sense of crippling despair upon finding out where he was—hedged in, still caught. He went a little crazy in a claustrophobic fit of effort to free himself. He gathered all the rage, grief, and fury of his throbbing heart; but the more he struggled to free himself, the more he felt trapped. The brutal fact that he was still hopelessly smashed somewhere in the entrails of the granite mountain of Skullsdoom roused him to the harsh reality, to his horror, that he had only been dreaming, as the bitter truth came to sweep Zuree from his grasp.

He lay alone in the silence that crackled against his eardrums, like an inert, static humming, resounding, reverberating in his mind. Izz's sense of the thread of time had been unsure. The tunnel seemed to grow steadily darker, but the mounting darkness was more than the mere absence of light. It was more of a physical thing. With the growing darkness came a piercing chill. His knotted muscles were stressed, aching for relief from lying in the same twisted position, fixed in such a restricted space for so long. Izz was feeling the effects of the constant darkness, of breathing his own second hand air, and the lack of food and water. He was half starved and exhausted to the point of death. Far too hungry, too parched, too fatigued for a reason. His stomach churned with unruly agitation, belching gas as it convulsed on empty. He suddenly grew fully aware of the tightness surrounding him, and of the weight of the world that seemed to be collapsing upon him, pinning him into his earthen prison. He felt encrusted in rock dust, with his mouth full of grit. He lay there, squished deep within the entrails of Zia as despair more profound than he had ever known seeped into his bones. He could feel himself dying; he was sure of it. But he did not want to die, not now. Not before he held Zuree again, if only for the last time.

Izz could feel the thickness of the rock walls pressing tight all around his hips, shoulders, and chest, cutting off his circulation. Deductive thinking told him he would never see the light of day again, but hope said to him that he had to someway stay alive. Somehow, he had to keep breathing, even though Izz knew he was closer to hopelessness than he had ever been.

He dug his feet against the constricting passage and wiggled, shimmied, and maneuvered himself as he exhaled as much air out of his lungs as he could and pushed forward with every tendon stressed to its limit. He tried to turn and twist, but he was wedged in too tight to move. He could feel hundreds of jagged edges ripping into the surface of his skin. His bulging muscles only served to hem him in tighter.

The futile attempt to move made his desperation to free himself virtually worse than the bleakness of his first state. Without being able to move forward or back an inch, Izz knew he was thoroughly done for. Sweating and straining, breathing heavily with growing panic, Izz drew deep breaths, trying to calm himself, knowing that utter madness waited at the end of that mental path where hysteria could just as soon kill him.

Izz's spirit was crushed, and despair riddled his faith with gaping holes. He slumped back, sliding into the bitterest surrender, and closed his eyes. He could barely stand the heat now. His mouth was parched, and he needed a drink of water; and though it was only inches away, he could not get to it. He desperately wanted to move, to stretch, scratch, anything. His limbs were becoming rigid and numb from lack of blood flow. He knew nothing could save him; and worst of all, he was separated forever from the only soul he had ever truly loved.

He was brutally aware that he had made a critical mistake at the crossroads of his life that would cost him his and Zuree's life. Where did he go wrong? Moreover, where did he not go wrong? He wondered. The more he thought about it; the more angered he became. Why had fate toyed with him, at the risk of failure and eternal loss?

And what of the so called Creature? Did He not care about his doomed fate? Izz just lay there in total disbelief, utterly frustrated and disappointed at his own stupidity, cursing Ammiz for getting him into this precarious predicament. For allowing the seer to convince him that he was the One—whatever that meant, he still was not sure.

Izz thought about it long and hard; but in the end, he knew beyond a doubt that it was not the old man's fault, not anyone's fault but his own for daring to believe. Looking for Zuree was an impossible task: it was worse than trying to find a needle in a straw heap. With all his heart, he wished he could just go home to Zollerzon. What did any of this have anything to do with saving the world of Zia? Perhaps it was never meant to be. For all he knew, Zuree could even be…no, no, he could not even begin to think it.

Izz hurt his head from the things that he thought. He felt anger at himself. He knew he needed to get a hold on his thoughts. Solace began to rekindle in him with every beat of his heart, building a hedge between what was important at this point and what wasn't—for what purpose, he did not yet understand. His thoughts turned to Zuree—the only reason that he was still alive. How he wished he could see her just one more time, even if it was for the last time. The hurt, the love, the extreme desperation began to mount inside.

Right then, Izz missed Zuree most acutely, so much so that it was killing him more assuredly than his dire plight. "I miss you so much," he declared with a weighty, winded moan. How he missed the sparkle in her eyes when she laughed, and how it filled him with such joy that he could almost hear her laughter ringing in his ears again. There was a tear forming at the corner of his eye that he did not want to cry. What good would crying do now? Izz sought hope and found none. He felt as if a weight was increasingly compressing, pressing down on his chest, a weight heavier than the mountain above him. On top of the weight building on his shoulders for having failed Zuree. He felt his heart crunch and clot against his ribs as it marked the passage of time. And now he truly understood what it meant to suffer a fate worse than death.

His heart trembled like that of a fawn caught in the jaws of a lion. It was more than he could bear. Fear swallowed him up alive as completely as the Noragore Rim had. Izz lapsed into stunned silence as he deteriorated into a deeper state of disorientation. The reality, as he had known it, ceased to exist. It was his darkest hour.

This fate truly worse than death had already surpassed every horror in his darkest nightmares and was progressively waxing worse. In a final act of desperation, Izz drew in as much breath as he could and screamed for help at the top of his lungs. "Help me! I do not want to die not, like this!" His scream echoed and withered before the endless inner silence, and Izz did not care if Baddlock himself heard him and personally came to kill him.

Izz waited and listened intently for a response as if one might come. When none came, he agonized with the reality that chilled him to the marrow and rattled his very spirit. He had voluntarily descended into his own tomb of solid rock, buried deep within Zia, where he would die a fool's death, just as the gate guard had rightly predicted.

He began to see, feel, and smell reality with an acute sense of false clarity that came from an elevated state of depravation. He then began to wonder what it would feel like to die. Why resist the inevitable? Life was a battle that everyone ultimately lost anyway. So what was the use? Death would not be so bad despite everything. After all, to die is natural. It would be like falling asleep, except for the part of not waking, at least not to this world. He somehow knew he would see Zuree in the next life, one way or another. All he had to do was wait for the intimidating spirit of death to finally come and take him on the path to his rest, where he could look forward to his eternal life. Death had finally found him out…again. His luck had been ever so extraordinary, but there was an end to everything. He was the cat that had finally run out of lives.

Izz winced at a sudden regret that tore at him. But it could not be compared to the pain he felt in his heart for letting his king down. And still, that was not as excruciating as the unbearable guilt he felt for having let Zuree down. Moment after grueling moment he was hounded and tormented by the constant reminder that Zuree's sweet, beautiful soul was in Baddlock's evil clutches. The thought sent bolts of grief through his imploded heart. In a tearful and wailing voice, he whispered the words that he dreaded to speak, "I am sorry. I did not mean to let you down. I am sorry, please forgive me. I did not mean for it to turn out this way. I am so, so sorry, Zuree!" Izz emitted an ungodly shriek of anguish at the top of his lungs, totally eclipsing the underworld tomb's complete silence.

While he was yet shrilling, his choking urge to weep released all his held back tears, and he broke apart and wept bitterly. His panicked eyes darted all about as the notion of going crazy seized his mind. As he grew cold inside, Izz listened to his heartbeat slowing in his ears and whispered, "So this is it, this is the place where I will spend my last miserable moments on Zia."

Izz of Zia

Izz strove to shake and cast himself away from his thoughts, but he could not. Between sniffles, he affirmed, "I am not afraid of you, Death."

After some time had passed, Izz screamed into the darkness, "Death! Come and claim your prize. Why do you linger?" He spiraled deeper and deeper inside himself, where he found a quiet and peacefulness in his small crawlspace, beyond his sense of hopelessness. It was as good as any final resting place, as good as any tomb. It was only a matter of going into a profound sleep without dreams, without pain, and worries. He did not care anymore. Izz made his peace with his fate. For a moment, he pondered what death would be like. Only death would tell. By now, there was resignation in his soul. All he wanted was to remove himself from his miserable mental state of defeat.

In a maddening fury, the continuous cluster bombardment of incendiary pots whizzed over the defending walls, aimed at the civilian quarters, spreading more devastation throughout the already crippled Kingdom of Edawn. Old men, women, and older children formed fire suppression crews, scurrying around in chain gangs, running water buckets, from the river and wells to the flames, trying in vain to douse the consuming beast. Whole families perished; burning people ran to and fro, hopelessly trying to slap out the ravenous flames. As chaos reigned, parents screamed for their children. A young mother had to be restrained as she looked on with horror as her toddler's little hands stretched up from within the inferno of a direct hit. Within an instance, she saw the child crinkle like charred parchment, and then crumple to ash.

Baddlock's never ceasing three ton catapults were incinerating whole sections of the kingdom. The Edawnians one ton catapults, which could not reach the Norticlan encampment, remained silent. As the fury of a one sided war closed in on them, Edawn's generals gathered to their king. All stood on the edge, waiting to hear their king's next command, any command.

The king showed no outward emotions to the crisis besieging them. No one questioned the king, and none challenged him. All remained faithful to their tradition of honor and loyalty to their emperor king that transcended their fears and doubts. After a long silence, Ozzdon spoke, "We are virtually defenseless against their long range catapults. We must somehow spill their blood before they spill all of ours. I for one, would rather die with a sword in my hand, preferably stained with my enemies' blood."

There was an uproar of approval among the generals and the surrounding troops. Rumors of a counterattack spread quickly.

The king called for a map and spread it out before him, smoothing out the corners so that it would lay flat. He studied it intently for a moment, as one would a mathematical quandary. Then after a ponderous moment, he said, as if saying it could make it possible, "Once we get under their catapults, they will be useless against us. If we then send our main forces in an all out frontal attack and draw their full defenses to the middle while two war parties break off to swiftly flank their outer forces; and then double back in a sweeping arc, pivoting like a pair of jaws working together in opposition to slip around their main formation. We could then envelope and attack their outer borders, get to their catapults, and disable them somehow. It will require tremendous sacrifice, but I believe it is our only chance in the world."

A murmur, of agreement, rumbled among the inner circle of generals and troops. As for the king, the idea of an all out frontal counter attack was unsettling. King Ozzdon had to be sure of a total commitment among his generals, so he offered them an indirect ultimatum: "A head to head confrontation will be risky. We are outnumbered, and our weapons are outmatched." The king countered. "I am sure we could outmaneuver their catapults, but then we would have to face their armor piercing crossbows and who knows what else they may have up their sleeves. Our present situation is grave, but not entirely hopeless. Reinforcements from the northern kingdoms should reach us at any time now." The king fell silent again, knowing all along that without reinforcements, a counterattack, however crazed, was their only alternative.

Itching for a fight, Zandor responded, "That is true, my Lord, but if our reinforcements were anywhere near, our scouts would have reported it by now. Here, we are sitting ducks. At least out there, we can die like men, not like sheep in a slaughterhouse." The ripple of unity became more boisterous, especially from the younger warriors.

Zandor continued, "We must stand up now, or fall forever!"

The spirit of allegiance and brotherhood swept over young and old alike.

"If we do not confront them now, we shall be tied down as long as it takes for their superior weapons and numbers to overwhelm us."

The king did not like its ghastly probability, but the alternative was just as unimaginable. He dared not play the counterattack card unless all else was lost. His eyes scanned slowly across the whole Edawnian military unit within his sight, and he saw resolve and courage on every man's face. He was filled with a total sense of pride in the lion heartedness of his countrymen. At that moment, the king realized the truest test of strength and courage was not in the willingness to kill but in the willingness to lay one's life down for those they loved. Every warrior was ultimately willing, and yet the thought was unthinkable. Ozzdon contemplated the battle to come. He felt his chest constrict, and it brought a pang of dull pain to his heart. He gathered himself up. His voice then rose loud and clear. "This day, hatred and cruelty have joined hands with madness. Outside these walls, there is a vast and sadistic war beast, and it is hunting all of us. Baddlock, the deranged madman that he has become, is demonically driven to grind us all into dust, men, women, and children. He will make no exception, he will have no mercy, and he will yield at nothing less than our utter annihilation." The king paused for a moment so that his warriors could grasp the weight of his words. The king unsheathed his royal sword, pointed to the heavens and cried out, "Gird yourselves! Rise up, you are warriors of truth, lift your hearts. Be it known unto you, and to all the people of Zia. You are worthy of your kingdom, so hoist high the royal banners of Edawn!"

A deafening shout went up among the troops in one continuous voice. The roar was awe inspiring, yet at the same time, a chilling finality resounded within it. The warriors began to chant in unison, "Long live Edawn! Long live Xylenia! Long live King Ozzdon!"

The shout echoed off the kingdom's inner buildings, over the shudder of the crashing fireballs and over the walls to reach Baddlock's ears. Baddlock disgorged a burst of evil hissing laughter and asked, "Do they purpose to defeat me with their futile incantations? Make ready!" Baddlock ordered. "I do believe the rats are about to come out of their trap."

Tigbone could not remember when his master had been more pleased.

"Spare yourself the anguish of waiting for what ultimately awaits you at my hand Ozzdon." The Wicked Warlock Wizard spat the last word out as if he was spitting out something unpleasantly bitter.

The command was spread down the line among the vast military forces. Baddlock wheeled Nightmare around violently to face the catapults and ordered the masters of the sky, "Continue to consume the kingdom. Tighten the noose and pulverize their will." Then he turned to Dandork and Darkon, "Position every archer to the frontlines, and bring up our short range catapults." Then Baddlock said, "I believe it has dawned on our illustrious king that the quickest way to end this war is to lose it."

The archers' banners were hoisted on tall poles, and a surging mass of humanity shifted forward. Each man carried with him an armor piercing crossbow and was followed by an arm bearer, who carried with him a bulky bundle of razor sharp, hardened steel tipped arrows.

TWELEVE
THE COUNTERSTRIKE

Behind the kingdom's walls, the Edawnian standing forces, smaller but no less fierce, were making last minute adjustments. They wore steel breasted vests and metal helmets. Long metallic shields would protect them. Having been given their general assignments, they formed into battalions; no one would shrink from the impending encounter. All casual conversation ceased as they readied themselves in silence as the tuning fork rang in their hearts and gallantry fortified their loins. Generals broke the rising tension, only to say what was essential as they assembled their men for the frontal assault.

Men from all walks of life, of every rank and class, waited impatiently, eager to challenge their enemy face to face and show their leaders their fearless courage. From cobblers to blacksmiths, from bakers to stonecutters, the soon to be combatants readied themselves. Despite never having experienced real battle, they had their hearts set on doing their best. Whether they died in their attempt or not, they preferred the grim risk of death on the battlefield to the terrible passive waiting to be crushed or burned alive in the fiery assault that continued to rain down on them. The training they had received from the War Games did little, or nothing, in preparing them for what was to come. Young warriors readied themselves with a mixture of curiosity and uncertainty, determined to be as brave as they could. Every warrior bore within him the grim realization that he might die in the impending battle to come. Each man tried to imagine what would happen beyond the Edawnian walls. Every man, throughout his life, had thought of death many times. It was something they all knew would eventually be the end of all men, but until that exact moment, they thought of death as something that would not happen until they were old and gray.

Time had ceased, yet Izz's mind continued to flicker somewhere between reality and a state of illusion. Pensive thoughts, images, and random, vague memory flashed in and out, like the forerunners to an all out hallucination. The human mind in this condition of utter hopelessness had to occupy itself, to keep the onset of absolute insanity from seeping in. Izz could see images forming in his head. What he saw in his mind's eye suddenly became a reality as his existence took on the essence of a protective form of consciousness beyond the realm of a mind disconnected from all that was time and space, present, past, and future.

A tiny spark of light lit up somewhere behind the fathomless depths of his eyes, like remote impressions of footprints lift behind by a repressed dream. His fading mind transported him back through time and space to a long forgotten moment in his distant past. From within, Izz saw a vision of two transparent figures, as if from a vast distance, calling to him. *We are here. We will always be here waiting for you, our precious son.*

The voices brought back to Izz's memory an echo from another time. They were the first voices he had ever heard whispered to him while still in his mother's womb, stirring the painful embers of long lost emotions and images of his mother. In his delirium, Izz called back, "Mother, I seem to be lost." He moaned in memory and despair.

His spinning thoughts regressed to his first concept of self. He was not, and yet he was what he was going to be. He was wrapped in affection and nurtured in well being. It was a radiating space of warmth and buoyancy. He felt snug and secure. His eyes were open, and in the bright light, he could see shades of reds and oranges. He remembered turning and reaching for the light but never being able to touch it. He felt as if he was dreaming a dream within a dream from which there was no waking. He remembered his emotional thoughts, thinking, *So this is life, and it is beautiful.* He could not want for more. It slowly dawned on him that he was somehow bringing into mind the remembrance of being inside his mother's womb. He recollected the feel of the inner lining of his nest, smooth and warm to the touch of his hands and feet. He could see, hear, taste, and feel the velvety warmth of the fluid that supported and surrounded him. Izz remembered how he had learned to distinguish between different sounds of voices. He relived a moment when two hands, one bigger than the other, caressed the walls of his refuge; loving sounds of adoration reached his ears from two voices radiating their love for him. That was the first time he knew true love, and he leaped for joy inside of his mother's belly. Life was good, life was beautiful, and life was a thing to be cherished.

Feelings formed in his mind of the rocking motions of his mother's long garden walks that drew him into deep, sleepy dreams in which he would go through an open door into an extraterrestrial existence beyond the forces of limitations. His thoughts carried him beyond the vague rife of the physical, beyond time and space, beyond disillusion and decimation. To a continuance so far back. Before time had been set in motion. Before the stars were spread across the macrocosm. Before Zia was cast across the expanse of the constellations. By some means unknown to him, he recalled from this time, being told that he would be born into a material world with a physical body. That in this physical body, he would have to face many diverse trials; and at an appointed time, would have to die. At which moment, he would then return to his eternal home and family beyond the stars.

In his pre infantile memories, his mind was filled with his mother's gentle love. Then suddenly, his mind dredged up a startling remembrance that wafted a shadowy flashback through his mind. He recalled that a sudden loud noise, though muffled, had startled him. He now recognized that it had been his own mother's distressful voice. The fearful feeling, for some reason, evoked admonitions that he was to suffer and someday die.

Tom Icon

Izz remembered swimming back from deep, sublime sleep to find himself no longer suspended. The protective cushion that once surrounded him was suddenly gone. Several moments went by, and then his mother's womb began closing in on him, squeezing and crushing down on him. He was suddenly turned upside down, with the walls of his mother's womb forcefully tightening down around him. The first thing that came to mind was, *This is it!* The death that was foretold just before his life became flesh. *My time has come to suffer and die,* he remembered thinking. Spasms of contractions began to press down on him violently. He could hear cries of pain from without. Each time a contraction subsided, he thought himself to be dead. He remembered thinking, *That was not too bad. Now someone will come for me and carry me into the eternal bliss beyond.*

Then another contraction would start, with more squashing, squeezing, and screams of pain from his mother. *My heavenly family must be mourning my impending death.* He remembered wondering, *Why is it taking me so long to die, and why does it have to be so painful?* Once more, the contraction subsided, and Izz remembered thinking, *Surely I am dead now? That was not too bad now that it is over. Where is the heavenly being that will guide me back home?*

When he realized that his shoulders and head were painfully pinned, he knew that he was still alive. Then there was a more forceful contraction, and his head was forced through his mother's birth canal. *Why do I have to be squished to death?* He had wondered again. The pressure was unbearable. He had tried to open his eyes but could not. He felt his head as it contorted to the compressing tension. *What a way to go!* He recalled thinking. Then his head suddenly emerged, and he felt a cool breeze on his wrenched head and flattened face. His shoulders and chest were still constricted, wedged in an embrace of death, and now he could hear the wrenching screams of a young mother bearing her first child. Any moment, his strangulated heart would be unable to beat!

Izz of Zia

He heard his mother's shrieks of pain with scarcely a pause for air to be gasped back into her lungs. His mother's distressed wailing finally came to an abrupt stop, and her body went limp. Izz had been torn from his mother's womb. He was a wailing baby boy who could—would not be comforted until he was snugly swathed in a blanket and put to his mother's breast. Almost every drop of life seemed to have been squished out of him, yet he was the most beautiful human being his parents had ever beheld. Izz remembered his first infantile thoughts after birth were, *If I am still alive, life must be extremely cruel!*

Izz further remembered the chill of the outside world, and how it had revived his wrung out little body, and how its coolness spread exhilarating sensations across his sensitive skin over its entirety. Light pierced his eyes, and the fresh air burned his little lungs as he drew his first breaths. He was in pain, bruised, and battered; his stretched muscles were throbbing, his tendons were drawn out, and his joints felt sprained. His back and limbs arched in resistance to the gravity that now pulled on him as he wailed at the top of his lungs.

Izz would never forget how he was held briefly in his mother's reverent arms and the look of love in her dimming eyes as she whispered, "His name shall be Izz." He remembered how he had thought, *Surely I am finally back home in heaven now.* He did not realize it then, but his mother had died shortly after giving him life. The midwife pulled him from his mother's lifeless arms, held him up from underneath his tiny arms, and smiled down on him. In one way or another, he realized that he had been thrust into a whole new world of sight, sound, and space—into the beginning of life, not the end. His father had loved his mother so much it was said that because he could not bear to live without her, he had died of a broken heart the following winter.

Meanwhile, back in the present, Izz's eyes were wet with sorrow. Then his memories rewound and started over again, over and over again, until his consciousness began to slowly float back to the surface for the last time, returning as if to pay his final respects to himself. He halfway woke to find himself sapped from his last vestige of will to live. Just when he found himself wishing for the end, his sixth sense picked up the tiniest trace of external stimulation. Somewhere in the most profound recesses of his mind, flickering through his perception centers were fleeting images roused by a dwindling far off sound, from somewhere in the void. In the innermost cognizant layers of his receding existence, a faint internal three way conversation began between his subconscious, his soul, and his inner spirit. The exchange penetrated past a hundred foggy similes. It was a haunting sensation. The conversation with the self began with his inner spirit, "Did you hear something?"

"No, it was just your imagination," the subconscious responded.

"I am sure I heard voices," the soul joined in.

"They were only hallucinations caused by the darkness," the subconscious refuted.

"Listen, there it is again. Someone is out there, and I can hear them!" the spirit maintained.

"They are only illusions brought on by the dying process. Let it go. We are almost there," the subconscious insisted.

"No! No! You must wake now! Please! I know I heard something!" the spirit persisted.

Like a drowning man coming up from the deep, Izz's consciousness slowly and reluctantly fluttered one eye open, fighting the heaviness of eternal sleep, with hazy memories of his birth pangs still kindled in his mind's eye. He lay in the darkness with his ears vigilant, as if listening for something, unsure of what, simultaneously half conscious and half unconscious. In the same moment, he wasted away in the twilight of life between whispers and total blackness, yet he could feel the minutest enduring ember of promise still smoldering.

Izz woke fragmentarily like a half extinguished cinder twinkling among the dead coals of his lost hope of living. The very exertion of waking wearied and weakened him. As it was, his life hung by a tread. He was just as good as dead. The darkness of his entombment had already merged into his mind. With his will to live failing him grievously, he wondered what death was waiting for. Why should he have to suffer so? He could not fathom the purpose of this prolonged misery, of dying. He hardly felt it worth the effort to have regained consciousness, only to repeat the prolonging question, "Why will you not just let me die?" Izz fervently cried out for an answer. None came. Apart from his shallow breathing and the heartbeat that implied that he was still alive, his tomb was deathly still.

The imminent, irreversible process of dying had stopped just short of its final tracks and began to retrace its steps back from the brink. He began the crossing back from the outer fringes of the afterlife. Izz's vital signs responded to the tiniest glimmer of he knew not what; he was like a man briefly reprieved from a death sentence. The silent emptiness was so odd. It ridiculed him, cursed him. He detested it.

The first significant thing Izz felt was the whole weight of Skullsdoom still crushing down on him. Then came the acute pain of stiffness, like the early signs of rigor mortis. His stomach was letting him know about the wrenching hunger in his belly. The pain was nasty as if the acids in his stomach had started ingesting the entrails pressed against his backbones. His eyeballs burned, his nostrils were filled with rock dust, and his throbbing temples seemed ready to burst. He was severely dehydrated. His tongue clung to his jaw. His stomach had a sickly feeling and had shrunken to the size of a little knot that felt as if it was stretched across his spine. There was an odd subtle glow in the tunnel. Summoning up all his energy, he rimmed his eyeballs along the bottom of his sunken sockets, focusing to see that Zuree's amulet pressed to his heart, was glowing faintly. How ironic, he thought, as he laid his heavy, reeling head back against the broken rocks. He wanted to send up a prayer but thought it hard for it to rise through the dense gray mass sitting on top of him. He tried to humor himself. At least nothing could sneak up on him here, not while he was buried alive in the center of Zia. It was also a good place to seize upon a few moments of much needed rest; at least he could get a good idea what his tomb was going to be like. Death might not be half as bad as he thought it would be if only it would finally happen.

Suddenly, just on the edge of his hearing, a sound reached his acute sensitivity. And then, with a gasp, as if coming fully awake with a jerk, Izz's eyes snapped wide open. He whipped his head around and cocked his ear in the direction of the noise as tiny shards of rock cascaded down on him. He tilted his head slightly to one side, and then the other, trying to pinpoint where the sound had come from. Then there was silence—so absolutely quiet was it that it unnerved him. There was nothing but him, in the still of his stone tether. And yet, suddenly out of nowhere, there it was again; and this time he was more than for sure he detected the faintest sound, resonance, reverberation…but could not quite make it out. He went on to say in a low voice, "I am hearing sounds and seeing things that are not there."

Then it was there once more. Izz concentrated on the very dampened but discernible impressions. His dazed mind and straining ears picked up ominous, muttering, unintelligible sounds, vague and indistinct like that of two distant crows arguing back and forth. He froze and listened, separating the noises from the arbitrary mineral sounds of the tunnel. He thought he heard something—something muted but without a doubt human coming from the farthermost point of somewhere.

There were voices. Izz heard voices! At first, he thought he might be losing his mind. He shook his head to shake out the shadows. He gathered his wits and listened again. The reverberation of voices seemed to be coming from within the emptiness just beyond the walls of the tunnel's dead end, just ahead of him. Was his hearing playing tricks on him? Izz's mind raced as he tried to focus. A forlorn hope sparked in his spirit. If his faith was a mere fabrication of his desperation's own making, hoping against hope, it was hope, nonetheless. Out of despair, he called out, "Is anyone there?" The faint sounds that came back to him included nothing he could construe as an answer. He dismissed the sounds as his unrelenting imagination, but then he heard it again, becoming progressively louder.

No…yes…yes! Someone was talking; however, he could not make out what was being said. Hope sent a pulsing wave of life oozing back into his struggle for existence. Izz's spirit seemed to burn with a renewed fire suddenly. The fog cleared from his brain as he regained full awareness. He gathered his senses, trying to think out what to do next. In his excitement, somehow, unexpectedly, the enclosure seemed less restricting. Was it just its imagination, or had he lost some weight, because he suddenly felt less cramped? The lack of water and food and his profuse sweating had caused him to lose enough body mass to allow him to turn his wilted and shriveled upper torso to the right slightly. He exhaled all the air from his chest, causing it to collapse just enough to enable him to flip onto his belly in one rotation. He lifted his head, blinking the dirt from his eyes; peered into the blue black darkness ahead; and saw a ray of faint light that managed to squeeze its way in from just ahead of where he was stuck. Once again, he exhaled completely and dug in hard against the floor with his toes. He was able to scoot forward on his belly over the sharp rocks, only a few inches. Exhaling and fiercely jerking, twisting and pushing, Izz forced himself through at a snail's pace.

He scraped along a thousand sharp edges that cut into his back, shoulders, and chest along the opposing walls as his ironclad will negotiated and angled him through the tiny crawlspace. Izz's face stiffed in agony as his desperate movements nosed him forward one finger's breadth at a time. His clothes snagged on the pointy rocks as he squirmed ahead, pushing his lantern before him and dragging his satchel behind. He could feel the tunnel walls scarping, rasping, and cutting into the surface of his skin, especially on his chest and back. It was like dragging himself across a trail of fire, guided only by the speck of light at the end of the tunnel. He used the fingertips of his right hand to pull himself forward by inches.

Izz concentrated all his energy and mind on squeezing from one impassable slip to the next, to the next. This was going to be a lot harder than he could have ever imagined. With every forward thrust he took, pain exploded through his spine and neck. Izz reached a nook in the passage where he was not sure he could make it through, but Izz was prepared to give everything he had left. He pulled at the rock, trying to pry open a bigger hole. All the stones, which had at first looked loose, appeared to be solidly cemented in. Izz scooted his lamp forward; he had no other choice but to force himself through or die. Impatient to get out, he positioned his face into the smaller passage, trying to angle, twist, and wedge his face forward. He slid his shoulders in sideways through the long opening. Like threading a needle, he pushed himself through a few more inches. But when his shoulders reached the walls of the slot, he immediately knew that he was most likely not going to get through, as he had feared all along. He squeezed his eyes shut; he exhaled and inched forward a breath.

As a result of a tremendous act of will, he squeezed through another breath. He tried to free himself, but there was just not enough room to scoot any farther. And he had done it again! He was stuck! His adrenaline was pumping, his heart was thudding, his blood pounded in his ears, and his legs and free arm were thrashing against the rock as he tried frantically to break through the constricting walls. His cuts, sprains, blisters, bruises, bites, and pulled muscles on his neck, shoulders, chest, arms, and fingers were bleeding; but strangely enough, he could not feel their pain. He knew he had ultimately sealed his doom, and that there would not be much chance of a second chance. After having built his hopes up, the inability to move forward quickly became unbearable. Utterly overwhelmed, he suffered a catastrophic, most dismal breakdown.

"I am finished!" He was going nowhere. It was too much to bear. Grief hit him, and all he could see before him was nothing but the total blackness of eternal damnation.

Izz closed his eyes to the anguish that washed over him. Once again, feelings of helplessness tormented his thoughts. Izz was going crazy with anxiety and self condemnation, breeding the thought that was escalating uncontrollably toward his greatest fear of going insane. By slow, painful degrees, he was beginning to feel a weightless distance in his soul. His faith was broken. *Why did I not go from womb to tomb?* At that moment, Zia seemed to tremble under and above him, and he heard faint rumbling like rocks falling deep beneath him.

He needed to clear his mind or go crazy. *Just relax!* Izz heard an inner voice shout in his head. "Relax! I am done for!" *How can I relax!* He did not know how he could go on living one more second without going ultimately out of his mind. Tears leaked from the corner of his eyes as he wondered why he had suffered more than any man should. He was so close, and yet so far; if he could only control his nerves. He wrenched himself from his thoughts and replaced them with thoughts of loosening up.

Finally, his momentary relapse was behind him. Slowly Izz felt his tense muscles relax with each moment that went by. He just had to somehow make one last dying effort with all the last strength of his battered, worn out body. He took in several deep breaths and managed to relax his stiffened spine. His constricted body triggered a conscious daydream in his mind; thoughts that were still fresh in his memory began niggling and replaying in his head. Drifting into a deep state of thought, he flashed back, in and out, back and forth, to the time of his birth. It was a hauntingly familiar situation. He caught his breath as mirrored images, feelings, and memories flooded through him. And now he realized why he hated tight enclosures.

From the traumatic experience of his birth, he knew that if he would collapse in on himself, he could make it. He dared to have faith when there was nothing left to hope for. And his panic receded farther and farther into the darkness. Izz's body became aware of itself. He sucked his shoulders in, allowing his body to take on the shape of the tunnel; and by some mysterious force of will, he pushed himself forward. Izz loosened up every muscle and fought the instinct to tense up in the squeeze. With his jaw set, he gritted his teeth and vigorously wiggled, twisted, and squirmed, forcing his aching body on, millimeter by millimeter, trying not to buckle under the agony crushing in against him. He pushed himself with all his might to remain calm and resist the reality mounting against his odds. No matter what, he dared not stop for fear of falling just short of the prize. Izz put all he had left into it in spite of the outcome. Placing each foot carefully against the crumbly rock, as his fingers dug into the crust of the bedrock, his shoulders scraped against the tunnel walls as he slithered along headfirst, corkscrewing through by the skin of his teeth, dragging hope alone. As Izz perilously called out on all his combined strength, will, and faith, he pushed himself against the enclosure that threatened to constrict him to death.

Like a cat being pulled tail first through a knothole, he forced his bruised and bleeding body through the shaft. As he scraped his head, he left behind patches of hair along the way. He could sense that he was on the edge of breaking through. He was bathed in perspiration and was so exhausted that the pain that surrounded him did not matter anymore. He rested for a fleeting moment. He could feel his pounding heart vibrating as the walls seemed to close in tighter around him with every beat. He could almost feel the entire tonnage of Zia above him as he felt it rotate beneath him.

One last superhuman surge and he finally reached through to the end of the tunnel. He could feel there was a manmade seam outlining the impasse. Izz struggled forward until his lead arm was bent against the dead end. In final desperation, he braced his back against the wall as he pushed against the stone block with crazed, brute force. He felt the stone face that imprisoned him give slightly, allowing an utterly hopeless situation to become hopeful. A hallucination of Zuree beckoning to him kept him moving. A love that refused to fail made him believe. *I am truly close*, he thought. With the last of the strength left him, he gave a mighty shove. This time, being wedged in was to his advantage. As he pushed, he felt the barrier move forward, like the cork out of a bottle, and fell out and away from the tunnel. The immense darkness that had surrounded him suddenly cleared away like a melting fog.

A voice, which he could distinctly hear now, at once asked. "Did you heard that?"

Izz froze to listen intently. Another voice answered, in a matter of fact tone. "It be just another stone felling itself, nothing more. Now get back to work. Our taskmasters be very angry if we have nothing showed in the time they be gone" Izz wanted out of there as fast as possible. Like a bound moth struggling to free itself from its cocoon, he struggled forward. The exertion was a pure back breaker, but finally, thwarting the embrace of death, Izz barely managed to free himself from the rim of the overhang, emerging from his stone chrysalis like prison. He let out a relieved breath, feeling pleased that he had, after all, made the right decision…or had he jumped from the fire into the frying pan?

As his ears sought the source of the voices, he hesitated for a moment, like a wild beast coming forth from its hollow, trying to sense if the threat was worth the risk of venturing out. Shrouded in bedrock dust, he dropped out of the opening, crashing over the side into another darksome chamber, landing on the hard stone floor with a sickening thud and a muffled groan, as his legs and arms were not able to support him. His lamp and satchel clattered down after him; his lantern lay broken beside him. Frantic that he was making too much noise, he lay still, doubled over in pain, not daring even to breathe. Then he crawled, against the wall exuberantly, overcome with relief. Again, Izz had miraculously cheated death, for the moment, at least. "You almost had me again," Izz whispered as the divine feeling of release flooded through every inch of his being.

Then almost immediately, the voice again came out from the darkness. "What be that? That be no rock falling!"

Izz pushed himself deeper into the shadows against the corner of the stone wall, dragging his pack behind him, and took a long, desperate gulp of water. Looking like a scalded cat, Izz breathed a sigh of solace. Suddenly he saw movement against a torch lit background. He tried to melt even deeper back into the darkness where the shadows thickened with imagined images of sharp edged knives. Izz stayed as flat as he could against the wall, daring a look only after hearing someone say, "I knowed it. I seed something there." The voice came again as a silhouette stepped forward.

"Come back! Could be the masters returned early. Get back to work!"

Izz silently spat out long muddy drool from his mouth and rubbed dirt from his eyes, as he worked to untie his satchel from his leg. He leaned back and examined his shredded shoulders; one had a deep gash in it. After a moment, he attempted to stand but did not have the strength to keep his knees from buckling. Hampered by the lack of light, he gathered his things in the dark. He was covered from head to toe with dust marks along his face and clothes caused by the squeeze. He quietly brushed at the light brown cave dust that covered his entire body, and then he strapped his dagger and satchel back on. He tried to get to his feet again but was unable to make his legs function normally, and fell forward onto his hands and knees. His arms and knees were wobbly and unsteady. After an instant of uncertainty, he took hold of the side of the overhang and pulled himself upright. He rubbed firmly at his bruised and battered knees. He straightened up on his rickety feet and somehow managed to use the walls of the cave to slowly stand up without falling over. Izz could not stand straight without hurting due to his stiff back. Once on his feet, feeling began to return to his throbbing, deadened legs.

He stood there on trembling legs, in a hot, dusty world, carefully trying to regain his equilibrium as he studied the lay of his new surroundings. Then he took a few tentative steps toward the torch lit background, wondering if he should not be going in the opposite direction. He shook his legs every few steps to bring them back to life. He moved slowly, carefully trying not to make any noise as he used the wall to steady himself. Izz winced and gritted his teeth, racked with pain as he walked gingerly, trying to ignore the aching numbness of his legs and arms. After a few more steps, his pain was subsiding. Feeling more or less human again, Izz made his way up to a rocky trail toward the torch lit area. The spongy dust on the cave floor absorbed the sound of his footsteps. An unexpected gust of sulfur laced air swirled in his face and drifted into his nostrils. The foul, sulfuric mist that came from the direction he was walking smelled like something between rotten eggs and burnt ash. The cave's bleak atmosphere was comfortless.

Suddenly Izz stopped dead in his tracks, just at that instant something forced him to look over his shoulder as a dull realization dawned over him. He neither heard or saw anyone, but this time for sure, he knew in the depth of his spirit that where he stood, he was not alone. All at once, the air was filled with the sour aroma of unwashed flesh and moldy clothing, and Izz could feel the warmth of human breath on his neck. There was a sudden movement in the darkness; and without warning, he felt a bony hand on his shoulder that made him leap, almost causing him to jump right out of his own skin. His alarm and astonishment nearly gave him a heart attack. Nearly paralyzed by fear, Izz had to restart his heart before he could reach for his dagger. With his feet seemingly rooted to the cave floor, he quickly drew his weapon to the attack position and turned his upper body to face his assailant.

Izz's eyes opened wide with surprise when he saw a face, or rather, the likeness of what was once a face; and he almost screamed when the skull faced man came into view in the dim torchlight. "Easy, boy!" said the skull faced man standing in front of him as he stared back at Izz.

The strange little man peeled and curved his dry, withered lips back into a grin that revealed a set of yellow stained stump teeth. "I be Zappa," the little man said as he extended his skeletal hand.

The skin of his emaciated face was colorless, rigid, like a mask made of taut goat parchment stretched out over a skull. His unkempt, plastered hair was a weedy mess covered with a wet muck smeared over his head, making it hard to see where the hair and dirt started or stopped. The body was nearly naked, skin clinging to bones where the flesh should have been, covered with grime and draped in tattered rags. He could not have weighed more than fifty medium stones, just skin, and bones.

Izz's heart dropped back into place as the old man's hollow eyes suddenly widened and he gazed, fearfully around as if expecting someone to come out of the shadows at any time. The raunchy odor that reeked from him was repugnant, nearly overwhelming; and Izz had to scrunch his nose as he struggled to keep from retching. In a hoarse, disembodied voice that sounded like crumpling paper, he asked, "Where you came from? You not supposed to be here… are you? How you get here?" His dim eyes darted back and forth, unblinking in his thin face. "You must not be found here," he said as he motioned with his bone thin hands. "Come, come quickly." Rusted, clinking chains hung like bracelets from his scrawny wrists and ankles. The old man struggled as he shuffled along; his chains clanging over the stone floor as he walked.

Somehow Izz did not perceive this walking skeleton as an immediate threat. To tell the truth, it was almost impossible not to like him. Although in chains that ran from his wrists down to the ankles, he walked quickly, unhesitatingly, before Izz, urging him to follow. Izz's heart, which had jumped into a rattling thunder, was beginning to bounce back to normal as he followed the old man toward the burning torches.

"I comed from the northern kingdom of Nadda." Zappa spoke to Izz as they walked toward the torch lit area up ahead. "I was taken from the North borders of the Ebony Forest in the strength of my youth. I have not seed my family in mostly ten cycles of the sun…may haps more. I have not seed the moon, the sun, or the stars in as much time," Zappa continued as he took long, awkward sideways steps around Izz, stopping only to point the way.

"My name is Izz of the Islands of Zollerzon," was all Izz could manage in response.

Up ahead, he could hear the rattling and clinking more chains. When they reached the torch lit cove, Izz saw that the walls on both sides were lined with blazing torches, with yellow flames dancing on their ends; and choking black smoke pluming upward from their tops. In the dim sphere of light, Izz saw men and women with sunken bellies chained to the scum laden, slime covered walls. Izz could trace the outline of the unfortunate group, with jutting ribcages, bowed elbows, and pale skin stretched over bulging bones. There were piles of rubbish in the corners from which reeked a smell somewhere between perspiration and stagnant sewage water. In the back, there was a holding pen. An iron grid barred its entrance and framed with sagging timbers. The enclosure was low roofed and floored with stone. Zappa disappeared into the shadows and could be heard scraping the bottom of the barrel and then quickly returned.

He approached Izz carrying a small covered bowl. With an outstretched hand, he said, "You look hungry. Take this."

Zappa offered Izz a wooded bowl of some unidentifiable, uncooked food that smelled rotten, and a wedge of stale bread, a piece one would have not thrown to their dog. "It be fresh," Zappa said, as he licked the spoon he had used to scrape the bottom of the barrel and dropped it back into his breast pocket.

Izz took the bowl and looked down at it. He finally removed the lid and stared wearily at what looked like something between a bowl of pudding and a stew that jumped and shuddered nervously. Its smell was foul. Its aroma made his shrunken belly contract a little more, and the feeling that came with it rumbled through his intestines. But even as hungry as he was, he found that he had suddenly lost his appetite. He tried to return the bowl, saying, "I just could not…" as he stared at the half starved looking people leering hungrily around him." Give it to one of them."

Zappa pushed the bowl back toward Izz and said, "Go on, it be all right. We all eaten."

Not wishing to offend Zappa and those staring with expressions of generosity stain across their skeletal faces, Izz slowly wiped his hands across his dirt encrusted shirt. With two fingers, he scooped out an unpleasant green colored swill, dripping a sticky liquid. He reluctantly raised his fingers to his mouth and took the muck in. It was disgusting! Izz swished the mouthful around, half expecting the taste to improve. It did not. He gulped it down and waited to be sick. When nothing happened, he ate a little more. They had to have bellies of metal to stomach this.

Izz looked around, with pity on his face as he shook his fingers over the bowl and then, much more concerned in the welfare of the other prisoners than the offering, he gladly turned his attention to them as he picked some of the rank bits and pieces from between his teeth. From behind the garbage, there came odd shrieks and groans from the background. Izz put the bowl aside and took a torch from the wall. There, underneath his flare, against the walls the torchlight flickered, drawing his attention to where roll after roll of men and women were chained, crouched and hunched down in their places in silence, crowded together in appalling conditions. Some were all but naked. Others were in filth worn rags, all covered with scum and open, running sores, making a perversion of the meaning of humanity. What greater hell was there on Zia than this?

The stench of body waste made Izz gag in absolute disgust. He resisted with every ounce of will he could summon not to shrink back with repulsion. In the deeper shadows, he saw more human body shapes and found more bleak faces, behind boulders and rocks. The rags that still clung to their emaciated bodies revealed more than they concealed. They were scarred all over, as tattered as they were thin, caked with dirt and blood from routine beatings. Still farther back were even more tangled bodies of imprisonment, wrapped in chains, living by torchlight, shadows being the only reality they knew. Everywhere he looked, Izz saw a sea of pale fleshed, shrunken people, living ghosts too long starving to death, waiting only for their final demise. Their large eyes widened by abuse, torture, and exhaustive labor stared glassy eyed with uncertainty and permanent fear. Izz could not believe what he saw there lit by the flickering torches. It was the vilest, most loathsome place he had set eyes on. It was a place without fresh air, where swarms of flies would have endlessly droned if they could exist in a hole so remote from the sun.

From the far background came a faint, melancholy, whimpering sound; and Izz saw movement in the darkness. He took the torch and swept it toward the noise. In the light, he saw small, sleazy cages filled with tiny, gleaming, terrified eyes looking out through the bars like caged animals. They were the hollow eyes, of dirty faced children, with runny noses and bloated bellies, penned in metal cages with scarcely enough room to turn around, with a cruelly barred door to let rank air out and keep the children in when they were not needed. Their expressions were fixed and glazed imprisoned not only physically, soul, and spirit as well. Thick dust caked the remnant rags that still cleaved to their fragile bodies. The smell of decay rose from each cage. Izz felt the blood drain from his face. "What is the purpose of all this?" he asked in a stunned voice.

Zappa stepped forward. "We were brunged here to this evil, too wicked place, made beasts of burden to look for lost treasure of Dark Lords. Legend say be hidden in belly of forsaken mountain when last days of ancient Great War of Zia be. I myself was stolen away in the primes of my youth, taken from my families, from edge of Forbidden Forest of Zia. When we be sick or be too wored out, we be taken away, never seed again. We falled sick and dead too many."

Zappa's eyes suddenly seemed to gloss over with remembrance. "Freedom promised to who find the golden Book of Foretelling. I myself find book in my youth, but I still here, chained, worked near death, punished bad for the smallest wrong." Zappa held up his left hand defiantly, where three fingers were missing, a wound he wore with pride. "This is for tempt escape. But now, I be empty, worned, and living under black shadow of death," he muttered. "The treasure trove said be hid by greatest earthquake. Nother bigger one coming soon. I knowed. I did not haded an education but I be smart. I heared Baddlock self say prophecy foretell one that find treasure be king over Zia."

On hearing this, Izz's eyes widened slightly and then narrowed. He pushed that thought away, abandoning it to the present. "Why the children?" he asked in a confused tone.

"The childrens be use search out deepest shafts only small child, can get, in where small for man. It sad, most die in collapse tunnel. Sometime childrens go down hole never seed again. We all worked until dead from tired. Most children be sick and die if they keeped with no sun and clean air for more than one Zia turn of season. The price for treasure be too, too so big."

"Where are the guards?" Izz asked as he feverishly looked through his satchel to find his unlocking tools.

Zappa answered, "Since I beronged I speak to none but my new family. Guards thinked me be death, mute, they speak free in my hearing. There be much talk of war on the Zia world. There be big talk about alignment in sky, and pure maiden of royal blood be kill to darkness god on evil altar to be let go foul wicked."

Izz found his tools and quickly worked to open Zappa's crude, pockmarked rust stained lock. "Do you know where this altar is located?" Izz asked, trying hopelessly to contain his desperation.

"Yes, it be not far for here," Zappa pointed to a passage that led to a manmade altar like archway that seemed to glow with a pulsating glare. "It be a too, too much wicked place, it be."

As time slipped by, time pressed in and became more vitally critical. Izz reached again for his satchel and pulled out a small ax. He handed it to Zappa and said, "Here, use this to break the other locks." Zappa snatched up the ax like an owl would snatch a mouse and held it to his face, gazing over its sharp edge with a crazed look. Some kind of energy seemed to surge from the ax into his hand, and there pasted on his face was a disturbing excitement. He paused for a moment as he clasped the ax to his breast and then stepped up to the nearest wall. Zappa ran a dirty hand through his hair and used the sweat of it to wipe away the grime on the wall to reveal a scratched in map. "I knowd a way out. I be smarterest," he said as he tapped his temple. Zappa had recreated a map from details filed away in his brain of his very near escape.

Izz came close as Zappa pointed to the map with his bony, two fingered hand and explained. "Along northern path there be passage. It lead to grand chamber. On north face be open to green valley where there be water, food, and freed." Zappa pointed to the other end of the map. "This be where wicked altar be. I never goed beyond this mark"—Zappa pointed to a scratch on the wall with his two good fingers—"where awful scream of the lost never end. It be the heart of evil self. But I seed the maiden took there. Most beauty she be." Izz was made painfully aware that precious moments were ticking by, gathered his wits about him. He turned to Zappa and said, "I must make haste."

Zappa looked deep into Izz's eyes as he scratched his bony chin. "You be coming among us, be you not?" Zappa seemed to read Izz's mind. "No! You can no go there! I seed men drive mad from what they seed there. You no know. You must no go there, my new friend." He could see in Izz's eyes that his mind was made up. "I beg for you, Izz of Zollerzon, please say to me you no go there. It be heart of evil self!" He saw that Izz's mind was fixed. "Oh no, my friend, why," Zappa moaned woefully and repeated the plaguing question, "I beg you, why ."

The look in Izz's eyes told Zappa that he was wasting his breath. "Fare ye well my friend," Izz said as he took a torch from the wall and turned away. Stunned into silence with an inner feeling of despair, Zappa turned quickly with a blank expression on his face and began frantically chopping away at the locks of the cages that bound the rings that freed the child slaves in droves. Zappa collected his frayed scarf and ragged cloak; his two fingered hand trembled as he knotted it around his thin neck, watching as Izz walked away. He whispered to the whiffing haze, "Is there no thing I can said to change your spirit, my friend." These were the last words spoken on the matter between them.

With torch in hand, well aware that he was running short on time, Izz lost none. When he had reached the archway, he heard Zappa call out, "I mark path for you my friend. Luck with you be."

Izz turned back to see that most of the slaves had already thrown off their yokes and were on the move. Freedom up to now had become something they thought they could only dream about. He could hear the doors that imprisoned the children creaking on their rusty hinges as they were being forced open. The children began to crawl out with a whine, their skeletal forms covered in dirt like grubs. They came hobbling out of the darkness like little animals escaping from a caged trap. He watched as one slave followed Zappa, then another. Like a procession of scarecrows, they followed one another, the stronger ones supporting those who could barely walk. Izz could see the yellow glow of their torches in the darkness as they hurried to free themselves. Some went back and assisted those who fell behind as they encouraged them with words of hope. One by one, they helped one another out of the living nightmare of death.

As Izz briefly looked on at the pale faces of these people, these children, leaving the now empty slaveholding behind them, he could no longer feel sorry for himself, nor pity his situation. In the corner of Izz's mind was the realization that if he did not leave that moment, he might not find Zuree in time. Fearing that he might already be too late, he turned to face the unknown. Down here, it was always night, and night had become his most dreaded enemy. His yellowish sputtering torch sent shadows skipping over the jagged surface as he quickly moved toward the arched entrance. As the footfalls of the escaping slaves faded, the place suddenly grew strangely still and silent like the calm before the next tempest.

As Izz took his first step beyond the archway, he thought things could not possibly get any worst. But he had no way of knowing he had unwittingly walked through the threshold of what would turn into a hellish nightmare beyond his imagination. He felt an urgency to hurry, as if the infinite time structure of the universe had, by some means, been suddenly quickened. The cave floor before him was hidden beneath a shroud of thick, smoky mist that crept along over the stone flooring like a cauldron of vapor that gave off smelly sulfuric fumes.

With no perceivable ventilation, the smoke turned into a haze that hung in the air like a creeping cloud. From where Izz stood against the torchlight, he could see there was absorbing darkness up ahead. Izz put his best foot forward and began to walk along a path that seems suspended between two sheer drops of obscurity on either side, where dislodged pebbles plunged for lengthy counts before finding the bottom. He was swept along, guided only by a torch that guttered and almost went out at every turn. He followed its light into the darkness as he swept it from side to side along the walls guided only by the glow of Zuree's stone. In a small, still voice, Izz heard someone from beyond the slave station say, "Quickly, let us get out of this living hell."

Thirteen

Doorsteps of Doom

Izz had lost all track of time, nagged with the foreboding feeling that he may have lost too much time that perhaps he was already too late. Led by the stone through various turns, he made his way through the creepy passageway Zappa had claimed led the Altar of Damnation. Almost immediately, he was met by a gloomy, airless, and stuffy mist that threw shifting shadows crossed his eyes like the same eerie, rippling motions his torchlight cast with every step he took. At times, Izz could not distinguish whether it was he who was moving, or if it was just the movement of the deep, dark ghostly shadows that seemed to drift past him in obscurity? He looked overhead and saw repeating bonelike ribs that buttressed the walls and ceiling, lined in random order along the span of the corridor. The floor was an empty extension of nothing but bare, broken stone.

Izz reached a juncture where he sensed an abrupt change in the atmosphere. He felt the air around him thicken abruptly, warming as if an intensifying heat was seeping through the walls. The rising, sweltering temperature seemed to pierce him. The air currents seemed to pick up considerably, and the shadows looked graver than ever. There was a detectable crackling of electricity all around him as if evil itself was insidiously lurking around every crook, set to ambush him without warning. For an unfolding instance, Izz trembled; he forced himself to wipe his mind clean and then stepped forth. Izz continued along the passage deeper into the underworld. After almost another half a zetta with only Zuree's stone and the dingy light of his torch to find his way he found himself standing beneath another ominous entrance.

The irregularly arched opening was framed with pockmarked stone blocks interwoven into the cavern's walls. The door, half shrouded in darkness, was a large black stone block three times the height of a man, and twice as wide, framed in huge spiraling stone pillars and carved globes. Its entire surface was roughly cut with numerous cluttered, graven images. The massive door rested on no visible hinge, yet it seemed ready to swing open at a touch. At the center, the large black stone door structure bore the primitive marks of an ancient tool that had been used to chisel its pattern into the solid black block. What was written seemed to be yet another warning, in a style of lettering strange to Izz. He studied the makings carefully and puzzled out some of the words, but most of the graphics were too primitive and too strange. Izz thought long and hard, musing out some sense of their meaning. He peered at the markings through narrowed eyes, as if staring more intensely was going to change anything. However, from what he could make out, it was an ancient warning, for sure. The warning stated something like: *Beyond this point is imprisoned the heart of evil*, something about *impending doom and extremely unforgivable abominations,* and so on.

As if by a gravitational pull, he was drawn to the black stone door. It was covered with dust and cobwebbed from long disuse, and looked as if it had been sealed until the end of all time. Izz stepped onto the worn and bucked raised platform. The array of thick columns that supported the black door was covered with peeling spots and streaks of different shades of age stained red oxide fused with darker yellowing colors. He reached out and touched it, and the door moved.

Izz withdrew his hand quickly. The feel of it was as hot as the doorway to an infernal hell. He watched as the unbolted door opened before him, as if of their own accord. The outline of the door changed, as shifting shadows moved across it. The massive stone had to be perfectly balanced for it to have moved at his slightest touch. Izz gave the black stone a simple push, and the door flung wide open like a gaping black mouth into purgatory. Its stony creak was high pitched like the cry of a cat. The door scraped an arc along the dusty stone floor as a black fog seeped in through the bleak doorway and hung in the air around him. Beyond the doorway, there was the ever present blue black darkness of the underworld. The lightlessness entered Izz's eyes and merged with memories of the deepest, darkest, starless night. The air within was oppressively heavy, sticky with dank odors that permeated the hot breath of repulsive heat. He froze for a moment lost in thoughts of *warning* and foreboding premonitions. And as soon as Izz took one step past the threshold of the odd black door, the door closed and whispered shut behind him.

He almost at once felt something foul afoot. An impression of utter wickedness hammered him like a hard blow to the gut. As he entered, the opening noticeably darkened. There was something, beyond any doubt, undeniably amiss. Izz nervously chewed on his lower lip as he stepped forward, plunging into the liquefied darkness, dauntlessly going where no man in his right mind would dare to go. Crazed with love and concern, his heart would not permit the reason that logic was pounding into his senses to deter him from his quest to save his beloved. A kind of seventh sense that Izz could not name urged him on. He forced his tense muscles to relax as he pulled almost blindly through. He convinced himself that he was not afraid of the darkness—that is until a mental scream in his head stopped him in mid step.

His spirit was perplexed by a repetitious sound that he could not place at first. Whatever it was, Izz got the sense of a concerted outcry. As if thousands of souls were lamenting all at once. Suddenly, as he listened, he knew what the noise was that came in waves—slightly louder, then fainter, then louder again. He could hear screams! He remained motionless, rooted where he stood, listening, unable to pinpoint the source of the faint, faraway wailing. The mournful clamor seemed to float toward him from deep within the far end of the cavity and bled through his resolve.

Izz of Zia

The only other sound was that of his frayed breaths and the thump of his blood pulsating in his ears.

Izz tried not to listen to the horrible high pitched screams and took a moment to bring himself under control. But still, the distant mindless screams continued at the edges of his mind in the back of his head. Izz next thought he heard a deep, doomful voice that came out of the darkness beyond, seemingly through the stone walls. "Come forth! Join those that eternally beg for death. Never is sooner than you will ever leave this place," the dark, cruel voice whispered. It was not a voice at all but a savage, animalistic snarl. Spooked, Izz looked around to see who had spoken, but he could not know where the words had come from. Izz waited for the pummeling in his chest to subside before continuing. *Calm your mind,* Izz told himself.

Thoughts of impending doom made him jittery. "No!" Izz resoundingly pushed the bristly feeling of fear away and held it at bay with every ounce of courage he possessed. Again and again, he heard yet other distant sinister screams, disconnected in pitch and rhythm, but continuous, like the spirit of death venting its last throes. No matter how hard he tried, he could not shut them out, and somehow Izz knew that he would have to follow them to their source. He felt an icy, prickling fear begin to crawl up his spine, refusing to let him rest.

Suddenly, for no understandable reason, an eerie draft wafted a thick, foul cloak of air from nowhere. His torch flame sputtered, flickered, and was almost choked as if blown by a forceful wind. However, there was no wind down there. There was a rustling like something moving in the realm of the dark, swirling shadows in its path. Now and then, Izz stared into the darkness ahead of him, hoping not to see anything approaching, wishing with all his heart not to discover the source of the screaming. At the same time, he was afraid that something was sneaking up behind him. All the while, fragmented thoughts whispered like phantoms in the darkest crooks of his mind of dreadful danger that lay in wait for him. But it was not the darkness itself that concerned him; it was what might be lurking within the darkness that terrified him. His concerns were compounded by the scream like wails that seemed to whip around him like a spiny weft periodically and then flutter away. Izz had to persuade himself again and again that he was not afraid.

Time seemed to roll away from him like a receding tide in a timeless sea. Eventually, he found himself in a passage laden with the odor of brimstone. He thought he could feel a burning breeze drifting through the corridor. It was different this time as if he had crossed a barrier where evil itself originated. He could feel resistance against his movement as if he was traversing through a viscous, burdensome fog that seemed to be growing, spreading, and closing in. It was so odd, almost as if the air itself was jeeringly mocking him. Izz increased his pace through the unfamiliar play of inexplicably hot, swirling shadow patterns. He could feel a tormenting kind of doubt that began running like a corrosive, liquefied alloy through his veins. He was overwhelmed by the feeling that he would not be walking away from this place. The part of him that had become his enemy whispered fragmented thoughts like evil phantoms from the dark corners of his mind. *Your flesh will rot on your bones in the depths of this realm.*

He could feel his hands getting very damp. He drew in a shallow breath as he attempted to dry them on his pant legs as he passed the torch from one hand to the other. Suddenly the monotonous sinister feeling of being watched returned and fell upon him. He arched his torch back and forth, but saw nothing; and yet he could not rid himself of the feeling that he was being watched. He turned in a slow circle to be sure nothing was sneaking up behind him. Then he heard a bitter sounding voice, "You will never leave this world."

Startled at the sound of the voice, Izz paused and looked all around. All he saw was his own shifting shadow casting deformed and twisted silhouettes on the irregular walls of the abyss as he crept past them. Yet on he went plunging even deeper into the chasm of the underworld. Was it all just in his head? He did not want to believe he heard anything. They were only inner imaginations forming in the deepest recesses of his head. He decided his time would be better spent hastening to his journey's end, where ever that may be. But the words remained hanging in the air. Then out of nowhere, Izz felt an unsettling feeling as if someone or something was about to reach out of the darkness and seize him. He felt his stomach muscles tighten in anticipation. There was something infinitely evil up ahead; he could feel it in the very depths of his soul but was unable to place it. He wished with all his heart and soul that he had never come here.

In the foreground, Izz thought, he had seen the flash of a moving shadow. His steps slowed as the illusion vanished, and when he reached the spot where Izz thought he had seen something move, he found nothing. This time it had been only a shadow and nothing more. Izz straightened and squared his shoulders and forced himself forward, bracing himself against what he might see, ever rebuking the malignant existence growing in the vibrating darkness. Then off to his right, he heard a strange, unexpected noise. He turned his head slowly and saw a shadow pass over his face. He had no clue what had caused it; then he caught a fleeting blur of something disappearing like a ghost out of the corner of his eyes. He stood there, watching and listening, ready to spring backward the instance anything gave a hint of movement. Then again, he turned full circle, straining his eyes to see through the darkness. There was nothing there. He turned back, and one after the other rubbed his eyes with the heel of his free hand. He thought his eyes had to have been deceived by the drifting mist.

Suddenly something growled—a bottomless, low, thrilling, forceful, and beastly growl out of the dark. There had to be someone or something there! He gave all ten of his fingers a preparatory twitch. He tightened his grip on his torch, and then his dagger slipped quietly from its sheath with a soft metallic ring. Before he saw anything, he felt an ominous presence pricking against his skin, and Izz knew beyond any doubt that he was not alone. Something was about to happen at any moment; he could sense it in the nub of his spinal cord as he felt fear run up his spine like a chilling steel rod. He felt the hair on the nape of his neck crackling as they stiffened on end. Just outside the limits of his torch, just past his field of vision, in the shadows, circling shades of doom threw their flickering fragments in the darkness.

At a distance, beyond the point where his torch's light refused to go, Izz could make out a dark outline. He sensed that something stood there, as still as oblivion, taking in his measure, waiting, preparing to strike suddenly and unexpectedly, when the first opportunity arose. He timidly moved a few paces forward to get a better look. Then suddenly, *whoosh!* Whatever had been, there was unexpectedly gone without a trace. Frowning in confusion, Izz stared blindly up the path and then turned and gazed back to where he had come. The awareness of a lurking danger grappled with his nerves and made his stomach go queasy. Fear clutched at him from the darkness. Izz forced himself to push on, overriding all the ominous warnings. At this point, it would have been just as easy to go forward as it would be to go back. After all, he had endured so far; he dared not fall short now.

A stone's throw away, in the twilight, Izz could make out some kind of wicked imposing labyrinth that presented an ominous foreboding scene before him. Jagged, tombstone like rock formations jutted up like ribs protruding from the spine of the monstrous, craggy ridgeline, looking much like markers in a cemetery. The strange landscape created an entangled vista of countless weird abstract forms twisted by buckling titanic selves. Izz threaded his way through the tall outcrops as he shone his torch over the rocky maze. As the light from his torch traversed across odd brown and yellow strata and formations, he noticed configurations of symbols etched into the wall that was covered with a layer of something that looked like soot. Izz took a long look up the boneyard–like passage and saw strange stalking shadows everywhere merging and disappearing into the inky blackness as they stretched into the farthest depths. He could feel evil waiting for him to come into its nebulous pitch darkness. Shadowy, creeping, lurking things called out to him, threatening him and daring him to come forth. Izz's iron will to find Zuree clad him with the armor he needed to go on. Very slowly, very carefully, he went forward into the caliginous murk. He had one eye on the subterranean stone forest ahead, the other on the passage he had just come from. And he had his third eye's vision bending around the corners of every rocky pillar in the distance.

King Ozzdon watched from the battlement of the main keep, were down in the courtyard below zealous warriors armed for battle assembled along the southern end of the kingdom. What the soon to be combatants, drawn by duty and commitment from every class of society, knew about war, they had learned from books. The Sons of Zia, civilian and military personnel alike, bowmen, spearmen, and swordsmen were all fully clad in armor. The gleaming of their boots and brass evoked the common member of Edawn's society to feel as if they had inherited a manner of nobility and princely affluence. The incendiary bombardment continued, and most of the Northern Kingdom was engulfed in flames or lay in ruin. The king's heart ached with the thoughts of the impending carnage and worried sick over the state of his missing daughter.

As he waded through the ranks of his generals he conceal the vexation of his spirit among his troops, instead he radiated valor, confidence, and optimism, while a thousand conflicting thoughts clashed in his mind. He thought about changing his plan to launch a retaliation strike at least every few moments. The idea of an all out counterattack was unsettling. There had to be a better way than this. He whispered to himself, "Why am I going along with this bad course of action?"

It's unthinkable madness! What will happen if we fail? All too aware of the time it would take the reinforcements to reach them from the outer kingdoms, he surmised, *This is our best gamble. It will at least buy us some time. I wish I could be positive about this decision, but I am filled with doubts.*

The desperate situation was forcing him to take drastic action. King Ozzdon gathered himself up, knowing he would need all his wits for the battle to come. In a loud voice filled with conviction, with his unsheathed royal sword high in the air, King Ozzdon addressed his troops, "This will be a day to remember! Any man who has nothing worthwhile fighting for, and is willing to die for, is a miserable creature who has nothing worth living for. War is a loathsome thing, a thing that should be despised, but it is not as repulsive as living under the tyranny of those that will to be our masters. Our homeland is in peril, the transgressors that are on the march have come against us, seeking to steal, rape, and destroy our entire way of life. War is, at times, an unavoidable evil. Never, ever believe that it is anything more than pure hell on earth. There can never be any honor in the killing of men. Many here will undoubtedly shed their blood on this day, and some will surely die, but you will live forever in the hearts of those that go forth before you with the truth that makes men free."

"We must fight as one. Every man is a vital link in this great chain. Watch your brother's back, and he will watch yours. Do not fear to be afraid. There can be no true courage without fear. Let us now send these disciples of darkness back into the deepest hell from where they came. Sons of Edawn, we must answer the threat. Rise up now and let the storm of war break loose."

While the king secured the strap of his helmet, a tumultuous awakening of lion heartedness roared in agreement all through the kingdom, as the battle cry rose until the kingdom's towers seemed to tremble.

Hearing the uproar and its unmistakable meaning, Ammiz ordered that anything that could be used as a bandage to be collected and every available person, including those children of age, be prepared to assist the wounded that were sure to flood in.

On the northern hilltops, Baddlock, who had been working himself into a terrible temper, widened his eyes and cocked his head toward Edawn upon hearing the commotion. He knew that fast approaching was the moment that was sure to make him shiver with delight. Tigbone leaned to one side on his shorter leg as he chewed on his dirt blacken nails and was relieved that Baddlock's anger was subsiding. Intoxicated with the lust for blood, the Wicked Warlock Wizard laughed with sheer delight as he said. "Come, come, we are yearning to receive you. What do they wait for? My warriors are eager. Come forth and feel the bite of our razored steel."

Tigbone laughed a little laugh of glee. "Methinks they be chickenhearted." Then his smile drained from his face as if he had again suddenly remembered the ill fate of his pet chicken.

Baddlock ordered the archer into formation along the front lines. He commanded Kuvazo, the Catapult Master, "Gauge our stone catapults for a close range attack."

Meanwhile, in the belly of the beast, the droned out screams continued, and Izz could not be sure he did not just imagine it. His senses stayed astutely alert, his eyes never stopped moving, searching out every nook and corner. His uneasiness was growing with every passing instant. His dagger was in the strike position like a coiled spring, prepared to react to the slightest sign of danger. Deeper and deeper Izz went down the long path that Zuree's stone marked, without any other reason than the fact he had no other earthly clue where to find his beloved. He kept listening, looking, and feeling things out. Izz kept seeing, sketchy apparitions just beyond the edge of sight, shadows that seemed to stretch out and reach toward him. Every so often a darkened image seemed to flash across his vision, making howling sounds that had no logical explanation, strange noises, disturbed pebbles crunching underfoot. He forced himself to rule over his fears.

Izz crept silently in the direction of the noise, preferring to face the faceless thing he just knew to be lurking in the shadowy darkness. He held his breath as something black flashed across the passage ahead of him. Izz suddenly noticed that he was clutching the hilt of his dagger so tight that he had lost the feeling in his hand. His pounding heart thundered over the persistent screaming that faintly echoed in the foreground throughout the chaos and was by now becoming more and more monotonous. His breath quickened, his eyes narrowed, the surface of his skin prickled, and his chest tightened. Izz reached the spot where he thought he had caught a blur of motion but again saw nothing. He wished for a real flesh and blood adversary to battle, to see, to strike at, one he could draw blood from. He swept his torch along the cave floor; there were no signs, and no footprint marked nothing.

You see, it has all been just a figment of your mind, he told himself. *Only a trick of the light, toying on your overactive imagination, making you see things that are not real, only mere shapes and shadows. It was a trick of the wits, or the drifting smoke deceived my eyes.* If only he could convince himself, it would have made him feel much better.

And just when he was starting to feel better, suddenly out of nowhere, by some dark instinct, Izz was made painfully aware that something was standing right behind him, charging the very air around him. He froze, choking on a gasp! Every hair over the surface of his entire body stiffened and began to vibrate. Izz felt as if someone had pressed cold fingers to his throat. The back of his neck bristled from the draught of breath hot upon it. Each nerve along his neck and back was pulled taut as twisting wires stretched to their breaking point. Too afraid to turn around, Izz closed his eyes as he fought to catch his breath. He gagged a deep, ragged breath and held it against a sudden awaited impact, not knowing when death would strike.

Right there and then, he was overpowered with a sudden, flesh crawling terror he had not ever felt up until that moment. He thought he was about to soil himself, expecting an icy blade to fall upon his neck at any moment. Izz forced himself to react. He peered quickly down over his shoulder with dread, whipped around, warding off the unseen with his torch, and then slashing out with his blade against the supernatural evil that threatened to envelop him. His razor sharp blade stuck out so fast that it was lost in its blurred arch as it droned in a flash through the thickening air.

Izz of Zia

The room erupted into depraved laughter. Izz peered into the darkness as he whirled around wildly, prodding with his torch, expecting to catch the hidden enemy by surprise. He believed that an army of bizarre entities was moving out of the dark against him. He feared that some hideous power from deep within the underbelly of Skullsdoom was about to engulf him. Yet there was nothing there. The foe, if there was a real foe, remained unseen, and elusive.

For a moment, he watched for a sign of anything unexpected, staring into the dark unknown until his eyes hurt. When he neither saw nor heard anything, or sensed anything ready to pounce on him, he lowered his dagger and laughed a hollow laugh, amused at the madness forming inside his head. *It was just the trick of the light or the lack thereof.* He relaxed his grip on his dagger but did not return it to its sheath, not just yet.

In a conscious effort, Izz forced himself to reason. When he turned to continue, he was abruptly confronted by a strong gust of biting wind. It was no ordinary wind, however. It was a perverted, spine tingling, burning wind that carried with it the powerful scintillations of ghost movement at its edge. Izz wheedled his dagger and slashed out at the onrushing tempest that somehow seemed to have an eerie awareness of its own. His torch beat against the air, batting at the intangible, unseen phantom as it whirled around and careened past him. Izz took a step and swung to his right to face what felt like a disturbance laced with evil in the air. Then as suddenly as it had arrived, the flurry just vanished. Gone with it were the dreamlike negative images that had drifted before his field of vision. How could anyone defend against something that intermingled with the darkness? He kept moving forward as his gaze roved over his immediate surroundings.

Izz reluctantly took extra time searching out here and there, to the right, to the left, in front and behind. He made far reaching circular sweeps with his torch, avoiding the deepest, darkest shadows as he went. There was something inexplicably ominous in the air as if someone was holding their breath waiting in the shadows just ahead. The darkness itself felt as if it would suck him into its core. As he advanced, the light from his torch seemed to cause the very shadows to cringe away from themselves as if trying hopelessly to ward off the light.

"It is all an illusion," Izz said out loud to himself as his shaky legs forced his feet to move forward, as his toes seemingly curled back in the opposite direction.

Through thin ribbons of drifting smoke, Izz moved, turning in slow loops to be certain that nothing was encroaching on him. But little did he know of the horror that lay ahead. Just then, he heard a movement that was not of his making. He listened to a quiet, strange rustling from his right, left, or somewhere slightly behind him; he could not be sure. Izz turned around, trying to detect the source of the noise that sounded just above the ever persistent distant screaming, but before he could pinpoint its origin, it suddenly ceased and disappeared. Every strange sound left him rattled and jumping involuntarily. At the slightest noise of any wind or unseen spirit seemingly passing on their way to and fro, he turned to look but saw nothing, not a solitary thing. His senses were all concentrated forward, for movement, smell, or anything that indicated danger.

Suddenly, Izz stood frozen in the middle of the next step. Again out of nowhere, slightly off to the right, he could perceive the physical presence of something in front of him, something out of place, and something breathing heavily. Izz edged forward, drawing closer for a better look. His hand trembled around the hilt of his dagger as he clutched his fist down on it so tight that he could not feel it in his hand anymore. Suddenly, he saw a shadow within the shadows, keeping perfectly still and hidden. A pair of nonhuman eyes cloaked in the darkness stared back at him. His attention centered now on the shadow. "Who is there?" Izz called out. His only answer was a voiceless snarl. Without blinking, he stared at the glassy eyes in astonishment. Then a drifting haze crept in and obscured them from his vision. The mist cleared briefly once again, revealing two motionless, animalistic eyes with no human traits, glinting like two dim red globs through the gloom.

Izz of Zia

For an eternity, Izz stood there, numbed and immobile. He stared at the piercing eyes glaring back at him with sinister, steely observation. It seemed it was trying to determine if Izz himself was real. Unsure of his own eyes, Izz raised his torch toward the abnormal silhouette until he could make out some kind of head, neck, chest, and shoulder. All at once, a figure, out of a nightmare, appeared amid the darkness, clearly not human. It flickered in and out of sight in the discharging light that fluttered before him. Cloaked in darkness, an image surpassing his most horrified phantasm emerged from behind the clouded curtain. Izz's eyes enlarged in shock, and his heart smote him with fear. Izz searched wildly, for a place to retreat; but instead, he froze in startled distress at the shadowy vision before him. It was like one of those dreams where one wanted to run from a monster, but the harder one tried, the more that their legs seemed detached. He opened his mouth and strangled on a long, silent, shuddering scream. He wanted to cry out, but he could not draw a breath. Then he heard an agonizing mournful groan, and it took him a moment to realize that the deep, prolonged grunt had come from him.

Izz's mind was racing. *This cannot possibly be real!* His brain tried to convince him that it was just a figment of his wild imagination. An illusion brought about by a mind that had been in the darkness for too long. Izz fixed his torchlight. It took a while for his pupils to focus fully and much longer for his mind to acknowledge the dreadfulness of what the torch revealed. As the light revealed, the creatures obscured features Izz looked the beast up and down. The grisly thing was beyond the bounds of his capacity to make sense of.

The monstrous presence looked upon Izz as if something had been plunked from the mind of someone's demented madness and given form and shape. Like a giant cross between a warthog and a reptile, it was more grotesque than Izz's conception could have ever conjured. Its oversized shape was remotely like that of a man, with the utterly unnatural, grayish skin of a reptile that appeared and smelled as if it had just dredged through a lake of putrid scum. It seemed to have a crablike skeletal exterior studded with warty projections the size of walnut halves and bony ridged protrusions everywhere. Its huge twisted limbs hung in disarray at its side, along its bloated belly, seemingly possessing the power to crush him like a worm.

Izz's eyes were gaping wide and staring, blinkingly trying to believe what they were seeing. Then gradually, he took in the detailed terror of the creature before him. Its outward appearance was like no animal he had ever seen before. It looked more man like than a beast. The decrepit, humanlike carcass looked more dead than alive, riddled all over with small holes from which long tubular maggots crawled in and out of. Its head looked like a badly butchered turkey buzzard with teeth. Its face was one from a horrid hallucination, a mass of putrid, pustule rot, but somehow it managed to open what looked like a mouth that came yawning wide open. It let out an inhuman scream that electrified the atmosphere, making the surface of Izz's skin prickle with goosebumps.

As the creature let out a roar that echoed from every wall, it's sound almost ending in a whimper, it exhaled a black cloud like a puff of stench and bellowed out a decayed tooth. All Izz could manage to do was stare wide eyed at the demonic ogre glaring back at him as nasty flicks of spittle pelted him. Izz held his torch out in front of him in an unconscious weapon like position and raised his dagger to thwart off the petrifying, gnarled creature.

At that instant, Izz wished nothing more than to bolt wildly like a frantic chicken being chased by an ax wielding butcher, but it was too late. The abnormality seemed to swell up as it stepped forward. Izz's eyes became twin spheres of bulging wide eyed terror as he took a step back and halfheartedly raised his dagger defensively in front of him. Whatever it was it was up in Izz's face, eye to eye, to have stabbed it would have probably only anger it. But even if he had wanted to, he could not move for the sear fear that pressed down on his heart. Izz held his breath when he saw a burly, warty hand reaching out of the darkness to clasp him by the throat with its giant clawed fist and drew him in closer. Izz wanted to slash out with his dagger, but hesitated and only glared back like a startled deer seemingly waiting for the motivation of pain to set in. The ghastly beast seemed to be studying Izz. It could smell the undefiled blood that flowed in his veins and was perplexed. It had never seen anything that still possessed an untainted soul within it, not since the great fall. Still not believing what it beheld, it leaned forward, squinting, uncertain of what it was looking at. Izz was the most unusual flesh born thing that it had ever encountered in the underworld.

Izz's mind focused on pure horror as the sight he was looking at surged through his wits' end. He could scarcely bring himself to look directly into its unholy, smoldering eyes. As the demon creature tightened its iron, viselike grip on him it drew him eyeball to eyeball, as whatever it was bore its jagged teeth. Izz's presence should have been impossible, inaccessible to those in living physical bodies, and no unbeguiled human had ever entered this sector of the realm before. Izz gagged, barely able to breathe! Then unexpectedly, as Izz looked into the two orbs that mimicked eyes, he thought he had seen a fleeting glimpse of fear flash across somewhere beyond the monster's eyes.

Out of nowhere, a sudden immortal roar of terror tore throughout the darkness, vibrating the very walls of the cavern. The outcry sounded like something between a falling stack of iron rods and the high pitched whine of hundreds of agitated pigs. The shrill reverberated and rumbled over the oscillating darkness, drowning out the uninterrupted screams in the background. It was almost as if all evil had suddenly sensed his presence at once. The creature took a long, raspy breath and stared unflinchingly for a brief moment. Then its glassy, unblinking eyes suddenly went wide with terror and seemed to glaze over with the shroud of death. Everything Izz had heard and seen chilled his blood with fear as terror pounded in and out of his heart.

Just then, the creature unexpectedly released Izz. He fell to his knees and, in sudden fright, bolted to his feet. The beast cringed and fell back, moaning. As it twisted away to seek refuge in the darkness, it turned briefly and spoke in a strange, scary tongue, which sounded like nothing more than ranting gibberish. In its next breath, its mouth continued shouting words in a peculiar unknown tongue. And yet from its tone, Izz somehow understood that the words that were roaring in his ears was a foreboding, warning for him not to enter. There was no way out. It was an outcry that Izz knew he could never get out of his head, nor would he ever forget those haunted terror filled eyes.

Get out! Get out before it's too late. Run! Run, you oaf!

Izz recoiled at the voice exploding inside his head. The nightmarish creature's receding, a long, loud, piercing screech of fright ripped agony and torment into the air. As the frantic living dead thing withdrew, it left a trail of stinking globs of scum that oozed out of the soles of its feet. The rhythm of slogging footsteps and heavy breathing and moans faded away as it slipped back into the darkness until it was just a blurred, inky shadow. From the farthest recesses of the cavern, a boiling black cloud appeared that seemed to reach out to drag the tortured phantom back into the ebbing shadows. It turned misty and transparent, until it faded into the void from which it came, as if it had never been. Real or unreal, he wished he had never seen it at all.

Izz's eyes refocused on the subterranean chamber around him. He fell back trembling against an outcrop of rocks. His nerves were raw and blistered. As he tried to catch his breath, he stared in disbelief, trying to clear the searing images from his mind and ridding himself of the stench from his nostrils. Despite the horrible up close encounter, and in spite of having seen with his own eyes, the logical part of his mind still attempted to persuade him that it just could not be true. It was too ghastly, too unsettling, and too unbelievable to be real. It had to be a hallucination created of a brain that had been deprived of sleep, robbed of sunshine and in need of fresh air for far too long.

None of this could be real. That was what Izz's mind told him. Izz repeated the evasion until he almost believed it.

Izz's stomach churned as he sucked in a short breath through his teeth and pulled his face into a tight lipped grimace.

Then his torchlight picked up something in front of him, and he noticed the decayed tooth in a small pool of slime at his feet. He probed the tooth with the edge of his dagger and raised the stained blade to his face as acidic bubbles boiled on its tip. Then he gulped. "A footprint!" And he knew by the nausea churning in his belly, that he had experienced something that had been far worse than any human mind could have possibly just imagined. Again, conquering fear, and panic broke through to him and made him tremble. It was far too strange. All the essential boundaries of his most central beliefs crumbled. It was madness. Knowing that worse horrors might even now be gathering against him in the dark, an overwhelming urge told Izz to run away to anywhere but where he was going. But his undying love for Zuree held him fast.

Out of the midst of nowhere, there was a sudden flash of light, which split the darkness, blazed outwardly in every direction and bathed every inch of the enormous vault with illumination. For the tiniest fraction of a moment, the cavern became brighter than midday. Izz closed his eyes against the brilliance as his pupils dilated and its innermost filters instinctively strained to screen out its vivid brightness. The astonishing and startling light flared from floor to roof and wall to wall with such bedazzling intensity and speed that Izz could not be sure that it had even occurred. In its pulsating wake, he heard an agonizing scream that sounded over all the other remote, distant screams. By the time Izz reopened his eyes, the light that had lasted no more than a twinkling of an instance had already slipped away as suddenly and unexpectedly as it appeared. The only indication that anything had ever actually happened was the blinding afterglow that was burned into the back of Izz's throbbing retinas and the swirling sensations of dancing patches of color.

After a moment of uncertainty, Izz stood and straightened himself up. For another moment, he stood trembling, bewildered, and amazed, feeling lucky to be still alive. He surveyed the scene before him as his torch continued to reveal nothing but the same unchanging shadows and the wearisome monotony of the darkness before him. In that brief instant, Izz stood stunned and reeling, his mind staggering at the unfathomable magnitude of depth into which his quest had swept him away. He remained bound up in knots as moments of profound silence passed, leaving him numbed stiff—that is, until something that had escaped his notice seized his attention.

At the farthest corner before him, from the same direction the faint screams were coming from, Izz saw a dim pulse of a yellowish orange phosphorescence glow, like that of an immense flickering torch waiting to set the entire underworld ablaze. Unable to turn away from his fate, Izz girded his loins. From there, he would go forth that he might fulfill his destiny, wherever that may lead him.

FOURTEEN

GATEWAY OF THE DAMNED

King Ozzdon's resolve to do what was in the best interest of his people was by now a foregone conclusion. For once, he did not both to consult the power of his crown. The king mounted his warhorse, Ivory. The mighty white stud was fitted with long silver armaments covering most of its face, neck, chest, and flanks. With its muscled haunches and legs, he easily carried his full armored weight and that of his rider. Ozzdon wheeled Ivory toward his army, gathered his reins back, and brought the horse to a halt before his generals. They all had one thing in common—a love for their king and a deep seated hatred for Baddlock and Dandork.

The great king for the first time was about to lead his forces against a fierce foe whose men greatly outnumbered his troops three to one. They were going up in opposition against armed forces that were equipped with immensely superior weaponry and held the upper hand of the lofty hillsides. They were in no doubt to bear grave losses. Ozzdon turned to encourage his troops, speaking not as their king but as their equal: "With all speed, let us wield our forces. I will lead the main attack up the middle as it is my obligation and privilege. Zandor and Kondor, you will lead the flanking forces. Do not separate yourselves from the main contingent until you are certain the time is right. Arius," the king, addressed his oldest friend and Chief Commander of Skymount's forces, "you bring the foot troops up the center and reinforce our frontal attack."

The king's stallion pranced back and forth as the king yet spoke: "Very soon we will confront the dreadful beast that has come down upon us, and there will be many losses. But the control of these lands must be held at any cost. We will have to lean heavily on stealth and strategy. Failure to stop Baddlock at Edawn's gates means the unthinkable. We must throw everything we have at them, in the hope of hindering and delaying them long enough for our reinforcements to arrive from the outer kingdoms. We cannot fail. If we fail, we are doomed to destruction, and all will come to darkness. An all out frontal attack seems like a blind craze, but I do not see any other alternative. Our ultimate objective is to rid the world of Baddlock and Dandork. Our plan is very straightforward, to forge forward and to keep advancing whether we have to go over, under, or through the whole Norticlan world to get to them. May the God of Ammiz be with us."

As the generals turned to assemble their men, King Ozzdon drew Zandor near and placed his hand on his shoulder as a father would a son, and spoke from the heart. "If I fall, grid my armor, take up my sword, and drive these rebellious sons of demons out of our kingdom back into the abyss from which they came."

"Nay, my Lord," Zandor answered, "you shall live to cut their hearts out with your own blade."

Kondor approached the two and reported, "All is in ready, my Lord."

The three commanders joined their brigades. King Ozzdon raised his voice to the heavens. "Sons of Edawn, grid on your armor, fit your helmets and grip your swords and shields. By the blood of our fathers, when tomorrow dawns, may Edawn still stand against the principalities of darkness, our common enemy. Stay separated until we are well under their catapults, then surge toward the center. Our main forces will attack up the middle, while our flanking forces attack their catapults. The fate of Zia is in your hands. May the Giver of all things grant you the courage to fight well."

Thousands of noble would be combatants knelt in a concentric circle of brotherhood and prayer. With their heads bowed to the ground, they sought spiritual encouragement in wordless worship each in their manner.

Izz of Zia

All the northern inner gates began to raise simultaneously, breaking the solemn spell.

The king once again drew his sword and raised it to the heavens and vowed, "From now on, we will do our talking with our swords, and if need be, we will fight to the death."

Ring, ring, ring rang out the sliding of metal. Thousands of swords forged in the same fire, honed to razor sharpness, gleaming with a familiar metallic shine were drawn. Steel slashed through the air, resonating and tracing a glimmering trail of light, as each warrior pledged his sword to their king. Then the war cry of the thousands reverberated all at once. And strength coursed through them with each escalating reverberation of their roar. Men bound their headgear. Cavalrymen swung up into their saddles and heeled their warhorses into position before the gates. Up and up groaned the main outer gates, to the North, east, and west. Massive metal grids rose, pointing their soot stained pikes toward the smoke filled skies.

A skeleton force, mostly those too old or young to bear arms, would remain on the northern battlement to keep up the appearance of a defense. The kingdom's colorful flags and pennants were unfurled, as restless horses snorted, jerked, and wrenched under their riders seemingly sensing what was to come. The Edawnian legions clamored, encouraged each other, and raised their voices to the heavens. Each knowing full well that they were just evading the thought of what they were about to confront face to face. The world stage was set, the lunatic offensive was about to begin, and there would be no illusion about what was soon to unfold. King Ozzdon's mission was to keep the enemy off balance until the reinforcements arrived. He realized that once he gave the signal, there could be no turning back. Once outside of the kingdom's protective walls, he would be carried away into the unpredictable realm. He would be just another vassal of in the grip of unknowable and uncontrollable fate.

With sword held in fist, the king gave the command: "Onward, Sons of Edawn!"

With Zandor and Kondor at his side, Ozzdon spurred his mount, Ivory, and led his armies forward. Thousands upon thousands of men emerged gallantly and poured out from all of Edawn's northernmost gates. The mass movement crowded in tighter behind their king. Outnumbered and out weaponed, yet their self assurance was the absolute assurance of those who had never been in a life threatening battle thinking they were ready for what awaited them.

Regiments and battalions gallantly executed a balanced, fluid patterned exodus in indescribable numbers, like a maddened sea's torrents breaking from their bounds. King Ozzdon quickly nudged his stallion into a gallop, moving to the head of the main frontal assault, while Commander Zandor and Commander Kondor led the outlying attacks. The cavalry was followed by the rushing tide of infantrymen led by General Arius. The dauntless leadership and personal courage of their king, commanders, and generals so inspired the men that they threw caution to the wind and rushed forth to seize victory at any cost. The open field stretched before them. Riders heeled their warhorses into a fast trot. Hooves thundered, and riding beast screamed as they were driven into a full speed gallop. The Edawnian military force bolted forth, horses pounding the earth like an unbridled storm. The flags and banners of Edawn snapped as they slashed through the air. The Edawnian army charged headlong, surrendering to the exhilaration of war, driven forward by the ethics of male gallantry and feat. Succumb by faith and obedience, spellbound by the legends and folklore and histories of the Great Wars that were mostly unknown; they went forth.

The Edawnian forces went up on the breadth of the earth and quickly closed the gap between them and Baddlock's opposing forces. As Edawn's cavalry came into the greatest kill zone of Baddlock's short range catapults, their reign of terror immediately began. With a clattering of trigger mechanisms sounding Baddlock's brutal stone catapults unleashed their payloads all at once. A shroud of huge stones that weighed almost half a ton peppered the sky overhead. In the time it took for several heartbeats, the screaming discharge of stones made landfall, pelting the oncoming riders like monstrous fists. So forceful was the barrage that it caused Zia to tremble under their stallions' thundering hooves, smashing horse and rider like worm and bug under a millstone. Striking stones cratered the area, tearing huge paths into the files of the oncoming riders, yet the surging front lines, instead of falling back, did not falter. They followed their king forward at a hastened pace. The king and his mounted troops charged headlong, into the waiting arms of destruction, and Baddlock obligingly devastated them as they rushed within the range of his catapults. It was a massacre, especially since the Edawnians had no catapult support because they were too far away, rendering them worse than useless.

The cavalry now neared the foothills, braving the full brunt of the cruel onslaught of the crushing stones. Fearlessly, they rode straight into the jaws of annihilation and mayhem. Man and beast toppled to the ground in twisted knots of flailing arms, legs, and hooves. Shocking screams of men and riding beasts rent the sky. Entangled horsemen were dragged mercilessly across the battlefield by pain crazed horses that rose and still had enough life in them to run. Once the advancing forces were under and out of the catapult's range, they hurled themselves forth with a terrible raging force against their hated enemies. They charged forward, seamlessly executing their inward maneuver in perfect oneness. Each unit responding as a whole, riders followed their leaders unquestioningly into the unfolding chaos.

As they approached the uncountable numbers of their enemy, the fermented odor of the Norticlan was thick in the air. Under the command of their tribal elders, the vast, dark opposing throng of archers sprang to life as the Edawnian armies came into range. It was a nightmarish cockroach's nest. The archers massed in military formation, like an animated monster, swiftly moving its tentacles into position like great snakes coiling and threatening to strike. A long drawn out animal like growl, made up of a thousand distinct rattling sounds, arose as the bowmen cocked and nocked their armor piercing crossbows. One arm extended over the fore grip, and the other braced the stock to the archer's cheek and shoulder. The oversized razor edged blade of the hooked tips was designed to cause significant tearing and bleeding. The nasty barbed tips were almost impossible to remove. The unique design of the feathering gave the arrow a spin that added flight range and affected the travel and impact, providing greater armor penetration. Regardless of the appalling carnage, of the deadly catapult, the massive incursion of Edawnian warriors reached the range of the archers. Sensing the building tension in the background, beyond the top of the hill, the terrifying, roaring screams of the chained Zomborges could be heard like the sickening macabre wails of a wounded beast.

Zandor turned to the rider at his side and asked, "What on Zia is that?"

Zandor, Kondor, and King Ozzdon drew their swords almost at the same time and held them up high. A forest of light reflecting Edawnian blades suddenly flashed and came forth, held overhead in muscular arms in a fierce plunging charge. And like a heartless, evil beast, thousands of merciless Norticlan archers stood by, primed to massacre them. In a remarkable display of bravery and tenacity, the Edawnian's first wave rushed forward following their fearless king, galloping onward with shields raised and swords at the ready. Hearts and hooves thundered as the storm surged ahead against the approaching battle line, throwing the whole of their conviction behind their charge. The champion within their hearts allow them to go forth for what they believed. They relentlessly advanced with great courage in the face of death no matter what, and that is what left no doubt of their noble valor.

The eyes of anxious Norticlan marksmen took on an icy glare as they held their twitching trigger fingers fixed, as every crossbow zeroed in on their target. The scent of looming death was like a nectarous fragrance in their nostrils, like a narcotic surging in their veins.

Izz of Zia

Baddlock waited until the last possible moment, just as the onrushing force reached the uttermost killing zone. Nearer and nearer, as they shouted their battle cry, the Edawnian frontlines ascended straight into the verge of the storm about to rupture upon them. With one swift downward jerk of Baddlock's bony hand, a blizzard of countless arrows darkened the sky like an eclipse of the sun. Projectiles were sent whirling through the air at direct point blank range. The unleashed hailstorm made the air drone with intensity.

Hardened steel tips suddenly pelted the frontal assault, an overbearing majority of them finding their mark, slaying and mangling their targets. A succession of agonizing shrieks came from the front ranks as almost the entire frontline of men and beast fell like a great sea surf tumbling and crashing onto a rocky shore. One by one, horses screamed as they crumbled to the earth under their riders. The cream of the crop of Edawn was cut down like rippling waves of grain stalks falling at the sweep of the reaper's razor honed sickle at a great harvest. Regardless of the slaughter, generals relentlessly shouted out commands for their troops to advance.

The unyielding front lines of Edawn were armored from head to toe with thick plated steel, reinforced with chain mail. Unfortunately, their armor was no match for Baddlock's armor piercing crossbows, especially at that range. It was like ramming their heads into a stone wall. Down they fell in untimely demise by the thousands, cut down in their prime. Anyone that fell wounded was trampled under hoof. As each frontal line of Norticlan bowmen launched their deadly volley, they merely stepped sideways and back, and from behind them stepped up the next group, ready to deliver the next volley. Each ensuing storm pitilessly burst upon those who dared to come within their range. Again, almost everyone on the frontline wave was massacred, falling in their battle formations where they took their last step forward, in a flood of crimson carnage. Men and animals were cast back, with a murderous fury of tempered steel, like chaff before the wind. Slashed by thousands of armor piercing blows, the living knew the next moment could be their last. It was beyond comprehension. No one had ever witnessed such death, let alone such a continuous massacre.

Suddenly, out of nowhere, the hilltop reverberated with the multitude of high pitched screams as the Zomborges caught the scent of blood in the air and cries of the dying. The frenzied, prolonged bellowing sounded like something between the roar of an enraged grizzly and the bray of a crazed yakox, and the squeal of an impaled pig. The clanging of chains sounded as they came taut and were stretched, twisting to their breaking point. Unable to escape, they vented their frustration on each other in appalling ways.

Miraculously King Ozzdon rode on into the raging storm of death. The critical realization of the situation sunk in with the shocking grasp that he was now fully committed to a suicidal attack of self annihilation from which there would be no reprieve. The cost was proving to be too great; they could not possibly sustain these kinds of losses and expect anyone would walk away alive. King Ozzdon roared, "Spread out!"

As he witnessed the devastating consequences of his frontal attack, the king watched the hillside turn red with the lifeblood of his men hewn down in wave after wave of indiscriminate butchery. Still, up the ridge, the Edawnian warrior drove, expecting death at any moment. They advanced without hesitation, and they fought back fearlessly firing their longbows and casting their lances. But it was as nothing before the murderous strength of the enemy. Like a dense horde of angry hornets, the arrows repeatedly descended upon them, inflicting shocking casualties. And Still, the living did not falter. They were more than willing to die for their king, their kingdom, their families, and their lands. If they had had more than one life to bestow, they would have laid it down, a thousand times if need be.

The all out frontal attack resulted in nothing more than a series of tumbling dominos. Men staggered from loss of blood and fell by the wayside. Incapable of soaking up any more blood, the ground began to puddle everywhere pooling ankle deep, spreading around them and then ran like water. First flowing in rivulets into trenches, swelling into ditches, and then gorging into streams down the slope of the hill. Those that remained standing did not doubt that it would only be a matter of time before they too were going to their death.

All Baddlock's archers needed to do was calmly aim their crossbows at the oncoming troops and had only to open fire. The pitiful slaughter devoured men and beast indiscriminately. They could have fired blindly and could not have missed hitting someone. The crossbow infantry shot their arrows with such force and quickness that their tides of razor sharp arrows were swallowed up by the flesh of men that courageously threw themselves onward. Like a swell opposing a cliff, against the waiting arrows that tore them to shreds, they charged forward. Red pools of blood kept rising as the Norticlan archers picked them off like sitting ducks. The main frontal force, led by King Ozzdon, continued the attack, directly drawing Baddlock's main firepower. Zandor and Kondor were given crucial time to outflank the outer catapult units.

As the elite of the nation was systematically cut down without mercy, astonishingly, King Ozzdon remained unscathed. Even though he carried in his shield a dozen arrows and his horse, Ivory, had taken two bolts deep through the chest plates he charged onward. Ivory trudged on until he stumbled to the blood soaked ground mortally wounded. With a high pitched sound between a neigh and a whine, Ivory tried to get up but could not. The king dismounted and patted his horse on its neck and whispered, "You have done well, my old friend." Then he mercifully cut Ivory's jugular vein.

Anger and adrenaline exploded through the king's veins amid the chaos, confusion, screams, anguish, and pain. He was risking everything, his own life for the defense of his people. Maybe it was the right thing to do, but if he wanted to command his army, he had to stay alive. As crossbows continuously clicked, a blink of an eye later, more screams bellowed out, followed by infantile wailing sounds. Soon he was encircled by atrocious sights and sounds. The mortally wounded were strewn on the blood drenched ground, twisting, squirming, and screaming. The air was thick with the damp mist of blood that made the king's vital fluids curdle in his veins and made the pit of his stomach twist with sickness. It was too late to rethink the situation. He was appalled at the massive losses they were suffering. He did not want to sacrifice his men. He hated it, but somehow it seemed like a necessary evil. At this point, it would have been just as suicidal to retreat as it would be to go forward, so the king chose to go head on.

When the Sons of Edawn saw that their king had not fallen but stood tall with nerves of steel as a bastion against all the odds, they rallied around him. They had two choices, charge on and die or just die. They repeatedly charge only to be easily beaten back with heavy losses. The familiar voice that they had always believed in was now calling them to rise in defiance of the grim beast that bathed their beloved land in their o blood.

The Wicked Warlock Wizard gazed over the carnage he was responsible for and shook with depraved laughter edged in lunacy. He coiled his hands together and then twisted them as if a black widow knitting a silky web of entrapping horror. Blood thirst overcame him and filled him with the lust for death. Then out of the haze in the middle of the bloody cesspool, to his surprise, he spotted King Ozzdon. His face twisted into a quizzical stare. His upper lip arched until it touched his crimped up nose as he blinked his squinting, unbelieving eyes. "King Ozzdon! There!" Spittle spewed from his mouth as he screamed and pointed his withered forefinger in King Ozzdon's direction. "The audacity of his brazen arrogance is beyond crazed!"

Dandork was instantly at Baddlock's side, staring in amazement that King Ozzdon himself would be leading the attack. He could not help admire the fearlessness of his once friend and king.

Izz of Zia

Thinking that he had King Ozzdon exactly where he wanted, Baddlock turned to Dandork, and said, "Well, we will just see how heroic he is once my butchers start flaying the hide off his screaming flesh, one strip at a time." And he might even have been right, but for the courage of the Edawnian heart, it would prove easier said than accomplished. Baddlock then commanded, "Move all the archers to the center of the attack."

"But our flanks, my lord," Darkon protested.

"Do as I command, or my dogs will dine on your heart this twilight," Baddlock insisted as his eyes glazed over with madness.

"Immediately, my master." Darkon bowed his head and pounded his chest.

The command was given, and the flanking archers thronged and swarmed to the center of their defenses. The combined volley that they then unleashed again eclipsed the light of the sun and cast a blackened shroud of doom overall in its wake. Warriors in selfless feats of courage stepped in front with shields forward and took the full force of bolts meant for their king. The gut wrenching horror at the scandalous loss of life was so appalling that it sickened the least hardened Norticlanders. Blood fountained out of the lacerated flesh of the dead, dying, and wounded, flowing into the depressions and grooves of Zia. The air suddenly was thick with the smell of blood, it reeked in the nostrils of those still alive with a sour coppery lead scent, intermingled with a hint of rust and salt. And the wails of the Zomborges intensified to a gruesome pitch. The charge continued despite the rattles of death and the cries of the dying. Those at the front fell back, and those at the rear pushed forward. The escalating arial assault came to a head as men fell away from their protective circle around their king like peels of an onion. Surrounded by the dead and the dying, the king inadvertently led his followers deeper into the death trap.

The Edawnian plan to coax Baddlock to react to the king's affront was finally working, but the cost was vast. At that exact moment, the twins peeled away with one sweeping swing. Each spreading out to either side hoping to find the enemy's flanks unguarded, hopeful their surprise attack would do some serious damage. Zandor and Kondor pulled their mounts out of formation, breaking away from their forces from the main attack into two separate flanking strategic assaults. They split and angled in from two directions, in a complicated, highly tactical maneuver.

Moving swiftly to the West and the East, the twins split in two directions toward the rear long range catapult assault. While Baddlock's full attention was turned on the king, Zandor and Kondor moved their divisions swiftly, almost unhindered by the opposing fire of deadly crossbows. The twin warriors led their men thorough maneuvers, positioning themselves for the assault ahead. While what was left of the king's cavalry relentlessly charged up the middle, followed by the arriving foot soldiers. On the sideward battlefronts, both attacking flanks reached the opposite hillsides almost at the same time and began to climb the hill slop to press the enemy's edges. Zandor's mind raced ahead as arrows from the outposts started to fly across Zandor's vision, he reined up sharply, rode past, and then circled. Zandor's mount pulled forward as he studied the enemy's position. He concentrated on their every move, sizing them up, trying to determine their numbers, searching out their weaknesses. There was a certain logic to their ploy; darting this way and that, they kept shuffling their pattern of movement, outmaneuvering their enemy. Long distance marksmen picked off each other's moving and unmoving targets almost at random. The flanking attackers probed the Norticlan defenses for any vulnerability, seemingly following no plan at all. They sent two or three fighters in as if to attack, firing on the enemy systemically with their longbows then retreating. As they neared the top, arrows from Norticlan longbows whistled and zinged all around them. Zandor made his move, galloping ahead of everyone, veering his charge, speeding toward a slanted path. He let go of the reins and raised his nocked longbow into firing position, took aim, and dropped the first defender with one arrow.

At the top of the rocky ridge, all the trees had been burned or cut down. The rows of stumps presented a sector that looked very much like a giant graveyard. The largest, tallest trees had been cut to brace the catapults. What was left of the hilltop forest had been used to erect barriers of thorn vine entanglements around the entire encampment. The barrier was something Zandor had not anticipated. Dense thorn thickets were tangled together to create an impassable boundary. Zandor knew he could not just stand around, waiting for a revelation to magically manifest. He ordered his warriors to dismount before the thorn barricade. Men attempting to clamber over the ensnarement of thorns quickly found themselves blundering into a deathtrap. Many were caught in the barbed vine entanglement, unable to break free. They were easily pierced with spear, sword, or shot through with arrows, and then left to hang there in all positions, kicking and jerking like toy puppets dangling on a string. Willing to die for the greater good, bodies piled up on the thorn barrier. Neither the horror of the painfully sharp snare nor the number of the dead halted the men that launched themselves unto the barbed fortification.

Oncoming troops climbed over the bodies of their fallen comrades that lay twisted beneath them in gruesome angles that only a dead body could assume. They took turns covering one another as they crossed, men who first cleared the twisted thorn coils dashed forward with their swords drawn. Inexperienced civilian recruits fought to the death against the well equipped Norticanian veterans of many fierce inter tribal wars. They were not too smart, but they were strong, brutal, savage men of war. Zandor, stirred by bottled up anger, flexed his muscles as he shot toward the enemy. Quick witted, he impaled the first foe and disemboweled the next Norticlan swordsman as his deadly blade stuck like lightning. His target was the bull catapults that were devastating his people. He slipped through the clutches of several adversaries, then dove and zigzagged toward his objective. Zandor was not bothered, unduly feeling perfectly at ease, even fervent about killing his enemy. His daring heroism turned common men into fearless warriors. The Edawnians fought like lions, driven to destroy this murderous pack of Norticlan hyenas in spite of their superior weapons, regardless of their greater numbers. Uncommon valor was a common virtue despite the continuous substantial loss of life among the Edawnian ranks. Zandor's bowmen sporadically picked off the enemy from their catapult stations as they came into the range of their longbows.

Zandor, with a handful of Edawn's bravest warriors, was among the first to reach the monstrous bull catapult lines. He conveyed a measure of strength, courage, and control to his men. Zandor stood his ground as he swatted arrows away from the longbow catapult defenders with his formable sword and shield as he advanced with the speed of a panther on the hunt. He saw several guardsmen draw their swords and charge at him, while the long range catapult lord kept right on firing upon Edawn. He glanced behind him and saw two swordsmen approaching fast. Amid the quick and the dead, Zandor consumed by the absolute intensity of combat, readied himself for whatever confronted him next. He flung around his sword, and it flashed, throwing off sparks as torrents of blood fountained full. Zandor was more than ready to confront his enemies face to face, prepared to fight, and fight bravely to the death if need be.

As a handful of Edawn's finest reached the summit of the hilltops, they attacked the western catapult line, and quickly found themselves isolated in a death defying battle with little hope of deliverance. The first assailants maneuvered to confront them, and Zandor wasted no time in hesitation. Forgetting his entire well thought out plan, he cast all sensible caution to the wind and charged straight into the jaws of death. His instincts were fully awake, honed to their fullest equilibrium. Out of nowhere, a foe's enormous blade swept downward at an angle toward Zandor's neck, and just in the breath of time, he managed to deflect it with his shield. Another thrust came straightforward toward his midsection. The razor sharp edges clanged as he parried his powerful adversary's broadsword away. He then spun and swung at lightning speed. Before the Norticlander could react, Zandor's blade sliced his throat with a devastating slash, severing his two jugular veins. The Norticlander dropped his weapon and clutched his detached windpipe with his two hands, gave out a bloody, hissing gurgle, and dropped to the ground, dead.

The next challenger reached him with an arching overhead vertical, descending drive. Without stopping to think, Zandor dropped to one knee, turning sideways as he ducked, brought one hand over the other, and plunged his sword upward, to the hilt, into his rival's chest. His quarry violently shuddered as he let out a bubbling murmur. Then Zandor yanked his sword out, as it trailed an arch of deep crimson that splashed across the battleground. The victim then dropped into a lifeless heap. Zandor rose, spun, and swung and spun again, swinging his blade to and fro in powerful, slashing arches. He cut off an arm of one adversary and then severing the spine of another with two successive slashes. With a single two handed stroke of his weapon, he struck down a pair of onrushing Norticlan warriors. Zandor did not stop to consider how many barbarians he had killed or mangle. He only thought of them as vermin that must be exterminated that he might save his people.

Fury reared up and raced through his veins, urging him to rush the next attacker with a double fisted decapitating blow. As the slain Norticlander fell to the ground dead, he felt suddenly horrified by his own black, deep hunger and thirst to lash out, to maim, and to kill. *I am only sending a few depraved, savage pagans into their heathen world,* he thought when unexpectedly, out of the corner of his eye, he caught the flash of steel. Too late to react, Zandor turned in horror to see a sword coming down for the final blow. An unutterable woe twisted upon his face at the nightmarish sight coming down upon him.

Then a second flash of polished metal clanked and locked for a moment, arm against arm. It was Rayzar, Zandor's closest childhood friend stepping in to save him just in the nick of time. A third flash of cold steel sank deep into the would be killer's rib cage. The Norticandor dropped instantly, as he hit the ground, he clutched at his gaping, bleeding wound. Immediately Zandor's men were all around him wielding their whistling blades, elbow deep in hand to hand fighting in defense of their commander.

Meanwhile, on the opposite side of the embattled hillside, the forces Kondor commanded had swiftly moved uphill and then doubled back in a sweeping arc. They converged on the eastern slope in the same pivoting move. A metallic ringing echo of razor sharp edges sounded as Kondor attacked the East end of the hillside. Kondor was the gentler of the two twins, but in battle, he proved to be very quick, powerful, and brutal when the situation called for it. Every man that Kondor commanded took on the onrushing gauntlet to his optimum ability, and no one gave less than better than his best. Surrounded by danger on all sides, they breached the thorn barricade, in the same manner, Zandor's party had, at the loss of many brave men. Every Edawnian fought like a mighty warrior, regardless of the overwhelming odds. The more that rushed them, the stronger they advanced against their mortal enemy. Consequently, they suffered grievous casualties, yet they relentlessly advanced on their death march toward the catapults, spilling a trickle of blood for every fistful of dirt they gained.

Archers shot each other within spitting distance. Blades flashed, dancing with death; armors clashed; razor sharp shafts pierced the flesh of men. The warrior next to Kondor was suddenly hit with an arrow in the face at close range, shattering his skull. Mortally wounded, he dropped his sword gave a muffled sob and reached for his injured face as his body fell dead across Kondor's arms. Kondor let him slip out of his arms and continued his own epic battle for life. Rent bodies all around him stumbled, collapsed, and rose again, sometimes falling forevermore.

At the very same time, the king's frontal assault was sustaining the heaviest casualties in its legendary struggle to forge ahead. But despite their superhuman execution of courage, their swords were useless, and their longbows were of little use against the steel piercing crossbows. Those wounded that were still alive huddled on the ground behind their fallen horses with their shields up, trying their best to avoid the down pouring barrage of deadly shafts. There was little protection against the storm after storm of arrows that fell systematically upon them, and there was no escape. As a result, most of the Kings Imperial Cavalry and foot soldier contingent was locked in a fatal entrapment of agony and wretchedness. King Ozzdon's forces had only managed to get as far as the foot of the hillside. Above them were the Norticlan trenches and barbed thorn vine. The grassy slope had become slippery with blood, turning the field of battle at their feet into a blood soaked snarl of the fallen.

Nevertheless, they kept going, forging their way into hopelessness, shedding their blood like water on the gore drenched battlefield. The frontlines of self sacrifice devoured men like sheep for the slaughter. And yet, the never wavering warrior was willing to follow their king, no matter what the cost. No matter what the loss, even if the fruitless quest had become a quagmire of unthinkable madness.

Zandor led the western flank assault farther up the blood swept hillside with the mightiest of men to his right and his left. They concentrated their full effort on reaching the dreaded bull catapults that ceaselessly continued to decimate their kingdom for no other reason than to exterminate the helpless citizens of Edawn. They had to disable them somehow, or everything would have all been for nothing.

"Aaayh!" came the sudden, deafening war cry from Zandor's powerful lungs as he roared at his men, driving them forward beyond human endurance. And the whole western hillside instantly converged into an explosive clash of blinding blades. They fearlessly fought their way farther and farther out on the limb of the living. It all became one big gamble now—whether any of them would get near the catapults, let alone bring them down was quickly becoming an ill fated mission. Yet they cast all to the wind and slammed deeper into the hoard of advancing defenders.

Zandor's bloodstained sword endlessly flashed and shimmered, jetting wide arcs of spattering blood across the air and forcing the Norticlan savages back. Norticanian bowmen, charged with the defense of the long range catapults, and the advancing Edawnian warrior came eye to eye with death and shot at each other at point blank range. But in the end, the muscle bound Northerners were no match for Zandor's lighter, quicker marksmen.

Finally, miraculously, Zandor and his men were able to reach the line of murderous catapults. As they blindsided the catapult crews, they were met with little resistance from the handlers, although outlying, long=bowmen relentlessly continued to rain down death on his men. Arrows zinged all around them so close, so dangerously close, some finding their mark. With little warning, many Edawnians were picked off without knowing where the deadly arrow came from. Catapult guards rushed down from the upper ridge to thrust at them with their razor tipped lances. A torchbearer had just lit an incendiary pot when Zandor drove his sword's sharp point into his throat, dropping him where he stood. Zandor resheathed his sword, took the lit kindling pot, lifted over his head, planted his feet firmly, and sent the incendiary crashing against the base of the catapult's launching support beams. Fueled by the volatile mixture, the green, rich sapped beams quickly reached their flashpoint and erupted into raging flames. Zandor Immediately ordered his men to do likewise.

From the other side of the battle, Kondor as if of one heart and mind with his twin reached the bull catapults on the opposite side almost at the same time. It was an all out, animalistic frenzy of killing as Kondor's forces held off the hordes while a handful of Edawnian warriors set the Eastside catapults ablaze. Zandor and Kondor's bittersweet victory, however, short lived; at least had managed to salvage some of their bludgeoned pride from what was otherwise a complete disaster.

Izz of Zia

The strength of brave hearts failed as the Edawnian forces were driven back by the accursed storm. King Ozzdon felt the flow of slippery blood underfoot. He turned to see the death and mayhem that surrounded him everywhere he looked. His golden chain mail and armor that once gleamed in the sun was now covered in his countrymen's blood. He was mortified as he witnessed the appalling bloodshed in all its horror. His eyes filled with tears, he closed them tight so that he could see the slaughter of his kinsmen no more. The screams that would forever haunt him echoed in his soul, searing themselves across all his senses of sight, touch, taste, and smell. Cold misery twisted inside of him as his mind, heart, and spirit broke all at once.

Soon Baddlock's most prized catapults were bursting into mounting flames at both ends of his encampment. And it did not take long to catch the Wicked Warlock Wizard's attention. "My catapults!" Baddlock screamed. "My beautiful catapults! Quickly, everyone! Exterminate those vermin that dared set fire to my imps."

The veins in Baddlock's neck swelled, and it seemed that they might burst as they pulsed with unrestrained fury. The Norticlan crossbowmen and their arrow bearers then shifted their attention from the bloodbath that was once Edawn's elite frontal attack. "Move your worthless carcasses." Baddlock hurled curses and insults at anyone he thought was not moving fast enough. *"Immediately!"* The harsh taskmaster shrilled as his anger burned out of control.

As if in a dream, King Ozzdon stood in the center of the chaos. He looked around at the stunned, hollow looks of men that stood like lifeless toy tin soldier replicas of themselves. Oh, the looks on their faces. His blood chilled. It had been a disheartening defeat, and the living were at the point of disappearing all together among the dead bodies that by now were beyond count. The very air seemed to reek of gloom and wretchedness. In the heart of the terror, in the back of his head, he could hear in the background a distant echo of someone calling out to him.

"Your Majesty…what is your command?"

An eternity passed before the king came to his senses and became aware that there was a sudden reprieve in the intensity of the slaughter. He perceived a window of opportunity that could be their last chance to retreat. He was left with no other choice but to fall back. The king suddenly raised his voice, loud and clear. "Sons of Zia…retreat…help the living, leave the rest, fall back! Now!" Thus began the bloody withdrawal.

As the overwhelming Norticlan killing machine concentrated on Zandor and Kondor, the twin warriors stood their ground like bait for the lion, setting ablaze as many catapults as they could. Delaying their retreat until the last possible moment while the king and his men made good their retreat. Then and only then did they halt their ruinous wreckage of the bull catapults. Both twins turned and ran for their lives at the same time before they could be engulfed, trapped, and slaughtered in an indefensible mounting snare. Bowmen took turns to ward off their hooting, and shrieking attackers as their band of brothers quickly retreated, working their way over the top of the thorn barrier. Some deliberately forfeited their lives so the others could live.

In the frenzied race for escape, suddenly, Rayzar found himself caught in the thorns. The more he frantically struggled to free himself, the more he became entangled. The Edawnians could hear the dreadful howling sounds of the full Norticlan force at their heels. Those who could not be saved were left to die.

Zandor turned to survey the over boiling hilltop and saw that Rayzar his best friend, was caught with one arm stretched out at an awkward angle. While Rayzar was desperately breaking his back to free himself, the oncoming crossbowmen were rushing toward him. In a hail of howling crossbow arrows, Zandor made his way back in Rayzar's direction. Seeing this, Rayzar screamed, "No! Get back! I am done for. Turn back Now!"

Izz of Zia

Amid a hundred screaming arrows, Zandor's mind seemed to have shut down, while he stood there eye to eye with Rayzar as he dangled there helplessly. A thousand lifetimes passed before an arrow sliced across Zandor's cheekbone, bringing him to his senses.

"Get out of here!" Rayzar screamed louder.

It tore at Zandor's insides. No matter how much he wanted to force his way through to him, there was nothing he could do to save his best friend.

As if in a daze Zandor turned against his will, and it took a huge piece of his heart to tear himself away. Finding his steed, Zandor swung up onto his horse with one mighty leap and heeled his mount into an all out bolt. He looked back one last time to see a Norticlan warrior butt Rayzar with the back of his crossbow, instantly knocking him senseless. Helpless to do anything else, Zandor turned his attention to his men; and as they retreated, into the distance, he saw that his king was in grave danger. He raced around his fleeing troops and raced toward King Ozzdon as the frontal forces disengaged and fell back.

On the opposite side of the hill, Kondor was almost wholly overrun when he finally called out the retreat. Men withdrew hastily grappling over the barbed barrier. Those that could find their horses mounted quickly and bound away. Others ran in a jittery, unsteady way, breathless, half mad, trying to escape the undertow of the nightmare, threatening to sweep them out into an endless sea of obliteration. Kondor, out of fearlessness, returned with a few brave others to retrieve some of the mortally wounded. They refused to retreat until they were driven away by the encroaching Norticlan counterattack.

From every side of the hilltop, the Edawnian wounded, those refusing to die, delirious in the throes of death, left trails of blood and gore as they crawled in the direction of the kingdom. Groaning and whimpering through their blood filled mouths they pleaded for help with upraised hands. Those more dead than alive begged, between moans of agony, to be put out of their misery. Most who could not be rescued were left behind to an uncertain death.

As King Ozzdon urged his men on, he suddenly heard hoofbeats approaching swiftly from behind him as he ran. Relieve surged through him when he saw his faithful Commander Zandor over his shoulder, slowing to a trot and preparing to whisk him up and away. The king fell into step with the approaching stallion and leaped up as Zandor rose in his stirrups and offered his king his strong arm. With one mighty swing, Zandor lifted the king up and onto the back of his horse behind him. They galloped back toward the kingdom until they had reached a safe distance. At the command of the king, Zandor drew back on the reins and brought his horse to a halt just short of the northern Edawnian gate. The king dismounted as both men compelled and encouraged their downtrodden men back. As many severely wounded as could be carried, were hauled off the field of battle.

King Ozzdon turned to Zandor and spoke from his heart. "You saved my life. How can I ever repay you, my true friend?" "Your well being is my reward," Zandor said, and he meant it.

Dandork approached his master as the grieving Wicked Warlock Wizard lamented over his damaged catapults. "Shall we pursue the quarry?"

Baddlock did not respond, seemingly lost in his remorse over his prized weapons, the backbone of his assault force.

I tried to warn you, you old goat, Dandork thought.

And as if Dandork had spoken the words out loud, the Wicked Warlock Wizard's eyes suddenly widened and shifted toward Dandork. His eyes narrowed as he asked in a poisoned tone, "What did you say?"

Izz of Zia

Nothing…only that our quarry is getting away…my Lord and Master. Dandork bowed his head and shoulders low in submission.

With his attention shifting to the fleeing Edawnians, Baddlock spoke with a hint of concern in his voice, "So they are."

"Shall we give chase, my Lord?"

"No," the Warlock answered in a long drawn out whisper that sounded more like a hiss from a venomous viper. "That would only shorten our amusement." Then he spoke as if speaking directly to King Ozzdon himself, "Fight or fly as you will, either way, you will never stop the coming world order that is dawning." Then he turned to Dandork and said, "Let them run back into their hole, where they will be mine for the taking."

"Why not kill them all while the opportunity is upon us?"

"*Enough!*" Baddlock screamed as he ran his bony fingers through his stringy hair in distracted frustration. "Enough of your bothersome questions, I care not for your idle inquiries!" He waved Dandork off dismissively with his upraised hand. "See what you can do about repairing our damaged catapults," and with revenge twisted on his face, he ordered, "gather the Edawnian dead and wounded."

The reign of terrorizing catapults was forced to come to an abrupt halt. The conquest battle for Zia was cut short—for the time being. Thousands of Edawnians had been killed in the retaliatory strike, defeated and dishonored, reduced to less than half their original number. They had gained nothing, except perhaps a precocious few hours to prepare for the next onslaught of wrath to come.

The skies overhead had already thickened with gathering flocks of vultures over the bloody panorama, as if called in by some primordial instinct, impatient to feast on the dead and the dying.

The Norticlan barbarians swarmed down like a pack of scavengers to claim their trophies of the dead and wounded. Those with head wounds but still alive were stripped and mutilated. The Norticlan believed that the soul of a dismembered body would be forced to walk Zia for all eternity and could never enter into the afterlife. Those that were severely wounded and unconscious, even those that were dead yet whole, were gathered to join their Zomborge armies.

Those left alive continued their exodus, forced to flee from a staggering loss, the worst defeat ever inflicted on the Empire of Xylenia in all the written memory of Zia. They ran from a place from which few returned, their numbers drastically dwindled. In the lengthening distance, between one moment and the next, the painful screams of the dying diminished until all grew still and those that had cried out in pain were presumed dead. By all accounts, the attack had ended in slaughter and disgrace. Anyone that had not been able to keep up with the retreating armies was presumed as good as dead.

With frayed nerves, the never ending procession of dispirited, bloodstained combatants retreated toward Edawn. Their bodies were torn their hearts rent, their morale sapped. Their defeat was stupefying. It was the single bloodiest day in memory. Most of the elite were dead; the brightest, bravest, and most promising had been lost in the assault. The disseminated survivors trudged away from a catastrophe that defied belief. Dreadfully swollen faces stared straight ahead as ripped bodies, bearing each other up, stumbled forward on their wobbling knees. Some went back and forth as if they were dumbfounded. Others did not even look like human beings, and some were physically unscathed but mentally broken. Darker yet were the cries of those that were barely hanging on to life and in excruciating anguish. Some were so severely maimed they were beyond help, and only begged to be put down along the way and permitted to die graciously on the ground where they lay.

No one said a word, too weary to bellyache, and too bewildered to rationalize. The men of Edawn had found out firsthand what war, and killing, and dying was all about. It had been a horrific and frightening introduction to the mortifying wails of agony and death. Some scoured themselves for having thought that war would be the most exciting exploit they would ever experience. A glorious crusade in which they could prove their manhood and boast of their bravery for a lifetime to come. But they had been sadly mistaken. Instead, it turned out to be the most gut wrenching and fearsome thing they had ever lived through. It had been a futile effort, more a rout than a battle, doomed to destruction from its inception. The mightiest war machine of all the kingdoms had faltered and failed miserably. The tragic retaliatory attack had only ended in carnage and almost reaching the brink of total annihilation. Smitten with defeat, lacerated bodies, fractured minds, broken hearts recoiled from the field of destruction and death. It had been a terrible thing to have to experience. Men, breathless and drenched in sweat, moved along looking back at the frightening slaughterhouse they had come from. What made it worse was that it had been almost all for naught. The result was virtually worthless, senseless self destruction. At best, they had only been able to disable a few catapults, delaying the inevitable for the moment. At worst, the retaliation had only further provoked the terrible ruin of Edawn.

Darkening clouds moved in from the North like a death shroud cast over a dead man. The murderous day suddenly blackened as if heaven's eyes had suddenly filled with sorrow and raindrops began to fall like silent tears, wept for the fallen.

FIFTEEN

THE UNFATHOMABLE

Izz had been walking for an unknown point in time now, following his unexplained insight, perhaps for another zetta or more. Or maybe it only seemed like it. The feeble yellow light from his torch crawled along the pathway ahead of him. His trek carried him to where just beyond, the glowing entranceway waited. The faint scorching pulsation flickered against the walls, like a billowing blaze that oscillated and throbbed like the beating of a huge wicked heart. And the persistent sounds of continuous anguish that were like no other sounds he had ever heard before dragged on uninterrupted. From a distance, Izz could see that the entryway was a crumbling pile of mismatched stones so ancient it seemed that it had been swallowed and lost in time. It was a structure that had never been seen by any earthbound human—at least none that had lived to bring back the tale to tell that is anyone apart from Baddlock and he was not telling.

As he approached, Izz could sense a wrathful, infinitely black, evil presence in its hazy reddish light and its depths. The screaming and crying lengthened, coming in increasing waves, louder and louder. The wicked opening seemed to flare and blaze with an inner flame like that of a furnace lit to its most intense red heat. A low shroud of smoke drifted out of the entrance and hung in the air just above the ground drifting toward him and curling around his ankles. Izz raised his torch for a better look. The ingress was framed with two rough hewn gigantic standing stones, across the top an enormous lintel marked the throat into the next hidden vault of the unknown. The structure, crooked and off balance, made it seem as if its design was based on brokenness.

Suddenly out of the dark shadows from somewhere above came a hoarse, muffled sobbing, a whimpering sound. Izz looked up, his eyes searching the darkness. In the middle of the top stone lintel, there something was moving. As Izz's torch sought out its source, he could again feel that same intense alarming dread beginning to uncoil deep down inside once more. Fear was quickly replacing his dread and escalated into ever mounting terror, bringing to life all of his darkest fears yet again. It was the identical distressful dread he had been trying to shake off, ever since he had first descended into this forsaken underworld. As he moved in closer for a better look, his mind worked furiously against the panic rushing up his spine, through his heart, and into his head. When Izz came about, his torch flame for a second time almost died for no apparent reason. The glow suddenly muted to a minute flicker…just as if the light was not welcome. Virtually as though darkness had rebuked the fire back into its twisted fibers until it looked like little more than a cumbersome firefly.

Up ahead, the tunnel turned sharply to the left as the dark specter of fear stalked him. All the while, the screaming noises were getting louder still. So loud that he could imagine them emanating just around the next corner. As he advanced, he waved his torch before him. A clanking noise grated into his consciousness, and he stopped to listen. He heard breathing—a sound that was labored and pained, between gasp and snarl, followed by more strained breathing. A ghostly image fading in and out up through the fog caught the corner of his eye as he passed; and just then, he realized anew he was not alone. He wheeled around, and once again slid one hand to the hilt of his dagger. Something as dark as the cavern he had entered was up ahead in the same chamber. He flashed his torch at the figure right before his path.

In the rising darkness, the vexing fright returned full force. Every muscle in his body tightened. It felt beastly. It felt perverse. He began craning his neck around as he neared the corner that might, after all, cost him his life. He felt the familiar bristling feeling of his back hair as fear stiffened the backside of his neck.

Izz suddenly sprang back, in ever escalating horror at first startled, next frightened, and then horrified. He slammed himself against the passageway wall. He held back a retching scream. He closed his eyes tight and drew the back of his hand to his waxing face, backpedaling as his disheveled hair fell over his grimacing expression. What he had seen was something he could not explain. As he braced himself, he reopened his eye a fraction to see, it was the creature he had encountered earlier. His eyes went wide with complete astonishment. It was nailed to the jagged gray, soot covered stone, by its hands and feet. Each hand was fastened at the wrist and stretched out so far that its shoulders seemed dislocated. Its feet were spread eagle, and each foot was spiked with one single long spike through the anklebone. Its fingernails from all its digits had been ripped off. Its eyes were squeezed tightly shut in the purest misery as it savagely tried to free itself, coiling, writhing, and thrashing about violently.

At first, its lips moved without sound; and then babbling cries surged from its gaping mouth. Izz suppressed a shudder. Its face was a mask of torment, torture, and untold terror. Its eyes became slits as it squirmed and fidgeted as if it was trying to clutch at the source of its pain. A bleeding fungus covered its entire body. A festering wound in the middle of its upper body caught Izz's eyes. Its left side oozed with the stench of putrid entrails; its heart had been ripped from a gaping hollow in its chest. The maggot riddled skin around the wound hung from its body like strands of infectious tissue progressively dripping leprous pus. Now and then, it struggled, trying to free itself as it twisted in its own gore. The thing turned its head slightly, and as it did, Izz could hear the bones and cartilage in its neck grinding and crunching. Its eyes were half opened, but there was no light in them. One of its eyes seemed to be missing, blood and goo oozed out of its empty socket. Then it turned its head fully around. The popping and grinding of bone told Izz that its neck had been broken. When his torchlight cast itself along its face, Izz saw that it had no eyes, only vacant cavities where its eyes should have been. It sobbed uncontrollably, making a weird whimpering sound as it seemed to be reaching out to him.

Appalled, Izz could only stand there speechless, mouth agape, detached in a stupor of disbelief. The creature drew a long rasping, strangled, gurgling breath, and Izz half expected it to break out into a long agonizing scream suddenly. Instead, it seemed as if it was trying to say something. It coughed and choked on some gross thing it had hacked up from the bottom of its ruptured lungs. Its mouth trembled as it tried to speak, but only expelled a hot breath of black vapor that laced into curling wisps from its nostrils. Blood spewed from its mouth between unknown words that it was only able to mouth.

Then the strangest thing happened. Izz began to hear the creature's thoughts whispering in his mind in the same way he had heard his eagles, wolverine, and the fish. *These are the gates of doom. Turn back. This is the mouth of the condemned underworld,* the creature wailed, with pain tearing through it. And then the beast looked down with pleading empty sockets that seemed to beg, *Please, kill me! Put me out of my misery, please! Please, please, for mercy's sake, kill me!* It ground its gums in pain against the bloody sockets where its teeth had been pulled.

Izz wished there was something he could have done to lessen the misery of the tormented creature. But he sensed that on this side of reality, there was nothing he could do for the writhing spirit. He stepped around the messy puddles of unidentifiable gore that was trickling out of its mutilated remains. The creature continued its angulations and spewing out its warnings as Izz stepped toward the marked boundary. *Turn back! You're doomed, you fool!*

The entity from a dimension where the real and the unreal merged continued its faint, jabbering, drooling rant of warning as it stirred violently. It made an effort to scream, but instead, it only groaned. Muttering, hissing, slobbering in a twisting mass of pain, it could only lament and choke on its attempt to speak. *Please end this nightmare. Come back!* The hopelessness of its silent plea was what haunted Izz the most.

Despite his fears, he continued to follow his gut feeling. Ignoring the creature's stern warnings, Izz held out the guiding stone. Its response was unmistakable. Izz stepped into the threshold and instantly knew that one more footstep, one more pace, one more stride, and he would be at risk of being lost forever. Never to come out again, never to return to the surface of Zia! The slumped figure rose up on its nailed feet, heaved forward and raised its head as it chucked and chugged a convulsed, stagnated scream at the top of its lungs. What looked like blood spurted from his tattered mouth as the passage filled with a loud, eerie, whining, whistle like wail. Unable to maintain the intensity of its outcry, it collapsed back down, and continued to weep, groan, and moan silently.

Through the threshold, passed the pathetic creature, Izz found himself in an expansive hemispherical space. The enormous cavity had a surprisingly high domed ceiling. The entire void was lit with the crimsoned glare of a great fire and filled with smoke, tremendous heat and little breathable air. From the floor to the roof, the cavern reached to unbelievably lofty heights. Its elevated roof was lit and dimly highlighted with the most tenuous facades of strange black reflections of faint red lights. The ascent arced so far up above that miniature clouds drifted at its vertex. Izz continued his daring trek, knowing nothing of the plight that surrounded him on each side. Suddenly a rush of confused sensations shook him. Had the evil of this place grown stronger or had he become more acute to its presence? In the background over the never ending drearisome drone of intensifying screams, his ears picked up a faint fluttering, a deadened stirring like the flapping of wings. He inhaled deeply, striving with his greatest effort to keep himself focused. He looked up to the ceiling where the sounds were coming from. Like a physical touch, he projected his senses up to the heights and perceived a shadowy jerking against the surface beyond the mysterious mist. Izz felt his stomach muscles stiffen in opposition to an instinctive impulse. He braced himself against the impending unknown as if he were inches from the crushing jaws of some fiendish beast he could not see. He paused and looked up for a moment as his eyes scanned slowly across the immense stone canopy of the cavernous expanse. The walls themselves were so high, and the ceiling so vast that they were invisible in the darkness. He swept his torch over his head as if that would somehow shed some light on the lofty heights. He reminded himself that each moment he hesitated was valuable time wasted.

Up ahead, at the far end, long red tongues of fire cut through the cavern like auroral clashes of lightning that flickered between oranges and yellows, flashing and twisting with a terrible rage. The shadows against the upper walls and ceiling seemed to be moving and twirling and shifting along with the circulating currents of heavy warm smoke. The sense of evil in the room congealed like a black liquid that swirled about in the darkness. Along the cave floor, Izz began to see occasional flashes of a few pocket sized fires. Solitary flames began to flare here and there, burning along the well worn path that helped light his way. The flames, smoke, and heat appeared to escalate with every pace. There was a faint smell of death and the sulfurous scent of evil everywhere. It was hot down there, and getting hotter. The smell was growing stronger the farther he traversed into the strange cavern.

Izz did not know what the nauseating smell could be that was making his empty stomach recoil and turn. He wrinkled his nose. The odor was horrific. It was the most revolting smell he had ever experienced. He would have vomited if he had anything to throw up. He had a bad feeling about this place he was entering. Just being there seemed so wrong. And by now, the hideous, never ending screams from the far end were becoming ever more hideous. He found himself vexed by unclean spirits, wishing over and over he was anywhere but there and then. Over the wailing, he could hear the feeble sound of claws scratching on the walls and ceiling. He could feel something insidiously evil and could sense in the glittery darkness powerful hate. The perception was so forceful that it made the entire surface of his flesh sting as if suddenly pricked with hundreds of piercing needles.

Izz thought he heard groaning and threshing body movements, almost visible there in the stark gloom. Little by little, the darkness had begun to recede, and shadow images on the walls and ceiling began to manifest before Izz's eyes. At first, the upper walls and the ceiling looked like a vast, thick, brisling organism. The oddity appeared to be transforming into innumerable black objects with shapes moving individually, becoming lost within the shadows. As the cavern lightened up, the incomprehensible shapes took form out of the hazy living blackness. There in the obscurity, he saw outlined silhouettes suspended from the ceiling and against the walls. In the seething mass of activity, Izz thought he saw mysterious human like configurations. The outlined figures were practically indistinguishable from one another—ghostly shapes ominously obscured in the darkness. They were so tightly packed together that they touched and melted against each other, resembling one massive entity.

He whipped the tears from his smoky eyes and took a closer look at the scene that unfolded. It was one of those things that took time to register fully. Izz focused his fixed gaze toward the walls and lofty ceiling and prepared for the worst. Just what it was, he could not precisely say, but it was everywhere, entirely covering the walls and cavernous roof. Out of the clustered, stirring agitation, a multitude of shifting shadows churned and frothed like a huge waking nest of evil, hideous black insects.

The returning troops remained silent as the bloodied, pierced, and tattered poured back into the broken kingdom, through the severely damaged northern gate. Repressed in a stupor and demoralized, the ragtag army entered the kingdom, looking tired and despondent, their faces gaunt. Their noble actions proved of no use and had only served to shatter the hearts of the survivors. The bloodline of the most courageous heroes was no more. Their illusions of grandiose glory were suddenly ghosts of the past. The remnants of those that managed to weather through the storm of the one sided extermination were acutely altered; their lives forever changed. Those that were younger were made to grow up fast. They said nothing. They did not even have the strength, nor the will, to even try to make sense of the mind boggling tragedy that had just overwhelmed them. They tried desperately to blot out the unforgettable images imprinted forever in their minds, images that called out to them and haunted their souls. Every able man assisted the wounded, swaying from side to side and staggering forward, propping each other up as best they could. The survivors reentered the kingdom as if returning from a different world. They barely even recognized themselves, so altered were their minds by the unspeakable horror they had managed to live through. The whole kingdom met what was left of the returning Edawnian forces with a sudden draught of outrage as they reacted with a refusal to believe the staggering losses suffered. Worried sick wives and mothers poured out into the northern courtyard to look for their husbands and sons. Soon the wailing of wives, mothers, and children filled the kingdom; and they could not be comforted as darkness fell across the land and night stars wept red.

The healers gathered to render assistance, but for many, it was too late to offer salvation. The women moved among the wounded, providing water and any other comfort they could manage. But for some, it was all over, except for the weeping of their loved ones.

Upon entering the kingdom, the king immediately dispatched a lookout up the badly ravaged northern watchtower. The tower was heavily damaged, but was still sound—at least that was what the lookout hoped as he precariously climbed to the top.

Nonetheless, it remained to be the best vantage point from which to observe the enemy's movements. Once the lookout cautiously reached the uppermost post, his intense gaze played over the expanding plains bearing witness to the tremendous death blow as far as the eye could see. Pain wracked bodies, twisted in all positions, lay alongside their broken weapons and equipment. Most bodies near the foot of the hill were riddled with countless arrows, still lying where they had fallen, waiting only to be covered with dirt. The scene of the senseless butchery further unfolded like a progressive, developing, cancer that covered Zia with its foul scab like canker. It was an overwhelming human disaster that defied all comprehension, and almost too impossible to take in. At no other time in the world of Zia had more blood been spilled and soaked into Ziaian soil. Edawn's finest, brightest, most promising young men, the youth of a nation, the next generation, men of great strength and in the prime of their lives cease to exist. Men marked by their ability and energy and great force of character that had been willing to march out into the jaws of death for what they believed and loved, were no more. At long last, in a quivering voice, the watch reported that there was no enemy movement. The lookout was instructed to report on the next mobility, no matter how slight. The king spent a solemn moment dispensing comforting words to the wounded and the bereaved, trying to comfort the mothers and wives.

Dozens of candles blazed as a handful of overworked healers aided Ammiz. Mothers and wives assisted as best they could, while Mistress Aria and her staff did what they could, tearing lengths of cloth from everywhere, tailoring bandages. And even Queen Zahra and her most trusted servant Atta pitched in to change bloody bandages. Wounded soldiers who, even though injured themselves, hobbled about carrying water and bandages to their wholly immobile and wheezing comrades. It seemed that the number of incoming dying and wounded would never cease. There was a couple who had lost their eldest son huddled in the corner, weeping. The wounded, weak and shaken from agony under the knife, gritted their teeth and bore the pain without complaint. King Ozzdon looked on in silence, too stunned by all he had witnessed to do more than look disheartened at the carnage around him. He had sustained enormous casualties in their failed attempt. Even though they had failed, it had been with honor they had done so he tried to convince himself. Yet he only felt the bite of guilt for the men that had poured out their full courage for him and now lay dead or dying. The screams would forever haunt him. The blood of the dead would evermore course through him leaving a stain upon him so deep that it could never be blotted out. Were they sacrificed for his ego? His eyes smoldered with suppressed tears.

"I am the only one at fault, the only one to blame," the king whispered as he turned away to take time to rethink and recover.

All the while, the scribes of Edawn captured the grim realities of that time as they consolidated their account of the death defying counterattack. They recorded every signpost as they had been seized in thoughts. The astute hand of the scribe attempts to transcribe the entire experience into their ledgers, which in turn would then be written to the official annals of war. The scholar read the words as they were written as they wrote as if they were reciting a living prayer. The witnesses to the fateful truth took a moment to calculate the toll. For the scribe, it was the official records of death in print, names, dates, and a few scrawls to note other specific details.

After some time, the king emerged from the upper keep and looked down over the courtyard, staring a hopeless outlook in the face. He was surveying the remnants of bloodstained, downcast spirits; most disturbing were the expressions of defeat on their faces. With a grim look on his face, King Ozzdon knew he had made a bad mistake inspiring a failed strategy, and he regretted making that tactical decision. It was easy to reprove himself, in hindsight; but how could he have known that his unwise counterattack would have ended so disastrously? But now it was too late.

He came into the view of his men and was spotted from below. Those men that could, abruptly snap to their feet and stood rigidly. For a moment, there was stunned silence. "Sit yourselves down," the king demanded.

Those who managed to stand up flopped back down. The king's voice then rose loud and clear. "I am most proud to be your king. Because of you who have shown yourselves brave beyond the call of faithfulness, in the face of death. Our retaliation has cost us dearly, but for now, we have managed to hinder their catapult attack, and it has gained us valuable time."

There was a low, continuous ripple of agreement from the demoralized troops.

"Whether we will ever see tomorrow, I do not know. Only tomorrow itself can tell. What I do know is that every one of us—men, women, and even our children—must stand strong and fight. Not just for Edawn but our very existence as a people." He paused again, and his men grew deathly quiet. "We can and must survive, but only if we fight and never lose heart. We must show Baddlock that the few of us have more heart than all his vast armies will ever have." Still, there was silence.

To keep his troops from farther plunging into despair, the king solemnly asserted, "I am more proud than ever to be an Edawnian…the world has warriors none finer. I stand here with a sense of profound humility and utmost pride. Retribution is on its way. As I speak, the greatest armies from the farthest reaches of Zia are at this very moment converging upon us. Our atonement draws nigh with every moment, and soon the traitorous ones will regret their damnable rebellion. I promise to avenge the blood that has been spilled on our lands this day."

At that, hope was rekindled, and this time, the battle weary men united in one accord and raised a cheer, as they appeared to find some strength and solace in his words.

"We must be prepared to defend our kingdom and to be willing to resist to the last drop of blood if need be. We must not fear death, for, in time, death is the end of all men. If I were to say to you that I was not fearful, I would be a liar. Yet I know that the only thing I must be fearful of is the figment of fear itself. Know that your enemy is just as rattled even more so, for they do not hold in their hearts the promise of life in the hereafter. Your enemy will bleed and die. They are not invincible, and they are not Edawnian warriors. Every citizen, no matter how young or old, will be vital in the outcome of our defense. Remember what you do in this life will have eternal significance in the next. If every man does what he is sworn to do, if every woman renders assistance, if every child of age will give a helping hand, we can, and will, endure."

The kingdom once again rallied with courage and wholeheartedness, because every man knew full well, there was no other recourse.

On the northern hilltops overlooking the Kingdom of Edawn sat the Wicked Warlock Wizard, like a hideous scavenging hyena patiently waiting for its mortally wounded victim to bleed to death. A dreadful hush fell over the campsite as a steady drizzle fell. The only sound was the clinging and clanging sounds of the catapult engineers frantically working to repair the damaged catapults. No one dared to speak to the spiny little man, or even question what he might be thinking. Tigbone only stood there at a distance twiddling his thumbs. Only Dandork hazarded an inquiring look toward him now and then. But the hardness of Baddlock's facial expression remained unchanged as he muttered under his breath. He seemed to be formulating the finishing touches on his next plan of attack with an invisible advertiser. All the while, in the waning moonlight, he surveyed the waste pit of carnage that had swallowed up men and beast alike. They were to him no more than cow dung on the hillside. Finally, he evilly hissed as he raised his nose into the air and said, "There is nothing more savory than the smell of fresh blood. Soon their rotting flesh will fill the air with its sweetness." Then he turned to his generals and ordered, "Bring all those that remain alive. That we may embrace the darkness, that our honored guests may curse the day they were born, and wish that their mothers had kept their legs closed."

As the moon fell against the western horizon, it shone as red as blood. Long shadows gathered over the war torn battlegrounds where the dead waited in vain to be buried. The moon dipped below the skyline and vanished beyond the end of the world. As darkness fell over the kingdom, the watchman reported torch bearers moving among the dead.

"What are they doing?" was the question everyone was asking.

"They seem to be collecting those still alive from the piles of the dead."

An unnerving silence descended over the kingdom, broken only by the gasps of those who realized what that meant. Most people hope they will die at a ripe old age by slipping away in their sleep, peacefully, surrounded by loved ones. But for these lamentable spirits, their last screaming breath of life could not have been farther from that reality. What demonic position could have possibly driven men to commit such depraved atrocities on other men? Do they not realize that their own torment will be a thousandfold greater? New campfires began to spring up all around Baddlock's encampment. Weeping widows, mothers, and children unable to find solace stayed close to the gates looking out toward the foothills in search of a reason to hope as darkness swallowed the night.

Nothing could have prepared Izz for the sight that met his eyes. He whirled around, his eyes darting over the ceiling and the walls of the cavernous yawning he had entered. Tightly cluttered as far as Izz could see on the walls and ceiling was a simmering cauldron of black spirits. With humanlike bodies, they twisted, contorted, and pathetically squirmed in agonized torment. Their count was beyond numbering, obscured by their density. They, like the creature at the entrance, were impaled against the rock surface of the walls and ceiling.

Izz's head snapped back as his mouth dropped open. He gawked wide eyed as if he did not quite believe what he was seeing. Looking uncomprehendingly, staring with ever more intensity, he froze with fascination and awe. Every wretched form he looked upon was fixed onto the igneous rock surface by their long, spindly scorpion like legs and arms with three huge silver spikes. Each wrist was pierced through, and their feet were folded one over the other and skewered like four legged spiders pinned to a stone slat. Each impaled being had two large wings that looked like black drapes clasped to the rock ceiling and walls with huge grappling hooks. Their wings scintillated and their long clawed talon clenched and unclenched as they struggled to free themselves. Large barbs suspended on chains were hooked to the backs and legs of those that dangled from the top of the cavern face and the shoulders and neck of those that hung from the walls.

What Izz saw he could still not believe; he recoiled in disgust, struggling to comprehend what he was witnessing, trying desperately to separate the real from the illusory. His fingers tensed on his dagger. Izz gasped, the taste of scorched sulfur filled his mouth, muffling the cry in his throat.

Izz perceived that this was some sort of prison for the principalities of darkness, the first fallen angelic bings into the underworld, those that Ammiz had made mention of so many times. He felt the dread that sprang forth from the creatures above and around him. For a passing moment, he could feel their acute and profound pain and fear. He could see their thousands and thousands of glowing yellowish eyes paired like dim stars against the sooty dead of night. Izz's blood quickened as shivers and tremors prowled up and down his spine. His skin crawled as every hair on his body shudder. Cold fear cringed through his heart as his courage seeped away like sand through a tight fist. Stabbing horror as never before came upon Izz and relentlessly, clutched and carried him away beyond terror, beyond shock. From above and along the walls came swelling waves of movement as the hordes of anti-dimensional demon beings seemed suddenly empowered by the fear they evoked. Their strangely unseeing eyes darted around as they sensed and fed on the negative energy of his fear.

Their struggle to free themselves suddenly became so savage that it sent dust and stones tumbling from aloft. Izz gasped in shock, touched by a sudden fearful trembling in his stomach. The intensified restlessness was unsettling and upsetting as it seemed that all hell was on the verge of breaking loose. Izz was petrified as if held by an invisible, clenched fist until his fear quickened him. Like arousing from a waking, living nightmare, he reminded himself that fear was only a distortion of reality as Ammiz often alleged. The urgency to move forward in the direction the amulet pointed to, no matter what, suddenly became critical. Izz bridled his fear and forcefully uprooted his feet. He knew that each moment he hesitated was precious time wasted. He was on the move. With each step he took deeper into the cavern, the brighter Zuree's amulet glowed, and the more agitated the demons on the walls and ceiling became. Izz kept his eyes forward and moved as quickly as he could. The flames, smoke, and heat ahead appeared to intensify and grew heavier in the air with every approaching step. He felt the thick air heaved into his lungs, and surge out of his throbbing chest again as panic rose from within. The screams of horror and pain of the demon hordes increased to a pitch so intensified that Izz had to hunch over with one hand clamped over his ear in an attempt to block out the madness. The very air seemed to taste of agony and terror, and as he put distance between himself and the impaled demons, his heart pounded, and his head ached at the nightmarish anomaly he thought he had just seen. Izz moved cautiously down the path, still shaken by the encounter that kept him ever on his toes with fear. As he hastened to move forth, an eerie orange haze drifted slowly toward him, bringing on its breath a sudden flare up of suffocating fumes. Like meat that had been left over a flame for too long, the odor of charred hair and seared flesh became fierce as the greasy stench thickened. The ghastly smell that was almost overpowering got worse with every step he took toward its source. All the while from above, the screaming, moaning, wailing and struggling against some impending doom persisted. Izz dug out his neck wrap from his satchel. He wrapped it around his nose and mouth in several layers to help keep the horrid smell out, but it did not help very much. Suddenly a strange, overpowering red glow appeared against the shimmering haze of a backlit ring of fire. Izz squinted into the brightly lit cavern and perceived an aura casting deep shadows like the faded rust color of dry blood against the cavern walls. The smell of the burning of unclean things grew stronger.

Izz of Zia

There seemed to be a dingy scarlet fog before his eyes, reflecting thousands of licks of ravenous flames that snaked up the walls nearly white, like lightning. He could feel the howling of hate in the winds created by what appeared like an intensifying inferno raging before him. The heat increased twofold, then doubling and redoubling up to a point where Izz was sure his skin would melt off his flesh.

Squalls of unbelievable heat came swirling toward him, so brutally that he thought his clothes would burst into flames. He felt his hair was bristling. From within the vast inner chambers, he could hear ghostly cries of tormented torture and pain. The horrific sound gushed vividly upward, growing louder and louder, more and more intensely eternally. Izz felt droplets of sweat begin to bead on his face and trickle down from his forehead.

Was he sensing reality, or was it delusional fearful imagination? Was he on his way to who knows what unspeakable doom? A flash of images of Zuree calling out to him cascaded across his mind. Izz could now see ever increasing scorching flames glowing red hot and dancing off the walls in the distant chasm. It all made dreadful sense at this moment. It was the ancient entrance to hell, the eternal abyss of death, damnation, and evil. The gate Ammiz often spoke of was before him glaring forth from across a chasm of thousands upon thousands of years.

Izz reached for Zuree's stone, which was now pulsating like an anxious heartbeat. If he just kept moving, he would be all right. Izz kept repeating to himself. Step by step, he was drawn onward by some unearthly influence that had taken his will into its grasp. He heard the noise of combustion make crackling sounds that grew deafening as he approached its source, compounded by the beleaguered screams of the tormented within. Izz froze in his tracks. He inched his foot forward, then pulled it back. *This is as far as I go*, he told himself. *This is as far as I go, and not one step farther—this far and no farther*—Izz repeated over and over in his mind, as he took another step and yet another and another. *No love could stretch that far*, Izz repeatedly heard an external voice pound in his head over and over as he moved forward. He tried desperately to reassure himself while probing his guts and heart for something to hold on to. But above all an inner sense told him that he must go on. Even if the gates of hell themselves had burst wide open at that moment, he would not have, could not have been able to stop himself from going forth like a doomed moth to a flame.

The pendulum in Izz's inner clock swung with a loud tick-tock in his head like the clanging bells of doom. Panic pounded and pulsated its never ceasing rhythm, making his headache with the realization that he was losing his race against time. As he walked through clouds of smoke, Izz could see the ever glowing background in the distance was brightening with white and yellow flames that oscillated slowly, listlessly, as if to the beat of a massive remote dark heart. The smell of smoke was spreading thicker in the air. He heard the terrible, amplifying screeching, screaming sounds of demonic pain from the outer chasm from wench he had just come compounded by the nerve racking screams from within. The air crackled with tension as the eerie warnings of impending disaster hammered in his head. His uneasiness was growing by leaps and bounds. Izz's heart was assaulting his chest, and his palms were so wet they were slithery. Izz's skin was prickling, and he felt something deep within him jitter, as though parasitic worms were crawling just beneath his skin. Again, he cringed at the nearly unbearable screams from within and without as it were from a mortally wounded monster agonizing its last moments of existence. Izz began to feel as if he were walking along a path for the damned, in line, waiting for death to call his name.

In the ebbing red haze, Izz suddenly ran into an almost solid wall of deep smoke that curled and billowed up, roiling its way around him, making him gag. The smoke seemed to rise and take a gruesome form as the sound of screaming drifted within it. The unbreathable air started ghastly and only got worse. Izz was afraid he would suffocate but found he had breath enough to move on. He did not want to see what was beyond the smoke. But he had to know where the mystical stone was leading him. He adjusted his scarf and continued through the boiling and rumbling clouds of choking gas. He tried to slap away the poisonous gases to no avail. Through the smokescreen, Izz could barely see what looked like eerie illumination frolicking before his astonished eyes. In the drifting stale, asphyxiating air, a bright ball of light like a giant ember just flew past him and then shot up through the darkness and disappeared. The multicolored vapors continued to thicken and eddied voluminously in streams that hovered about and surrounded him. Orange, red, and yellow puffs expanded in the obscurity of the smoke, and then blossomed and were caught in an up drafting current that surged upward.

More bouncing, kaleidoscopic bulbs appeared like sentinels blocking his way. Izz drew his blade, slashing and stabbing at them in vain as he convulsed in a heartburn coughing fit. He gazed at the top to see the smoke plumes rushing up through a vent extending to the surface, whipping themselves into miniature storms, accelerating as they rose as if they could not wait to escape this place. All at once, Izz almost stumbled forward as if an impenetrable power suddenly opened to allow him passage. The air around him suddenly began to somewhat clear. He gazed ahead, and the first thing he realized was that he was entering yet another cavernous macrocosm that was very different from the one he was leaving.

Sixteen

The Lost

arkness closed in over the Norticlan encampment on the hill, as huge campfires were set ablaze that the catapult crews could complete the final repairs on the damaged catapults. The wide eyed wounded Edawnian warriors craned their necks around, trying to figure out what the approaching torchbearers had come to do to them. They could sense that something was dreadfully wrong, but what that was, they could not quite imagine.

The Norticlanders that surrounded their captives only glared back at them mercilessly, their faces lit with the dancing flames of their torches. Among the Norticlan warriors came the black robed Dark Priests with their eyes glossed over with pure evil above their heinous rotten toothed evil smiles, ready to inflict the worst woe imaginable. Baddlock's Dark Priests were incarnate demons who hated all men with an insidious hatred that had slowly festered out of embittered self hate. They stuck out viciously at others who had succeeded in the real virtues of men such as honor, charity, and love, where they had so miserably failed.

Their methods of torture were rumored to be the most hideous forms of execution. It was said that they were able to keep a man alive for days, screaming at the top of his lungs, suffering more pain than ever dreamed a man could experience. Their every waking moment was spent incessantly striving to dream up something even more horrendous. A feeling of panic set in as the Edawnian warriors were loaded on to railed wagons like animals and carted toward the inner encampment. Legs and arms dangled through the rails as the carts that were packed to capacity jolted along. Before this night would be over, each helpless captive would regret, a million times over and over, the day of their birth. The fortunate had died while they were being gathered, transported, or shortly after reaching the invaders' encampment.

The living were separated into groups according to the severity of their wounds. Those that were too mutilated were cast to Baddlock's prized dogs to be eaten alive. Others that were just barely alive were thrown to the Zomborges, where they were brutally ripped to shreds without the minutest mercy or remorse. Those that were expected to die within the hour but were still fully alert were dismembered in the cruelest methods possible. The Dark Priests made unholy signs and dedicated those that would be sacrificed to their underworld gods. The first victims were then strapped hands and feet to four draw animals, which were then whipped viciously, sending them bolting to the four winds at the same time. Once the straps snapped together, what happened next was inconceivable. Human flesh was pulled, wrenched, or otherwise dismembered in opposite directions, making savage ripping sounds, as muscles were torn, and gruesome popping noises as snapping cartilage was ruptured. Ligaments and bones were rent limb from limb. A loud, appalling baby like squall escaped from lips that made their last sounds, cut short as a mist of blood burst, into the air. The fatal eruption sent cheers throughout the blood crazed encampment. Those with wounds that had not pierced vital organs and those that had been entangled in the thorns were brought before the Wicked Warlock Wizard. This would be Baddlock's most amusing hour. Such a thing had become his favorite, loathsome method of dealing with prisoners or, virtually, anyone else that displeased him. Those wounded that were sure to live for at least a few hours were separated from the group. The rest, still in shock from the unbelievable carnage they had lived through, looked on in horror, their shoulders slumped down dejectedly and their hearts filled with a doomful dread.

Once again, the beastly Dark Priests called upon their underworld gods to bless their offering. The wounded men were slapped into full wakefulness and their clothes ripped off from the trembling bodies. Then the condemned were taken to paired poles that were buried and wedged into the ground. The naked men were hung upside down, stretched, and constrained in an X position. A long, wicked saw with long, ragged teeth was brought out, and the executioners lifted the saw across the victim's crotch and slowly sawed the men in half, down the middle, while they cried out and begged for the mercy of death. This method of torture and execution was the most inhuman punishment that only a twisted demonic mind could have conceived. Because the victim was hanging upside down, his brain received a continuous blood supply in spite of severe bleeding. By the time the saw reached the lower intestines, blood was streaming from nose and mouth. When the saw reached the stomach, a blast of blood spewed out of the victim's mouth as he let out a gargled howl. All the while, the condemned shook and trembled violently like a leaf caught in a web in a raging storm. The doomed remained alive and conscious until the saw severed the major blood vessels of the abdomen and lungs.

The next group of wounded were brought forth and staked to the ground. Then one by one, every bone in their bodies was shattered. As an executioner wielding a sledgehammer with brute force, blood was sent splattering in every direction with every bone crunching blow. Vital organs were avoided simply to maximize the pain and horror. If that was not cruel enough, a decrepit looking assistant carried an instrument that resembled an infant's rattle, only bigger, with a hollow, perforated ball on the end of a long handle. The ball was submerged into a small crucible carried by the tormenter, where it filled with molten lead. When the ball filled, the demented torturer walked from one crushed victim to the other, sprinkling droplets of molten lead onto their skin. The screaming and whining were incomprehensible as the internally broken men were seared to the bone, everywhere the liquefied metal splashed. As pain tore at them, insanity claimed their minds, one at a time. Anguished bellows permeated the air as broken men whipped around, flailing and thrashing wildly.

As Izz anxiously continued he all at once found himself in what seemed to be an unearthly dominion overlapping the physical and spiritual realm. He seemed trapped in alternating realities, surrounded by a graveyard of flames that leaped and hissed from everywhere. Then something unexpected happened. Suddenly, the screaming stopped, falling silent as if it had never been. For a moment, nothing happened. As if the abyss was holding its breath at his sudden presence. Then Izz noticed stirring within the smoke that shrouded the void and swirled about his ankles all around him. He peered through the streaming smoke beyond the ghostly mist and at first, was unable to see against the fiery backdrop. But as his eyes adjusted to the brightness, his mouth fell open in amazement at a span that appeared unbelievably endless lake of fire. Before him lay a yawning pit of an engulfing inferno that was lighting up the deep. There was no more need for his now ineffective torch. He doused its feeble flare and stuck it in his satchel, allowing it to poke out the top as it cooled. The brilliant tongues of flames were Izz's only source of light now.

The little breathable air that did reach him reeked of a mixture of choking smoke and burnt flesh so vile that he could barely stand breathing it. Cracking, and popping fires of eternal damnation suddenly fanned into consuming eruptions all around him roaring with the breath of a dragon. In the backdrop, tornadic columns of twisting magna belched out lightning like fingers that reached out toward him as if to pull him under. The strangely colored lake set ablaze was not fueled by any perceivable fountain, and yet, there it was. And here he was before it. Its flames flared with incredible power and threw up showers of sparks that dance across the path before him. Fumaroles, smoke, and ambers crawled up along the pit's walls like disjointed, projecting tentacles of a rampaging monster.

Izz looked down the terraced footpath. Everywhere spitting red flames surged and whirled down its course like wildfires running before a seething wind setting the whole underworld ablaze. Beyond that point, the cavernous abyss expanded into an even greater chamber of incalculable height, depth, and breadth. Izz found himself at the fathomless mouth of a heaving kiln of heat and fire gushing intently upward. Suddenly the stone responded as if to Zuree's proximity. With little hesitation, Izz stepped forth into what seemed like walking into a furnace. He had come too far to falter now. Izz forged ahead, into the realm of flames burning, ever violently where only angels dared to tread. Not heaven or hell, angel or demon could keep him from his appointed quest. Izz's gaze took in the breadth of the ceiling along its smoke shrouded length until its visibility was reduced in the distance and finally disappeared into an endless red haze that seemed to reach away into infinity. His first reaction to the mysterious subterranean phenomenon was awesome amazement, virtually too overwhelming to be fear provoking; and then sudden primeval fear set in because he knew that its existence should have been too far beyond the bounds of possibility. It was an immense gate into another world, an unnatural, supernatural universe of fire. The sheer physical scale of this abysmal, unfathomable gape awed him beyond his ability to phantom. He could feel the intense heat and the pain of its burning, but its outbursts of incinerating fury did not not consumed him. With all that fire and heat, he knew he should have been instantly burned to a crisp of smoldering smoke and ash. It was almost as if he had walked into a detached reality. "This is incredibly unreal. It could not possibly be!" he mumbled.

Suddenly, an onrushing wind of glowing red hot heat came upon him like pulsing waves of scorching fieriness, hot enough to roast a yakox. Izz's body felt so hot he feared he would ignite right then and there. He threw up his right arm in opposition to the fierce glare of the flames and shielded his face as best he could. But he was ill prepared for the blast of blazing heat that came off its swell and struck the unprotected upper part of his face. He knew that his flesh should have instantly incinerated, yet it did not. He felt as if the very air was wrapping itself around him in fans of scalding stickiness. His breath burned in his throat. The smell of scorched flesh was on its weft, and Izz kept wondering why he was not burned to a cinder crisp. With a startled question pasted on his face, Izz asked himself, *How could Zuree possibly be in such a profane place?*

Izz tried to ignore the crawling sensation of escalating fear tunneling its way up his spine. He forced himself forward through the hot zone, keeping his eyes on the hidden places. He braced himself against what he feared he might encounter next. Again and again, the thought of turning back entered Izz's thinking pattern. And the more he thought about it, the more his quest seemed like utter madness.

From within the Norticlan hilltop, the multiplying screams were so loud and intense that their echoes were heard within the Edawnian Kingdom. Every able man, woman, and child busied themselves, fortifying the damaged walls and gates as best they could. The men tried to carry on silently without showing emotion, but the women and children were greatly afflicted and resorted to pressing their palms to their ears to shut out the screams. Suddenly, men that were frantically building makeshift barricades and digging trenches came to an abrupt standstill. They looked at each other but found no words. The king paused and looked over the crowd. His face was soaked in the sweat of labor as he swiped the perspiration from his brow and said, "Get back to work... everyone."

A warrior with a brother unaccounted for nearing hysteria from the distant screaming raised his sword to the night sky and uttered in desperation, "Those are our friends and brothers out there!"

The king lowered his head and shook it pensively. Suddenly he set his jaw out, snapped his head up, and thrust himself erect. Facing his men aggressively, he roared, "Get back to your tasks, now!"

Commander Zandor and Kondor came to the king's side and stared challengingly over the silent ocean of men. Ozzdon's command was law; his word was final. He continued, "I carry what is in your hearts, but there is not…anything we can do for them now. We have once severely underestimated Baddlock's numbers and his power. We must now make our stand, here and now, to defend our kingdom and our women and children. From this point on, from these trenches, from behind these walls, our armies must fight a stationary war of defense. From here, within our kingdom, we must rise or fall…forever! Every drop of our sweat now will save a goblet of our blood later. Soon reinforcing troops will reach us, and I swear to you, by all that is holy, we will drink revenge to our fill. For now, be strong, especially for the children."

Determined not to give way to despair despite the discouragement and exhaustion of his men, the king ordered them to stay busy. Ozzdon then turned the corner with his twin generals, out of the sight of the others. Only then he lamented bitterly. He whispered, "To what level of depravity can the human mind possibly plunge itself? How can any human conscience perpetrate such evil, to any other living creature, most of all to another human being? I am ashamed to belong to the same human order." He fell upon the outer wall and could not help but feel a sense that he was leaning up against a sandcastle cast on a desolate beach. And there was a monstrous wave about to come crashing down on him and his people.

Back in Baddlock's encampment, the blood lusted orgy continued unabated. The next group of men was blinded by gouging, their noses were cut off, and their throats slit. To extend the agony of the torturous death, the cutthroats were careful not to sever the jugulars, which would have prematurely ended the excruciating pain. The men's tongues were then pulled out through the open wounds in their windpipes and hung down the middle of their necks. The butchered men were then unbound from their racks and nailed hands and feet to two crossed beams and hosted up over the encampment to the cheers of every Norticlan warrior. In each case, these forms of torture would eventually end in death, however painfully slow. The length of time required to reach death could range from a matter of hours to several days. Madness would typically set in after a few hours, but this in no way diminished the pain. Men of the Norticlan stood around the dying, making wagers on who would live the longest and who would die first. Dandork, on the other hand, had found a secluded spot away from the slaughter. He kept reminding himself that he was a warrior, not a butcher of helpless men.

Baddlock sat nearby the circle of pain, on his war throne, watching helpless men that did not mean a thing to him, softly whimpering, long past groaning, too far gone to cry out. He watched heartlessly as the lives of lacerated, broken bodies slowly seeped away. How he enjoyed their pain.

Throughout the empire, kings answering the call of their Emperor King Ozzdon, advanced day and night, over land and sea, suddenly paused. They stopped what ever they were doing to listen and to stare into the night. They wondered what had caused the sudden chill of terror that had unexpectedly jolted up their spines.

The tower watch on the northernmost wall of Edawn suddenly broke the strangling tension gripped over the kingdom: "Someone approaches the northern gate!"

Every archer on the northern wall turned their nocked weapon toward the incoming band of staggering footmen as they came into view. "Do not shoot!" a haggard voice came out from the darkness.

"Stand down!" Zandor's powerful voice sounded out. "They are our very own men."

Those that had concealed themselves among the dead were able to escape under cover of darkness. The run aways gave an account of the bloodcurdling things that none could have conceived and were at that moment being executed on those that had been taken, prisoner. As Zandor listened to the horrifying account, his eyes burned into the night. His best friend Rayzar had been taken captive and was at that very moment in all probability being tortured. His big broken heart was filled to overflowing with pain. He glanced skyward and watched the dwindling starlight as it was being squeezed out of the western horizon. For the first time, Zandor saw the string of brightly lit points of light that had been spoken of many times. Across the sky, one by one, the globes of fire appeared. Small spotlights of magical illumination shone in the darkness, one following the other on their appointed trek across the northern sky toward the western horizon. Zandor stared at the absorbing sight as he heard among the crowd below some rejoicing, ecstatically to see their loved ones alive and well. Others not finding solace wailed the more.

As if in a daze, Izz walked along the fiery shore of the restless lake of fire as it tossed about savagely spilling and splashing over. Obscure anomalies seemed to be dancing before him in the distance. Black clouds seeped in and appeared to gather about him, separating him from all that was good. He reached to wipe the sweat from his brow and noticed that as he raised his hand, it seemed to disappear and reappear as if he was oscillating between two dimensions. He was caught where the actual physical, visionary, and spiritual met and each seemed to infuse itself with the essence of the other. He thought he must have somehow stepped out of the existing real world and into an inexplicable and menacing, living nightmare that existed in some another reality.

Izz was sure he saw things that were not there. Then the screaming suddenly started up again. The intensifying wailings mingled with the sounds of the searing flesh consuming flames. He kept wondering where he was when something seized his attention. He could barely bring himself to believe what he thought his eyes beheld. Within the burning lake of fire, he saw withering, smoking profiles, flames shaped like the figures of bodies interwoven with the wailing sounds of their torment. The closer he came, the more the flames appeared to be the silhouettes of people. Their fiery bodies glowed with a faint yellowish red light like human outlines plunged into an incinerator.

At first, Izz thought his eyes were playing tricks on him. He saw or thought he saw, waves of fire lashing out of control, blazing over the human eddy of haunted people enslaved by some powerful, unearthly fixation that kept them bound in the lake of fire. Izz could not distinguish sex or age. From the depth, individual forms incessantly crawled up to climb to the top of a pile up of intertwining bodies. Those reaching the top shoved those on the crest back down into the pit of splattering fire, only to be dragged down themselves in turn. Izz looked to see other shapes in the background and found more faces, more thrashing bodies as far as his eyes could see. The burning lake was filled with more and more bodies agonizing in pain, stretching back into the farthest horizons. And still farther beyond the haze that reached back into infinity, where more lost souls screamed in ever increasing agony. And yet farther into the void, a veil rose to hide the very end of time itself, from where unquenchable screams echoed. Their deathless bodies flopped wildly like fish in a boiling sea and twisting like worms on a hot stone. He could feel the squalling of hate in the winds created by the unseen power in the amplifying inferno raging all around him. The turbulence created by the churning movement was filled with hissing whiffs of toxic gases, mixed with the thick stench of incinerated death. The stench rolled off the molten lake of fire like fog off the marshes of a wasteland. He saw the bodies of the lost blazing ever brighter, burning alive. But they seemed to have somehow been altered into an inflammable physical state that kept them from being reduced to ash.

Izz wondered aloud, "Just what in the world of Zia could this possibly be!" It had to be the abode of the damned that Ammiz had spoken of numerous times.

Izz refocused his sight up ahead where the glowing red hot magma splashed up against the banks. The rock embanks were so hot that they had been scorched into hardened crystal interfused with tiny glassy globules that had once been bubbling stone. The depths were roaring with the sound of a turbulent sea as blinding fire spouted and burst into yellow white cascades of turbulent flames. All the while like an enormous squirming maggot masse, people, young and old were hopelessly trying to step over one another to climb above the entanglement of bodies. Again and again, the mass buckle and warp at the outer edges, twisting and bulging out and collapsing back in on itself like a writhing heap of snakes. The lost were caught in a supernatural web, which had at long last, driven them utterly insane. Their tongues lolled in their full gaping mouths. Like a roaring storm, their screams rose to an earsplitting screech. Their bloodshot eyes wide and dull reflected their madness and the reddishness of the glowing flames around them. Some cried out loud, some wept silently to themselves, and there were those like ghosts from another time that just stared out through hollowed out eyes into the blinding abyss. Their scorched, decayed skin hung in shreds. A fetid and rank blast of odor reached Izz's nostrils. The unbearable stench of death and the stagnation of their waste rose from the gulf in putrid waves. Izz held his hand over the scarf covering his mouth and nose as he felt sick to his stomach.

His eyes and lungs burned, and he blinked as he rubbed his eyes and gasped chokingly. He saw thousands and thousands of hate filled faces staring into nothingness, with eyes that had the intense, rigid, off the centered look of those who had lost all hope. Suddenly he was hit point blank with the reality of where he was. Izz felt fear vault into him, striking terror in his heart that sent shivered down his spine, threatening to bloom into full blown hysteria. As his mind leaped back and his feet shuffled in reverse, he attempted to draw himself away. But instead of shrinking back, he stumbled forward instead, despite his frantic effort to back off. Izz's heart nearly stopped when he thought he felt an unseen claw reaching out to grab him and suck him under. As he teetered, awestruck and horrified, a devouring blaze leaped wildly up at him. Flames washed over his face with a red glow, and fire licked at his feet as if yearning to relish his soul.

Izz of Zia

Izz stared with bulging, glazed over eyes at the contorted faces that loomed from the smoke filled pit. They seemed to be screaming in his face with gaping mouths at the top of their lungs as if their heads would burst at any moment. Their arms thrashed spasmodically to rise above the liquid fire, only to sink back down into the maze of infernal flames. He heard individuals muttering crazily, some begged for death, others pleaded for water, while others appealed for absolution. Suddenly, the smoldering bodies began a weeping binge that quickly turned into insane, disgraceful wails caused by their compounding agony. As Izz tried to back away, the endless roar of thousands of screams vibrated off the walls and rang in Izz's ears with the deafening outbursts of howling misery. The sound amplified, filling the yawning cavern with tormented unholy crying that suggested inconceivable persecution and, or, the repeated infliction of unbelievable punishment. The unyielding suffering was multiplied by unbearable regret. Izz asked himself again and again, "What manner of place is this?" It was too terrible to believe!

The abyss that stretched across the vast spans of suspended time and space was filled with the souls of the lost. Souls set adrift in oblivion, no longer a part of the living world of Zia. They were no longer a part of the present, the past, or the future. Was this really happening, or was it all just in his head? His chest tightened, and his hands started to tremble, and his fingertips began to vibrate. *How could dead, unfeeling, decomposing beings live and feel pain? And how is it that they could be tormented day and night forever and ever?* Izz wondered as its reality dawned on him with uncanny knowingness.

The oddest thing of all was that the multitude seemed completely unaware of his presence as if a fixed gulf between two worlds separated them. Suddenly a massive torrent of magma erupted like a volcano, spouting from within the innumerable mass, spraying scorching cinders overhead. As Izz struggled to distance himself, a column of flames spilled over his escape, like the splash of a thick stew. Izz waited until the smoldering slag trickled back and was absorbed into the face of the roaring sea of magma again. The screams of horror and pain increased to a pitch so intensified that Izz had to hunch over with his hands clamped over his ears attempting to block out the madness. The odor of charred hair and seared flesh was overpowering as the greasy stench thickened. The very air seemed to taste of agony and terror. Izz heard a shuddering gasp, of panic and hysterical terror right from where he was standing, and it took him a moment to realize that the sound had come from him.

Suddenly Izz heard a voice like that of Ammiz inside his head: *You must hasten, before the eternal lost sense the presence of the living in the midst of the undying dead. Remember, fear will be your greatest enemy. And never forget: Your race against time is critically short.*

In that instant, Izz was able to break himself away from the pit's strange magnetic power. He mechanically stumbled away, jerking and kicking himself frantically back. He scurried backward on all fours like a crab over a rocky surface. His hands were clawed and trembling as he turned and scrambled back onto his feet. He found himself breathless and mortally afraid. Izz staggered away, crying out in desperation and distress, unintentionally running deeper into the fiery abyss.

Izz's face was burning, and the skin all over his body felt like it was on fire. He felt as if his hair, and even his eyebrows and eyelashes, were crackling and ready to burst into flames at any moment. He turned away, raising one arm to shield his eyes. And as he looked out in search of escape, his eyes felt as if they were broiling in their sockets. It was becoming increasingly difficult to see anything through the thick billows of smoke that rolled and seeped its way to the highest parts of the cavernous ceiling and into every corner. Yellow and orange flames ceaselessly moved as they hissed and made snapping sounds from every side. While from below came the hideous sounds of gashing teeth and shrills of terror. Just beneath the hideous haunted sounds, his ears were filled with the racket of his frantically beating heart. There was nowhere to run, nowhere to hide.

Izz of Zia

Izz was wheezing, and his eyes were watering with tears as the foul air seeped up from beneath. He felt nausea in the pit of his stomach, as his insides seemed to turn inside out from the smell of the ghastly fumes and broiled flesh. It was just too hot for man or beast, but strangely enough, despite the unbearable pain, he was still not being devoured into flames and ash. What was happening to him, he could not fathom. All he knew was that he somehow needed to breach the madness that was bleeding him out mind and soul. He did not know anything anymore beyond that. Despite his feeling of fear and repugnance, step by step, he backed away thinking he had escaped the worst of it. It could only get better from here he thought, but there was no way to imagine the unspeakable horror waiting to come.

When Izz thought he had reached a safe distance from the molten lake of fire, he stopped to gather his wits. He reached for Zuree's stone and in the seething, coagulating smoke, Izz held the stone high in hand and slowly rotated where he stood. As he turned the stone periodically brightened. Then suddenly, the stone glowed brighter than ever and was pulsating like a frantic beating heart, faster than it ever had before; and he somehow knew that Zuree was near. Izz froze and slowly lowered the stone. Could Zuree be a part of the endless sea of the lost? Impossible! The thought brought on a pang of empathy that thrashed him heart savagely against a constricting fear that threatened to stop his heart altogether.

A tiny fraction of a moment later, through the solid mist to his upper right, at a distance, he saw before him some sort of natural megalithic landmark. He was surprised that the unusual formation had thus far escaped his attention. The roughhewed blocks and geometric standing stones looked like an extremely peculiar gateway. The fixed towering structure overhead marked the passage of a stone earthwork that spanned across the fiery abyss. On the other side of the arched structure, through the hissing of the flames and spray of fiery cinders, Izz could make out a crested framework that resembled a stone bridge. He immediately set off along the unmarked path where the stone beckoned. Painfully aware that precious moments were slipping by as the endless cycle of bits of time trickled their way into the chasm of eternity.

Izz sensed that he had less and less time left before the Great Conjunction moved into alignment as Ammiz had foretold. The urgency to move forward, in the direction of the stone bridge, no matter what, became critical. With each quickened step he took toward the stone gateway, the brighter Zuree's amulet glowed. If Zuree were down here, he would not leave her here. He was prepared to search for her until he found her or gasped his last dying breath.

SEVENTEEN

THE STONE BRIDGE

In the Norticlan encampment where the nightmare from which there was no waking only grew worse as the night wore on. It was a time of bloodletting and pain, a time of unspeakable torture and execution. It was a time of ruthless debauchery and defilement that became more and more sadistic with every outcry from men that pleaded for death. It was the most wicked example of evil. The barbaric Dark Priests had had many years to learn and practice the techniques of their torturing crafts. The unholy priests took great delight in plunging themselves into man's grisliest depths of deprivation. And they especially enjoyed getting creative with their cruelty in ways that rational human beings would never think of, let alone doing. They committed the nastiest atrocities against men—things that could not be written anywhere, except upon the hearts of the evilest of evil men. The most brutal methods of execution of all time were reserved for the strongest, less injured prisoners.

The groups of men captured on the twisted thorns were brought forward. Except for a few deep punctures that had held them in the thorn barricades, they were virtually unscathed. Special racks were set up for these men. The most gruesome of deaths were derived, by the darkest, twisted minds, at their most inhuman decline of despicable wretchedness. Woe to these cursed men, scourged with this ravaging spirit that entered their minds and gave birth to the monsters within them. It would have been far better for them to have never been born. For their fate would be thousands of times worse than the victims that stood before them. Among the unfortunate, Rayzar was chained and waiting for his turn to fall victim to one of humankind's greatest inhumanities. He waited to be plunged into a world where empathy does not dwell in the hearts of men.

The captives were held down while their necks were fitted into long handed yokes that were used to maneuver them to their racks. Each victim's clothes were stripped from them as they were simultaneously shacked down to the rectangular wooden frames. Each rack was raised from the ground to the level of the specially skilled butcher that stood over his subject. Their heads were immobilized with knotted ropes that were tied back against their throats chokingly tight. Each butcher's sole objective was to inflict as much damage and pain for the longest possible time before killing the condemned. The victim's feet were fastened at one end, and the wrists were chained to the other. The tension on the chains was increased so that the forsaken was wholly immobilized, which in itself induced excruciating pain.

In some cases, the sufferer's joints were dislocated and torn from their sockets. One group of captive prisoners was to be flayed from head to toe and then taken and crucified. Others would be disemboweled, and those remaining were set aside for impalement.

At a rack where the first unfortunate soul had been readied, one of the most wretched of the Dark Priests approached his helpless victim. He ran his long filth and blood encrusted fingernail across the forehead of the Edawnian warrior as the warrior tried to twist and turn away. The executioner lowered his face until he was eye to eye with his victim and said in a low, gravelly voice, "I am going to have to hurt you, very, very much. And believe me when I tell you that I will try to make this as painful as possible, for as long as possible." His putrid breath was sickening and smelled as if the miserable subhuman creature had eaten a bucket of pig excrement for breakfast. "You," he continued, "are about to experience more pain than you could ever imagine. You are going to be sorry in ways you cannot even begin to fathom."

Izz of Zia

The unfortunate man, now petrified as his fear surged through his spine to an unbearable pitch, stared back blankly, his eyes filled with shock and despair. In every case, each victim first had to endure castration. Next, as the young man whimpered and bawled like a terrified infant, the Dark Priest carefully made a surgical incision through the skin and the muscle, between the navel and breast bone. He was extra cautious not to puncture the abdominal cavity. The executioner inserted his finger in the incision and pulled up. Then carefully, the butcher parted and peeled back the skin as he cut away. Another cut was made from the stomach down toward the inner thigh, continuing down to the end of each foot. The skin was flayed meticulously away with the sharp point of the honed razor blade of the knife. Then a circular incision was made around each ankle. The peeling away and complete detachment started at the limbs and worked inwardly. The neck and face would be saved for last. The victim was slowly killed by skillfully, methodically detaching portions of the skin, inch by inch, over an extended period, striving to keep the bloody sheets of skin in one piece. The professional skinner watched excitedly as his victim's muscles twisted and rippled as nerves flexed like tense springs.

As the victim was wholly separated from his skin, every inch of the body convulsed with unspeakable agony. All the while, the condemned vented out one ear splitting, muffled squeal after bloodcurdling scream after another, only letting up just long enough to suck in another whimpering breath. His outcries and trembling were so violent that it shook the rack out of its place. So terrifying and so horrific that it sickened even the most hardened Norticlan warrior. Every Zomborge in the camp joined in unison with their own hideous screams as they salivated streams of drool out of the sides of their mouths. All the while their eyes darted from side to side as they rattled and stretched out their chains. Horses had to be held down as they jerked their heads up instinctively and stepped sideways with every blaring screech.

On other positioning racks, the shuddering forsaken were prepared for disembowelment, another ungodly and excruciating method to die a hundred deaths. To die as quickly as possible was the most one could hope. The quarry was stretched out in the same manner as those that were being stripped of their skin. The slavering sadist bore down on their unwilling participants. The unbending executioner slid the honed razor blade into an Edawnian warrior's abdominal cavity, adding to the pool of blood underneath him. The screams were so agonizing that they sounded like the brays of an enraged bull. The evil priest pushed the blade in farther, slowly slicing through the stomach muscles between the pelvis and the thorax. Then cut along the rib cage with deliberate slowness, de-skinning his victim like a strung lamb while his legs and arms quivered and quaked violently. The pain shot through the victim's nervous system with jolts of nauseating pain as a pungent mist of gaseous vapors rose from his butchered body. The evil slaughterer inserted his hand into the cavity of the stomach, like a child searching out a box of toys as he sickeningly sniggered. Finding what he was looking for, he wrapped it around his waist and forcefully jerked on the entrails, spooling them out like a feline unwinding a ball of yarn. The Dark Priest stopped each time the pain threatened to incapacitate his victim. The extraction of the intestines and organs from the gastrointestinal cavity of a conscious person was a method of punishment that could only be inspired by a demonically induced insanity. Oh wrenched sons of evil, what have you done? How is it that you have not known the costly price you will be brought to bear for your wicked deeds? Do you not know, how is it that you have not heard that your name shall be blotted out of the Book of Life forevermore?

As the disembowelment progressed, the slayer worked slowly removing entrails and genitals, throwing the detached parts to the campfires. He removed remaining organs as he strived to avoid the lungs and heart to keep the condemned alive and in pain as long as possible. The butchered sent horrendous infantile cries in all directions as he banged his head against the rack and dug his nails deep into the hardwood.

Izz of Zia

At the same time, on other wooden tables, men were being impaled, yet another inhuman way of torture so hideous it defied reason or understanding. The small end of a long pole was rounded to cause a lesser amount of internal damage and avoid as much vascular injury as possible along its track. The long blunt shaft was slowly and forcefully inserted and driven by two draw horses through the pelvis, between a man's legs. The stake gradually traversed the small and large zigzagging bowels and pierced through the stomach and diaphragm. Essential organs were pushed to the side, bypassing the lungs, through the throat and out the mouth. The unthinkable debauchery left the victim profusely bleeding internally and in great pain, but still alive for an extended time. The unendurable spasms of pain evoked ghastly screams, making this cruel method of execution one of the goriest. Impalement was one of the most grueling and gruesome inflictions of the purest, hate filled evil ever conceived in the human mind. What could have possibly gone so wrong in the human conscience? What self hatred, what madness could have driven a man even to consider, let alone carry out, such a ruinous act of outward animosity and inward self condemnation? The skinned and the disemboweled were crucified on crosses that were set in the ground. The impaled were erected on stakes as well. One by one, a forest of broken souls rose to the night sky.

Thus was the witnessing of the barbarity of man's cruelty to man, and this was humanity at its worst. The Wicked Warlock Wizard watched from the distance of his mobile throne. Watching the pain of how men died an endless death from which he drew a black force of energy from the diminishing auras of the suffering. Tigbone was curled up at Baddlock's feet, cringing as if he was the one on the rack. As the torturers simultaneously continued to mutilate their victims, a unified chorus of screams let out of utter anguish and agony filled the encampment. Its profane pitch reaching the Edawnian Kingdom, resounding over the entire empire. The cry was heard throughout the most inaccessible reaches of the heavens and reverberated unto the deepest underbelly of Zia. The demonic world fed and extracted a mystical, ever increasing strengthening from the pain and fear of human suffering. Large, black, warty yellow eyed demons shuddered fiercely in every direction, shivering with delight as they gorged themselves on man's misery. Was there no compassion left to be found in all of the world of Zia? And where was Ammiz's Great Creator? Had His lovingkindness come to an end forever? Some in the shocking storm of inward anguish cried out to the Greater for quick relief. But in reply only heard a deafening silence that drowned out any other feeling but that of being forsaken. Why did the Great Creator seem so far away when they needed Him most? Yet there were those that traveled their dark paths to complete their journey in trust, peace and living hope.

EIGHTEEN

MISSION OF MERCY

In the belly of the beast deep within Izz continued his undying search for his beloved princes Zuree. In the innermost abyss Izz found himself what looked like a dilapidated bridge structure. Izz moved toward the crumbling archway, and as he approached, he observed that the bridge was laid out in one segment that rested on six pillars of granite blocks. The overpass spanned high across the abyss, which blazed below with the fury of an infernal holocaust that set the underworld alight. As he neared the archway, through the thick shroud of billowing smoke Izz was suddenly met by an eerie sight of fleshless skeletons. The bony structures were impaled on formations of serrated, razor sharp pillars of molten cinders and ash. Both sides of the path leading to the bridge were lined with bones. Izz moved past each one carefully, braced for any surprise. He dared not to turn his back to them as if at any moment they could come to live and attack him. Revulsion constricted his throat and swept over the surface of his skin. He hurriedly maneuvered his way around the skeletal remains, checking behind and stepping around.

As he stood before the archaic archway, he studied the bridge structure that lay immediately before him. It seemed that out of the prehistoric well of time, eons ago. A colossal vertical stone wedge split and flaked off from the cavern wall and fell across the deep sea of flames to inadvertently span its length. Izz stopped and looked across the length of the enormous granite slab of stone. Ahead, at the farthest end of the elongated bridge, his keen eyes noticed an iron door embedded into an outcropped tower of hardened black stone. The upheaved stone island was perched in the middle of the burning lake, precariously clinging where it was fixed, its base all but melted away. At its very top on the brink, could it be the accursed chamber of the Altar of Damnation? Izz stared anxiously across the bridge, how could he know where the line was drawn? What did he have to lose—his sanity, life, maybe his soul?

In the act of trusting faith, Izz some way or another reasoned that this iron door was significant. He hung Zuree's stone amulet over the empty void. The stone was pulsating even brighter and brighter than it had ever before as dots of slashing lights and shimmering streaks shot out of the stone across the bridge towards the iron door. Izz took his first step onto the bridge in the direction of the iron doorway on the far end. The moment he stepped on the first stone, it sent a wave of tremors across the entire bridge. The ripple extended along the walls and ceiling so noticeably that he could feel its building vibration seep into the marrow of his bones. Like a waking of a sleeping giant, he felt the hideous evil of the chasm intensifying and curdling around him from every direction. The disturbed atmosphere seethed, and its force was so fierce that the walls of the cavern shook with the violence of its vexation. Could the bridge be aware of his presence beyond the realm of the natural?

It seemed as if he had somehow invaded a deeper dominion of an unfathomable oddity, where nothing existed but the thought processes of those within it. Had he wandered too far into the forbidden enigmatic labyrinths of the infinite mind? Just then, he seemed to have become one with the hellish underworld. And from that moment on, deepening thoughts of impending doom kept rearing up in his consciousness. He did not know what this all meant. The not knowing was much worse than knowing the brutal truth. But the one thing he was sure of was that his burning love for Zuree was stronger than his fear of the unknown. No matter what happened the pure clarity of his purpose would push him forth. And with that love motivated faith Izz set off across the rough hewn stone deck of the ancient bridge. How the crumbling trestle defied the ravages of time and the inextinguishable, raging hellfire lake that blazed below was a mystery.

Izz moved forward quickly, ignoring the ever escalating heat that singed his throat every time he drew a breath. The stale air at the heightened level was so thick that it seemed it would choke the life from him. He tried to hasten his pace, but the faster he attempted to move his feet, the more it felt as if he was dragging leaded weights. He traversed forward, taking each quickened step with critical care, as if the bridge might liquefy under his feet at any instance, without warning. Over the edge, he could hear amplifying noises, escalating frantic cries; bubbling, gulping, drowning, submerging sounds filled the air. There was a sudden commotion below, a stirring, churning, tossing disturbance. Drawn by movement, his eyes snapped over the side. He looked down into the inferno below, where the enkindled depths seemed to drop off down to the center of Zia. All at once, the questioning look on his face turned to wide eyed shock as he realized what was happening. The entire lake of fire seemed to all at once come to a brisling boil. Izz swallowed hard, his throat was raw and burning from the heated stench that permeated every molecule in that ensnaring moment. The air around him crackled and hissed with hidden activity. He felt the first pangs of desperation as he stood there alone, attempting to steady his nerves, while all the time. Feelings of insidiously paranormal terror engulfing him.

Izz focused on the scene of frenzied activity over the side as he quickly continued to move toward the iron door. He hurried along as massive, molten orbs leaped and threatened to envelop the stone bridge with seething fire. Yet somehow he was supernaturally protected from the unbelievable radiating heat. Beads of sweat trickled from his forehead, and ran down off his face, falling in drops off his chin. Suddenly just at that moment, a frenzied movement made him look down over his shoulder again. He nudged to the edge, not sure what to expect, and what he saw made the blood in his heart run cold. Below beneath the boiling clouds, he could see in the smoke a ghostlike vision of human images massing like drowning rats in an overcrowded sewer. In a flash, the swirling mass of living dead turned simultaneously, drawn to the edge of the bridge. Their hollow eye suddenly widened fighting to ascend, crawling their way up out of the fiery pit that held them. With an explosive, milling bellow, the throngs of dead flesh tore themselves away from the abyss. The sound of their cries and wails rose to an almost hideous pitch. Izz saw the sea of agitated, decaying, bodies as they lifted clear of the molten surface. They reached up to climb the foundation pylons toward him with gnarled fingers clawed at full stretch. It was as if he had suddenly been found out. It was as if his presence had been sensed in the vibrations of the bridge echoing off the intensifying rings of flames that seemed to be reaching up to get at him. The living dead were clamoring everywhere, lining both sides of the chasm crowding the bottom along the bridge.

Raging cries howled in Izz's ears like one gigantic lost soul. The force from the rear ranks pushed the front horde up against the rising tide at the base of the bridge. A grayish mass writhed in the smoke and rose as human linked chainmail joined in dripping shreds of hanging flesh, as they climbed with inhuman strength in pursuit of him. The ensuing throngs of madness each, in turn, struggled savagely to break free from the eternal bonds that seemed to hold them in the lake of eternal fire. In a great clatter and rattle of bones and shrilling screams of horror, the endless procession climbed, dragging, pushing, or pulling themselves over one another to get to him. He saw angry faces affected with advanced gangrene, toothy mouths peeled open, with loose brownish teeth crumbling around their screams of dread and hysterical desperation. Globules of dangling and dripping rotten flesh, teeth, globs of hair and tattered pieces of cloth ripped away and sloshed back into the unquenchable deep. The gravitational pull of the imprisoning vortex countered their surging upward attack with an equal opposing force that worked to drag them back down. Izz put his hand on his dagger. It was not much of a weapon, but it gave him some comfort. His fingers started to tense on the hilt as he gripped it tightly, pulled it up, and held it at the ready.

But how could one fight something that was so boundlessly unreal?

Izz stood frozen in place, staring in horror for the longest moment; this would be his one last chance to take flight. Every nerve ending on the surface of his body screamed for him to turn and run from this evil place. Then as if suddenly waking from a trace, he marshaled his courage. He did not run out, he braced himself and ran in, toward the iron door across the stone bridge. He was not leaving without Zuree! He broke into a jostle, then a trot, and then an all out full run. Sensing that this window of opportunity would not last, Izz drew on the full vestige of his strength. He ran faster than he had ever run before. Faster than he ran away from his childhood tormenter. Faster than in his race against Rizan. Faster than his flight from the pack of wolves, and faster than he dash through the arrow gauntlet. In the next instance, it seemed that every undead cadaver in the underworld was rushing to the top edge of the stone bridge. The bridge shook violently from beneath as unseen fists pounded it from just below his feet, and scurried along beneath the deck like giant spiders as he ran. The hammering of climbing hands and feet interwove with an evil melody that thundered in his ears. From within the fiery entombment of living death, the nightmare came forth, as the grasping fingers felt around the edge of the bridge. Adrenaline pounded wildly through his heart, and fearlessness coursed like a hot fortifying liquid through Izz's veins. Monstrous sounds came from just beneath the bridge. Screaming and crying sounds like the bellowing roars and snorts of wild yakoxen, like vicious animals trying to get to him. Suddenly a rolling wave of slimy, clawed fingers shot forth from within the entanglements. Twisted hands stretched over the edge, grabbed at him with ugly, crippled fingers. Long charred nails reached out at him, leaving oozy trails of pus on his pant legs.

Overpowering panic began to pour in. Izz tried to keep his rising dread under control, but fear was gnawing away at what grit he had left. Izz's eyes filled with unspeakable terror as he saw a sudden surge of the condemned come crashing over the edge of the stone bridge. From both sides, they came, like a giant sea swell from the shear depths. As Izz ran, terror ran right there, just behind him, moving upon him with every step. The voice of a nameless terror haunted after him, condensing within his mind as he ran on. *Now you are surely doomed,* a familiar voice sounded in his hearing.

Herded on by their parasitic, demonic tormentors, in wave, after wave the undead came upon the bridge from beneath. They attacked not in a solid wave, but in a frenzied jumble of crisscrossing directions. The abomination that exploded against him took his breath away. Spurred by a mixture of fear and courage, Izz accelerated his single minded effort to reach the iron door. He never stopped once to wonder what he would do if by some wonder, he even managed to make it there. Reaching the iron door would be the ultimate test of his will. The mounting immovable object was about to collide head on with the unstoppable force of his love for Zuree. At the same moment that Izz hit his peak stride, the sea of lost souls arose and screamed all around him, all at once. The deciding factor would be his agility, endurance, and speed. Crazed into delirium, the haunted all rushed in as if, they were ready to jump right out of their rotting skins to get to him. The suddenness of the assault knotted Izz's stomach and forced him to weave about spasmodically. He drew more profoundly from every remaining ounce of endurance he had left. From reserves so profound that came up from the deepest part of his bowls, he kept up his daring dash for the iron door. Trying with every ounce of effort Izz had left in him, he stayed balanced and on his toes as grisly intercepting hands reached for him. Frantically they tried to cut his legs out from under him as he hurtled himself across the gulf of decomposing flesh and bloodless hands that were coming at him from everywhere. As Izz struggled to catch his breath, a thick, foul smelling haze of repugnant odor struck him like the breath of a murderous slaughterhouse that threatened to heave him into a gagging fit. With nothing left to give, Izz exploded into a hopeless all out run toward the iron door, without stopping to consider any other option but reaching the iron door.

The chances of reaching the Iron door was quickly stacking up against Izz's favor. The outcome was pivoted on the faithfulness of his heart and soul. He held his dagger before him as he zigzagged, twisted, and turned. Izz dodged slashing claws of ruinous fingers that desperately reached out to seize him. The anguished, angry cries of the lost souls that thought they had him in their grasp, but were cheated by his agility, flocked after him. Continuously prowling, clutching hands, and gnashing teeth drove onward to take hold of Izz, only to be met by his slashing dagger. Many that lost their grip on the bridge were swept back, sucked down into the wild whirlpool of a universal law set in motion by an unseen hand. But yet in unyielding desperation, the damned, with jerking muscles, tried time and again to force themselves upon him. With heart pounding, breaths coming in gasps Izz rolled, whirled, pushed, and bypassed his pursuers, continually fighting as he struggled for his life.

The increased activity caused a drift of black plumes of smoke to flow up over the bridge filling the air with poison and ash. The vapor crept in all around Izz like a heavy, darkening cloak, making the air impossibly hard to breathe. As Izz turned on his heels, spun, and raced past the animated dead bodies, he felt a condensing rush of arms reaching out for him. The feel of their dead flesh made him retch. From the puffs of thicker and thicker smoke, emerged more and more heinous, enraged faces, distorted with hate and malice. His weapon was in his hand wildly slashing as he made a hard ninety degree turn, narrowly avoiding the demon possessed creatures that tried to block his way. Izz turned on instinct, and smashed through shoulder first and shot straight past the midst of seeking clawing hands; bulging eyes; jutting jaws; gaping mouths; and lolling tongues. He bolted, edging forward, ducking just underneath their clutching hands as they closed just an instant too late to cut him off. At this point, Izz was more prepared to died than relinquish.

Tom Icon

As the escalating danger coagulated, Izz's determination only waxed the stronger. He picked his way through the chaos like a slippery bar of soap, lunging forward in long, wobbly strides, running on blind instinct. The principalities of evil brooded in anger that the intruder was still moving and could not be stopped. They mauled at the air with their spidery arms, desperate to halt his movement toward the iron door. His heart suddenly seemed to jump from his chest to thud violently in his parched throat as he glanced over his shoulder at the shadows that chased him. Izz shuddered when he felt the scraps of flesh that fell away from bony hands that gripped at his shoulder as he forcefully broke away. He cut away with his dagger as he spun and dodged across from one end to the other. Severed, clenching hands fell to the bridge deck, still trying to clutch at him.

One grotesque corpse after another tried with all their might to catch him, only to be knocked off balance and siphoned away into the unquenchable inferno below. With widening, stunned, blind eyes, they were absorbed back into the devouring flames as they tried to drag him down with them. Izz kicked viciously back at them as they screamed and shrank away. He desperately had to stop to catch his breath; his throat and nostrils were baked with dryness as if he was breathing in fire. But he dared not even hesitate. He knew that if he faltered, he could easily be swallowed up, driven to madness, to become one of the countless half rotten, soulless bodies that begged for death.

The next swarm was upon him with blinding swiftness, attacking like mindless, wild, hyena like beasts that barreled murderously toward him. As the lost souls closed in, he saw them up close for the first time; he had never seen such evil, or such hate, so clearly. Their dredging hands like tentacle raked out and reached toward him. And Izz stuck back endlessly with his dagger to clear his way. Izz's blade ripped away in grayish blurs at the rotting flesh, exposing bones and cartilage. He angled off one way and then the other, guided by will and raw gut feeling. Blood was thundering in his ear, and his breath was burning in his lungs as he suddenly smashed into the crushing hordes that were closing in fast like a tightening fist. All movement was distorted like a whirlpool of rags in a cyclonic storm. The infernal hordes pushed and pulled, and twisted in until they were standing shoulder to shoulder, blocking his advance.

Izz knew he was in over his head, but he could not give Zuree up. The cluster closed in, overwhelming him, and he tried to pivot, to turn, to backup, but they were drawn in behind him too, choking off his retreat. He reeled around and was thwarted at every turn. He stood rooted to the spot, unable to move forward, back up, go over, under, or around. He would have to turn and fight. Despite it all, Izz still managed to hold out a tiny corner of hope. His eyes narrowed combatively as a deep animal like warning sound rose out of his throat. He was as steely and gladiatorial as a cornered lion. He stepped forward as the crush of figures pressed in to encircle him with crooked monstrous claws. He suddenly released a startling, powerful force, hacking, tearing, slashing and chopping with his dagger. The encroaching demonic powers ripped at him like crazed animals, as he desperately squirmed like a slippery eel trying to elude them. Pandemonium ruled with unthinkable madness.

As the inner circle tightened the noose, suddenly, the whole bridge began to quake as the surface of Zia slightly shifted in response to the approaching Conjunction. Izz maneuvered the mass to the edge, letting fly with his elbows and prying his hands away enough to push a band of corpses over the side back into the chasm of hell. The dead souls clung to him like giant leeches threatening to sweep him over as they fell. He was like a wild beast kicking and jostling against a tangle of arms, and hands with tattered fingernails raking toward his eyes. The situation was growing uglier with every pounding heartbeat. Izz felt the dizzying waves of hysteria as the screams of the dead fell away. The wailed like the long, cursed cry of the wind as they plunged back into the magma with a great spattering splash. Izz leaped for a step, but the mob kept coming. Hands were immediately on him again, clutching at him, and he knew at that point it was not even remotely possible that he could escape them. Through the lattice of arms and hands, he could see the iron door. He had one foot in a sinking hole, and the gaping hole was getting deeper. Yet he refused to give up. He swept and slashed out with his blade faster and faster, with more and more forcefulness at the infringing presence before him. In his final throes, the onslaught surged around him like a riot in full craze, pulling him in every direction at once. The rage of the beast was squeezing in all around him now like a tightening noose. The evil power battered him with unyielding cruelty, pummeling him with dreadful black fists that fell to crush and obliterate him, flailing at him from all sides, whipping into a frenzy of jarring and malevolent violence. It was useless. They were everywhere, clutching, pulling, and punishing. Izz danced on a razor's edge with every heartbeat at any moment bound to lose his footing.

Izz felt a heavy blow slam against the back of his head, and another caught him in the belly. Then another descended and then another bringing him down hard as his strength gave out. He tried to resist, but his best efforts were easily overcome. There was the sensation of falling helplessly, and he hit heavily on his face on the stone deck with a sickening thud that drove the air out of his lungs. The taste of blood flowed in his mouth. Izz was a trapped animal, instinctively scrambling to get loose. He struggled to get to his feet, fighting for his life. But it seemed that the whole crushing weight of the underworld was pressing down on him.

At last, he accepted defeat. He would conserve the strength left him until he hoped for any chance of escape. He had trouble catching his breath. He opened his mouth to scream out his stark horror, but his wind was locked as if his chest were collapsing under the weight of the sheer numbers.

Izz lay overcome, unguarded; his face flattened against the stone floor; his clenching and unclenching outstretched hands were helplessly pinned down. Gripping hands held him by the shoulders from behind as wisps of foul breath closed in on him and strangled his breath. He could feel their drizzling mucus drool dribbling down on him. He watched in terror as hundreds of rotting arms and hands reached for him and grabbed to tear at him. Hands clawed and turned against him embedded fingernails tore deep into his flesh, scratching the skin from his arms. He could feel his strength poured out like water. He tried desperately to escape as he slashed, punched, and kicked in all directions, but it was pointless. He was taken hold of, pushed and shoved to the edge of the bridge as the lost prepared to drag him below.

Izz could no longer see anything amid the grinding, swirling confusion of arms and legs. Severely beaten and abused, he was contemplating the impending terror of his demise when suddenly, without an inkling of warning, out of oblivion, a powerful armed fist grabbed him by the nape of the neck. The force of the unexpected abduction yanked him to his feet, up and away from the grasp of the murderous mob below. The strangling fingers spread, encircling entirely around his neck and throat as talons interlocked over themselves as Izz gasped and shrieked.

Instinctively, both Izz's clutching hands went spontaneously to his neck. Now as unlikely as it would seem, a patrol of roving demons drawn by the commotion had appeared out of nowhere, suddenly and unexpectedly. The devilish being that held Izz high over the mob of the damned was the demon lord caretaker of the eternal lake of fire of the deep. The cluster of pyromaniacs was allowed to leave their imprisonment for short whiles, from time to time so that they could stoke the flames of the abyss, for they were the keepers of the lake of fire. While Izz dangled in midair, kicking and squirming, the blood crazed throng lashed out with their spidery, bony arms and hands as if destroying Izz would somehow lessen their torment. The demons and the lost shouted back and forth at each other, but Izz could not understand what was being said. The dead souls were screaming angry abuses as they ripped at the air with their clawed hands. The demon lord unleashed the evilest of evil roars. Izz could scarcely stand the piercing scream that strained him to the very edge of insanity. The attacking assemblage of ghouls shrieked back, shrilling and yowling in soul searing agony until they had backed over the side to the point of no return. And once again, the lost were trapped in the wrenching grasp of the imprisoning, eternal lake of fire. The condemned were locked into an imploding nexus of toppling dead flesh that was sucked back down. The living dead fell away like fractured figurines, from their broken strings. The chain reaction set off pitiful wailing cries of horror as the damned were plunged deeper into the bottomless flames than ever before, for daring to defy their masters. They pathetically begged for release from the prison of their minds as they sank back into the swirling fog of their nothingness existence. As the lost souls continued to squeal frantically, the band of demons took great delight in their heightened agony.

Meanwhile, Izz dangled there in midair with a startled expression twisted on his face, looking on with wide eyed despair as the few caused misery of the thousands. The crowned lord of the flames raised its head and sniffed the ill stench of death that filled the air. The master of the flame paused for a moment as if to savor some delicious aroma. He joked in a crow's voice, "There is no sweeter smell than the aroma of charred, rotting flesh." Tilting its head back, it let go an ugly blast of laughter as he trembled with glee. A pale yellow, suffocating odor of sulfur puffed past its teeth in billowy plumes of rising vaporous drifts. The head demon spoke in an utterance that Izz understood somehow. The lesser demon warriors all laughed noxiously, like a flock of squabbling vultures. The demon lord turned its malicious attention back to Izz, as it carried him, leading him weightlessly, effortlessly. It studied him at arm's length as Izz continued struggling, kicking and gasping. The head demon squeezed down on its chokehold until Izz's kicking movements slowed. Its jaundiced eyes steadfast bulged out of his face and fixed. "I see you are a new arrival here. Whatever are you doing on the bridge?" The keeper of the flames spoke as if Izz had been a lamb that had wandered out of its pen.

The other dark figures stepped forward and encircled Izz, dragging with them a staunch, contaminated fog that nearly concealed their shadowy presence. More demon sentries came out of their hidden demon domain to arrange themselves around Izz. Each one of them was more hideous and tormenting than the other. The deformed creatures, with their rounded grotesquely exaggerated bellies, and florescent glowing yellow eyes, looked both frightening and laughable at the same time. Izz's stunned eyes suddenly focused as he tried to make sense of what he was staring at up close. What he saw were two huge, peering, amber snake eyes. Its horned eyebrows made its hooded globs even more malicious. Its facial skin was stretched tight as a drum over its pointy over seized canine fangs that protruded outwardly and down past its chin. Its head bristled with twisted thorny barbs and out of the top sides; two gnarled horns crowned its misshaped head. It was an ugly warted thing, half manlike, half animal, pure evil. It looked like a malformed buzzard, but with bigger leathery wings. It's shadowy, flat black figure seemed to ingest the light of the blazing labyrinth and not return it. So unbelievably hideous was it that Izz could not imagine anything more horrendous. In a state of fearfulness, never had the demonic been so real to him. Again, it took in a deep, sniffing breath, taking in Izz's scent, and then turned its head chokingly as if it had smelled something discussing. The chief keeper of the flames slowly turned back to Izz and asked, "Just what is it that we have here?" Its eyes narrowed with disdain.

From the elevated range of view, Izz tore his eyes away from the sinister creature that was now glaring at him with murderous hatred. He focussed up ahead and saw that the iron door was just beyond reach. Suddenly the keeper of the fire's intake of breath came short. It gasped a visible sulfurous vapor as its peering eyes flashed with extraterrestrial, evil intelligence. "A lifeblood, where no life is possible?" The ringleader's huge viper like eyes protruded from their sockets as its nostrils flared in shock. "This one yet lives!" the tormentor of spirits wondered aloud.

The startled demon followers screamed in a tone mixed of unexpected dreaded and horror as if the foretelling of Izz's arrival was well known. Each demon within an earshot of the alarming revelation screamed, shrieked, and shrank back as if Izz was the bearer of a foredooming woe. All the demons within sight scattered back like a flock of buzzards, fleeing the impending jaws of a deadly predator.

An under lord, peering intently through cleft eyes, stepped toward the taller and darker figure among the order of fallen angels. "Are you sure he does not bear the mark of our master as Baddlock does?"

Another lesser demon voiced his apprehension: "He belongs here not."

The circle of demons shifted, squirmed, and whimpered in confusion for a time like a herd of dumfounded goats. Agitate the keeper of the flames shook Izz so violently that Izz was left hanging limp in his outstretched hand. Then the head demon spoke to the others in a reassuring tone, saying, "I will deal with this fresh meat from the other side, myself." Meaning that he did not want any of the others to interfere with his intended amusement.

The rest of the subordinate demons stepped farther back to give the dominating devil room to deal with the intruder. Izz tensed up, beset with a gripping sense of helplessness. He tried to swallow, but his throat was too constricted. Nor could he stop himself from trembling. As Izz struggled to ease the stranglehold that was cutting off his air, he looked longingly at the iron door. Sensing that his life was in great peril, Izz sucked in as much breath as he could manage as he struggled like crazy and called out at the top of his lungs, *"Zuree!"*

The keeper of the flames drew its free hand back and flexed its talons. Its merciless glare was accented by the reflection of the flames from below. Slobber dripped from its snarling mouth as it reared backward, lifting its hand to strike Izz down into the frenzied mob below. Izz's heart pounded with terror as if it were about to bust out of his chest.

Inside, in the dark altar room, Zuree having learned to sleep standing to escape the hunger pangs and the numbing pain that radiated through her whole body, suddenly woke with a start. Her head suddenly sprang up like that of a wild animal all at once become aware of the danger. She stared blankly toward where the sound was building beyond the iron door. All at once, the screams and wails came more intensely, coming from seemingly everywhere around her. She flinched, forced open her eyes, and whispered in a groggy voice, "Who is there?" She tugged on the metal clasps that held her and pulled herself upright. Her wrists were already raw from having done this repeatedly. A trickle of blood ran down her arm, down to her elbow, forming a droplet that spotted the stone floor at her feet. Thinking that she had only imagined hearing her name, she closed her eyes to the darkness. She tried to find solace in imagining her father on his way at that very moment to set her free. Her thoughts turned to Izz. She so longed to see him that her heart ached more grievously than her bloody wrists.

Zuree's faint response popped into Izz's head, and he just knew that behind that iron egress, his beloved Zuree was being held. Suddenly as if the stone had sensed the two hearts beating as one, it seemed to draw in the combined love from both, the key to its power. The stone began to sizzle and hiss, and all at once, there came a burst of light more brilliant than the noonday sun at Summer Solstice. Then the stone shot a blinding blue light beam through the air like a flare fired from a weapon. The light struck the head demon and went right through like a flash from a shooting star. The light ray pierced the iron door and suddenly lit the chasm with what appeared to be a white patterned likeness of pure energy. The light waned gradually, and a few moments passed before Izz could once again see.

Zuree stood astonished, with an enigmatic look etched over her face as if it would be there for life. The light seemed to leap into the pit of her heart and left it slamming a wild beat inside her chest. The logical part of her brain was instantly forced to reconsider what she thought she had just seen.

Just outside, Izz winced and tried to draw back shaking in terror, unable to escape. He braced himself against what he feared to be the deathblow that would finally end his life. But to both Izz's and his assailant's great surprise, the demon lord, keeper of the flames, let Izz slip out of its clawed grasp and slowly dropped to its knees, with eyes wide. And its form went limp with shock. It stared down at its chest where a smoldering crater honked out powerful blasts of nauseating stench with every gasping breath. The cauterized cavity began to crumble into ash from within until the only thing that remained was a heap of disintegrated ash.

Dozens of pitiless eyes stared at their fallen lord, or what was left of him like a lump of manure. Terror washed over every demon's faces as they turned and looked at each other for a fraction of an instance. Then they scattered like a flock of cackling crows whooping and wailing as they took flight on leathery wings. A black cloud of dusty ash rose over the parched bridge floor and swirled around Izz. With another explosion of rushing, gristly wings, the demons rose into the darkness. They dashed away across the chasm like hemorrhaging phantoms, bleeding a torrent of vapor until they were all gone as if to escape a voracious slayer. The amulet's bright burst of light had appeared to have burned a crater through the darkened energy that had held the demon lord together.

Suddenly a quiet eddy reverberated throughout the cavernous space. From afar, two of the wickedest of wicked eyes trained on Izz. Then out of nowhere, there was a sharp crack, and the eerie silence split end to end. Out of the nothing, a drum began to sound in Izz's inner ear as if a heavy mallet was rhythmically being pounded against an anvil inside his head. Millions of rampaging flames transformed the caverns into a turbulent sea that vibrantly flashed and danced in his eyes. Izz gathered himself, wavered a moment, but then he hastily rose up onto his elbows. He told himself to get up and run, to run as he had never run before because his life depended on it more than ever.

In the next heartbeat, Izz staggered to his knees, and then sprang to his feet. He recovered his dagger, which had slipped out of his hand. Then was off like a jackrabbit being chased by a pack of jackals. As he ran toward the iron door below, he noticed a great disturbance in the tossing fiery sea that could not rest. The sound of the huge drum pounding in his head hastened as he pace. Hot magma spouts fountained as if a storm in the depths was brewing. Bright orange and red pumpkin size globules emerged and burst like giant soap bubbles, spattering in disarrayed patterns. Waves of red hot, molten lava splashed and sloshed back and forth, unpredictably across the depths like a thick lake of stew about to boil over. Out of the bubbling cemetery for the living dead, returned the hordes of the lost. Up the foundation towers and pylons, they climbed with such a vengeance that it caused the girders and the deck of the stone bridge to tremble and shake. Izz's eyes narrowed when he saw the outlined silhouette of thousands of tortured souls quickly making their way back up. He had to make it to the iron door somehow before they reached the top, and fear lent him speed. The iron door was within reach, and the only remaining obstacle was the growing mob of multi-possessed corpses as they began to reach the top and over. There they stood in ranks, braced against each other and poised to attack. Their lifeless sunken eyes were trained on him. Their long nailed hands clinched in renewed determination. A sudden surge of fortitude sparked from Izz's guts to his heart and mind.

Izz was thinking fast; then in slow motion, turning over, weighing in his mind the chances of surviving through what he was about to plunge headlong through. With every accelerating stride, the welcoming committee was growing. The images of glinting eyes rushed a frantic riot through Izz's head. He did not slack his pace. His eyes registered the odds mounting against him. His intellectual deduction accepted their visual intake as they considered their input thoroughly from top to bottom. And even though his eyes were insistent, he utterly rejected the hopelessness that they saw. Those indwelled of dead flesh would not keep him from his appointed meeting with inevitability. Without breaking his stride, Izz crucified his fear, and left his feet, diving through what looked like a weak point in the opposing whirlwind of dead flesh.

Racing with destiny, engulfed in evil, Izz twirled and turned, kicked, elbowed, and slashed blindly with his blade. And as he forced his way through groping arms swung closed, just narrowly missing their intended target. He felt a sensation of wild willful momentum shoot through him like hot coals burning deep inside his belly. Nothing short of divine intervention could have stopped him now. At full stride, he launched himself toward the door, shooting through the air as if fired from a catapult. By hook or crook, he managed to bust through the rotting, maggot infested wall of flesh and bones, mindless of the rife of stench that engrossed him. He pushed past the undead that roared about him like a living, frenzied sea of gore. On the other side of the putrid wall, he fell forward. As he slid across, the bridge deck seemed to jump up. He flung himself forward and then rolled and slammed up against the iron door with a terrible thud. Although suddenly feeling depleted, at long last, Izz finally had reached the iron door.

For no apparent reason, as if an unseen force seemed to surround and protect Izz, pure evil sensed that its attack had been frustrated for now. Or perhaps the threshold of the mysterious iron door was somehow off limits to the underworld. The horde quietly slipped back into the fiery abyss, and just like that, they were gone. For whatever reason, the indwelling principalities of darkness called off its assault and shrank back into the shadowy depths. For the moment, the onslaught of torment came to an abrupt end as if evil had paused to catch its breath and revise its failed strategy for its next attack.

Living Hell

In the face of the heavens, in the dark side of the night, the orbiting Great Conjunction was barely a sliver of afterglow radiating in the black vacuum of space. Its finely tuned orbit seemed tuned and in alignment with the mind of the Great Creator. The circling dance of planets disappeared beyond the western horizon and was gone to the other side of Zia. Below the overcast sky, a lone band of warriors dressed in black flowed into the pitch black pool of the night on their suicide mission. Without King

Ozzdon's knowledge, and against his wishes, Zandor and some of his bravest warriors made their way north through the killing fields. It was not the safest thing to do, and it sure would have never met with the king's approval. But Zandor did not know what else to he could do.

The band of volunteers with nothing to lose, pressed on silently, no matter what the consequences, surrounded by bloody gore and corpses, with the stench of death all around. The darkness was adequately concealing. There was nothing but the sound of insects, the soft hush of the wind, and their footsteps sloshing through the slaughter in the still of the night as they followed one another in a straight line, picking their way respectfully, trying not to step on the dead. With every stride, they fought the encroaching panic attack and the paralyzing phobia that grew beneath their feet, of a fear that death would open up a gaping grave at any time and swallow them up into its black pit. From time to time, lightning from a faraway storm lit up the bleak, gray horizon, revealing the land of the dead where hundreds of confused horses roamed about, still wearing their body armor, refusing to leave their fallen riders. If death was a place, the place was here. They forged ahead with a sense of urgency, moving through the haze, each form drifting into the drizzle. The small band was completely shrouded into the blackened night, guided only by the distant campfires dancing like fireflies in the dark hour before them. Cloaked by fog, the enemy's encampment loomed like a wicked island in the midst of a haunting sea.

The rogue troop gathered along the foot of the hill and peered up toward the encampment. And even though the forces waiting at the top overwhelmingly outnumbered them, there was no fear on any of their faces. Zandor turned to his men and whispered, "If there are any among you that would rather turn back, now is the time to do so." There were no takers. "You know what to do. Trust your instincts." And with that, he turned and stealthily led the elite force up the hill. Each figure crept noiselessly, moving smoothly and quickly up and into the dark mist until they were enveloped by its vapor, like melting honey into hot tea. At that point, Zandor led his men up the ridge, tensely, sensing the night, depending on his gut feeling, for survival as he traversed the open terrain up the hill. Halting his men, he edged up to the top of the slope alone, weighing his every move against sudden death. Along the way, Zandor ran across several dead Norticlan warriors abandoned were they fell because the Norticlan command did not have the decency to scatter a little dirt over them so that their bloating carcasses would not be exposed.

Under the cover of darkness, he reached the crest of the hill to find that most of the invading encampment slept. Zandor signaled the others to follow, and each man made his way up the steep incline. Huddled in a tight circle at the top they cut through the thorned barricades with their sharpened pincers and crawled across. The dead Edawnian bodies bound in the barbed thorns still hung from the grasp of the ghastly barrier. They crept stealthily ten paces apart with longbows strapped on their backs and blackened faces and hands. Flattened to the ground, they inched their way past the outer perimeter guards. Herbs rubbed into their skin , masked their scent from Baddlock's vicious dogs. Three arrows sliced silently through the still of the night. There were three hushed yelps that no one heard, and three watchdogs fell to the ground. Other inquisitive dogs that came to nose around fell one by one.

About a stone's throw away, around the campfires, could be seen figures gathered about the dancing flames. Zandor turned to his men, pointed to a lone guard patrolling and safeguarding the area, and motioned them to wait, and then peeled away. Zandor's entire body relaxed as if it were dissolving into the night's terrain. As he approached unnoticed, the danger of discovery closed in, and Zandor's blood pumped wildly. Around the catapult campfires, the darkened camp seemed alive with movement, sound, and the silhouettes of workers repairing their killing machines. But the element of surprise was on their side, a probe this far into their encampment was the last thing the enemy would have expected. Out of the darkness, Zandor rose, and with one stroke, his blade drew blood, slitting through flesh, slicing the night guard's throat, sending another heathen to his pagan god. He covered the watches mouth while he bled out so that no one could hear the soft, muffled cry of death. Zandor signaled for his men to spread out, and they advanced quickly at a crouched pace.

The Edawnian phantoms slithered toward the unguarded, tortured prisoners, skirting the twilight about as close to the brink of disaster as they could come without being detected. Along the way, they saw on long poles human skins fluttering like torn banners shaking in the currents of the wind. An indefinable smell of guts and gore was borne on the wind. The pungent air reeked of blood and raw flesh much in the same way as that of a stockyard slaughterhouse. From the glow of the campfires that burned around the fringe of their slowly dying comrades, they could all see the pangs of agony etched on each face. Their eyes reflected the flames like two glowing blood red coals glowing in the gloom that filled the night. The exposed flesh of those that had been skinned alive had turned purple and blue, with patches of dark reds. Those disemboweled were covered with streaks of watery blood, their exposed chests showed the inside and outside of their hollowed out ribcages. Those impaled spasmodically arched and shuddered uncontrollably from time to time. For some, the agony was beyond endurance, and mercifully, they had passed out; their only link with life was their own harsh, irregular breathing.

The surreal scene was out of an unbelievably nightmarish phantasm. Butchered men's screams had by now softened into muffled pleas for deliverance from their living hell. Men groomed to be the fiercest warriors in Edawn were sickened to the pit of their stomachs. Suddenly Zandor noticed one of the youngest of the elite had ventured a bit too close to a sentry at his outer post. Too close for Zandor's comfort, Zandor cringed. Courage was all well and good, but there was more than enough time to get one's self killed on this suicide mission. The young Edawnian warrior felt his stomach roll. He tasted the bile as it came up his throat and filled his mouth. He cupped his hand over his nose and mouth, desperately trying to gag down and silence the rush of vomit that came spewing out from between his fingers. The gurgling sound aroused the nearby Norticlan night watch that was slumped against a nearby crop of rocks.

The guard wiped his hand across his face several times before rising and looking suspiciously around for a few moments. As he walked across the myriad of dying men, the sentry thought he must have imagined that he had heard something out of the usual moans and groans of the dying. The smell of vomit came to his nostrils, but he did not think twice about it as it mixed with the other rancid smells of death that surrounded him. The watch continued to patrol the outer perimeter of the encampment along the circumference of their campfire's twilight. He suddenly froze in his tracks, sensing something out of place; he paused for what seemed like an eternity. He stood there trying to figure out why he had stopped, while the young Edawnian lay on the ground with his face pressed to the dirt at the sentry's feet, still holding a mouthful of bile and looking up, his eyes wide with terror. There was nowhere to hide, not even in the darkness. The sentry was so close that the young warrior wanted to bury his head in the ground. He could see insects crawling over the muddy, blood wet ground, bloating themselves on the coagulated carnage just beyond his nose. Adrenaline pumped wildly through him, as his body contorted with tension, and his heart was thumping so hard against his ribs that he could scarcely believe that the watchman could not hear it. He was shaking so severely that he was sure the enemy could hear him vibrating against the hard ground. The junior warrior glanced toward Zandor, who had an arrow at the ready. Zandor moved a finger over his lips, to tell the youngster to be perfectly silent.

After the most prolonged moment, the Norticlander moved away, distracted by his urgent need to relieve his bladder. The barbarian walked in front of a tree to urinate. Drenched with sweat from concentration, the fledgling warrior slowly let out his breath, and the rest of the contents in his stomach spilled out. Zandor signaled his men to be still as he drew his bow's string back. In the next moment, an expertly loosened arrow pierced the back of the guard's head, forcefully pinning his skull to the tree. The slain guard's body convulsed as he made the most awful muffled, retching noises and then sagged against the tree. Zandor waited for a reaction from the camp, praying for none. His expectations were answered.

Zandor turned his attention back to the mission at hand; and as he turned, suddenly his woeful eyes fell upon what was left of Rayzar's tortured, gutted body, strung among the dead and half dead prisoners. His heart and mind were long since gone and void. Zandor clamped his jaw shut, but could not help himself from groaning through quivering lips. What he saw made him look away immediately, as he withered back to shield himself from the sight, but his eyes came back to the pitiful figure that was left of his childhood friend. Quite unexpectedly, as if sensing the presence of his best friend, Rayzar's eyes open and focused down on Zandor. Rayzar's body twisted and jerked as it bled white. His lips parted, moving to form the words, *Kill me!* The faint agonized whispered plea reached out to Zandor. Then Rayzar opened his mouth to speak again, but the rest of his words were meant for a lip reader. Then Rayzar's eyes closed, and his lips trembled as if readying a scream but failed. The release of death was the only earthly thing he could look forward to. No matter what lay beyond, nothing short of hell could be as appalling.

For the most extended moment, Zandor merely stared at him, bringing his arms around himself from hurting for his boyhood friend. He could not hear anything but Rayzar's gasping breath between his own moaning. Rayzar's eyes opened again, and again he begged for the worst heart rending relief imaginable. Zandor could not stand to see him this way, but neither could he leave him to die like this. No man ought to die like that, and nothing was going to save him this side of death.

Sensing his dwindling opportunity drifting away, Zandor drew his nocked longbow, and everyone with him followed suit. Zandor rose to one knee, and everyone else did the same. There would be no joy in it. Through teary eyes, Zandor took careful aim for a kill shot, and through dimmed eyes, he fixed his sight on his intended target. Rayzar nodded his approval; he tried to wet his withered lips with a tongue that felt like a charred piece of wood in his mouth as he tried to smile. He moved his lips, but no words came. But the words his lips formed were unmistakable. *Thank you!* Then he clamped his jaw shut and squeezed his vacant, sightless eyes that seemed to be staring inwardly, down tight. A trail of bloody drool dribbled from his lips as he anticipated his solace. It took a big piece of Zandor's heart. The arrow flew from Zandor's fingertips, instantly killing his cruel fated compatriot. Rayzar jolted forward, and his death pangs faded with merciful speed as his head flopped and his tortured body sagged down into the release of eternal rest. The Edawnian warriors shot again and again and again, and then rolled and disappeared into the darkness, dissolving into the night like vanishing ghosts.

By the time the relief sentinel arrived in the early morning hours, just before daybreak, every prisoner had been slain, released from their misery. The watchman stood there, eyes and mouth gaping, trying to make reason of what had happened.

Baddlock and his generals were gathered around a central fire plotting and congratulating themselves when the watchman approached, babbling, "They're all dead. Every one of them—all dead."

Baddlock looked up at Dandork and said, "Go and see what this jabbering fool is talking about!" He sounded edgy as his face twisted with irritation.

Dandork departed at once, and soon returned to report, "Every captive has been slain through the heart by an Edawnian arrow."

"Edawnian spies within our camp!" Baddlock flew into an unbound, volatile rage; and in a voice that sounded like ripping wrath deep within his throat, he screamed, "Awaken everyone and assemble them before me, immediately!"

Dandork and Darkon complied at once, and the camp erupted into a jumble of movement. Search parties of torchbearers spread out in every direction facing the Edawnian Kingdom, but Zandor and his brave men were long gone.

Not noticing his dogs anywhere, Baddlock asked, "Where are my precious?" He called out to his dogs, not knowing that in the distance lay his dogs, each bearing an Edawnian arrow.

"Here is one of them," a Norticlan warrior called out. Baddlock ran to where three dogs had been discovered and dropped to his knees. He repeatedly lifted his favorite dog, Slayer's head in his hands and releasing it, and repeatedly it fell to the ground, blood bubbling from its nostrils. "My precious! My precious," he cried.

Dandork and Darkon gave each other an odd glance. Human life meant nothing to Baddlock, but his dogs were the only living thing on Zia that he truly cared about. Big tears welled in Baddlock's eyes. He balled his fists up ominously tight, so tight that he lost the feeling in his hands. He quickly swiped his fists across his eyes and held his clenched hands up to the sides of his face. Baddlock was suddenly made aware that his Warlords had gathered behind him. He narrowed his eyes into slits as his beady eyeballs rolled back and forth in their sockets. Then he cocked his head to his left shoulder and hissed out of the corner of his mouth, "Prepare the exploding pods. Go! Leave me!" The Wicked Warlock Wizard continued to lament over his dogs while hundreds of crates were being pried open, each one containing a sinister brass pod that glistened in the light of the blazing campfires.

***

Meanwhile, behind Edawn's walls, the king had discovered too late Zandor's irrational plan to spy out the Norticlan camp and was at that moment chastising Kondor for having let Zandor go. "Why did someone as wise as Zandor make such a costly mistake?"

Kondor responded, "You know as well as I do, once Zandor makes up his mind, he seldom acts cautiously. He leaps into the raging fire and considers the flames only when they are licking at the soles of his feet."

While they were yet wrangling, the tower watch reported a far off movement in Baddlock's encampment just as Zandor's party of mercy was approaching the kingdom. The tower watch called down to the yard below, "Sons of Edawn! Someone approaches the northern wall!"

A warning rang out. And because it had been a night when sleep had been unthinkable, immediately hundreds of swords were drawn simultaneously, chiming out their ominous warning against the intrusion. Scores of arrows were at once trained on the suspected attack. A heartbeat before Zandor and his men were riddled with a wave of deadly arrows. Kondor recognized the camouflaged face of his twin brother as it came out of the darkness. "Stand down!" Kondor screamed. "It is our Edawnian brothers."

King Ozzdon was almost at once at the northern gate to meet Zandor as he came through the fortified entrance. Despite Zandor's insubordination, the king received him with a relieved embrace. Then with his eyes fixed and unyielding, he pretended hard, over his relief, to be outraged over Zandor's defiance. "What makes you think you can undertake such an extraordinarily dangerous mission without the approval of your king?"

"Save your anger for the enemy," Zandor snapped and began to walk away. But then he paused, hesitated briefly, and then spoke in a calmer tone, "Forgive me, my Lord, but I could not bear one more moment of knowing that our Edawnian brethren were suffering such an ungodly death. Not even the most savage of animals should die like that." Zandor sounded exhausted but confident that he had done the right thing.

The king nodded in carefully measured agreement, deciding against prodding him for any further explanation.

Zandor's voice was anguished; and mumbled, more to himself than to the king, "I just executed my best friend...I killed him to set him free," he finally choked. "It was like murdering my own brother. It was the most grievous thing I have ever had to do."

Izz of Zia

As Kondor approached, Zandor reached out and drew Kondor to him, forehead to forehead. "I would not have done it for any other reason, not to save Edawn, not to save Xylenia, Zia, or anything else."

The king could not prevent shuddering at that thought. "I understand. I would rather that a loved one died mercifully under my own hands than to die in agony at the hands of the lunatic Baddlock has become," the king somberly said as he remembered his own best friend, King Kozar of Skymount. "Yet," the king continued, "understand I could never have allowed you to go. I could have never forgiven myself had you been lost." The king leaned closer and whispered, nonetheless, loud enough for Kondor's benefit too, "But now that it is done, I am proud of you. You are one who has proven himself worthy of being called a true Son of Edawn. A real warrior who has not let the threat of death deter him from his sense of duty to his fellowman. Well done, true and faithful servant." And the king gave Commander Zandor another manly hug in the manner only a true friend could. Zandor was the most selfless person he had ever known.

"It has been a long night, my Lord." Zandor turned to his king, waiting to be dismissed. The set of his jaw signified he was not in the frame of mind for any further discussion.

The king led Zandor away, and when they were alone, he drew him close and looked him eye to eye as he asked, "If death would be my greatest gift, would you deny me?"

Zandor looked back at his king, eye to eye, and replied, "I would deny my king nothing." Then he broke off, turning briefly only to say, "Heaven help us all if our reinforcements do not get here soon, very soon."

Zandor's thoughts turned to Rayzar. His worst memories came crashing in on him. He tore himself away, moving to get away from it all, retreating to a secluded corner, but his memory followed him there. Zandor slid down with his back against the wall and sat there, silent, his heart cut to pieces and his mind broken. The man in all of Zia less likely to ever cry buried his face in his hands closed his eyes and began to sob. Tears streamed from his eyes. But after a moment, he rebuked himself, "There is no point in grieving over what cannot be helped. Remorse has no place in a warrior's heart," he whispered to himself as he raised a hand. He wiped his tears away and then covered his face with both hands and mourned softly in the darkness.

Izz stared wildly about, looking and feeling like a crazed man. Dark shadows dueled with the light cast by the lake of molten fire against Izz and the rust streaked iron door. He pushed himself up against the iron door, bracing himself for the next attack as red fog and deathlike stench filled the air. Izz was for the moment still reeling, overcome with a petrifying fear that was nearly unbearable. He was almost delirious with a foreboding panic that forced him to struggle to regain his sanity as he pressed himself up against the heat pitted iron door. Inside, in the dark, Zuree had heard the heavy thud against the iron door over the perpetual screams and roar of the flaming furnace outside. Her eyes grew wide as her arched brows narrowed. Again, she tugged on the metal clasps that held her fast. Raw pain shot through her aching wrists as she pulled herself upright as best she could. Her body had had just enough time to stiffen up; everything hurt, mostly her elbows, her shoulders, her knees, but especially her wrists. For the most part, she had finally given up all hope of ever being rescued. She had already learned to accept not only the bondage of her body but that of her spirit's and soul's as well, yet she had tried to save her strength until she saw perchance the unlikely glimmer of an opportunity to escape.

Outside, Izz was a mess of anxiety and frayed nerves. Physically and emotionally spent, he cradled his head in his hands, struggling to get a grip on his mind, trying to clear his head, trying to think. As Izz pulled himself together, the shock gradually passed, and rational thoughts began to dawn. Something told him it was the eleventh hour, and its mark of time was late. The gravity of the situation was compounded by the jittering sensations that flashed back and forth and shuddered through every cell of his body.

Izz was able to calm himself down enough to finally reach down and fumble through the pouch tied to his waist, searching to find the tools that he needed to jimmy the mechanism of what looked like a complicated hodgepodge combination of locking gears. Izz ran his fingers through his unkempt hair. It felt dusty and stiff and unpleasantly soiled. He studied the lock; his breath came fast and deep in the thick atmosphere. He swiped at the perspiration beading on his face. He wiped his sweating hands on his grimy shirt. Izz knew he could somehow unlock the iron door if only he could stop the shaking of his hands and knees. Izz pushed every distraction from his mind, awkwardly fumbling for the latch and focused on the locking mechanism. The first thing he noted as he suspected that the lock was one of a complicated kind, not vulnerable to the tools of intruders. With impatient fumbling fingers he tried one tool, then another. He tried again, going slower this time. The pressure mounted within him as he groped with his tools. He cursed softly at the door, to no avail. He jiggled the lock picks and wanted to shout as he shook the lock until the whole door seemed would begin to rattle. He jiggled each tool hard. Still, the lock refused to yield. His hands were shaking too much.

Inside, Zuree could hear, in the middle of all the other noises, shuffling movement somewhere right outside the door. She braced herself, drew in a sharp breath, and looked about wildly.

Izz found the extra tools he needed and turned his total concentration to the iron door's unyielding lock. He studied its intricate interlocking system, then inserted several thin, needle shaped tools and twisted them into several positions. Zuree could hear the tools rattling in the lock, and she drew a deep breath as she fully straightened her trembling self up. Her stomach knotted up in dreaded anticipation. She stood cringing and shivering, feeling suddenly faint inside.

While Izz worked on the door's lock, his eyes were drawn to the markings above the door. He noticed that the top of the metal door bore a rusty plaque covered with odd symbols of an unknown origin. He paused and wiped it with his sweaty hand. He held the brightly radiating amulet up to the plaque to illuminate it farther; however, he could not begin to understand the markings it bore; but he was sure it was another curse, warning, or a jinx. He went back to work with his unfettering tools with jittery hands, frequently stopping to wipe his sweaty fingertips against his pant legs. This was the most complicated lock he had ever tried to open. Despite his failure to keep his hands from shaking, his eyes were steady. He inserted one unlocking tool after another. *Click-clack*, the tumblers in the lock turned as the first set of multifaceted tumblers lined up. Izz frowned in concentration, his mind working furiously, every nerve in his being strained. No matter how many locked doors stood in his way, nothing was going to keep him from reaching Zuree, if in fact, this was where she was.

Izz ran his fingers across his hair again, then interlocked his hands before him and crackled his knuckles, limbered up his finger, then pressed lightly on each needle tool. He jiggled his tools ever so carefully. Sweat dripped from his forehead as he wiggled several of the tools he held at one time against a stubborn tumbler. And at the end of his last nerve, snap went the mechanism that unlocked the iron door, a turn, and a click, and the lock's bolt sprung open with a loud *clack*.

Zuree heard a distinct noise of metal on metal at the door. She could not bear the thought of another encounter with the likes of Baddlock. She held her breath, biting her lip until she finally gained control of her fear. She cast off her slippers and waited for her opportunity. If it were Baddlock, she would be ready this time. She would scratch the old weasel's eyes out with her toenails if she had to, but she was not about to let him have his way with her again. At least not without a fight.

Taking a deep breath, Izz unlatched the bolt, pushed on the heavy iron door, and its steel hinges let out a muffled creak as it opened slowly with an eerie groan, like the trespassed seal of an ancient burial vault.

Zuree heard the door and held her breath.

The iron door stood ajar open into the darkness within. Izz entered cautiously, inside it was a spooky place. Within the room beyond the iron door, the chamber was hewed out of solid stone. The ceiling was too high for the width and breadth, the entrance passageway too constricting for Izz's comfort. As Izz pushed the door fully open, there seemed to come a heinous, terror stricken cry of fear from the dredges of the deepest pit of wickedness that swept across the boundless depths of its inky darkness. Izz looked warily inside; there was no sign of Zuree anywhere in the foreboding space. Had he come the wrong way? The amulet stone's illumination remained steady. He hesitated before the warning plaque for a moment. The pitch black rectangle seemed to have somehow anticipated his entrance with the expectation of a cavernous mouth waiting to consume him, heart and soul. Izz staggered into the chamber. He wanted to turn away, but he imagined he could in, some way, feel the presence of Zuree's heart.

Izz left the iron door open a crack behind him to allow just enough light from the inferno to seep in.

Having heard the entrance of someone, Zuree opened her mouth to draw in a jagged breath, and despair rushed in and filled her. She peered into the darkness. Her sight was blurry. All she could manage to see was a dark silhouetted figure of a man approaching. She took a deep, shuddering breath and sent a soft voice out into the darkness, "Who is there?" Her voice was harsh, with a cautious tone of emotional uncertainty. The soft echo of her voice was the only faint comeback, "Who is there?"

Izz recognized the voice. He stood there, immobilized in time. Izz called out, "Zuree, is that you?" He advanced as if he were fearful of scaring off an unnerved fawn he was closing in on.

There was no answering call. Only silence replied. The light from the amulet continued to throb, suddenly releasing and propelling an outward burst of energized light that leaped throughout. Izz held the stone up high, and its glow lit up the room and painted the inside of the Altar of Abomination in a bluish shade of light.

Finally, there came a weak, trembling voice out of the shadowy darkness: "Izz, is that you?" Thinking that she had recognized his voice, she hoped against hope. "Please…please! Let it be you," Zuree whispered, scarcely able to make a single word emerge from her lips. As a tiny breath of faith escaped her tightly pursed lips, she tried to call Izz's name out loud, but she could not get another word past the lump in her throat, too terrified to even utter his name again for fear it was all only an unfolding illusion.

At the far end of the underworld's altar room, Izz could make out the form of a person, slouched and bound to an upright stone beam with hands restrained above their head. Izz could see that the person was stricken with fear.

"Zuree," Izz called once more in hopeful desperation, as expectation hardened like a knot in his chest.

Again, Zuree thought she had recognized the voice that called her name. She bowed her head and shook it to clear the blood that seemed to be clotting in her mind. She feared that she was imagining things again; but no, this time Zuree was almost sure she had heard her name called. It occurred to her that beyond any doubt, it was Izz's voice and that perhaps she was not imagining things, after all; and she forced herself to raise her hoarse voice. "Izz? Izz! Izz!" And as Zuree called back, her eyes teemed with pleading hopefulness. The trill of her voice echoed through the evil altar room like the wings of a small flock of messenger doves taking flight.

Izz was dizzy with excitement, vigorously filled with joy. His spirit soared when he recognized Zuree, and relief swelled inside him as he caught a full view of her. Instantly, every trace of fatigue, all weakness, every wound, every ache was immediately wiped away. He was a whole man again, radiating renewed power and wholehearted tenacity as tidal waves of reprieve swept over him. She was grubby and unkempt, but she looked noble even in rags. She was haggard; and her gown was torn, soiled, and appeared soaked through, but to Izz, she looked more beautiful than ever, and in that first moment, it was more real than ever. Izz was haggard and tattered, smelly and battered, but it was Izz and nothing else mattered. As they faced one another for the first time in forever, Zuree stood frozen for an eternity, waiting to be touched by Izz to be sure he was real.

The heaviness of the universe was lifted off Izz's shoulders as he quickened his pace. Excitement lit his eyes as his spirit sent a quivering flash throughout every inch of his body, coursing a mighty flood of joy with massive blasts of love from the depths of his heart and soul as he called out, *"Zuree!"*

Izz's voice reached out and touched her like a searing light in the darkness, and out of the shadows, a glorious sight met Zuree's eyes. Her face was a visible picture of unmistakable gratitude, surprise, and relief. Her eyes brightened immediately in the dark, like warming sunshine. Then she felt a great rushing sensation of deliverance flooding her spirit. Her heart leaped as Izz came into full view, filling the air with his magical presence. "You found me! I knew you would come. You came to save me! Ammiz's great God does exist! Thank you, thank you. Thank God for you. I almost thought I would never see you again. But somehow I knew in my heart you would come." Tears glistened in the corners of her eyes as joy raced through her. "Get me out of here. Please get me out of this awful place."

Izz's eyes lit up intensely as he emerged from the pale shadows. "Nothing on or under Zia could have kept me away. You have given me such strength."

Restoration came to Zuree's soul, and the apprehension that had coiled within her heart suddenly eased, and the mental suffering that had been strangulating her spirit, instantly let her go. His forthcoming presence set Zuree's spirit on a course of bliss, thwarting the whole gloomy atmosphere of that dreary place. Up close, he saw how careworn Zuree looked, and how fatigued she had become from her imprisonment. Her once lustrous hair was tousled and drooped loosely, hanging in tangled disarray around her face. She had been crying from the torment she had endured. Her eyes were reddened and puffy, and there was such a vulnerable expression on her face. In the dim light, he could see more clearly that her nightdress was tattered and torn around the shoulders and down her legs. Her countenance was marred just as a beautiful rose wilts from being too long in the dark, deprived of fresh air and sunlight.

Zuree was conscious that she needed washing, yet Izz looked upon her in that same loving way as he had looked at her in that same moment they first met. It broke his heart to see her like this. But even in her exhausted, overwhelmed, and unadorned state, her savage beauty made her look like a golden goddess from a magical fairytale, and her unyielding grace was the only vestments she could ever need. There was something there that was precious, to be sheltered, safeguarded, something worth dying for.

Izz exploded in a moan of relief as he ran to Zuree. She arched toward him, as though to test the fact of his existence and to assure herself that Izz was flesh, blood, and bone, not just a dream. The feeling was beyond measure, only to be quantified inside the rational understanding of the spiritual. Zuree shifted her position slightly, unconsciously showing a little more of the soft flesh of her inner thigh, leaving little to the imagination. Izz forgot to breathe as they collapsed closer in full contact. Pressing against each other, they became very near tipsy with sudden intoxication, caught up in the energy, happiness, and excitement of being together again. He touched her cheeks, cupped her face, and wiped a smudge from under her shining eyes, so gently that she wanted to cry for his sheer compassion.

"Do you have any water?" Zuree asked in a parched voice.

Izz raised the last of his water to her lips as he gently supported her chin. She shifted her mouth to the water skin, and thankfully took a long, deep drink. When Zuree had finished, she asked, "You are not alone, are you? Tell me that you are not alone! Where is my father, the king, and where are his troops?"

"I will tell you everything after we are far away from this foul hole of a crypt," Izz muttered.

Without tearing his eyes from Zuree's beautiful face, he reached up and tugged on the chains that held his beloved. He dug into his pouch as if suddenly remembering something forgotten, and pulled from it his locksmithing tools. As he wiggled and fiddled with the lock, he could not seem to catch his breath because he just knew Zuree was close. His hands trembled; his fingers fumbled. *Come on, come on*, he urged himself.

It was then when Zuree got a closer look at Izz's many injuries. The lesions along his face were by now only dimpled scabs instead of pitted holes. She observed the deep wounds on his arms and his bloodstained clothes. She gasped. "Your arms! Izz, what happened?"

"Just a few scratches, scrapes, and tears. A few bites, cuts, and bruises here and there. Nothing serious."

Zuree noticed a deep wound along his shoulder and traced the mark, tenderly following the line with her eyes. "Is there anything that can hurt you?" Zuree asked with a sympathetic expression fixed on her face.

"Only the pain of being without you," was Izz's reply.

The next thing she noticed was that Izz's pale, thin face was blatantly marked by traces of fatigue, hunger, and stress. Up close Zuree could see more clearly the exhaustion that lined his face. He looked weary to the bone, beyond that which mere sleep could restore. She saw the disarranged, stringy hair that hung over eyes that were etched with strain. Izz's face was gauntly and stony from having had too little to eat and being too long deprived of fresh air and daylight. His clothes were unraveled and torn to shreds, and despite his joy, he looked as if he had not slept in days. Astonished beyond words, Zuree only smiled, he was the love of her life, and that was all that mattered. Her eyes blinked to hold back a flood of tears as she felt a surge of empathy that could not be suppressed. "You look unwell," she finally said.

"Actually"—he triumphantly smiled as he turned over the last tumbler—"I feel rather invigorated. In you is where I find my strength." Despite it all, he wore a kindly, and even jubilant expression.

Zuree heard the final click, and at that exact moment, the iron bracelets that held her came open, and she felt the cold pair of shackles break loose. Her relief was enormous. She slipped her slender, aching wrists out, pulling her arms down. Her spirit was set free, and like a bird, it flew from its captivity and soared to the heavens like a snow white dove. But when she tried to stand on her own, she lost her balance. Zuree's body, weak from her imprisonment, sagged against Izz, almost falling to the dusty floor. Izz reached out, caught, steadied, and scooped Zuree into his arms. It was pure bliss to be near Izz again, to feel his strong, reassuring touch.

She wrapped her arms around Izz's neck and fell against his chest. She would need some time to regain her equilibrium. "How did you know where to find me? And where is my father?" Her question was a hoarse whisper.

Izz unclasped the chained amulet and put it around Zuree's neck. "Your amulet has led me to you." He cushioned Zuree in his arms, rested his head on hers, and he held her so close for the longest time, enclosed in her soft warmth.

Zuree was sobbing now as she curled herself against him like a child. Faint with relief, she gasped, groaned, and trembled in his arms as her heart danced. His reassuring embrace, concern, and sympathy was like a warming blanket suddenly spread around her, radiating not just warmth for flesh, blood, and bone, but warmth for the soul, making her feel safe and sound. The feeling went beyond exhilaration. She burrowed her face against the solid, comforting expanse of Izz's chest, and she could hear his heart racing. She tried not to twist a grimace as life flowed painfully back into her hands as love fluttered through the pathways of her veins like millions of swarming butterflies, flooding her heart to its deepest core. Suddenly she began to laugh and weep at the same time, and she wondered how it was possible to feel happy and cry all at once, yet she persisted in doing just that. Then she composed herself as she drew Izz in closer and said, "Baddlock and Dandork have betrayed us, and they have treated me as if my life meant nothing to them. I thought I was going to die in this forsaken place."

Izz clasped Zuree's face in his hands as the distance that had kept them apart for so long disappeared. All of a sudden, the situation did not seem so overawing. He traced every curve of the face he had seen so often in his darkest hours, and his profuse longing faded into the past. To touch her was celestial, as warm as the morning sun. "Are you well?" Izz's voice was filled with tenderness, and that was enough to make it seem that everything would be all right. To hear his deep voice warmed Zuree's heart, and as she looked up, she felt at that moment as if nothing in the world could ever hurt her. In the gravitational force of his love, even the bitterest of her aches and pains were sweet. "I will be well as long as you never, ever let me go," she whispered.

He embraced her fiercely and whispered, "I am bound to you."

Face to face, with eyes locked, Izz's gaunt, bruised and grimy face was the most handsome thing she ever wanted to see. His profound ebony eyes transfixed on Zuree's liquefying blue, green pools and the hours they had suffered faded farther and farther into the past where they ceased to exist. Izz smoothed back the damp strands of hair from Zuree's face as he gazed at her through loving eyes. Her heart began to beat wildly, bursting with thanksgiving, casting every nerve cell of her body into a responsive and boisterous reawakening.

Izz gathered Zuree even closer into his warm and strong arms and whispered, "I was so afraid I would never see you again." Then he crushed her to him.

Zuree immediately felt that she was wholly immersed in love. She felt peace and solace soak through her as Izz almost flattened her to him, and she felt safe and secure even though they were surrounded with so many unknown uncertainties.

For a moment, words failed them. Instead, Izz gently drew Zuree ever closer, clutching her against him until he could feel her heartbeat pounding against him as he felt her respond to his closeness. Moved nearly to tears, Izz tucked her head under his chin so that she could not see how misty his eyes had become. When he had regained his composure, Izz took Zuree's face in his hands again, hoping that she could see how much she meant to him. "I longed for what seemed like forever to feel the joy of being near you again, which has now become the greatest joy in my life."

Zuree wanted to tell him everything; her eyes revealed what she could not put into words. As their souls joined as one, the bliss inside was suddenly overwhelming. Izz's heart swelled with rapture, and all the stress, fatigue, hunger, thirst, and the pain all seemed merely to drain away from his flesh suddenly. From deep within a renewed strength and hope came bubbling to the surface. Izz surrounded Zuree with the strength of his love, which had become a raging flame of its own. She was vulnerable now, and she knew she must not look too deep into those eyes that drew her away to a different time and place.

And even though they were still caught in the heart of evil, they could not seem to tear themselves away from their momentous reunion. As the two were drawn in by each other's magnetism, Izz stroked Zuree's cheeks with the tips of his fingers. Izz tenderly tilted Zuree's face up by her chin and brushed back her golden hair. Even though her thick hair was undone and hung in disarray over her smudged, tear streaked face, he was amazed by how her inner beauty radiated from within despite it all. She was still and would always be the most beautiful woman he had ever laid eyes on.

Zuree leaned back and lost herself in the unbelievable piercing power of his eyes. Her blue, green eyes lit up like jewels in the dimness as her whole face grew radiant while the air around them crackled with anticipation. Izz finally came to a conclusive decision, the only logical one, and without another thought, he leaned forward. When Izz's lips were just a breath from Zuree's mouth, passion burst within him. And just before Izz gave Zuree his conquering kiss, Izz spoke—as an oath whispered upon her lips, "My life is not my own. I love you, Zuree, and I live only to love you. Without you, my life would not be worth living. I would gladly lay my life down for you a thousand times."

"Take my heart. It is no longer my own. It belongs to only you," Zuree murmured against Izz's encroaching lips.

That one point in eternity had arrived like an ending looking for a place to start. There was no turning back now. Not even a thousand demons could have turned them away from what would be their first kiss. Zuree felt at this magic moment as if she were utterly bathed in Bless. It was a moment not even the bleakness of their predicaments could ruin.

Izz drew Zuree's face in as gently as he would the most fragile blossom, his mouth seeking hers. Their lips came gently together, as their hearts touched and danced the eternal dance of love. Even though their physical presence remained cornered, their souls were set free. At first, the kiss was gentle and undemanding. Their mouths melted together like warm nectar. Then Izz adjusted the perfect fit, deepening the kiss and taking in the depths of her sweetness. Zuree felt as if she had been struck by lightning. Souls knitted together in something so binding that neither would ever set the other free. Their hearts gushed out the language of devotion, and everything written in their heart spilled out in a moment of complete and utter surrender. Unconditionally, the lover and the loved in both breathed each other, tasted each other, and were pierced by each other's gift of love. They felt the other flowing in their enraptured, innermost gasp of life.

Zuree went limp against Izz. Their mouths dueled in a dance with equal abandonment. She clutched his face in her hands and forcefully pulled him down to her, and his fingers threaded through her hair, becoming a fist to hold her captive. Zuree had never longed to kiss any man the way she yearned to kiss Izz at that moment. Her hands dug into his thick mane as she kissed him back with a fervor that left him shaken, momentarily stunned. Izz enfolded her into him as she pressed in with undaunted insistence. Their first kiss was searing with lips crushed together. Both lost somewhere in the realm of passion and sensations.

Neither could hold the other close enough. Izz and Zuree clung to each other as though both were trying to make the other part of their very soul. If they had held each other any closer, they might have become permanently conjoined, never to let go, never to let the other out of their sight again. The kiss turned scorching hot, ravenous, immediately seizing all awareness as they surrendered and let the raw feelings take over. An unspoken vow gushed out to tell each everything that was in the other's heart, the message was clear, sparing nothing. She accepted his pledge with her whole heart, body, and soul as he kissed her with abandoned savagery. With this first kiss, they spoke from the depths of their souls, saying so much without saying a word. Resistance was abandoned as they passionately kissed one another back and forth again, again, and again.

Izz tried to redirect his focus, given the weightiness of their present predicament, but it had become an impossible task. After what seemed like an infinity, Izz gently pulled back; however, she followed him, and he had to kiss her again. He knew then and there that she unconditionally loved and needed him every bit as much as he loved and needed her. This time, his kiss was more profound, longer, and thoroughly intoxicating. Under the power of their embrace, their lips felt as if to turn into hot honey as they were swept away into an enchanted, mystical, celestial realm where they seemed to dissolve and merge into each other.

At long last, Izz breathlessly spoke just above a whisper as he continued to kiss her. He cradled her face in his hands as his kisses bathed her face in a baptism of love. Finally, the words he had yearned to say since the first time he had laid eyes on her rushed to the forefront of his mind. "I love you more than I can say, Zuree." His voice cracked with long held words that for too long had remained stuck in his throat. "I have thought of little else, but of this moment for as long as I have lived, it seems. As it turns out, I love you more than anything, even life itself." The look on his face said it all.

There was an insight into a wholeness that went beyond the tangible. The two discerned a sensation of completion that reached out to Izz and Zuree from somewhere the two never knew existed. The tinderbox kindling between them, from the first time Izz and Zuree had met, suddenly set alight and then erupted into a blazing outburst of heat that consumed them both completely.

Everything Zuree had kept locked deep down inside her heart suddenly gushed from fountaining wells that knew no depths. She felt Izz's vigor, and strength coursing into her soul, enkindling her from the inside out, overflowing and gratifying every unfulfilled yearning her heart had ever felt. She could feel her unbridled heart slamming inside her chest, swelling and making rapturous sounds that ripened into murmuring tones as if drowning in love. In each other's arms, they found a secure sanctuary where time and space became irrelevant as if reality was at their mercy as if Zia had suddenly stopped spinning just for them. In all their lives, there could never come another moment like this, and the moment held space for nothing more. Izz's spine clenched when he felt her soft full breast press against his chest. Zuree's gasps turned into moans of raw, unbridled yearning.

Then both became suddenly very still, and deep silence followed. Nothing could have ever tarnished or marred the pure beauty of Izz and Zuree's heightened passion, but it was time for clearer heads to prevail. They continued to hold each other tight, and it would be a long while before they would release each other. The moment left both lightheaded with their hearts pounding a thunderous beat. Never before had they felt the inexplicable sensations their closeness had stirred. On the tips of their tongues, each would always carry the taste of their first kiss and the unspoken promise of a lifetime of unbridled devotion. Izz finally forced himself to ease slowly away from Zuree, ending what had been so faultless between them and with this—reality reclaimed its presence.

Suddenly, the enchanted spell, along with the silence, was utterly broken when out of nowhere, just outside the door, there came a long mournful howling straight from the most bottomless cesspool of hell. At that same moment, as if drawn by an unseen force, at the edge of his vision, Izz noticed the black doorway that led into the next champers He looked nervously into the yawning darkness, and at the apex of the rearward room, he spotted a familiar black structure clearly hewn out of one solid, black stone. He did not want to believe, let alone turn his fixed eyes to see it was the black altar of desecration.

NINETEEN
THE EXODUS

I zz heard Ammiz's voice. *Time is not on your side.* Suddenly the love encounter was cut short, both true lovers appeared haggard again, reflecting the fact that neither had eaten or slept for days. All at once, urgency seemed vital. Logical thinking was imperative and was most critical now more than ever. As instances ticked and moments tocked, Zia was turning, and the Great Conjunction was converging. It would only be a matter of time before Baddlock's Dark Priests came back to subjugate their sacrificial victim to their unspeakable horror.

The storm outside grew louder and louder as it echoed off into the profoundness of the deep. Izz's heart jumped, startling him. Instantly, the outer world came crashing back into focus as Zuree and Izz exchanged a suddenly worried glance. All at once, Izz was abruptly reminded that they were far from free and made painfully aware that precious time was slipping away. Moment by moment, bit by bit, the unceasing pulse of existence conspicuously marked the incremented calibration of itself with precise perseverance. To delay one more moment could only bring them closer to failure. Izz clasped both Zuree's hands in his and said, "Now all we have to do is get out of here, all in one piece."

Zuree did not like the sound of that. Both knowing their nightmare was far from over, they looked to one another for courage.

Zuree's eyes fluttered, and as soon as she could find her voice, she asked, "Where exactly are we?"

Izz answered with a gasp, "We are below the surface of Zia, but I know the way out." His shaky voice, however, did not convincingly convey the confidence of his words. Still, his nervous smile made her believe anything was possible. Izz's expression turned somber as he looked straight into Zuree's eyes and asked, "Are you able to move?"

"What is out there!" she asked with an uneasy shrill in her tone as she unwittingly smoothed down her tattered dress and nervously worked on a clump of knotted curls behind her head.

"It is nothing to worry yourself about. As long as we are together now, nothing can stand in our way." They looked at each other with a spark of hope kindled in their eyes.

She nodded. "I will be fine. Just give me a moment." She slipped into the shadows, for a few moments of privacy to attend to her personal needs.

While Izz waited, it suddenly occurred to him that because he had been so intent on finding Zuree, now that he had at last found her, Izz realized that he had not once given any thought beyond that. Izz would figure something out. Now that he had found what he came for, he would find some way out of this most unhallowed side of hell. He considered what he was going to do next and had to conclude he had no real course of action, except to follow the same vague strategy. All he could do is to simply take evasive action and keep moving onward until destiny showed him what it had in mind for them. In the time Izz had gotten to know Zuree, Izz had recognized that she had a courage heart in her. It was the same sort of inner strength that was present only in women who had lived their lives in much less privileged circumstances. He hoped for Zuree's sake that she possessed half the strength he saw in her. The vilest evil was out there waiting, he could feel it. Whatever happened, he would dare not falter.

When Zuree returned, Izz asked, "Are you ready?"

"I am as ready as I will ever be," she answered, with a strained voice.

Izz reached out and offered his hand, and after a moment of hesitation, she took hold of his hand and let him pull her to him. They walked to the entrance together, leaning on each other. Once

Izz of Zia

Zuree started moving her feet with Izz's help, she regained her fortitude and gave a forceful smile. When they reached the iron door, Izz turned to Zuree. "Do you trust me?" he asked as he ran a hand along the contour of her face. As Izz spoke, Zuree searched his eyes. Most assuredly, she found an overflow of hopeful optimism there. However, there was an unmistakable, peculiar uneasiness beyond his eyes. She raised her head, and her trusting eyes rested on the man who held her fate in his hands. The odd foreboding in his eyes unsettled her, but the reassurance in his smile caused a little of her fear to ease away.

"Yes, I trust you," Zuree finally replied.

"I mean, do you really, truly trust me…with your life?"

"Yes, I trust you with my life! I have faith in as far as you bestow it on me." This time she did not even think before answering. "I know that you have risked everything for me, and so I have no other choice but to trust you with all my heart. I will not only follow you anywhere you lead me, but I will also follow you all the days of my life."

They stood close together before the iron door and gave each other a quick hug. Then Izz pulled his scarf off from around his neck and began to wind it around Zuree's head and eyes. Zuree held her hand up between the veil and her face and forced a laugh. "What are you doing?" she asked as she studied Izz's face. Was he groping for an answer?

Izz could only ask, "Do you love me?" His gaze was fixed.

"Hopelessly," was her reply.

He clasped both her hands in his. "Then please, please trust me."

Izz did not sound fearful, which was reassuring. He did sound anxious, which was not. Zuree lowered her hand, and Izz continued to wrap the scarf around her eyes.

"No matter what you hear, no matter what you feel, no matter what you sense, do not dare look. Believe me; this is the only way," Izz licked his dry lips and tried to smile.

"All right, my life is in your hands," Zuree said with conviction.

The hour that the whole of the underworld throughout the universe had waited for, for millennia was fast approaching. The planets by now were spinning so close to one another that they began to form one huge chaotic system, pulling each other into an unusual dance. The light of the imminent conjunction was brightening now. Their temporal juncture was unchangeable, and its cosmic season had come around once more. What happened on Zia would affect countless other worlds. The wickedest of the wicked powers of darkness drawn by the approaching galactic alignment were beginning to assemble themselves around their prospective altars of abomination in anticipation of their long awaited release. The malignant spirits gathered themselves according to rank as they crowded around the altars that served as universal markers. They were exit and entry points that they believed, would allow the release of the wickedest of demons, permitting them access to the entire cosmos. Their material existence awaited, squirming and twisting in their imprisonments, in different dimensional realms. So vile were the evil entities, deemed too violent for the Ziaian planet that they were restrained in uninhabitable planets apart from all their other coconspirators in different galaxies. The window that they anticipated to open soon they conceived would permit them to quickly overrun Zia, from where they would invade other planets and launch a second assault on the Universal Powers. And even if in reality they were dead wrong, this was what they believed to be true.

In the lower column of Phantomsdeep's Dark Temple, in the sinkhole of human misery where all of Zia's filth collected, where the stone floors were stained with splattered blood. The Dark Priests Several shining silver implements of ritual torture and death were strewed on tables throughout the room. Damp black shadows whispered of eternal pain and disturbed the restless spirits of the departed, where the dead did not die. It was a lightless hole where wicked men dressed in black hooded robes, with sagging white faces, crept through the dark temple like emaciated black sewer rats intoning the supplication of utter darkness. Evil men consummated their forbidden rites concealing their presence, working in the dark, thinking thoughts of things one cannot imagine. They wallowed in the pigsty of debauchery, preparing themselves for the multitude of ceremonies that would usher in the long awaited conjunction.

Their repetitive recital of invocation to commemorate the great approaching event droned throughout the ghoulish temple. Their chant filled the dilapidated building to its highest vaulted ceilings with unpardonable blasphemies. The dark hearts that gathered there seemed intoxicated with the ecstasy of their approaching task of anointing with royal blood a new era of darkness. They were those that had sacrificed their sons and daughters, spilling their innocent blood to demons. They were those willing to sell their souls to eternal death itself for the right to be the High Priests of the damned. There was a cruel, pleased glint in their eyes, cruelty born of hate, lust, and greed; they were the ones seeking revenge on behalf of their fallen would be gods. Woe unto you wicked men of the flesh, mark the telling of these words well; an eye for an eye and a tooth for a tooth, you will most assuredly reap the whirlwind you so justly deserve.

They assembled themselves secretly, unnamed, and masked in the darkness with their vessels and steely knives. They formed their evil procession and made their way toward the underbelly where Zuree's precious, pure, royal blood was to be spilled on the altar marker at the exact moment of the Great Conjunction. Thus they hoped to trigger the cauterization of the collective consciousness of darkness. In essence, freeing all evil to disrupt the immutable intricacy of the universal matrix. In turn, the seven greater planets would enter into a spiral pinwheel whirl, spinning faster and faster and heating up to the intensity of a miniature sun. One world would then seize away stardust from the surface of the others until each planet including Zia was drawn into an inward helix. This in turn would gatherer the seven planet system into an eccentric elliptical fiery orbit. This unnatural force would instantly cause them to implode into one single cluster, releasing a chain reaction of uncontrolled doom. At this instant, they believed that all time would collapse into this singular moment in which all powers would be bound, therefore releasing every dark force throughout the mega cosmo.

Throughout the second heaven, around gateways far and wide countless legions of evil spirits from different dimensions were arriving. A rapidly growing storm of demon spirits boiled in a gathering around the portals that they believed would set them free. The demonic spirits of all ranks and principalities were all ready and waiting. They cheered lustfully with the expectancy of triumph. The anticipated power of unprecedented exaltation danced and burned within them. The haters of men were intoxicated with the foretaste of wild slaughter and supremacy.

Izz knew he had not convinced Zuree nor did his reassurance erase the fear he saw in her eyes. As he adjusted the scarf over her eyes, he asked, "Is it all right?"

Zuree nodded.

Attempting to appear calm despite the raging chaos he knew to be waiting on the other side of the iron door, Izz asked, "Are you ready, my love?"

Zuree nodded once again, standing there thinking the whole thing over, trying to persuade herself all would be well, but somehow seemingly unconvinced. Izz peered out from behind the iron door and scanned the bridge. All appeared clear. "Let us get far away from this dreadful place," Izz muttered as he made a feverish attempt to prepare for the terrible chain of events that had already been set in motion just beyond the iron door.

Zuree accepted his hand as if she was receiving an unspoken promise, one to the other that they would make it out alive. Zuree made him feel brave and invincible. His mind was set. The launch of their exodus was one heartbeat away. Izz braced his hand against the iron door and then stared out, contemplating the plight that must ensue as he unwittingly squeezed Zuree's hand the harder. His touch felt strong, vital, and alive. Unsure of what he might encounter, Izz slicked back his black hair with his sweaty, trembling hand. He felt his stomach squirm from the apprehension churning in it. He paused for the last moment at the threshold to get his nerves good and steely before he stepped outside where the only guarantee was that there no guarantees.

Izz's heart was prepared for the fight he knew they would inevitably confront. As he clenched his grip on Zuree's hand, all the fear she had felt oozed out of her. They both took a deep breath and held it for a moment, then Izz slowly pulled the door fully open. It was like opening the door to a furnace of seething oceanic fire. Yellowish smoke belched in from the wide open door, hissing like steam from an over boiled caldron. Outside, Izz shaded his eyes against the glare. The air felt more oppressive than before. The smell was much more intense outside of the altar chambers. The stench of charred flesh haunted the cavern and was barely breathable. Izz peered to the right, to the left, and above, scanning slowly; but he saw no movement, nothing manifesting to challenge them. His attention then turned to the bridge. The quake had weakened the bridge's support structures, but it looked sturdy enough to hold them. But looks could be deceiving; his sixth sense taunted him to think. It would be a trial by fire.

As soon as Izz set foot on the bridge, he had a dreadful premonition of horrendous lurking perils that cut through his mind and heart. And all at once, the way back to Zia's surface seemed half a world away. Same souled, they stepped out over the abyss, together with hand in hand, a force to be reckoned with. Zuree instantly fell into step with Izz, and her fate was inseparably bound to his. The first thing she felt when she stepped out was the wall of heat that hit her. Unable to see anything but white dots in front of her blindfolded eyes, she asked, "Why is it so hot?" Her breath caught in her throat. She swallowed hard, her mouth was dry.

Izz drew his breaths in sharply, fighting as best he could the searing sensation that began to fill his lungs as he pulled Zuree along. "Just hurry," he whispered in very soft tones as if afraid they were about to be found out at any moment.

They scurried down the bridge, leaving footprints in the freshly ash covered stone as their hurried footfalls echoed back and forth, like a public proclamation announced from a rooftop. Apart from their footsteps, there was a low rumbling, which seemed to be coming from the very center of Zia itself. There was a faint distant vibration in the stone beneath their feet. Izz quickly moved onward, cautiously alert, and aware. He observed here and there, within and throughout, from side to side, up and down, in front, and at his heels. The shifting movement intensified as he looked across the reverberating bridge; it seemed to be listing like the deck of a ship on the high seas.

Across the lake of fire, the flames raged on like remote dust devils twisting on the surface of a fiery wasteland. Balls of fire erupted and shot out of everywhere in all directions, like extreme wrathful resentment provoked by an entity of pure evil and profound darkness. Twisting cyclones of heat suffered them to taste the whirlwind of flames. Hot cinders surged, hanging in the air and pummeling Izz's face as they moved quickly across the stone bridge. Izz wrinkled his nose as the stink of rotten eggs wafted up from below. The bitter, sulfuric smoke caught in his throat and made him cough violently. On either side of the bridge, Izz could see the dazzling lake of molten fire. He could hear the terrifying squealing sounds from the bottomless depths that almost unhinged him from his senses. All the while, the engulfing sound of the unseen sucking vortex of complete extinction got louder and louder. Izz suddenly held his hand out to break Zuree's stride as he stopped to look over the edge of the bridge. He struggled to fight the ever increasing feeling that he would be overcome by fear from what he saw. Zuree immediately sensed that something was wrong, terribly wrong. "What is that…noise?" For a moment, she could not get that last word out. "Why is the ground vibrating, and what is that hideous smell?" came the nagging question from her lips.

Izz suddenly seemed mute as he stood there as if his boots were glued to the stone deck of the bridge. His worst fears were materializing as he stared at the nightmarish hordes that seemed to have been lying in wait for their attempted escape. And the principalities of darkness by now were well aware that they were on the move. Every lost spirit, empowered by their indwelling demons, lunged upward with paranormal strength. Up the subhuman bodies came by the thousands of thousands, zeroing in on them in such numbers that it seemed the very bridge itself would collapse under their sheer weight. The full horror of the approaching demonic armies, with their flashing teeth and their mauling claws, burned into the back of Izz's eyeballs. They all seemed desperate to prevent their escape at any cost. The clamoring sounds drifted up to Zuree's ears, and she clutched herself to Izz. As she pressed and molded herself to him she felt his fear seep into her very soul. Haunted by every anxiety she had ever known, Zuree asked, "What…is happening? And what is that horrible…" Her words suddenly broke off as her voice ascended to a shriek full of fear and misgiving.

And even if Izz had wanted to tell her, it was something he did not have words to describe or explain; thus instead, he said, "Just keep your eyes closed and do not look no matter what," he pleaded. Zuree could feel the ominous harbinger to something terrible about to happen. Izz could sense her escalating alarm, feel her hand squeezing the blood out of his. As she clung to him, her fear mingled with his. "They know that we are leaving," he thought out loud as he wondered about his gift for timing again.

"Who—or what—are they?" Zuree asked as panic trembled in her heart.

Early in the predawn hours, just before the first cock crowed, on the hill, the entire Northern army was assembled in front of their master, Baddlock. His generals stood up front before him as he walked before his troops with his hands clasped behind his back. With long, heavy steps, he walked back and forth, up and down the lines of his warlords, giving them all a stern, lingering visual examination. His sagging skin puffed with an abominable, twisted scowl never before seen. He challenged the slightest one wrong look, daring any of them to meet his eyes. To look upon him would have been construed as a great disrespect and taken as a direct insult, inviting serious consequence, possibly even death.

"This night…," the self proclaimed master of the Ziaian world barked, "our common enemy has infiltrated our inner circle, disrupted our tribute to our Dark Lord, tainting our most sacred celebration"—Baddlock moved through the ranks like an avenging judge—"all due to the stupid incompetence of a few. This intolerable dereliction of duty must not go unpunished. Those responsible will be exterminated like the mindless vermin that they are. If we do not purge them from our ranks immediately, they will go on to breed more mindless idiots like themselves."

Baddlock flashed the condemned a wrathful glare. "If this gangrenous infected is not amputated at once, it will spread like a plague among our ranks. I am forced to set an example. Therefore, every single man on watch during the breach will be executed at once." His decree caused a momentary stir, but the Wicked Warlock Wizard held his ground, more than anything to strengthen control over his armies. Power was all that mattered.

Darkon, the leader of the Norticlan tribes, stepped forward and asked, "All…is that not a bit extreme?" In the background, there was an unmistakable agitation in the circle of the hierocracy of the Norticlan leadership.

Baddlock, upon hearing the challenge, froze in his tracks, his spine became rigid, and he spun around, shooting Darkon an icy, predatory glare. His eyes riveted upon Darkon. In a flash, Baddlock came face to face with the Norticlan ruler and adjusted his eyes at the leader's eye level, staring Darkon down, forcing him to look away. The Norticlan commander turned and was astonished at the speed in which the older man had moved. The Wicked Warlock Wizard's eyes were filled with unquestionable supernatural evil. Darkon's eyes were drawn into Baddlock's menacing, mutating eyes. "What…what…I meant was…"

When Baddlock sensed Darkon's weakening resolve, he tightened the noose and crushed Darkon's will. The Wicked Warlock Wizard waved him to silence as though he had forcefully struck him. Darkon had never known real terror until that moment. The once fearless leader wrinkled his thick forehead, and fear dominated his startled expression as Baddlock's appearance, for a flash of an instance, was transformed into a terrorizing, macabre image. The WickedWarlock Wizard's appearance then altered intermittently from human to demon, with fiery eyes and a face locked in a grotesque contortion. In a voice not his own, Baddlock whispered through clenched teeth, "Embrace the powers of darkness, or embrace your own undoing."

Darkon stood there trembling breathlessly for a moment, as Baddlock's words buzzed in his ears like hornets waiting to sting him. His wild eyes widened with fear as a sharp, lacerating spasm pierced his mind like an ice pick through his eye to the center of his brain. Biting his lower lip to keep from crying out as he dropped to his knees and shook violently. "There is no other Master but you," Darkon muttered as he fell to his face. Half a world was better than death. At least he would not have to die.

Appeased Baddlock looked beyond Darkon, then asked in a loud voice, "Is there anyone else among you who dares to contests my decree?"

One look at Darkon's broken, whimpering mass was enough to send shivers throughout every Norticlan general that looked on with utter disbelief. The Wicked Warlock Wizard again raised his voice to the stars. "Who is your Master?"

The undulating masses before him appeared like a giant wave rippling across a vast sea of humanity as every man began to drop to their knees. Next they lower their heads in homage to their evil master, vowing their lives and their unwavering allegiances to their false would be god. With a wave of his hand, the denounced were herded forward. Addressing the faulted watchmen, Baddlock said. "If there were not more pressing matters that now demand my attention, you all would replace those men on the cross. However, this is your lucky day."

Each guard was dragged frontward, unceremoniously by the hair, by their Norticlan kinsmen, and then forced to his knees. With a foot placed between their shoulder blades, the strap that bound their hands was then stretched back by each strongman. Those sentenced to death were held fast as swordsmen positioned themselves for the fatal blow. A nod from Baddlock and well wielded blades sent decapitated heads rolling. Each body curled and jerked like a headless withering worm as blood spurted from their stumps. One head fell facing the generals; its wide eyes scanned the front lines as its lips formed a silent scream.

TWENTY

THE TRIBULATION

In his next strategy of devastation, Baddlock ordered his catapult lords to their stations. "And now the hearts of men will know why they fear the dark," he boasted. The squeaks of complaining machinery gears under too much strain were greased silent with the entrails of the disemboweled. Once again, overwhelming tension forced the giant catapult timber beams to creak and sag into submission. Then the armed catapults were carefully aimed.

This time the catapults were armed with exploding canisters. An invention Ammiz had meant to be used in celebratory ceremonies, its secrets stolen from the seer's private library. The Wicked Warlock Wizard made his own modifications. The paper cylinder design was replaced with thick brass, and Baddlock's engineers had increased the concentration of nitrate and added charcoal and sulfur to the mix. To make matters even worse, if that was even possible. The twisted mind of the Wicked Warlock Wizard thought to mix in the explosive of each pod hundreds of sharp metal shards and broken glass. The extra shrapnel would be violently spewed out in all directions as it exploded. Baddlock's canister was meant to inflict horrific maximum damage to any living soul. A crude fuse was made by soaking paper in water mixed with the explosive combination, then allowed to dry in the sun. The length of the fuse Izz was thoughtfully measured, calculated, and inserted in relation to the distance the canister was to travel. If measured correctly, these flying charges would explode right before or near the time of impact with the target. It was the most volatile manmade implement ever created, and never was it meant to be used against humanity.

The watchman on the northern tower reported movement on the hill, and the kingdom braced for the attack they knew all along would come sooner or later. Zandor commanded the East side of the northern wall, Kondor the West, and King Ozzdon took up a position in the middle. They thought that there was nothing Baddlock could do to top the devastating weapons he had already unleashed in his obsessive effort to wipe them off the face of Zia. They had no idea that things were about to get worse, infinitely worse. Zandor gazed through the predawn mist toward the haze shrouded ridge. A profound foreboding crushed in on him, and he could not shake it. There was no way any one of them could have foreseen or possibly prepare for what was about to unfold.

Noting that there seemed to be confusion among the catapult handlers, Baddlock screamed, "What is…the…*delay*?" The holdup only added to his volatile anger. Pongo, the head engineer spoke up. "Begging your pardon, most high, but darkness still covers the land, and we cannot calibrate our target until first light."

Irritated for being contradicted, Baddlock angrily ordered, "Use the remaining incendiary pots to mark your target. I want our whirlwind to be unleashed at first light. Do I make myself clear?"

"Crystal clear, my lord!" was all Pongo could say.

In the distant lay of the land, the gray light of dawn continued to seep between the northern Edawnian walls to the edge of the Norticlan encampment. The early morning mist rose from the ground, clearing like a melting fog under the warming heat of the rising sun.

From atop the tower, the lookout saw a shocking sight as the killing field to the North came to view in the clearing mist. Vultures that now numbered in the thousands were beginning to descend from their circling convoys in the twilight sky above. Eager to feast on the dead. On the ground, the watchman saw night foragers everywhere, summoned throughout the night by the distinct odor of death borne in the air. It was a terrible visual journey through hell, a festering eyesore to see, so vile that it caused the watchman on the tower to retch and heave.

The Catapult Masters first launched a few incendiary pots that were already calibrated for weight and distance to light up and fix their marks. The first strike was systematically fired to facilitate and usher in the fiery cataclysm that was to come.

From the kingdom, troops on the wall watched as once again the sky was scorched with streaks of fire. The tower watch gasped as a fireball hurled directly overhead, trailed by long streaming flames in its wake. The projectile narrowly missed the tower not more than a few paces aloft. Like falling stars, the fire pots descended from the dawning sky, preceded by outbursts of fire over Edawn. Suddenly a canister burst across the northern battlement: warriors' garments flared, and their hair crackled in flames.

The intended objective was marked, and the spring trigger mechanisms of the primary explosive barrage only awaited Baddlock's command. Vaingloriously, he leveled his hand, as if a magician with absolute power, casting a magical conjuration. His long bony index finger flicked out from his encircling thumb and pointed toward the Edawnian Kingdom. The fuses were lit. The bright, sparkling lights of the flickering pod fuses could be seen from the kingdom's battlement. All along the ridge line of the northern hill of the horizon seemed to burst into hundreds of small pulsating stars. And less than a half breath later, an odd shudder was set rushing through the air as hundreds of catapults were fired simultaneously. And the phosphorous balls whooshed from the catapults, instantly filling the air with whistling canister racing on a southern trajectory. They lit up the sky as they headed straight for the Kingdom of Edawn by the hundreds. High above, each canister was trailed by a tail of sparks, streaming behind them like the wake of a vast comet shower. The fierce storm tide of plummeting pods closed in with frightening speed, steadily losing altitude, ominously, relentlessly nosing toward the targets waiting to become heaps of rubble.

Suddenly the unforeseeable terror struck the kingdom, one by one, like so many iron fists. What happened next, no one saw coming; nor could they have ever readied themselves for what would dwarf their greatest fears. Upon the impact of the first pod, it's lit fuse reached its mother lode. A slight fraction of time later, the projectile exploded. Its detonation was so instantaneous that it was little more than a small flashpoint of light that belched, and flooded out an incredibly violent, red, and silvery outward hailstorm. Expanding, vaporizing, superheated gasses, under enormous pressure, suddenly ruptured its thick container, creating a shockingly loud, jarring concussion, like the thunderous flash and clasp that comes instantly after a devastating bolt of lightning. The blinding flash washed over in streamers of brilliant light thrown outward, flaring in every direction in solid lines as pieces of metal and broken glass splashed out everywhere. It was the first time such a thing had ever been seen. Like a giant slap on Zia's face, another ear splitting explosion rent space into obliterated minute fireballs of fine stardust and jagged chunks of metal fragments erupted. Explosive canisters slammed into the sides of buildings, leaving gaping wounds on already scarred and torn fortifications. The kingdom was ripped into immense fragmented wreckage, bringing unutterable woe upon the already doomed nation.

The noise, which set dogs howling and then whining, was unbearable; and the earth rattling discharge was incomprehensible. Simultaneously, the unbelievably powerful force unleashed its swelling blast wave. The burst spread across the courtyard with alarming velocity in every direction, sending out a monstrous calamity of destruction and mayhem of an intensity never imagined possible. Like the rumbling of a fast moving storm, the effective propellant hurled its shrapnel outward in flailing walls of energy that filled the air and spread like ripples from a disturbed pond. Over and over, ribbons of white hot burning light shot out in all directions like a flash fountain of blurred, high powered luminosity. Men screeched in fear and covered their ears. The blinding heat seared them, and they had to shield their eyes from the luminous blaze, like the scorching splash of the sun detonating before them. Those that survived recoiled from the explosions as they stumbled to their feet again, to stand awkwardly upright, bracing for the next discharge. In the wake of the blast that seemed to hang in the air, the echoing boom sounded throughout the kingdom. It was a booming roar like the clap of thunder, but much, much louder. It was mush more like the turbulent opening of hell, similar to no other sound ever heard on Zia.

Those caught within the immediate blast zone vanished, disappearing in the flash of bright white light. Those inside the burst rings were turned into a melted mess by a shroud of shrapnel. Shredded metal gouged flesh, shattered bones, and spattered blood. Broken glass lacerated flesh to minced meat. Those in the outer ring were flattened, or wounded, or maimed, or killed instantly. Then there were multiple flashes everywhere, and the energy release before the thunder sent sudden terrifying spears of vaporizing brightness thrown in every direction all at once. After a moment, there were other great explosions after another. Then another and another until the entire interior of the kingdom seemed as if it had begun to boil and bubble with bursting globules of massive orange and red fireballs splashing everywhere. Each exploding pod spawned a poisonous yellowish green gas that overcame men outside of the blast ring. One by one, they ran headlong as if mad, until they fell in a choking fit. Repeating blast waves sent out tentacles of death and destruction throughout the kingdom. On the battlement, King Ozzdon was stunned by the shocking swell of expanding waves that rushed out and over him like the surge of tremendous overpowering winds. The king was slammed against the parapet wall. Struck down, caught by the edge of a nearby punch packed blast. Massive devastation from every direction tore away at the defending walls. The king ducked as debris rained down all around him.

Smoke built up fast, filling the area with a charcoal haze and the smell of singed flesh. Ozzdon wiped what he thought was dirt off his face and then realized it was the incinerated blood and guts of what was left of the men that had stood close at hand. The general standing closest to him let out a gruesome scream and a shower of blood. Shrapnel from the blast had shredded his face and frayed his jaw off. Blood fountained, gushing high in the air from his mouth as his facial flesh fell away like cottage cheese. The general fell coiled in slime, in a writhing smear of blood.

The king allowed himself to breathe deeply of the clearing gas. Blood scattered in the air and the smell of it sickened him. Ozzdon bellowed in a deep, loud voice that echoed deadly "What in damnation is this!" His ears were ringing, but beyond that, the words that had come from his own mouth seemed not to be his at all.

Explosions were landing indiscriminately all around him, yet there was only silence as if the deafening sound of their detonations had been forcefully driven out of his range of hearing. Everything that happened after that seemed to unfurl in slow motion. It looked like all the fury of hell had broken loose, but so little did he know that it was only a sign of what was to come.

The ridge on the hill erupted again with another barrage of catapults sending a second metal storm of exploding pods, hurling through the air against the dawning sky. The next curtain of bursting pods fell from the sky like a never ending deluge plunging; then a third, fourth, and the fifth wave came. The pandemonium hissed, groaned, and growled with the sound of the heavens being rent to shreds. Repeatedly, the catapults were fired, reloaded, and fired again and again, weaving a sweeping, fiery fleece of streaming smoke trails that seared the Edawnian sky. The Wicked Warlock Wizard's brutal plan designed to make him master of Zia had been set in full motion. The victory was only a matter of time now.

Over Edawn, the thunderous barrage continued to descend to shatter the already scorched dawn. As if it would never end, one exploding brilliant light after another drove pieces of the container and its deadly contents flying everywhere. By now, Edawnian citizens had begun to pour out onto the streets. They had to see what had caused the monstrous roar of explosions heard all over the kingdom. They thought the bombardment had begun to fade away, only to be met by a much more massive expansion of blinding explosions.

Suddenly women, children, and the elderly found themselves caught in a ripple of total shock with nowhere to run. Throws of light and bursts of fire leaped into fanning flames. Unthinkable carnage and mind numbing terror ensued. White hot flashes detonated everywhere, like fountains erupting from a hundred volcanoes, all at once, and continued ceaselessly in an unpredictable, never ending cycle. The unrelenting aerial assault demolished hundreds of buildings, sending fragmented stone, shredded metal, splintered wood, and pulverized dust accelerating into the air in all directions. Thousands of inhabitants were annulated, rending flesh, blood, and bone alike in its slaughterous wake. It was the most awe striking decimation any mortal soul had ever witnessed.

Amid the indescribable noise and confusion, the violent firepower was overwhelming. Any form of defense quickly disbanded into disorganized formations of meaningless squads that did not know what to do. Grown men cried out like scared children, reduced to helpless trembling, dribbling, deranged maniacs plunged into shock and awe. The bravest hearts were defeated, their courage failing them for the things never seen by men had come crashing down upon them like a whirlwind of madness. Some young men fell where they stood, drawing their knees to their chests and wadding up into tight fetal balls. Their tears streamed down their faces as they screamed and whimpered uncontrollably, shaking like globs of jelly in a violent earthquake. Other traumatized men caught in a daze, went to and fro, in the chaos, unable to cope, insanity stealing away their minds. Men that had been knocked unconscious by the blasts suddenly regained their senses, only to realize that large parts of their bodies had been torn away. Dazed and confused, men emerged from what they thought was the last barrage, only to be met by another and yet another. A man blasted in half, chest open to the elements, rippling with torn muscles, tried to crawl for cover, while shoving fistfuls of intestines back into the hole in his upper body. Refusing to die, refusing to leave his lower half behind, he dragged himself along, leaving a stream of blood and a path of carnage behind him. Another man tried to run for cover on the stubs of bone thrust through his flesh where his feet once were.

A group of men huddled together suffered a direct hit, sending sprays and flecks of scorched blood and singed tissue everywhere. Some vanished without a trace, leaving only a gory, smeared stain where they once hunkered down. Men clustering close by were knocked flat by the intense blast wave and suddenly realized that they were splattered with what was left of their comrades. The scorching heat seared them as the furious blast of its fire hit them devastatingly hard. They shielded their eyes as best they could from the brilliant blaze, hotter than the burning core of a smelting furnace. Those at a distance stared in horror as they witnessed the heads, arms, or legs of their friends blown away before their very eyes. Men's bodies split like melons with their skin peeled back on every side screeched for relief like an overheated boiler.

A few brave men next to Zandor stepped down from the battlement and out into the storm trying to rescue their wounded friends. The next blast was so close that Zandor was scarcely able to keep his footing. As soon as he was able to regain his senses, he screamed out, "Take cover!"

The ill fated group was frantically trying to uncover and pull their dazed comrades trapped under the rubble of twisted debris, only to be caught out in the open by the next wave of terror. A vast cloud of dust was blown away in swirling bands by the next exploding pod to reveal that most of the would be rescuers had been blown to bits. Men were thrown in gruesome, contorted angles screaming in agony, flailing and twisting their crushed limbs—like insects smashed underfoot. One silvery starburst flashed after another, lifting mushrooming red clouds to the sky and leaving obliteration in their wake. The hysterical screams continued unabated as cauldrons of black clouds rained down blood, rock shards, and shrapnel. The crash of a falling stone sent Zandor ducking for shelter, hoping that he did not become one of the ones caught in the epicenter of the next murderous firestorm. Soot and cinders continued to pour down out of the air like clouds of death, and a hundred times, Zandor thought he was about to die at any moment.

In full view from the towers of Edawn, the catapults poured down as the watchtowers shook and rattled under the terrifying onslaught. The watchmen popped his head out to look around at the total devastation. He saw the never ending clusters of streaming canisters as they raced toward the kingdom, and proceeded to hammer Edawn to pieces. It was an eerie sight. It was the worst onslaught of all time; its sustained intensity by far exceeded even the vicious assault on Skymount. The lookout took in the whole rocking turmoil, and upheaval all of it, all around him. The sky was alight with the supernatural glow of fire blasts that came and went off like lightning bolts exploding in cavalcades of blinding light and repulsive sounds.

As all hell broke loose, catastrophic eruptions pulverized stone walls into collapsing fragments and stripped the flesh from the bodies of men to the bare bone. Each shattering quake gashed the soil out to the bare rock and left bloodstained patterns everywhere on the surrounding walls. Below Zandor could see men running around in circles like chickens without their heads. Before long, the skyline of the Edawnian Kingdom was engulfed in flames as whole sections of the kingdom burst into an all consuming inferno.

As the onslaught continued, uninterrupted detonations sent smoke clouds drifting over the kingdom to shroud some of Edawn's tallest buildings. With every shuddering strike after strike, the once mighty kingdom was coming apart in clumps like a sandcastle at high tide. To anyone within the walls of Edawn, the world of Zia seemed to be coming to its end. In an exceptionally brutal, intensifying nonstop massacre, Edawn was brought closer and closer to the edge of oblivion. With each catastrophic blast that erupted suddenly and flared outward, the decimated kingdom was brought closer to its knees.

Kondor, who was posted on the East side battlement heard projectiles screaming through the sky and getting louder as they approached. Too late, he realized that he and his men were in the direct path of an incoming pod. At the last moment, panicked men were sent scattering everywhere running for their lives. Sooner than expected the heavy brass container hit the walkway floor with a loud crashing sound. An instant later, the volatile materials exploded, and the dreaded crack came, followed by the deafeningly loud blast, and at once the burst of illumination with its prolonged pulverizing discharge forcefully rocked the bastion. The direct impact sent sparks flying like a million fireflies suddenly set free from a fiery grave. It was a direct hit, and like a fractured eggshell, the battlement infrastructure crumbled. Stone chards pelted everything, making loud zinging sounds as they ricocheted off the inside walls and buildings, like bouncing rubber balls. Torn bodies were sent hurtling through the air as men left their feet and were sent flying in different directions away from the blast. Sections of the stronghold wall came crashing down as the fortification broke apart into countless pieces that scattered in complete disorder. The footing below broke away, and Kondor disappeared in a cloud of smoke, dust, and pulverized debris. A man caught nearest the blast, fountained blood from several gaping wounds, took three staggering steps, and then crumbled to the ground below. He thrashed and gurgled on his own blood until his life seeped away.

Meanwhile, at the same ruinous moment, in the bowels of the deep, Izz suddenly felt the surging prompt of his spirit. He forced himself to uproot his feet from the inertia that seemed to have held him for an eternity. Izz looked to the end of the bridge and then back at the ascending throng. They were in over their heads in every sense. He knew there was only an inkling of a possibility that they were going to make it before they were overwhelmed. But he was not about to stand around and wait to prove himself right. He turned to Zuree and said, "Just hold on tight to my hand and follow my lead," was all Izz had time to say before he choked. In one giant leap, Izz burst into a frantic race against time. His desperate bolt almost unhinged Zuree's arm from its socket. As they darted off black ash flakes that drifted in uplifting drafts were left trailing in ribbons of coiling spirals that were set spinning in a circular dance behind them.

Prompted by fear, Zuree found new strength to quicken her step along the bridge as Izz urged her on. "Run, Zuree! Run as you have never run before."

And like two deer running from a starved fiery predator, they pounced and took flight, racing down the bridge as fast as their frantic feet could carry them. But it would prove to be too little, too late. From every direction came the churning masses that reared up in rising swells that grew to be a crashing wave as innumerable lost souls flooding over the girders of the bridge. The first assault wave blocked their advance, the next their exit. Izz slowed and came to a careening stop as they were enfolded into an ever tightening ring. Instantly his dagger was in his hand, ready and willing to lay down his life for Zuree without a second thought. His expression froze into a defeated moment of resignation. There came a growling of many throats, and then the screaming began and got louder and louder as they neared. With nowhere to run, Izz pushed Zuree back as he, stumbled on terror, fumbling, rearward to no escape.

Zuree gasped and hysterically asked, "What is happening, Izz?" as she reached for the blindfold. Izz stayed her hand and said, "Do not look…just hold on to me and do not let go!"

"Why will you not tell me what is happening, Izz?" Zuree kept asking persistently.

"It will all soon be over," was all that Izz could manage to get past his trembling lips.

"That is what I am afraid of! Please, please, Izz, tell me what is happening."

Izz cleared his throat. "I am here, and I will never let you go."

"Izz, I am afraid. I am afraid!" Zuree said, her breath caught in her throat. For a moment, she could not get another word out. Zuree swallowed. Her mouth was dry.

Given a moment of reprieve, before the next flood of wounded came crashing in on them, in the middle of the upheaval Ammiz climbed to the palace's upper stairwell. From the northern window, he scanned the skies with his looking glass as if he was monitoring the quantum mechanic pulse of the cosmos. He lowered his eyeglass, and there they were visible to the naked eye for the first time in the birthing light of day. Ammiz pulled from his inner pocket a scribbled ledger and entered into his records the simplistic equations of his most recent observations and figured them into his calculations. He computed his observations against the gigantic calendar in the sky. Influenced by unseen forces, they obeyed perfectly the fundamental order of their universal law. True to their stately, rotating voyage across the vast span of time, they marked the astronomical alignment in the celestial realms. They created within them powerful forces, exerting their mysterious powers on all other bodies of the heavens. Their chain reacting fields of attraction and repulsion would affect all other worlds in parallel dimensions and galactic systems throughout the macrocosm of the universal continuum. The prophecies were clear, and the seer had read them at least a hundred times. Soon it would be time to answer the most significant questions that the universe posed. Would the light of man prevail, or would darkness reign? Ammiz's thoughts turned to Izz and whispered as if in prayer, "Young Master Izz, be brave, my son, for the weight of the world of Zia is on your shoulders. Do not falter. Let not the doubt that dwells in the hearts of the unbeliever strip you of your faith."

Closer and closer, the harbingers came together, reflecting in the early morning sky, along the northern horizon. The pinpoint specks of light were rapidly arriving at a relative mark of increasing influence in proportion to their mass and distance to Zia. The approaching planetary conjunction at that very moment in time brought about a shift in the cosmic gravitational pull. This reorientation caused Zia's tectonic plates to realign to a new magnetic axis suddenly. Global slabs of shifting granite suddenly compressed and buckled, snagging and binding as they slipped. Its tremendous stress amplified and suddenly caused Zia's outer crust's plates to snap and spring back on themselves. The immense release of energy forced Zia to shudder and quake so powerfully that it knocked Zia momentarily off its centrifugal center.

All at once, in the next split instant, deep beneath Zia's surface suddenly, a fierce tremor ran through the bridge. Seismic waves began to shake the bridge from side to side violently and shift it back and forth as the outside surface of the planet sporadically ground against itself. Unexpectedly, Zuree and Izz found themselves caught at the epicenter of a tremendous quake. The bridge floor began to vibrate, and suddenly everything was shaking violently under their feet. Just when they thought it could not possibly get worse, the shaking only intensified. They were slammed from side to side, so violently that it became extremely challenging to remain standing. Then everything started rumbling, setting in motion an up and down rolling, oscillation combined with repeating horizontal jerking. This quaking was followed by some mighty jolts, of rising and falling back and forth movements. How could this be? Somehow the huge slab beneath their feet almost seemed fluid. The surface of the gray stone wedge heaved like the skin of a long, angry serpent beast. Parts of the bridge began to crack and fall apart as the aftershocks kept getting bigger and bigger and bigger. Suddenly the whole section behind them fell away, plunging most of their encroaching attackers dropped off into the blazing chasm.   Zuree's terrified screams were muffled inside the tightly wound shawl as the whole planet of Zia seemed to be descending into chaos.

At once, the throngs of bumbling assailants before them too started to lose their balance and then began to fall over the edge of the bridge. There was a single intense shock, followed by a lot of jolting that escalated into powerful, rapid jars. The quaking ripple shot out across the lake of fire in splashing waves that expanded fast in all directions. Its shock wave continued compressing and swelling, engulfing the lost in its path. There was one big final joggle that seemed to reverberate through the whole planet endlessly with powerful waves that sent Izz and Zuree's frantic thoughts hurling. Those clumsy goons that still clung to the bridge lost their grip. As they fell away, their indignant yowls turned into one long tormented scream as they splashed back into their eternal damnation.

Izz, agile as a cat, clung to Zuree, and amazingly enough, they were not swept off the stone bridge despite their uncertain footing. Like two frightened children, hand in hand, they pressed close to one another's side, against the unreal and unimaginable. The massive tremor continued to run through the stone bridge as cinders and brimstone were sent flying up from below, at the same time as dust and debris fell from the cavern ceiling. As the bridge behind them continued to crumble away what was left of the bridge before them seemed suddenly to be set off the center of its foundations. It was as if the cavern walls had been sent gliding away from themselves. The pillars of the universe seemed moved out of their place. Everything suddenly appeared disconnected from its fixed position of existence, as if moving at whirlwind speed in an order opposite to reality.

As soon as Izz was able to regain his balance, he wasted no time and immediately began to run again, grasping Zuree to him. The agitated fumes had all but overcome Izz by now. As he coughed and gagged, he pushed himself farther and farther outside the bounds of his physical limitations. He was running with his lungs on fire, but he kept moving, ignoring the pain; he let his momentum carry him forward. Somehow his mind seemed to have hatched out a bargain with his body. The agreement, it seemed, was, if his brain allowed his muscles to disregard the pain, they would keep moving for as long as they possibly could. He was running on the only thing he had left, the strength from which he drew from Zuree's love. Izz moved in complete surrender to his impulse, shutting out everything, detaching himself from his surroundings, from every sight and every sound. He focused on only one thing, the far end of the bridge. His pounding heart reinforced his commitment with every beat, and Izz's love for Zuree blazed in his soul hotter than in the heart of the inferno that burned beneath them. Before them, innumerable flames, leaping from the bottomless void as it continued to churn and fanning out as far as Izz could see. Like an unquenchable incinerator burning out of control the eternal lake of fire blazed brutally amplified illuminating the darkest shadowy corners of the cavern. Its inferno engulfed everything in its wake as if the whole world of Zia was melting away. The heat was unbelievable, and even though they both felt the incredible heat against their skin, not even one single hair on either one of them was singed. There was a cracking sound in the smoke filled air as sinister shadows began to emerge seemingly out of the nothingness in the shrouding mist. A loud noise that grew by the moment sounded like the roar of a stormy sea. As the noise intensified, the ground began to groan and tremble again, coming too quickly after the last quake. Dust and small lumps of stone rained down on them even more violently than before. Larger sections of the bridge began to crumble and fall away as rocks and pebbles from above continued to pelt down on their heads. "Brace yourselves and keep steady," Izz cried out. "Do not worry. We are almost there. Just hang on to my hand and do not let go and do not be afraid." Izz strengthened his ever tightening grip on Zuree's wrist as he quickened his steps. Rising fear forced Zuree to run faster than she had ever run before to keep pace with Izz's long strides.

All the while, Izz was desperately hoping to avoid the misstep that would send them both to their death as he dodged the enormous stones that come crashing down from the ceiling. Their hair and clothes fluttered in the winds created by the inferno that lashed out in aggravated fury. Finally, they reached the end of the bridge, but everything continued to shake as if Zia had become a planet pulled out of its orbit, mocking the laws of the universe. The dense clearing fog that masked the sheer drop on either side began to clear as they pushed on, without slowing. Voids and mysterious openings came in and out of view out of nowhere threatening to swallow them up at every turn. They weaved their way through the eye of the needle along the twisting path. Mounting panic disoriented them as the rumble of rocks falling from the ceiling, tumbled down and crashed all around them. The cavern walls and floor cracked, sending huge sections falling away, opening gaping chasms that seemed to drop off to the very center of Zia. The cave floor was fracturing all around them, and at any moment, Izz expected the surface of Zia to drop away from under their feet. As Izz saw visions of being buried alive flashing in his head, he wondered how long it would be before the ceiling would come crashing down on them.

After what seemed like forever, when Izz finally felt they were at a safe enough distance from the collapsing bridge and burning chasm, they both collapsed onto the vibrating ground. Both were exhausted to the bone as they clung to one another for dear life. The cave floor beneath them would not stop shaking and seemed as if it would go on forever. There was no place to go. No place left to run. Where could one run when the whole world was shaking? They prayed to Ammiz's God as they clung to each other and did what they could do to protect themselves from the scatter and shower of jagged shards. Then suddenly after what seemed like a time without end, the extreme global cataclysm began to subside until it was all over. And everything all at once was still and quiet—too still and too quiet. There was only the sound of dust falling from the ceiling, and Zuree and Izz's hearts simultaneously hammering, thundering, and echoing in their chests. Izz's lungs seemed filled with dust. But it was finally over. Izz held Zuree until she stopped trembling. Izz's reassurance offered her a little island of hope in the surrounding sea of chaos. Their nerves were still rattled, taut, twitching, jerking spasmodically, and prickling, just beneath their skin. They counted themselves lucky and unlucky all in the same breath. They were yet trapped, lost deep in the bowls of Zia; but they were still alive and in one piece. When Izz had scarcely caught his breath, and Zuree had eventually calmed down enough, Izz gently unlocked her death grip on his body and urged her to her feet. It was difficult to stand at first. Their legs were still wobbly. The solidity that they had always taken for granted seemed now to be still vibrating, but it was only them. Izz final broke the mounting silence. "It is essential that we keep moving," Izz insisted.

"Wait…I must catch my breath," Zuree urged between painful, choking gasps for breath.

Sensing that their lives were still in grave danger, Izz glanced anxiously around the darkness. He looked mostly to where they had just come from to see if anyone or anything was following. Izz prompted Zuree to move forward and said in an insistent voice, "We must not rest until we are far away from this cursed, unhallowed place." And Zuree forced herself to rise.

TWENTYONE

UNYORKED FURY

Within the in the palace walls Ammiz looked up at the violently swaying chandlers and knew that the surface of Zia had not stopped shifting. Then his attention was torn away to where the palace hallways were once again becoming a commotion of activity. Weary from the all night effort of saving lives, he knew that another endless day had just begun. But for the ravaged survivors that were pouring in, the tribulation was just beginning, as thousands of injured and shattered victims were brought into the makeshift medical station in an endless succession.

As Zia trembled beneath his feet, and the massive catapults swayed back and forth the Wicked Warlock Wizard hardly even seemed to notice. He was too engrossed watching as his catapult lords systematically demolished the Kingdom of Edawn. He danced around in tight circles as he joyfully bounced on his tiptoes. He was moving his hands, feet, and body to some imaginary music playing fiendishly inside his head as he frolicked his way up to his catapult master, Kuvazo. Tigbone, ever at his master's side, brought his hands together and bobbled his head, seemingly in tune with the same diabolical music playing inside his wicked master's head. While the monstrous catapults sporadically launched their deadly payloads, Baddlock stopped, took the overlord by the neck, and pulled him to his side. With no distance between them, Baddlock then turned to Kuvazo, face to face, eyeball to eyeball, and grinned devilishly, the bloodlust in his eyes insatiable. "Can you?" he asked as he turned and pointed toward Edawn as he took a deep breath and grimaced. "Can you strike the Royal Palace from this distance?"

The catapult lord thought for a moment, then shook his head. "Not likely, the tension required to reach that distance, even if the throwing beam could handle the stress, would be more than the cord bundles can handle."

Baddlock gave the taskmaster a cock eyed look and then said, "Do it!" The chilling threat in his tone was unmistakable.

Kuvazo, the catapult master, brought his fist to his breastplate submissively. Pongo, the overlord, drew near to discuss the command over with Lokk, the head engineer. The engineer glanced over at Baddlock and then quickly looked nervously away, but the expression was unmistakable. The *Have you gone completely mad* look was written all over the master builder's face.

The Wicked Warlock Wizard noticeably irritated, walked over to the threesome, and asked, "What is the problem?"

Kuvazo turned to Baddlock with an apologetic expression screwed on his face and said, "Your Most High, the target is out of range."

Baddlock lowered his head and then slowly rotated toward his overlord, Pongo. He unexpectedly drew the overlord's sword, and pretentiously admired the blade. He tapped the sword's sharp point a few times with the tip of his crooked forefinger as if testing its edge. Then without warning, he drove Kuvazo through before the catapult master could utter another word. Then he turned to Pongo, handed him back his now bloodstained blade. "Congratulations, you have just been promoted to headmaster catapult engineer, overlord, whatever or other," he said dismissively. Then he gave the stunned overseer a long quizzical stare as if asking, *Why have you not done as I have commanded?*

Pongo's backbone straightened as abruptly as if he had suddenly been prodded with a hot poker. "Yes, yes, Your Worshipness. You are much too kind." He turned towards the catapult handlers behind him without daring to look down at poor Kuvazo's still twitching carcass.

"Why are you just standing there, gawking?" Pongo bellowed. "Man your stations!" A wave of fear surged over those in the same proximity, as they stepped back. They uneasy, trembled, shrinking away as if terrified of some dreadful power that the Wicked Warlock Wizard might unexpectedly unleash upon them.

The catapult handlers already had their catapult set to lunch at the standard calibration, when Pongo ordered the mathematicians to recalibrate the new coordinates. When the catapult was painstakingly repositioned, the safety blocks that restricted the catapult's pivoting axis were batted away. Pongo gave the nod that sent the pulley system operators to their station. As the catapult's arm beam was pulled back beyond its safety marks, the tightly coiled sinew ropes twisted dangerously in their frames. The winches squeaked and screeched with every turn of the ratchet. its pawl loudly clicked as it engaged each tooth of the catch gear. Muscles bulged and strained as the winch's turning handles were pulled and pushed. They forced the crank drum to rotate against its ever increasing inability to capacitate the proliferating potential energy. Every man knew that at that point if any of the iron bracings failed, the result would be catastrophic for anyone on or near the groaning catapult. Every metallic clack of the catch wheel escalated the fear of the already petrified catapult crew. *Clink, clack,* the frame of the catapult began to tremble. "Halt!" cried Pongo, with his two open hands, stretched into the air.

Everyone around him froze except Baddlock, who started toward Pongo. "Bring a unit of Zomborges." The newly appointed catapult master commanded one of his underlings.

Baddlock stopped in his tracks and waited to see what Pongo would do next, as Tigbone scurried to his side.

Back in the palace, Ammiz and his assistants, drenched in blood and other foul smelling fluids were frantically trying to save the lives of the young warriors that were scarcely men. Blood squirted across Ammiz's blood stained tunic as several bleeding arteries were seared with a hot poker. But they could not stop the blood from seeping out of one young warrior in his care. Bloody bubbles gurgled out of his patient's chest and then were sucked back in with every dying breath he took. Yet Ammiz remained calm, informing the surgeons that they were running out of bandages as he reached for another hot poker. Screams rent the air as assistants and helpers seemed to be running around in circles. There was a steady stream of victims, some without arms and legs, some wrenched and contorted. And then some were little more than_hemorrhaging sacks of torn flesh with outward jutting bones. Knowing that those beyond help could not last long, Ammiz instructed them to be given powerful painkilling narcotics and hopelessly set aside to die. Their wailing shrills were quickly reduced to sniffling whimpers. Having done all he could do for the youngster, he was working on, Ammiz turned to the next mangled man still in shock and choking for air. His head was a mass of dribbled red and clotted black, with screaming white teeth and a protruding tongue in the center that was once his face. Weak and shaken, the seer momentarily closed his eyes to the spattering blood, ripped sinew, frayed flesh, and broken bones. His brain, for that moment refusing to recognize it all—until the sounds of long, painful cries penetrated his exhausted mind once again.

No sooner had Ammiz finished doing all he could for the faceless defender when he was suddenly made aware that a couple had carried toward him an even younger victim. They appeared to be the parents of the victim. The father was visibly crushed, and the mother would not stop screaming. Ammiz, exhausted, and covered in blood, wiped the sweat from one side of his brow with his right upper arm, then the other side with the other arm. He turned and carefully examined his new, blood soaked patient. The gaping hole, with several bones protruding from the young man's chest, left no doubt that he was already dead. The seer turned to wash his hands, with a slight nod to his healers, then turned back to the parents and said, "We will take good care of him. Please, go and see if you can help the others."

The two reluctantly tore themselves away with the aid of the healers. The husband led his wife away, who refused to tear her eyes from his mother's only son, the only one who had ever heard her heartbeat from the inside.

A group of Zomborges was brought forward, drooling, and grunting and snorting, ready to kill something, anything. The pair of Zomborges were taken to the pull pulley machinery, their hands placed to the winch handles as a catapult handler gestured the desired reaction. The Zomborges responded, turning the winch, oblivious to the impending danger as they continued to drool, grunt, and snort. *Crickety-crick-crick-crickety-clunk.* The basket end of the throwing arm beam came to its lowest possible position. The catapult lord standing by cinched down the throwing arm in its launch position, locked and loaded it with its payload. Pongo wrapped the explosive pod in an old oilcloth to cushion the lunch and accommodate the heavily overflowing charge of powder. While the catapult trembled with its bound up kinetic energy, the crew scattered, pulling the fettered Zomborges with them. All anxious eyes turned toward the Wicked Warlock Wizard. Baddlock twirled and flicked his pointer finger. The fuse was lit, and the trigger tripped, releasing the tremendous force, from the overburdened sinew rope bands to the throwing arm, transferring its unshackled power to the brass pod. *Whoosh!* The arm flung the exploding pod forward, into the air as the catapult's massive frame shuddered and shook with whipping and yawning sounds that reverberated throughout the encampment

The watchman on the tower saw the shrilling pod arch across the charred sky, well over the tower in a straight line. He watched as it plunged towards the King's Palace, the most beautiful structure in all of Zia. The direct impact struck and crashed through the magnificently stained glass dome, smashing a huge hole in the top side of the King's Throne Room. The thick glass exploded and rained downward like a crystal waterfall. A loud tinkling of thousands of razor sharp flecks and shards of broken glass cascaded to the floors below. A single heartbeat later, there was a loud blustering blast that shook the palace so fearfully with the full force of its intense explosive ignition. An eerie wide fan of white fire filled the palace interior, forcing everyone inside to fall back from its frightful impact. Hurling glass fragments and shrapnel sliced in all directions, with blinding intensity. Its terrible force stunned everyone inside. When Ammiz regained his balance, he went right on working on the patient before him. Before the smoke had cleared, another direct hit burst through the stained glass dome. And then its main charge detonated with another horrendous roar, rattling the arches of the dome. More glass pelted those below as the stone arches trembled. The dome groaned and staggered under the terrible blows as large sections dropped and overhead arches buckled. Pulverized glass rained down from the roof as the whole dome threatened to collapse under the force of its weight. Healers and their helpers scurried for cover, fearing that the whole ceiling could come down at any time. They dragged and pulled as many of the wounded to safety as they could, shielding them from the falling glass with their own bodies.

As the long range assault continued, Baddlock ordered the bombardment of monuments, libraries, galleries, and schools, as a final insult, in a full demonstration of his absolute cruelty. The world of insanity and wickedness had united in the ugliest manifestation of war's utter barbarity. It was an act that mortified the entire citizenry of Edawn, and further sapped the morale of all its defenders. Everywhere blasts shook the kingdom as bright fires burned out of control, and boiling smoke rose from everywhere. Igniting fumes turned the streets of Edawn into a nightmarishly horrifying, flickering hell.

Out of nowhere, two precisely launched pods collided simultaneously with the main northern gate. As the canisters slammed into the iron framed and studded gate, its contents was forced towards the burning fuse, causing an instantaneous detonation of wreckage. A cataclysmic fireball ensued spawning a monstrous mushroom of smoke and brimstone. The blast left the fortified gate turned inside out and ripped to shreds in ways that rational humans could not understand. The watchman braced himself against the tower's inside wall, knowing that at any time, the whole thing was in danger of all coming crashing down.

Then suddenly, unexpectedly, the last brass explosive pod fell; and all at once, the holocaust ended as abruptly as it had started. By the end of the offensive, the kingdom was scorched and scarred, laid to waste in every direction. Men caught in the annihilating barrage, stunned and disoriented, remained frozen in the coiling grips of crippling fear, as the last of the flashing fire globes disappeared. Without knowing what to expect next, no one dared even lift their heads. While rocks and debris still cascaded to the ground, and as the last booming shock wave quivered away into silence, an eerie calm drifted throughout the inner kingdom. The shaking finally stopped, and the air cleared. As a thin billowing fog lifted, the clatter of small falling stone slowed, and pulverized dust clouds slowly rained down around them. Time fell into a void of oblivion. Minds were held captive in a state of an uncertain stupor. The only sound that interrupted the crackling, out of control flames were the high pitched wails of the trapped and wounded. For some, their own screams seemed to be coming from someone else lost in a distant, displaced world. The intensifying stillness that followed rang on death ears in horrible, impenetrable silence; if anything, it was worse in its chilling, eerie way than the prior calamitous mayhem.

As the elongating moments slipped by, the twilit dawn passed into early morning etching itself along the skyline's crest in a crimson aurora stretched across the horizon by the rising sun. The cresting sun filled the sky in an ever deepening rust red as if some vast mortal wound in the fabric of the cosmos were pouring out wellsprings of heavenly blood. Moment by moment, sunrise topped the edge where the heavens intersected the Ziaian world and spilled over its eastern ridge.

Izz of Zia

From his precarious observation post, the watchman on the eastern tower peered out over the madness. It was hard to see anything through the smoke rising all around him. The taste of metallic tainted smoke soured in his mouth. As the morning sun splashed into his eyes, he saw through the glare the brokenness of the world that was once the opulent kingdom of Edawn. To the North, the valley was still dark as if under an evil shroud, except for the campfires in Baddlock's encampment. He turned and looked over the kingdom. His staring eyes focused on the shadows of obliteration as midmorning light broke over the desolation. And once again his ringing ears were filled with the sound of the dying. It was a bath of death. The Kingdom of Edawn was covered with shattered bodies, and blood flowed across the kingdom in streams. Bodies lay everywhere, torn to bits, stomachs ripped open, heads, legs and arms rent from their trunks, some as good as dead but still clinging to life. Many were too pulverized to be recognized. A few of the disembodied splattered across the courtyard were nothing more than dark bloodstains over broken bones. Puddles of darkening blood merged and spread slowly, seeping into the cracks between the stone walkways.

Edawn's fortifications lay in ruin. The tower to the right of the watch was in shambles, nothing more than a pile of rubble. The tower's top to the left had fallen to the ground, landing almost upright. The superiority of Baddlock's firepower had broken through Edawn's impenetrable walls. The reinforced main walls that once seemed impenetrable and unassailable were breached, fallen into ruin, little more than crumbling heaps of stone. As the fine dust and smoke above the smoldering ruins, cleared, in the full light, the outer kingdom appeared inverted, with the inside where the outside should be, much like the crushed, disemboweled shell of a giant tortoise.

Zuree and Izz, in their mad dash to escape, had finally managed to reach the volcanic vent. The point where the boiling and rumbling clouds of suffocating smoke were caught in the up drafting currents surging upward and sent venting out. Izz took in several deep breaths and hurried through, determined to put as much distance between them and the gates of the damned as fast as he could. As they entered the next chamber, again, Izz immediately felt a heightened sense of profuse evil such as he had yet to experience. Knowing what lay ahead, Izz slowed down and paused for a moment, turned to Zuree, and said, "I must admit, I do not exactly know what lies ahead. All I know is that there seems to be some prison for disembodied beings from a dimension not of the world we know." He took her by the hands and asked, "Are you willing to follow me to the end, whether it be to our freedom or our doom?"

"I will follow you to the ends of the Zia," Zuree responded quickly.

Izz held Zuree's hand firmly, and they joined hearts as he genially tugged her forward through the imprisonment of the demon horde. Under his charge, Zuree had almost begun to feel safe again. On the other hand, Izz's fears were just beginning as he entered the vast chamber cautiously. He made frequent checks behind and above him, as unseen noxious forces charged the atmosphere. The whisperings of nameless fears seeped into Izz's subconscious like the unpleasant beginning of a nightmarish dream. Its heaviness discharged its presence in the air. Its constant undercurrents of shuddersome dread suddenly triggered in Zuree sensations of foreboding. They moved quickly like two ghosts drifting through a world split between fragments of dilution and reality.

As they traversed through the next chamber, Izz looked up, slowly scanning the far reaching ceiling overhead. In the darkness of the immense stone canopy above, the cavernous space was filled with insect like clicking sounds, and things moved as shadows began to emerge from the obscured darkness. The mass of pathetic demon forms seemed invigorated from their feeding frenzy of pain and fear channeled to them by the Dark Priests on the surface.

Zuree, who had only let out an occasional whimpered moan, asked, "What is that noise?"

"Do not worry yourself. We will soon be safe now. There is no reason to over concern yourself." Izz attempted to ease Zuree's dread. But neither could deny the tremble in his voice, and his words did nothing to convince either of them.

The quake had somehow caused the mist to somewhat vacate from the ceiling and walls. As the shroud of smoke continued to clear like a melting fog, on its fringes an ever maddening nightmare began to unfold. What it revealed was some kind vast, evil repository of crucified demon hordes spiked onto the cavern roof above. The clusters of impaled demons were very disturbed. They squinted against and shunned the increasing light that filtered in from the fiery abyss, clearly favoring the darkness as if the light when cast on them caused them unbearable pain.

Going forward seemed like suicide, but there was no way Izz could stop or turn back. Not when he considered the even more terrible alternative that waited where they came from. Zuree could hear an unearthly evil not of this realm, sneering tempestuously in her head. The demonic multitudes flopped mindlessly like double jointed puppets dangling from their impaling spikes and simultaneously squirming like so many enormous black legged and winged vipers trying desperately to drop onto the floor.

The prince of darkness himself knew that he had only so much time before the Celestial Conjunction. And there was no way he could allow his prize sacrifice to slip away from his grasp. Knowing that the situation was becoming critical, he unleashes every tittle of power that he had absorbed from the misery of men and called his demon hordes to arise. The buildup of dark energy filled the cavern with an electrifying tension that caused Izz and Zuree to appear like two phantoms meandering in a world of illusion. Black rips in the continuum of space opened up and threatened to swallow them. Izz's jittery courage was shaken further, spreading a tingling, awareness of fear throughout his entire nervous system. That was the moment when he realized that the bonds that held the ever agitated demons hordes were weakening.

On the walls and ceiling, the quagmire of evil was making every effort to tear themselves free. The more they struggled, the more black blood like slime that oozed from their impaling wounds. Every pair of countless yellow snakelike eyes was glaring down murderously on Izz and Zuree below as the two quickly made their way past the midway point of the cavern. Upon seeing this, the evil beings overhead and all around the walls escalated their frantic efforts to free themselves, but they were kept in bondage by the Omnipotent Powers that reigned over the universe. Only the pure blood of innocence poured out on the altar of abomination at the approaching conjunction could set them free. All the while, their prize was slowly but surely slipping out of their evil grasp. The farther Izz and Zuree moved toward the exit passage, the more desperate the demons on the walls and ceiling became, turning into one long, rousing rhythm of purpose. Their noisy, frantic struggle turned into a rowdy vociferous screeching of hysteria. Zuree could not stand the deafening screams ringing in her ears and pleaded, "Izz, I fear the worst. What is that? Please tell me what it is!"

"Just trust me!" Izz implored. In the next breath, he screamed, "Run!"

Because of the mounting terror unfolding on the surface of Zia, the channeling of negative black energy into the underworld by the Black Priest and the approach of the Great Conjunction, separation of the spiritual and the physical became possible. One by one, the empty hearts twisted, wriggled, and rolled, ripping themselves from their physical forms held fast by impalement. With less pain and difficulty than ever, they began to detach their malignant spirits from their imprisoned material counterparts. The disembodied entities tore themselves from their physical forms. The detachment creating a sickening sound resembling something between a dead oak being plucked from a muddy bog, and a leg bone being twisted and torn from the socket of a broiled chicken.

Once detached, they unfurled their translucent wings and leaped from the walls and ceiling. By the thousands, they left behind, their dangling weak and motionless embodiments, like suspended rag puppets left lifeless in their state of eternal bondage. They looked and sounded like a massive colony of deadly black winged wasps swarming to escape their burning hive as shadowy blurs took flight in crashing waves. The walls and the cavern ceiling spewed out the most hideous of creatures. It was as if Zia's underbelly had suddenly become sickened and was disgorging a poisonous toxin from within its bowels of the deep. With an explosion of wings, they rushed into the air. Circling disfigured blotches of stench, wrench, and darted this way and that, like crazed vampire bats defending their nest.

Shocked by the unexpected sight, and motivated by panic, Izz felt the instantaneous rush of adrenaline unload into his bloodstream. Izz instantly bolted, almost dragging Zuree off her feet behind him. He felt the darkness suddenly jump alive like a smothering, filthy black rag cast down over them. Izz snapped his head and looked over his shoulder to see a storm of black winged demons closing in. Closer and closer, tighter and tighter, they rushed in. "Run, Zuree!" Izz cried out. "Run! Run as you have never run before!" he pleaded.

And even though Izz was moving as fast as Zuree's feet could carry her, he felt as if they were moving in slow motion, more like in a dream than in the real world. Zuree was far too winded to utter a word, as she strived with all that was in her to stay on her feet. The silhouettes of indistinct forms, in a blinding flash, began to descend and surround them like a rumbling cyclone hurdling itself at them. The crowded throngs could just be made out through a gritty black haze, like figures advancing in a blizzard infused with the ambiance of the end of life. Izz and Zuree were like life sized images of themselves, running in a delusion somewhere between a conjured up hallucination and reality. The surreal situation was numbing Izz's senses beyond his ability to think clearly. Then Izz suddenly found himself running blindly, madly, neither thinking nor caring about anything except saving his beloved.

By this time, Zuree was just barely able to stay on her feet. The air was thick with the sulfuric stench of demons suddenly whooshing all around them from all sides as feelings of a catastrophic end clung to them. Winged demons rustled and quivered with escalating excitement in the air as dark, foul spirits began to fill the hollow like a vaporous mist. More and more demons were coming at them, weaving through from all directions. They emerged from the darkness, looking down with glistening red eyes. Each with a toothy grin that drooled with sticky beads of oozing dribble from their gapping, fang fill mouths. All the while, Izz kept telling himself that matters could only get worse.

Above, in the Edawnian's northern tower, the single standing tower on the northern wall, the sun had long past its quarter mark on its trek across the sky. The tower watch unnerved by the end of the world like cataclysm braced himself, amazed that he was still alive. He was still trying to wipe the taste of bile from his mouth when he raised a shaky hand and pulled his chin over the lookout's ledge, to take a measure of the situation. The catapults remained silent, replaced by the sounds of revelry. Below, the eeriest sight of death and destruction met his range of vision. He looked down in shock upon the wounded atmosphere that overshadowed the mood that once was. His unbelieving eyes pinned over the kingdom's skyline which had taken on the appearance of a tattered, jagged jigsaw puzzle, never meant to be pieced together again. All the other watchtowers on the northern wall had been torn from their foundations and the massive defensive outer and inner walls laid in ruin. Through the eddying lull of the fumes, consuming fires continued to burn out of control. In some places, the dust and smoke hung so thick it could have been sliced with a knife. On the ground, survivors of the daunting assault were beginning to emerge from a disastrous upheaval cropping up as if men were sprouting out of the ruinous ground. At first, only the most courageous, fearless of men, well prepared to die, peered out from their hidden corners, overhangs, and wreckage. For the longest time, startled men stared unable to recognize whether they were dead or alive, conscious or dreaming, and wondering why they could not seem to wake up. The surreal scene that unraveled before them in every vivid detail greeted every eye that could see. One by one, they came to realize that they had awoken into a holocaustic nightmare too impossible to understand in human terms.

Zandor had not had time to think. The battlement floor seemed to just have heave upward, as the whole side of the wall had toppled, and caved in on him, spilling him into the rubble below. He had ducked as a shower of broken stone had bombarded his head and shoulder. Dust, silt, and debris had come crashing and pouring down on him from nearly every side, causing him to crash headfirst, and fall flat on the ground below. He was engulfed in darkness as he descended and had been nearly squashed under a rolling block. The last thing he remembered was feeling the air knocked from his lungs and the inability to draw in air.

Zandor rose from the ashes, dust, and rubble, reappearing like a ghost from a grave, shaking his head to clear the ringing. His face was caked with dust and blood. He rubbed the dirt from his eyes as he came to his wobbling feet. The surrounding air was enveloped in a cloud of fine particles mixed in a red mist dampened with the dew of blood. Shreds of clothing floated over a cluttered heap of twisted metal, splintered timbers, and broken stone. The near death experience had been too terrifyingly close for comfort. Zandor staggered forward. Recovering quickly, he waded through a surreal landscape of gaseous, grayish blue fume rolling back upon itself. The stench of sulfur, blood, and scorched flesh was thick in his throat as it leeched itself into every corner of the courtyard. He swept his hand before him as if that would somehow clear the air or help him focus on some familiar web of life that was not unraveling.

Tom Icon

When Zandor came to his senses, his first thoughts were for his twin brother, "Kondor…Kondor! Kondor!" Zandor staggered through the haze, over fragmented beams and large sections of smashed stone blocks, toward where Kondor had been stationed. Zandor ran faster and faster, trampling among the rocks as his mind raced ahead. Out of breath, his lungs burning from the bitter smoke, he stopped and rotated in a measured circle. His wild eyes frantically searched high and low amid the wreckage of blocks and beams for some sign of his brother. As his eyes shifted from one blood spatter to the other, he saw no trace of him, nothing. "Kondor…?" His voice sounded fragile and broken.

Then through the clearing soot, in the distance, he saw something, a hand was protruding through the wreckage. Something beyond the explainable told him that this was his brother. The heedfulness that only one twin could feel for the other surged like lightning through his veins as he flung himself to his brother's side. Zandor clasped Kondor's hand; it felt lifeless, and Zandor mournfully screamed to the highest heaven, "No! No, please, please, no!" Then suddenly, he felt Kondor's fingers clutch on to his, and relief surged through him to know that his brother was still alive. Zandor, frantic with despair, fear, and painful concern clawed at the refuse, with disregard to the jagged splinters that were once supported beams. Finally, Kondor managed to pop his dust caked head up, wondering if the world had come to its end. He looked around, barely conscious, which intensified Zandor's burden for his only blood brother. Gagging, groaning, and grunting, Kondor thought the sheer weight of the suffocating pile of debris that surrounded him would snap his ribs. Zandor uncovered Kondor's torso as they both mustered their combined strength and forced his body upward. At long last, Zandor pulled and dragged dust covered Kondor from the rubble. Zandor examined Kondor for any visible wounds as he asked, "Is anything broken?"

Zandor helped his twin scramble to his feet as Kondor concentrated on breathing, unable to speak for the breath that had been forced from his lungs. "I must look a lot worse than I feel." Kondor was finally able to wheeze.

Relieved that his twin was still alive, Zandor wrapped his arms around his brother, heart to heart, in a great big bear hug. He thanked the Begetter of the Stars that his brother had survived. Kondor willingly returned Zandor's engulfing embrace until the air was further squeezed out of him. Both brothers cherished the moment, glad to be alive, and virtually unscathed.

At the other end of the devastation, King Ozzdon emerged from the upper stronghold of the battlement like a drowning man coming to the surface from the deep, into a world of utter chaotic disorder, confusion, and destruction. In the first excruciating moments of realization, rage pooled in his dust rimmed eyes, for the cruel, senseless slaughter of his people. Like a splinter in his mind, the ruinous scene that was once his opulent kingdom, sent a storm raging through his broken spirit. King Ozzdon staggered forward, trying to take a breath as he felt the pain of an inconsolable sense of loss coiling itself around his heart.

Thick gray plumes of smoke slowly drifted upward, lifting gradually and sweeping across the kingdom below, meandered toward the East as they seemingly oozed from deadly, gaping wounds in the kingdom. The tang of death filled his nostrils. Hit by the terrible jolt of disgust, pity, and rage all at once, the king stumbled back. He cradled his head in his hands, interlocking his fingers through his hair and jerked as if to tear it out by the roots. He muttered to himself, "Is such an insane thing possible?" It was much too terrible to believe. As the reality of it all crashed in on him, he felt his already racing heart quicken a notch, and then rip into his throat. As he seethed, he raised his voice to the highest heaven in a vengeance seeking tone and screamed at the top of his lungs. "Baddlock, you son of a pig! I will tear your heart out of your wrenched bosom with my bare hands! This I swear upon the blood you have shed this day." He raised a tightened fist toward the northern horizon.

Hearing the king from a far off, Dandork turned to Baddlock from his mount. Baddlock looked back from atop Midnight, his fierce war stallion, as it neighed and struck out with his forefoot. Baddlock freakishly smiled as he released a blast through his nostrils and said dismissively, "Does the fool propose to defeat me with his threats?"

Both men chuckled arrogantly, feeding off each other's excessive pride, vanity, and malice, as Tigbone joined in. Baddlock then looked toward Edawn and could see the span of the plains in all directions. He drew in a deep breath and said. "There is nothing sweeter than the smell of rancid meat on such a fine day."

Dandork gave the Wicked Warlock Wizard a quizzical glance.

Baddlock's mind suddenly became shrewd and calculating as he spoke audibly to himself, "Edawn is a desperate and enraged wounded animal." He knew that his next move would be the final nail in the coffin. He took a deep breath and held it, finally letting it out slowly through his nostrils. With his next breath, the Wicked Warlock Wizard forcefully commanded, "Bring forth the Zomborges."

The command was passed back through the ranks. Everything had gone as planned for the most part, and now it was time for the prelude to the ultimate victory. The bloodthirsty Zomborges would be sent in to weaken the kingdom farther before the final assault, and the finishing onslaught, thus prolonging the pitiless cat and mouse cruelty.

To add horror to terror, the Zomborges were assembled to load the dismembered dead that by then were covered with the larval of egg laying flies onto the catapults. The exposed, hacked flesh dripped with blood mixed with clear and other yellowish liquids as it was launch at the kingdom to the utter anguish and disgust of the survivors of Edawn.

Eventually the standing army of walking corpses, their bodies bleached bloodless, were brought in chains to the front lines. Wild and crazy eyed, their hair clumped in sweat and filth. They gnashed their teeth that had been filed down to tiny, razor sharp points as they gurgled sickening sounds from the depths of their throats. Several strongmen held each Zomborge down while another strongman forced a goblet of bitter, foul tasting narcotic down their throats. The potent potion was designed to narcotically induce a maddening surge of energy to match their bloodthirsty vigor to kill anything and everything within their grasp. Every handler knew that at that point, the Zomborge armies would have to be dispatched as soon as possible. For, in a short time, control of these pitiful, retched creatures would be lost; and that control would not be regained until the powerful drug wore off.

The lookout on the northern tower caught a sudden concentrated movement on the hilltop. The watchman abruptly lifted his head and looked alarmingly through his spyglass toward the enemy's encampment as he kept watch. With shocking concern, he quickly realized that Baddlock was mobilizing. "There is movement in the enemies' camp!" the keeper of the tower yelled down below.

Everyone within earshot listened in breath held silence, cringing as their eyes revealed the fear of what they had heard. There was one short, sharp shock of realization as a profound, startling numbness fell over the kingdom, and even the very dogs seemed frightened mutes.

Tom Icon
To be continued in Tom Icon's
third book.

For further information, contact us at:
izzofzia@gmail.com
Or visit us at:
izzofzia.com

Izz of Zia

SKULLDOOM
PHANTOMS DEEP
NORTHERN RANGE
ZZYMATOPIA
WASTELAND OF WOE
WOLF DEN
SKYMOUNT
FORBIDDEN ZONE
N
NE
E
SE
S
SW
W
NW
WANNINGTREE
EBONY
FOREST
RING OF GIANTS
BAY OF TRANQUILLITY
THE EDAWNIAN KINGDOM
GREAT SOUTHERN SEA
THE DEEP ABYSSAL
EARTH'S END
POINT OF NO RETURN

www.ingramcontent.com/pod-product-compliance
Lightning Source LLC
Chambersburg PA
CBHW030651120726
47905CB00001B/152